# RILEY

**A Novel**

# RILEY

### A Novel

## Paul Martin Midden

ISBN: 978-0-9859223-8-2
Library of Congress Control Number: 2019906119

Printed in the United States of America
Cover and interior design: n-kcreative.com
Published by:

Wittmann*Blair*

—1—

Riley Cotswald sat at her desk staring at the blank screen in front of her. What do I write? she wondered. That's a stupid question, came an immediate reply from somewhere in her head. Questioning myself about writing never helped anything. The only thing that matters is putting words on paper. I learned this with my first book.

She turned her head away from the screen and peered through the window of her small D.C. apartment. The sky was a Washingtonian blue, she observed, and if she looked down just a bit she could see the cherry blossoms beginning to burst. Just like me, she hoped.

But she did not feel herself bursting; all she felt was stuck at her desk, like a child in detention.

Knowing that distraction and procrastination were the two big things that worked against her getting anywhere with her writing, she forced herself to turn back to her computer screen. She had been able to do this earlier in her life, and she always associated writing with a special kind of experience, a mystical or even a spiritual one, whatever that meant. It was something she couldn't put into words; the irony of that was not lost on her nonreligious self.

I can do this, she told herself; and she forced herself to place her hands over the keys. The only way to start is to start, she thought. And so she believed.

She took a deep breath, closed her eyes, and commanded her fingers to move.

They weren't listening.

Riley leaned back in her chair. This is harder than I remembered.

She lectured herself: It doesn't matter that you have no idea what to write about. Remember when you started? When you wrote that first book? The one that sold? The one that allowed you to write full time? It wasn't that long ago; just a year ago you were on a book tour, touting your image as an up-and-coming young author. And you promised yourself and your publisher that you would produce another. That is why you are here. To produce another saleable book.

She sighed. Back then, what felt like ages ago, writing just seemed to flow and took on a life of its own. All Riley had to do was channel it and type. This was, of course, the narrative she told herself. The fact is she cannot really remember how she did it. Not exactly.

But this mystical narrative seemed to her to be largely true, although in a corner of her mind she thought perhaps the whole experience was romanticized a bit by time. She believed that's how it should happen. Magically. The stories are inside me, and all I need to do is make my fingers move across the keyboard. The narrative will take care of itself.

But maybe not. Maybe there is some other way. An outline? A summary? No. Writing is an art. Being creative is just that: an act of creation, one that required, even demanded, discipline, but one which at base was artistic, creative. So create! Write!

She tried to stop thinking and closed her eyes once more. She knew what she was doing. All these thoughts were just distractions. And the more self-critical the thoughts, the more distracted she became and the further away she came from the act of creation.

Riley sprang out of her chair to move, to breathe, to stop the pattern of useless thinking that was preventing her from doing the writing she most wanted to do. She walked around her small apartment. If Cameron were there, she would engage him somehow; she would whine to him. She wouldn't call it whining, but that's what it would be. It was always whining. It was saying out loud what went through her head, albeit in a more articulate voice. She would berate herself, and he would reassure her, no matter how dismal she judged her life to be at that moment or how crippled she felt putting words to paper. Or how little he actually understood what she was saying.

On reflection, that seemed like one of the best reasons to be with someone: having someone to complain to. And to have that person reassure you, even if you knew that the soothing words were insincere, as in Cameron's case. He tried to be sympathetic, but that trait did not seem to exist on his genome; the fact was dismal on the listening end. She shook her head. She didn't need to go there.

Riley sat back down and repositioned her fingers over the keyboard. She took yet another deep breath. In the back of her mind, she could hear a familiar voice: Scream all you want, young lady. If this is what you want, this is what you must do. It's as simple as that.

She straightened her shoulders. Okay, this is what I want, so this is what I must do. She replaced her fingers over her keyboard and started typing.

*Adam Wilkerson did not want to do what he knew he needed to do.*

She sat back and checked in with herself. This is more like it.

*He had been thinking about it for weeks, maybe even months. Definitely months. A year? Could be a year. He tried to avoid it; in fact, he tried everything he could think of to shield himself and his wife from what he needed rather than wanted to tell her. He wondered about how she would take it. He didn't think she would take it well.*

*Adam was sitting at home, waiting for his wife to return. It was Saturday; she had gone shopping. Where or for what he had no idea. It was hard to imagine that she really needed anything. He thought she was just killing time until . . . until what? Until night fell and she could go to sleep and forget her own unhappiness for a few hours. That is, if she slept. That nocturnal pleasure has been coming hard for Mrs. Wilkerson recently. Adam knew this all too well; his wife wasn't the only one lying awake in silence at night. What he didn't know was what to do about it.*

Touchy ground, Riley mused. She felt herself pale a bit, and she noticed her hands were sweaty. Anxiety, she knew. And maybe excitement. Perhaps both. She did not take her eyes off the screen.

*Adam wondered, even at this late date, if there were some way to avoid this, to somehow give his marriage yet another lease on life. Then he could avoid the discussion he promised himself he would have. But his mind was blank. He had tried everything. He tried being assertive and firm and then warm and kind; he tried to be inviting and disclosing and a little removed and distant. Nothing, absolutely nothing helped impede the belief that had been growing in his mind that he was just out of gas. By which he meant that the marriage was out of gas. No more fuel in the tank. Running on empty. The relationship platitudes were coming fast enough to fill a silly daytime advice show.*

Riley leaned back in her chair without taking her eyes off the screen. This was a habit of focus: looking at the screen was still writing, even if her hands were not tapping on the keys. She knew the anxiety was there and she knew why. She didn't want to give her nervousness any space; nor did she want to draw comparisons to her current life. She was sure that would make it harder for her to write.

So she didn't give in. Her eyes did not stray from the screen; she forced herself to continue.

*He was fidgety. He jumped up from his chair and headed for the kitchen. Maybe he should eat something, but he wasn't really hungry. He was mostly just anxious. When he thought about his relationship with Suzanne, all her many positive qualities filled his mind. She was attractive, charming, and liked by almost everyone who knew her. She was respected in the community and was unfailingly kind. She would go out of her way for people she scarcely knew. Everyone who knew the two of them thought that Adam was a lucky man indeed.*

*But he didn't feel lucky. He felt hollow. Passion was gone, sex was infrequent and undiscussed. If he did allude to sexual contact, he was met by his lovely wife with silence. Not just silence, but stony silence. Maybe even something more potent than silence. Something more deliberate, as if she were willfully refusing to understand what he was talking about. He frowned as he opened the refrigerator door.*

*And the kicker was that even all that no longer made him angry. It was just part of the growing emptiness that was taking over his life, making him numb. And it was just another piece of evidence that the relationship was faltering. No, worse than that: it was dying.*

*There was a time when this did make him angry. He hated it when Suzanne just shut the door on sensitive or delicate topics. He would get mad; he would say so, sometimes in a hostile way, sometimes in a kind way. To the extent that one can express anger kindly. But none of that made a difference. Ever. If he asked her straightforwardly if she were still interested in him, she would dutifully say yes, but those words coming out of her mouth never felt as if they matched up with the message she seemed to broadcast beyond them, which sounded to his mind something like 'No, I am not interested, but I don't want to rock the boat. And I don't want to talk about this again, ever.' But those words never came out of her mouth. She just got more and more remote. Gradually, as if she had a plan that would one day result in her . . . what? He didn't know. But it felt deliberate, which was all the more galling.*

*Adam realized he had been staring into the open refrigerator for some time. He closed the door, not registering a single item his eyes may have scanned during the time the door was open. He was right: he wasn't hungry.*

*He turned around and left the kitchen. He returned to his desk in the small den where he worked on domestic stuff: paying the bills, doing correspondence, banking—anything that could be done on a computer, which included almost everything he did at home. He glanced at the clock on the desk. It would be another hour before she said she would be home. He wondered absently if he had the nerve to go through with it.*

Suddenly, Riley pushed back from her desk and took her eyes off the computer screen. She realized she was shivering a bit in the warm room. Maybe this is all a little too close. She didn't know how it would work out with Adam and Suzanne, but she had a pretty good idea of how it was working out with Riley and Cameron, the husband from whom she had been separated for some months.

Like Adam, Riley stood up and went to the kitchen. But she only wanted a drink of water, something to quench the thirst she felt inside her, a thirst she was pretty sure would not be slaked by a sip or two of tap water.

What she was thirsting for the most was elusive. In her real life, she was the one who sat around wanting to speak the obvious truth to Cameron, who seemed eternally tone deaf about anything but his natural inclination toward happiness. It came so easy to him; it drove her crazy. Riley never quite grasped the root or the nature of his sunny disposition. Why was he so impossibly happy? He smiled a lot; he was seldom nonplussed; he put a good spin on everything. On those rare occasions when he absolutely could not avoid his emotions, as when he was watching a tear jerker or heard about the death of a friend or a national tragedy, he would shed a tear or two, but very briefly and, if it lasted more than a couple seconds, apologetically. Riley had never seen anything like it. And then he would return to his preternaturally happy default state. At first this was charming to her.

"That drove me crazy," she whispered aloud. As she said it, she felt her words confirmed by a roiling in the pit of her stomach, something she often felt when she and Cameron were living together. She decided that the water would have to do in the quenching department. Whatever else she was really thirsting for would have to wait.

It was not completely lost on Riley that she was writing this story to help herself. One of her several therapists had suggested that she do this: that she use her talents as a writer to at least try to understand distressing events in her life, especially her relational life. Maybe, just maybe, said the Master of No Promises, it would provide some relief; and if not relief, then clarification. She wondered absently which therapist had told her that. It must have been the one before last, but honestly she couldn't recall.

Riley hated that therapist.

Despite her several forays into therapy, Riley was able to attain neither clarity nor resolution. Sure, sometimes therapy was consoling, as it might be to speak with a good friend about what's bothering you. And arriving at insight was occasionally fascinating. But despite those moments, the issues that plagued her remained for the most part unchanged and endlessly frustrating. As the consolation faded and the insights lost their initial charge, the same tacit but powerful desire to be fixed in some magical, mystical way reasserted itself. She kept waiting to be cured, when it was the waiting itself that was precisely the problem, a concept that finally, after years of struggling, dawned on her one day in an unusually candid moment. This desire, the belief, the fervent hope that a little more work would do it, that a little more therapeutic attention would change her and her world was hard to shake. It was not only a belief, it was an assumption. Why else put yourself through all that work examining the nooks and crannies of your psyche? And the harder she worked, the stronger the belief. Until that same loathsome therapist sat back in his too comfortable chair and labeled it magical thinking.

Magical thinking?

Yes, Riley. Magical thinking. The kind that we all do as children, when we believe that, for instance, if we wish for something really, really hard, it will come true. Most people grow out of it around, say, age seven or eight. Ten is late.

Left unsaid was that thirty was beyond the pale.

No wonder she hated him.

Why is this so hard for me to get? If I want my life to be different, I have to do something to make it different.

Simple. In theory.

No matter how much personal responsibility she tried to shoulder, nothing could shake her desire and belief that she needed something more, something from outside herself. As much as she liked to write, no amount of writing filled that need; nor did it give her surcease from the constant internal self-criticism to which she was so prone. At least therapy gave her some clarity about that.

What do you expect? This is life on earth. For the most part, for the gigantic part, it is conditioned and unfree, as averred, she recalled, by Daoists everywhere.

Another thought that did not give her peace of mind.

I don't think it's peace of mind I'm looking for. Curious thought. Of course, everyone wants a measure of peace, but peace is just an absence of turmoil. It sounds boring. Maybe it's not peace at all I want. It is something more complex, more nuanced, more . . . she didn't know what.

She sat back down and looked at the blinking cursor. She glanced at the clock. It was close enough to four o'clock, the time she set in her schedule to stop writing for the day. She had started late today mostly because she had been avoiding starting altogether. But she finally did and was feeling a tiny bit self-satisfied. Her schedule— the one she would initiate in full force tomorrow—was to remain at work three hours in the morning and three hours in the afternoon. An hour break for lunch, but few if any other breaks during the day. Bathroom breaks were okay, as was getting up to get something to drink. But not to eat or to snack or call anyone, unless it was writing-related. She knew herself well enough to know that any one of the endless distractions available to her would derail a day's productivity. To her this was a Spartan schedule, and she hoped it would be good for production and for the focus she needed if she was going to please her publisher. And herself. But every ancient, lazy, vaguely formed impulse in her body had to be disciplined daily for her to pull it off. As much as she loved writing, she hated the discipline part. In fact, at the moment, she hated everything.

Riley closed the file on her computer and backed it up on a flash drive; then she powered the machine down. This is enough today. I started. Putting the computer to bed this way at the end of every writing day was a ritual of sorts, signaling that she had completed her work. The material would not disturb her again until the next morning, when she could deal with it refreshed. That was the plan.

She noted as she was arranging her desk in preparation for the next day that this hatred of everything was mildly exhilarating. Riley felt something inside her shift. She walked into the kitchen area and began to think vaguely about preparing something for dinner, but this mild exhilaration commanded the greater part of her attention. She recognized that she wasn't really hungry; she was just going through the motions of her life.

She had done this when she and Cameron were living together. She did things because there were things to be done simply because she was the wife and Cameron the husband. She did not realize until some years into the marriage that this was not exactly something she had signed up for; it was simply what she fell into, as generations of women had done before her. That galled her even more.

Now, she felt the difference between doing things for another person because you loved and respected him versus doing them because you felt you needed to versus doing them for yourself alone. Alone she felt freer; that was easy. In a relationship, it was always a battle, and too often, the former behavior won. Once she realized just how obligatory this all felt, she began to resent it every time she caught herself in the act. She felt like a prisoner fighting a battle she was sure to lose.

In any case, the fact was that here, today, right now, she didn't have to make dinner if she wasn't hungry. Or if she just did not want to.

Even though she knew these ruminations were unproductive—the kindest way one could characterize them—it was almost impossible for her to stop. Did I really feel imprisoned? Yes, I did.

Riley was certain that she just did not feel so flexible or so free or so able to breathe when she lived with Cameron. Maybe it was about him; maybe it was about her. She had no definite idea, despite those long periods of time in therapy, and, truth be told, she didn't really care much. It was just how it was.

Of course, living alone entailed some loneliness, but it wasn't terrible. There was free time: time to do whatever she wanted or nothing; time to sit and stare, to watch television, to cry her eyes out if she wanted to for no good reason. She never resented preparing dinner for herself. It felt good not to be in her chair writing. It felt good to be by herself. It felt good to be moving around.

And this new idea did not leave its prominent place inside her head. What is it I want? If not peace, then what? Passion? Excitement? Purpose? This airy thinking went on until it gave way when she realized she was actually hungry.

Time to eat.

Life is full of weird paradoxes, she thought as she opened the refrigerator to examine the candidates for dinner. But she was aware that it wasn't just the idea, even the new idea that was so compelling just now. It was also an accompanying physical experience, the opening up sensation of her brain to a new experience. It was hard to describe. A feeling at the top of her head that did not immediately recede. One that seemed to energize her.

She wondered absently if she was having a stroke. She had no idea what that might feel like, but she felt like a poor candidate for such an event. Her age, general health, weight management, and typically sound nutrition habits worked against it. So she did not think she was in any kind of physical danger. She felt fine overall;

better than fine. Good really. She did feel a little light-headed, the way she sometimes felt when running a longer-than-usual distance or pushing herself hard in the gym after not getting exercise for a while.

I am way too wrapped up in myself.

Oh?

Yes, I'm too wrapped up with my feelings, with my physical sensations, with my life and with my own ongoing, mostly negative commentary. She could feel herself slipping into a familiar, if uncomfortable, hole. "I don't want to do this!" she said to the refrigerator.

When the refrigerator didn't respond, she turned, left the kitchen, and picked up her cell phone on her way to the couch. She called Jennifer, her best friend.

Voice mail. Ugh! "Hi, Jen. It's Riley. Call me when you get this."

She glanced at the clock. 4:15. Jen was probably still at work. Just to do something different, Riley picked up her laptop bag and her wallet, grabbed her keys, and left her small apartment. She needed to get away from herself.

Riley always felt lucky that she lived within walking distance to so many great places. Distracting herself was as easy as walking out the front door of her apartment building, an older one in a revitalized part of town. She walked down to the nearest Starbucks, which was largely empty, and ordered a tall coffee. She pulled out her wallet and paid with a card. It was an automatic gesture. With the rest of her consciousness, she looked around, at the server, at the counter, at the window, at anything that would distract her from her internal thinking. After paying, she turned and walked over to an empty table, pulled out her laptop, and logged onto the Wi-Fi network. At that point, she let out a long if silent breath in relief. She was not here to write. She was not here to think. She was here to distract herself, to play, to divert her attention: things she found easy to do while online focused on her laptop in the familiar environment of her favorite Starbucks.

Thank God, she thought. First, she checked her email to see if she had heard from anyone. A bunch of ads and the daily update from Cameron, who still seems after six months to believe that this separation is just a hiatus before he and Riley resume their married life. Then she opened Facebook to see what was new there. She hated Facebook. It always felt that other people were having a happier, more exciting time than she was when she perused the postings. Of course, she didn't post much. Almost never. Somehow, she never felt that what she did was newsworthy or could possibly be interesting to someone else. Nor did she think anyone would care.

And she was pretty sure she was right about that.

Absorbed in the small screen, Riley was startled when she glanced up and saw a man standing in front of her table. Where did he come from?

He was just standing there, not saying anything.

"Do you want something?"

The man flushed a bit, obviously embarrassed. "I'm so sorry," he said. "I was waiting for you to look up."

Riley wondered how long he had been standing there, but it seemed too inquisitorial to ask. Instead, she shrugged slightly as if to say 'Okay, what do you want?' What she actually said was "I'm looking up."

The man's flush did not improve. He started to stammer. "I'm sorry," he said. "I've seen you in here a couple times, and you've always been by yourself. And. . . and I was wondering . . . I was wondering . . ."

Riley's head was bobbing in tandem with each repetition of this phrase that was painfully trying to complete itself.

"I was wondering if you'd like some company," the man finally said.

Relieved that he finally made his way to the end of his sentence, Riley wondered what he was talking about. She looked at him with dismay.

"I'm sorry," the man said, backing away slightly. "I was just wondering if you wanted some company."

"Yes, that's what you just said." She looked at him sideways. "Are *you* looking for some company?"

Without a word, the man—boy? Riley was thinking—sat down across the table from her.

She sat back and looked at him more closely. Despite an almost grammar-school lack of confidence, this person looked like a fully grown adult. He must be in his early to mid-thirties. She observed that his flushing had given way to a pale, vacant look on his face and a slight tremor in his hands.

"Are you all right?"

The flush returned. "Yes, yes, of course. I'm just . . . I'm just . . . It's just hard for me to approach women."

Riley wondered how this strange person could talk without breathing. "I can see that," she said.

The pair sat in silence for a few moments, regarding each other with the kind of curiousness that arises when one is suddenly confronted with the unexpected. After a short while, Riley thought the boy's flush was returning, and to forestall that, she said, "Okay, so what's your name?"

"Edward," he replied. "My name is Edward."

Riley could not help but smile at the way he repeated his name, as if to confirm that it was really his. Is this guy autistic?

"So, Edward, what did you have in mind when you decided to get up the courage to sit here?"

Edward deflated a little. He looked askance at the floor near his chair and seemed to be thinking. Then he turned his head toward Riley and spoke. "I had in mind that we could get to know each other a little, and, if we liked each other, even a little, we could go on a date."

Unexpected clarity, thought Riley. "A date? Like a movie. Or dinner?"

"Yes," Edward the Formal replied. "Like a movie. Or dinner." He thought for a moment. "Or both," he said, as if to make sure he was covering all his bases.

"Okay. So how do we go about determining the first step, that is, deciding if we like each other or not?"

"I think we just talk for a while, as we are doing now."

"Well, okay, how are we doing?"

"Pretty well, considering the rocky start."

Riley chuckled. This guy may have arrived here from another planet, but he at least recognized a rocky start when he saw one. She found that perversely but only mildly charming.

"In all fairness, it's only been a couple minutes. Maybe we should keep talking."

"I'd like that," Edward replied.. "What's your name?"

"My name is Riley."

"It's nice to meet you, Riley. Actually, I have seen you in here a couple times, and I always wanted to meet you."

"Because . . . ?"

"Well, because you are attractive and serious, and you are obviously a reader. If not a writer."

"What makes you think I'm a writer?"

"Well, you are studious, and you are always reading when I see you. And you are in here at odd times. You do not appear to have a nine-to-five job somewhere. Here it is: 4:30 in the afternoon, and you are sitting in a coffee shop." Edward thought for a while. "You could be a teacher, I suppose, but, I don't know, there is something about you that suggests a writer." He squinted his eyes and looked at her with what he seemed to think was a discerning, grown-up look.

"We'll get to that later," Riley said. "What do you do, Edward, that you are also sitting in a coffee shop at 4:30 in the afternoon? And at other odd times of the day apparently."

Edward smiled. Riley wondered why.

Edward turned his head sideways. "I am a teacher," he said smiling.

"Why are you smiling, Edward?"

"Because teachers are usually outgoing, and I am not. I am shy, which is one of the reasons it's hard for me to approach women."

Riley nodded.

Uncomfortable silence. Both Riley and Edward were wondering what to say. And more than that, they were each trying to decide which direction they wanted the conversation to go.

Riley decided not to speak first this time.

Edward, his face scrunched up a bit as if he felt the burden of having to say the next thing, finally said, "So, Riley. What do you like to do? Besides read, that is?"

Riley for her part decided to be frank. "Look, Edward. I can appreciate how . . . how . . . anxiety-filled it can be to approach a member of the opposite sex. But the fact is, I am in the midst of a divorce, and the last thing I want just now is any kind of relationship or entanglement." She looked at him sadly. "I'm sorry."

Edward breathed a sigh of relief that seemed to radiate from the deepest stratum of his being. To Riley, it seemed like evidence that he was actually alive, a living, breathing human. Not only that, but he appeared to get more animated. "I really, really appreciate your candor, Riley," he said after a moment. "I can't say I'm not disappointed, but you wouldn't believe the things that women say to me. I just really, really, really appreciate simple honesty."

Riley nodded again. "Me too," she said softly. She imagined that Edward got himself hurt a lot. If most of his forays into the dating world were of this caliber, she could only imagine the scars that lay beneath his chameleon-like skin. It seemed to take so much out of him. She pitied him, but only a bit.

Nothing happened next. Riley sat there; Edward sat there. They weren't looking at each other: Riley was glancing at her laptop and Edward was looking at his hands. This is getting awkward, Riley thought.

Just as she was about to say something to attempt closure, Edward spoke up. "Well," he said. "Thanks for spending a few moments with me." He got up, bowed slightly, and walked away.

It was Riley's turn to breathe a sigh of relief. She had mixed feelings about the whole encounter. It wasn't that Edward was unattractive: he wasn't. He was socially awkward, but Riley felt she would never win any awards for being socially graceful. And truth be told she found his awkwardness at least a little dear. What surprised her about her own reaction—in addition to the unaccustomed candor—was how jealous she was of her own time. What she told Edward was true: she wasn't ready for another relationship. She didn't want one, at least not now.

Riley sat back in her chair and looked out the large plate glass window. She was feeling a surge of freedom having turned Edward down, and she was wondering if she would ever relinquish the feeling she was having just now. She recalled wondering about this in the past, before she met and got involved with Cameron.

This was the part that was so confusing her. She liked men. She liked Cameron. She loved Cameron. She even liked Edward a little. She liked a guy named Dean she met at a bar once. Liked him a little too much, as she recalled.

She also liked relationships. She loved talking about ideas, plans, how the other person felt, how she felt.

So what's the problem?

She straightened up and glanced at the blackened computer screen in front of her. The problem is that I also like being by myself. I like relationships but not all the time. She hit the space bar on her laptop, and the screen lit up.

This did not sound so bad to her.

Riley surfed a while longer and then shut down her laptop and began gathering up her things. She glanced up to see if Edward had left the coffee shop. She was relieved not to see him, and she slowly began making her way out of the shop and back to the safety of her apartment.

Once inside, she put her things on the table near the door and walked over to the kitchen sink. She took out a glass, put some ice in it, and filled it with water from the tap. All the while, she was thinking about Edward. And Cameron. She thought about how sure she must have sounded to Edward about not wanting a relationship. She wasn't sure that was entirely true. It was true she didn't want a relationship with him. Not now. Maybe not ever. Probably not ever.

She stared at her reflection in the tiny window above the sink and squinted. Truth was, even though she valued her privacy and her alone time, she did feel some loneliness. Not lonely enough to hang out with somebody like Edward, who for whatever charm and innocence he possessed was just a little too creepy. And not lonely enough to call Cameron, her soon-to-be ex-husband, the eternal optimist who drove her so crazy.

She put the glass down on the counter. For a moment, she thought she might cry. Her body was hosting a lot of different feelings that were each calling out for attention. She felt sad enough for tears, but what she was feeling wasn't only sadness. It was more a mix of confusion, resentment, dissatisfaction, and longing, a combination that felt toxic when all those feelings collided. It usually led to the kind of pointless uncertainty she was feeling now. And this kind of uncertainty infuriated her. It was stressful, and she hated it.

She picked up her glass again and refilled it with water. She took a long draught. Then she dumped out the rest and turned around. I can't stick around here with these thoughts and feelings. I've got to get out of here.

Just as she was deciding where to go and what to do, the phone rang. She glanced at the tiny screen and saw that it was her best friend.

"Hi, Jen," she said after hitting the talk button.

"Hey, Riley," Jen responded. "What's up? I'm returning your call."

"Absolutely nothing. That's why I called." She could hear Jen chuckling on the other end of the line.

"So, you're wanting to do something . . . ?"

"Yeah, I need to do something. I just got back from Starbucks and ran into this creepy guy who tried to ask me out. It was awkward. He sat down in front of me and asked; I said no. We had nothing else to talk about and all he did was fidget and sweat."

"Ah," breathed Jen. "Not a flawless male/female bonding experience."

Not even close, Riley thought. "What are you doing for dinner?"

"Meeting you at Carter's?"

"Sounds like a plan. Give me twenty minutes."

# — 3 —

When Riley got to Carter's Tavern—it was really just a bar with so-so food—thirty minutes later, Jen was sitting in a booth nursing a gin martini, her drink of choice for a pre-dinner cocktail. She spotted Riley immediately and waved.

Riley swept into the booth bench across from her friend. "Thanks for meeting me," she said as she sat down. "I was going a little crazy."

Jen chuckled. "Surprise dating requests can do that," she said. Riley was pretty sure that for Jen any dating request from a member of the opposite sex, preferring as she did members of her own, was unwelcome. She found most men, maybe all men, at least slightly distasteful.

Women, on the other hand, she found endlessly intriguing. The hair, the make-up, the curves: all of this held boundless allure for her. She was prone to intense but short-term relationships, the kind that mostly centered around fun and sex, sometimes fueled by drugs and always by alcohol. Jennifer respected her attractions and acted on them whenever possible. She had had an attraction to Riley for some time now. There was no question in her mind that she would respond to a request for company from Riley, no matter what the reason. For Jennifer, hope seldom died before a relationship was consummated, and the word 'no' rarely registered with her. She seemed to think at most that it meant 'maybe later'.

Jen understood that Riley considered herself straight, something that Jen wondered about but never brought up. She had made a tentative move on Riley a year or so ago and it went nowhere. That did not extinguish her attraction; if anything, it piqued her interest. Even though it was a long shot—she knew Riley was married to a man—she thought she sensed a yes in Riley's psyche somewhere. So she decided to bide her time. In her soul, she felt that she and Riley were destined for a romantic ride at some date to be determined, and she couldn't help looking forward to it. As with almost any woman to whom Jen was attracted, she simply did not believe protestations of exclusive straightness.

For Riley's part, she enjoyed Jen's company and loved the fact that her friend seldom turned down an invitation to get together, no matter how inconvenient it seemed. Riley knew Jen was gay; she was not unaware of the thwarted effort she made last year to lasso her into a 'closer' relationship. She felt then and felt now that she and Jen were close enough. Riley never really questioned her sexual orientation: it was just part of the larger equation of her being, maybe a part of some cosmic algorithm of relationships. It was one of the few things about relationships she rarely even wondered about.

And it wasn't that she didn't find Jen attractive. She loved her personality and intelligence, her good looks, athletic figure, and straightforward mannerisms. It all added up to a very attractive package.

She also knew enough about her friend's relationship style and her history to be wary of too much intimacy. One of the things that was clear to her was that a physical involvement with Jen—even if she were open to it—predicted a short-term joy ride followed by a steep and probably calamitous ending. The fact was that she valued Jen as a friend more than as a potential romantic partner even apart from the whole business about orientation. She didn't want to lose her. Especially not now.

It wasn't that Jen talked about her romantic entanglements a lot, but she did mention from time to time that she was spending time with this woman or that, and by Riley's estimate, the half-life of those involvements was about six weeks. Disgruntlement showed up after a month or so; flameouts after a couple more months. Another thing Riley liked about Jen was that she didn't whine or get depressed when these short-term flings ended. She just sighed a little, joked about it, and, after a respectable period of celibacy softened by the regular intake of gin—a couple weeks, at least—started eyeing around in earnest for another *objet d'amour*.

This assessment entailed a fair amount of guesswork on Riley's part, as Jen never got all that specific about her involvements. But she could tell by Jen's elevated mood when she was going full bore into a romantic escapade, and she could feel Jen's coming down from it in subsequent weeks. A few times, Jen even told Riley straight out that she was off the market for a while. None of this seemed to interrupt the schedule of their friendship.

Nor did those trysting relationships seem to impact Jen's relationship with Riley much: she was still unfailingly available and cheerful, if a little euphoric sometimes during their time together. Riley knew there was no one in Jen's life at present. At least there wasn't yesterday.

"So: details, sister, details," said Jen.

Before she could comply, a server was at their table looking for Riley's drink order. Riley looked up at her and ordered a gin and tonic.

"Okay, so I finish writing for the day, and I take myself off to the coffee shop to get some air, to get out of my apartment and out of my obsessive head. I'm sitting there with my laptop open, staring at the damn screen, playing. You know, Facebook, email, Instagram, Reddit. I was just about to head toward Goodreads when I look up and see this guy standing in front of me. I swear I don't know how long he was there."

"And he's sweating and shaking and pale as a toilet. He starts stammering. All of a sudden, he asked me if I want some company and sits down without an invitation. I must have made some barely discernible movement that he interpreted as assent because he proceeded to tell me how shy he was and how hard it was for him to approach women and, by the way, would I like to go out sometime."

"So I ask him what he had in mind and he says like a movie or dinner or something. And I'm thinking this whole time: Is this guy a grown-up or some kind of physically accelerated twelve-year-old?"

"And I say to him that I'm in the process of a divorce and I'm not at all ready for another relationship, and he just sort of nods and sits there and doesn't say a thing. I mean, this poor man!"

Riley's drink arrived, and she took a sip.

"Finally, and I am telling you this was only a few minutes, but it felt like a long, long time . . . finally I say 'Sorry' and he gets up and thanks me for being so candid. Then he just walks away. I glue my eyes back to my laptop and hope he's gone. When I look up about ten minutes later, I don't see him; so I pack up my stuff as quickly as I can and retreat back to my apartment."

Jen was chuckling throughout the story. "Who was this guy?"

"Edward. His name was Edward. He's a teacher. He'd been 'watching' me and tagged me as a writer. If he knew anything about writers, he would know they hate being identified or stereotyped. But he was pretty bold for a guy who is so freaking anxious."

"Stalker?"

"Maybe," Riley said without hesitation.

Both women took long sips on their favorite beverages. A cozy, funny silence settled on the pair.

"Men!" said Jen.

"Men!" said Riley.

# — 4 —

It was a good thing Riley and Jen could both drink with some abandon and still get up and go to work the next day. It was past 11:00 p.m. when Riley rooted through her purse for a credit card to split the check with the person she believed to be her best friend in the world. Filled with feelings of warmth and boozy connectedness, she walked home—unsteadily at times, leaning episodically on any sturdy fixture along the way. Lampposts were helpful in this regard. Once inside her apartment, she threw her keys on the table by the door and fell into bed without removing her clothes or visiting the bathroom.

And she slept until 8:45 a.m., fifteen minutes before the 9:00 a.m. time she set for herself to start writing. Her goal was for this time to be inviolate; she never wanted to miss what she regarded as the optimal time to begin creating. So when she realized the time, she shot out of bed, tore off the clothes she slept in and raced to the bathroom, where she completed her morning ministrations in record time, as if someone were clocking her.

With a minute and a half to spare she threw coffee in the coffee maker, filled the tank, and leapt to her worktable, which was approximately six feet from her kitchen. Once seated, she sighed deeply, flipped on the computer, and settled herself into that open-but-disciplined state of mind she felt was most conducive to putting words on the screen. She felt no signs of being hung over.

Riley reviewed the material she had written the day before, and a frown fell over her face. How am I going to do this? she wondered.

She took deep breaths to calm herself and to invoke whatever spirits might be available to help her carve out this new story line. What was it that Adam was going to tell his wife? That he wanted a divorce? That he didn't love her anymore? After a few seconds of this, she reminded herself that thinking was not writing, and she put her fingers over the keyboard and started typing.

*The minutes dragged by. Why is this taking so long? Adam tried taking deep breaths to calm himself. He thought of turning on the television, but there was little that came out of that fancy box that interested him. Then he had a sobering realization: There is only one thing I can do to quell this feeling. He stared at himself in a mirror along the far wall and beheld himself with a mixture of contempt and the promise of relief. I can choose not to say anything. I can just go on. Why does today have to be the day? Maybe this anxiety is telling me something. Maybe I'm not ready.*

*And at that thought, his anxiety immediately began to ebb. Coward, he whispered to himself across the room at his crooked image smiling back at him in the mirror.*

Riley sat back in her chair with a feeling of satisfaction. Not a bad start. She got up to pour herself a cup of coffee, relieved at how clearheaded she felt despite the drinking she and Jen had done the night before. Thank God for a sturdy constitution, she thought.

*Adam sat down in his usual seat when he was home alone. Working from home had its upsides and downsides. He greatly enjoyed the freedom it gave him; but it also left him with a lot of time during which his thoughts and his imagination could run wild.*

*He knew from long experience that his 'job' did not take more than half a day. The company that retained him set out a set of very specific expectations and tasks for each workday for their non-resident workers. Adam knew that they felt these were demanding tasks and ensured a diligent workforce. He also knew that none of these tasks was especially challenging, and he realized early on that completing them required about a half day of work, about for four or five hours. He had developed a schedule so that he completed his work around noon and submitted it at the end of the day, satisfying the requirements of his job and giving him a lot of latitude for passing the remaining time as he saw fit.*

*He was savoring the relief from the stress he had been feeling when he heard Suzanne's car in the driveway. His anxiety cranked back up. Act busy, he instructed himself.*

*He heard the car door slam shut and the front door open; then the sound of keys being thrown on the hall table. He heard Suzanne's footsteps on the wooden floor. He heard her walking toward the small study that served as Adam's workspace.*

*"Hi, Honey," he said when her face peaked around the corner.*

*Oddly, Suzanne did not say anything. She walked over to Adam's work desk and sat down on the only other chair in the room. After some uncharacteristic fidgeting, she looked him straight in the eye and said, "We have to talk."*

*Adam was surprised, and it took a moment for him to produce the requisite nod. Of course, he would talk. This suddenly felt like new ground, as Suzanne was never the one to initiate a serious conversation. His mind flashed on all the needless anxiety he felt not half an hour before.*

*Suzanne looked down at her hands and seemed to be breathing slowly and deeply. After a minute or so, she looked up at her husband and said simply, "I don't want to be married to you anymore."*

*Adam felt the blood drain from his face and thoughts flee from his mind. He felt lightheaded. In this moment, his world shifted in a direction that was perhaps in the long term not unwelcome but in the present was so shocking that he did not know how to respond. Maybe he did not hear his wife correctly.*

*"What?!" he finally said.*

*Suzanne looked at Adam calmly. She seemed to understand that this might have come as a shock to him. She paused for a long moment before replying.*

*"I have not been happy for some time," she said in a way that was so self-possessed Adam believed later that it was rehearsed or that someone had told her what to say. "And I don't think you've been happy either." Another pause. "We have no children; we both have*

*decent careers. We are free to do as we wish." She looked at him dead in the eye. "And I do not wish to be married to you any longer."*

*Adam turned away in a largely futile effort to get his bearings. If he had not been so shocked, he might have jumped for joy. As it was, he realized that a tear was running down his cheek. "I'm sorry," he finally said disingenuously. "I didn't know you were so unhappy."*

*The couple sat in silence listening to the minutes pass by until Suzanne finally got up and said, "I'm going to get a bite to eat. Want something?"*

*This seemed weird and unduly domestic given the explosive if brief conversation the pair had just had, and Adam shook his head absently. Suzanne walked out of the room. Adam sat in silence. He did not bother to wipe the tear from his eye.*

Jesus! Riley thought. This is close to home. She could not help flashing back on the fateful conversation she and Cameron had had when their separation started. In that scenario, much of the stage direction was changed, but the substance was nearly identical.

In that scene, it was Cameron who had come home from work.

Cameron: Hi, Riley.

Riley: Um, Hi.

Cameron: What's for dinner?

Riley: We need to talk.

Cameron: [Silent, looked in Riley's direction.]

Riley: We need to talk now.

Cameron: So talk. [Smiling]

Riley: I don't want to do this anymore.

Cameron: Do what?

Riley: Be married to you. [Tears start to flow.]

Cameron: [Silence]

Riley: I'm just not happy.

Cameron: [Silence]

Riley: Are you listening?!

Cameron: [Nods]

Riley: For Christ's sake, say something!

Cameron: [Pause] I don't know what to say.

The two stared at each other, Riley feeling relief at finally saying what she'd been wanting to say for months, Cameron trying to wrap his mind around a completely unexpected development.

He had no visible reaction.

This is what had incensed Riley the most. No reaction! Really?! She would have thought that even unflappable Cameron would have flapped a little. The fact that he didn't provided the additional courage Riley needed to follow through on her plan to separate.

Cameron's reaction came down to this: If this is what you want, Honey.

Riley (thinking): Honey? He never calls me Honey. He calls me by my name. Always. What's going on here? I don't know what to say.

Cameron (interrupting her train of thought): What's for dinner?

Riley: Did you not hear what I said?

Cameron: I did, but I don't know what to say. And I'm hungry.

Riley, in stunned silence for a few moments. Then: Chicken parmesan.

Riley snapped herself out of the familiar reverie of those events. Even now, she could not get over Cameron's equanimity about the potential loss of his life partner, about his impending divorce.

It was true that neither of them, even now, made a move to engage legal proceedings. She had talked to an attorney, who had advised her that divorce was uncomplicated in situations such as this, where there were no children and where both spouses had careers. It was simply a matter of dividing up whatever assets they had, which consisted of one car, a lease on a house, and modest separate bank accounts.

Riley wasn't sure why she had not moved forward with the legal situation. She and Cameron had talked about it only once, and he told her that if this was what she wanted she should be the one to file for divorce. At the time Riley nodded, still tranquilized by Cameron's rampant indifference.

And that was three months ago. Since then, he calls regularly. She dutifully takes his calls, but they don't have much to talk about. They both agreed that he would stay in the house until the end of the lease, something he could comfortably afford to do given his income, and she would move out. He would also keep the car, as she had no use for it in pedestrian-friendly D.C. As time went on these conversations became shorter and shorter. The about-to-be ex-married couple had less and less to talk about.

The real questions that Riley had were apparently not answerable by her soon-to-be erstwhile husband. Did he not care? Was tranquility his major goal in life? Did he not love her?

And then there were the suspicions: Did he have a mistress? Was he gay? When she broached these issues, her questions were met with silent nonchalance and casual head shaking. He's just not going to tell me. This did nothing to allay her suspicions. As time went on, she cared less and less about the reasons. She began to wonder if they had had any good times at all, something she figured was probably pretty standard for a person in her position.

And so she had been assured by her current therapist. What do you expect, the attractive, bespectacled woman in the chair across from her had said bluntly. You left the relationship for a real reason, not something you had conjured up in your mind. The fact was that, for all Cameron's superficial amiability, he was emotionally closed and generally unavailable to the feelings of others, including and perhaps especially you.

As she trudged through her therapy sessions, sometimes acutely grieving the loss that comes with the collapse of a major relationship, she began to understand how much useless energy she had put into coming up with reasons why Cameron's emotional insularity was 'normal'.

It wasn't. She hated it. She much preferred her friend Jen's authentic recklessness to the amiable but cold presence of Cameron. That realization remained with her throughout the months of the separation. Coming back to the present moment, she made a note to call the attorney in the morning.

She shook her head. In the meantime, best to get on with writing.

*Habit kicked in and dinner went on as it always had. Adam and Suzanne scratched together a presentable menu and then sat down in their usual places to eat, sitting directly across from one another around the small table in their kitchen. Usually they made small talk. This evening, there was nothing but silence.*

*At length, Suzanne spoke. "Rough day at the office today," she said, playing with the food on her plate. "I had to fire somebody."*

*That makes two firings in one day, thought Adam, munching on the ad-hoc dinner. He was quiet.*

*Suzanne looked over at her husband. "I'm sorry to be so blunt about all this," she said. "I am not trying to hurt you. I just don't want to be married anymore."*

*Adam swallowed the contents of his mouth. "You mean you don't want to be married to me anymore."*

*Suzanne turned her head sideways, thinking. "Yes," she said after a moment or two. "That's true."*

*"Tell me, Suzanne," Adam said. "Why now? Why today?" He flashed on his earlier decision to postpone the whole matter, remembering how relieved he felt. Now, he paused for a moment and in an effort to hold onto his pride said, "It's not that this is surprising, really. I know you're unhappy. Truth be told, I'm not very happy either. But I was wondering about the timing." He looked across the table at his wife. "Why now?"*

Good question, Riley thought. She couldn't wait to hear the answer.

*Suzanne put her fork down and stared at Adam for a long moment. "It wasn't any one thing," she said. "It's a lot of things. I'm not sleeping very well. I haven't looked forward to coming home for some time. Months maybe. I can't wait to go to work in the morning. Our sex life is shot." She bit the inside of her mouth. "You don't seem interested in me or in my career."*

*More silence. Suzanne was trying to think of ways to soften this blow to Adam, and Adam was trying hard to grasp that this was the woman he had come to see as avoidant, passive, and mostly—he was searching for the right word in his mind—superficial. Suzanne said, "We are really different people. And I think we want different things."*

Different things, indeed, Riley thought. But what were these different things?

*Adam looked down at the table trying to gather his thoughts before speaking. After a few minutes, he said, "Honestly, Suzanne, I know this is hard, but it is not completely unexpected. I have been thinking the same thing for some time now. We're not happy, but I thought maybe it was just a phase married people go through. And I haven't known what to do about it. I haven't known for a long time. Months, as you said."*

*Then, from some less wobbly part of his self-esteem and as if recalling an idea he had forgotten, Adam said, "Are you seeing someone else?"*

*Suzanne did not respond right away, but her ears reddened and her face took on a paler hue.*

*"Who?" Adam asked, mostly in an effort to mask his shock and hurt.*

*Suzanne looked away. "Nobody you know," she whispered.*

*Adam turned away from the table. He couldn't look at his wife. This was an entirely new piece. He was angry; he could feel his body temperature rise and his hands begin to tremble. He didn't want to lash out. He didn't really want to hurt Suzanne. But he was boiling inside. Unhappiness is one thing; infidelity is quite another. He took deep breaths to contain the rage that was still building.*

*"How long?" he asked, turning his head back towards Suzanne.*

*Suzanne looked away, trying to decide how much information to share. "I don't want to talk about this right now."*

*"What?! Just when do you intend to talk about it?" He could not mask the sarcastic tone in his voice.*

*Suzanne didn't say anything. Adam could feel her more typical pattern of silence and avoidance creeping into the room. "Say something!" he commanded.*

*After another long pause, Suzanne began: "It's, it's complicated," she said. "It started a few months ago, and honestly I thought it was just because I was so unhappy at home." She looked at Adam. "I wasn't looking to get involved with another person."*

*This is bullshit, Adam thought. She is being deliberately vague. He pushed back from the table, crossed his legs, folded his arms across his chest, and waited, staring at his wife, feeling wounded and righteous.*

*Suzanne looked out toward the window to her right, looked back at Adam, and returned to the window. This happened several times before she spoke.*

*"As I said, you don't know her."*

*Her. The word cleared the air and hung in the space between them. Her. Not him. Not a man. A woman.*

*Of all the things that Adam had wondered about over the course of this last year of their rocky marriage, he did not consider for once that he wife, his lovely, charming, witty, beloved wife, was gay. The slow-motion explosion in his head prevented him from saying anything, he was so shocked.*

*"Wow" finally came out of his mouth.*

*Suzanne looked up at him. "Yeah," she said. "Wow."*

This is getting interesting, Riley thought to herself. Of course, thoughts of her friend Jen were clamoring to be heard inside her head, but she kept her focus on the screen.

*"And actually," continued Suzanne, "You do know her. Or at least of her. It's Ellie, my boss."*

*The air in the room suddenly felt thinner. Adam's mind had trouble holding onto the thing that Suzanne just said; he felt numb. He didn't know what to say. He was trying to recall if he had met this woman, the woman who is Suzanne's direct superior. He couldn't place her.*

*"You only met her once, and it was a couple years ago," said Suzanne helpfully. "It was at the office Christmas party. I think you met her only briefly. She wasn't my boss then."*

*Asking one of the million questions coursing through Adam's mind might, he thought, help him get some focus. "So how did this happen?"*

*Suzanne, who was feeling the relief that comes from confessing the truth, continued in a soft voice. "We'd been working more closely together these past few months. She noticed that I didn't seem happy and was always willing to stay at work late." She looked at her husband askance. "She was kind to me. She listened. She was sensitive. She cared."*

*Adam knew that those were the things Suzanne didn't feel she got from him. This was an astounding thought, as he had come to think of her as the emotionally unavailable one; but he didn't say anything. He was beginning to realize that the situation he had seen one way had other parts that made it mind-numbingly complicated. In some ways this took him off the hook. He was beginning to feel a little smug and even a little more self-righteous. He wanted to hold onto that. "And?" he said.*

*"And one late afternoon, we were the only two left in the office. We were sitting on her couch and one thing led to another and . . ."*

*"And what?"*

*"And I don't need to go into the details. Let's just say we shared our feelings with each other."*

*More silence.*

*"Jesus, Suzanne," Adam finally said. "I don't know what to say."*

And neither do I, Riley thought.

She sat back in her chair. At least Adam had something specific to hold onto. He couldn't possibly in this day and age think that it was impossible for him to be in some kind of love triangle with two women. His ego should be intact, but one never knows about male egos.

Curious to find out more, Riley resumed writing.

*"I just have one more question," said Adam softly. "Is this truly it? Are you leaving me for this woman?" He thought for a moment. "Or is this a passing thing, something that we can perhaps get through." He was surprised at the olive branch and unsure if he even wanted a reconciliation. But there it was.*

*Suzanne looked at him with a mixture of curiosity, sadness, irritation, and even caring. "I don't think so, Adam. I mean I don't think I'm leaving you for her. I'm leaving you because, because there has just been too much water under the bridge." She looked across the table with a sad, sweet smile. "I think this marriage has run its course."*

*And as much as he didn't want to or plan to, Adam felt a flood of tears rising in his body. He tried to hold his breath, to remain immobile; anything to forestall what he was sure would be a humil-iating display of emotion. It didn't work: the tears flowed full force. He broke down and sobbed. It was all too much. He was mortified, all the worse because it caught him by surprise. He was hurt, despite Suzanne's intentions not to hurt him. Perversely, he was proud of his wife for stepping up to the plate, for being so straightforward. He didn't disagree with her diagnosis. After all, wasn't he planning on having a similar conversation with Suzanne just an hour before? He put his head in his hands in an effort to contain the grief that was suddenly his.*

*Suzanne did not move. She cared for Adam, but she had a definite sense that his tears were necessary. Let him cry it out, she thought. He'll get over it sooner. She couldn't stop thinking of Ellie.*

Hard-hearted bitch, thought Riley.

No, came a voice from inside her. A realistic woman. Riley could not help wishing that Cameron would shed those kinds of tears at the thought of losing her. But she wasn't sure she could be so patient as to wait for the eternity it would take.

# — 5 —

Riley's phone rang. It was Cameron. She sighed heavily and picked up her phone, trying to decide whether to answer it or not. She decided not to.

A moment later, she heard the familiar ding of a new voicemail. No doubt, Cameron left a message for her to call him. It's always the same sunny message. "Hi. It's Cameron. Call me."

She didn't want to call him. She did not believe that Cameron had anything close to the capacity for emotional candor that was playing out on the computer screen in front of her by characters of her own creation.

That's unfair, came the voice inside her head.

Yes, it is, she thought. She punched the voicemail button on her phone.

And the voicemail was mostly as expected, but something was different. Cameron's voice was not sunny and bright; in fact, it was almost shaky. It wasn't his normal, full-throated, confident voice. It wasn't 'Hi. It's Cameron. Call me.' It was more like 'Uh, it's, uh, Cameron. Umm, call . . . me.'

This was unexpected.

She punched the 'return call' button.

When Cameron answered he still sounded shaky. "Cameron, what's the matter?"

There was a long pause on the other end of the line. "Umm," Cameron finally began. "I, uh, I, uh . . ."

Riley stared at the phone as if Cameron could see her encouraging him to finish his sentence.

"I was fired today," he finally said in a voice that was palpably shame-ridden.

"What?! Fired?! Cameron, why? What happened?"

"I don't know exactly. They were pretty vague. They talked about downsizing the company. They said it wasn't about my performance." He paused a bit. "I don't know what to do, Riley. I thought everything was fine at work. It's always been fine."

"You're a hard worker, Cameron. I've never heard you complain, and I've never heard any criticism of your work." She too paused a moment. "I don't know what to say."

She could hear him crying on the phone. Not the usual here-one-moment-gone-the-next type of crying, but sustained, heavy sobs. She could almost feel his body shaking over the phone. She absently glanced at her watch to time the outburst.

"I'm sorry," Cameron finally said. "I can't talk anymore right now." And he hung up.

Riley stared at the now dead phone. Really? It's upsetting to lose a job, but Cameron is a computer technician. He will probably have another job by tomorrow afternoon. She put her phone down and looked around.

She was torn. On the one hand, she understood his reaction, but never before had she comprehended just how important Cameron's job was to him. She thought of his father, who was a genuine workaholic, often absent for weeks from his family. It was no surprise when they learned after his death that he had sired children with another woman in another city.

Slowly, an idea began blooming in Riley's mind that she had never recognized before: work was Cameron's top priority. Not me, not his marriage, not a family he might have had. But work. Just like his father, who died in his car at the young-ish age of fifty-seven.

Her phone rang; it was Cameron again. "I'm sorry, Riley. I just wanted to let you know. And I didn't know who else to call. Tomorrow I'll be busy looking for another job."

He said this as if to explain why he might not call her.

"Of course, Cameron," she said. "Tough break." Hard-hearted bitch, she thought about herself.

Cameron hung up.

Riley clicked off her phone again but stared at it for a few moments. Huh, she thought. So this is where he lives; this is what's most important to him.

She knew Cameron to be a hard-working guy, and she didn't think for a minute that he wouldn't find another job. She thought maybe she could have been more sympathetic, but the fact that he was so casual about their separation and so distraught about losing his job just infuriated her. She could feel her body temperature rising and her hands trembling. She was seldom this angry about anything.

She found the number of her attorney and scheduled an appointment with his secretary. She thought of calling Jennifer, but she was no doubt at work. Her heart was racing, and her thoughts were scattered. That son of a bitch.

And then she thought: Why didn't I see this before? Obviously, he was fastidious about work, but that was a trait common to young people who wanted to succeed in their lives. But the emotional tug of work for Cameron was something she had completely over-looked. She felt blindsided in addition to being angry.

She couldn't write when she was this angry. She shut down her computer, grabbed her keys and laptop and fled her apartment. Maybe the coffee shop, she thought, or maybe a bar.

It's not even noon. No bar!

She took deep breaths as she walked. Never during the course of her marriage to Cameron had she been this angry with him. In some ways it seemed like a small thing, but in her mind it was a huge thing. It explained everything: his studied insouciance, his indifference to anything she ever said. He probably wasn't even listening; he was probably thinking about work or planning about it. For the first time in Riley's life, she felt true *Schadenfreude*: she was taking glee in someone else's misfortune. Serves him right, the self-centered prick.

She passed by her usual Starbucks and glanced in the window. There, sitting nursing a latte and just looking around, was Edward, the strange man she met the previous day. Almost without thinking, she walked into the shop and headed straight for him.

"What are you doing here during the day?" she asked, the intensity surprising even her.

"We're off today. Something wrong with the HVAC system. Classes were cancelled."

This sounded suspicious to Riley, but she didn't care.

"You remember that date you asked me on?" she said, looking at him straight in the eye.

"Yeah?" replied Edward slowly.

"I'm ready," said Riley.

Edward looked confused. "Now?"

"Yes, now. Let's start here. Buy me a cup of coffee."

"Okay," said Edward, standing up and reaching for his wallet.

To the surprise of both of them, as soon as Edward stood up, Riley threw her arms around him and planted a huge kiss on his lips.

Edward, completely taken by surprise, did not have time to defend himself. He followed Riley's lead, kissing her back as much as his surprised self would allow.

The two stood locked in an embrace in the middle of a mostly deserted coffee shop. Not quite completely deserted, however, and the few patrons who had been otherwise occupied could not help watching the peculiarly intimate scene being played out within a few feet of them.

"Never mind the coffee," Riley said. "I live close."

Edward's eyes were not naturally prominent but grew large on the spot. "Oh, my God," he whispered.

And Riley took his hand and led him out the door.

# — 6 —

Fortunately, Edward turned out not to be a mad serial killer or some other variant of psychopath. Riley thought he was a little unpracticed at sex, but he was an eager student and Riley was an aggressive teacher. The ersatz couple spent the afternoon in bed, taking brief breaks in between passionate acrobatics. Around 4:00 p.m., Riley rolled over and turned to Edward.

"That was great, Edward. It's time for you to leave now."

Edward looked at Riley without protest. He rolled over onto his back and stared for a moment at the ceiling. He was worn out and didn't have much more to give. And, since he didn't know how he had gotten into this predicament in the first place, it did not faze him that Riley asked him to leave.

"Okay," he said simply. And he got up to retrieve his clothes.

All the while, his mind was fuzzy. Not an unhappy fuzzy—in fact, a delightful one. But he had no clue what he did to end up in Riley's bed in the middle of the day. He had had sex with girlfriends before, but it always had a tinge of guilt and self-consciousness about it—always at night; always in the dark—nothing like the go-anywhere, do-anything spontaneity of this afternoon's unanticipated tryst. The fact was, whatever insecurities he had in his life about sex were demolished twenty minutes into the afternoon. He was completely swept up in an unbridled passion he had never experienced before.

He felt a need to say something to Riley, but everything sounded bone-headed in his mind. What do I say? Thank you? Can I have your number? What is your last name? Any of these questions seemed to him to risk shattering the delicious balance of pleasure and tantalizing uncertainty he felt throughout his body.

And there was no question that he would do anything Riley asked him to do. She wanted him to leave? Gone. If she'd wanted him to stay, he would have stayed. He was completely powerless to do anything but what this woman wanted of him at the moment.

In this mental fog, he gathered up his clothes and put them on as best he could given his fatigued but sated state. He leaned over Riley's nude body to kiss her one last time, but her face had turned to marble, and he ended up grazing her forehead with is lips. He nodded to her and walked out the door.

After he left Riley got up to lock the door; then she lay back on her bed and gave herself a moment to check in with her body, her feelings, and then her thoughts. She felt completely relaxed in a way she hadn't in months. Her body felt warm, and she cherished the feeling. After a while, she stretched and breathed and waited for her body to return to its normal, non-coital state.

The anger she felt had dissipated. She wasn't so angry at the moment, although it was very clear to her that the reasons for her outrage remained unchanged. She felt the tiniest bit of guilt for being so aggressive with Edward; but he had wanted to date her, so she decided he was fair game.

She let herself breathe deeply the luxury of the moment.

Then she got up slowly and walked unclothed across the room. She was in no hurry to cover her body: she felt free and didn't want that feeling to leave her. She looked at herself in the mirror and liked what she saw.

Riley got back into bed, and her attention gradually returned to her soon-to-be-former husband. The anger that had been nearly extinguished during her sexual escapades with Edward stirred inside her. She dozed off to fantasies of revenge.

She awoke after an hour to the sound of her phone buzzing. She was instantly alert and noticed how good she felt as she glanced at the screen to see who it was.

"Hi, Jen," she said, hitting the talk button.

"Hi, Riley," came the cheerful response. "Are you free?"

"More than you know."

Jennifer chuckled. She had no idea what Riley meant, but she could tell by the tone of her voice that her friend had turned some kind of corner.

"Remember Edward?"

Jen thought for a moment. "The creepy guy in the coffee shop?"

"Yeah, that one. I spent the afternoon fucking his brains out."

Silence.

More silence.

Riley could not tell if this was approving or disapproving quiet. She thought maybe she had been a bit too frank for her uninter-ested-in-males friend. She didn't care. She started laughing softly.

"Jen?"

"Yeah?"

"Um, did I offend you?" She bit her lower lip.

"No. I'm just thinking."

"What are you thinking?"

Jen chuckled softly. "Lucky bastard: that's what I'm thinking."

Riley rolled over in her bed and laughed even louder. "I'm pretty sure it was one of the luckiest days of his life."

"I take it this is . . . a relationship?"

"Hell no, it's not a relationship. I don't even know his last name."

There was quiet on the line for a few moments.

"Look," Riley said at last. "I've got some work to catch up on. But let's hook up . . . I mean, let's get together sometime soon. Tomorrow? Dinner?"

"Dinner tomorrow, it is," Jen replied. "See you then, Honey."

Riley clicked off her phone, got up from bed, and walked into the bathroom. She again looked at her naked body in the mirror. I feel whole. I feel free. I feel ready to put Cameron in the past.

This feeling was so novel, Riley felt as if she had misplaced herself somehow. She wondered where she had been all these last months or years. Being involved with a self-obsessed workaholic must have taken a bigger toll than she thought. But now she no longer felt connected to Cameron. She felt free to look after herself. She felt an unfamiliar absence of guilt. She took in a deep breath and gazed at her face in the mirror. "Finally!" she said out loud.

She turned and threw on some clothes and sat down at her computer to resume her work. But this time, it didn't feel like work. It didn't feel like the oppressive work of writing so much as an opportunity to create something. By rights, she did not know what would happen to her characters. They have their own lives, and she has hers.

She put her fingers over the keyboard.

*Adam couldn't help but feel awkward when it came time to turn in for the night. The pair had not spoken since dinner, and he could not think of a single, sensible thing to say to his wife, whom he was now seeing in a completely new light. The torrential tears had subsided, and he felt, well, he didn't know what he felt. Empty, maybe; or resigned. He wasn't sure. It all felt so momentous. He looked at the clock; it was nearing ten. He glanced over at Suzanne, who was sitting on the other end of the sofa watching TV as diligently as she usually did, seemingly unconcerned about whatever events she had put into motion. And by all accounts oblivious to him.*

*"Uh, I'm going to bed, Suzanne," he said as casually as he could. In fact, he was agitated, and his stomach was roiling. He didn't know what to do; he didn't know what Suzanne wanted. His pride was still smarting from the disclosure about her affair with her boss. What was her name? Oh, yeah: Ellie.*

*He wasn't sure he could lie next to his wife and contain the impulse to strike out at her. He wasn't by nature a physical or violent person, but the more the thought of her indiscretion settled into his mind, the angrier he got. He had been pretending to watch television, but he was paying almost no attention to whatever was on. For all he knew, neither was Suzanne. He didn't care.*

*Because he couldn't think of anything else to say, he just turned and went into their bedroom.*

*Maybe I should sleep on the couch, he thought. Then he realized that Suzanne was sitting on the couch, and it just seemed awkward to ask her to move so he could sleep there. Maybe she would sleep there. He shook his head. He was completely unprepared for the role of a soon-to-be-divorced thirty-something.*

Aren't we all, mused Riley.

Through a series of texts the next morning, it was decided that Jen and Riley would meet up at a new restaurant, one they had both been wanting to try.

When Riley showed up for dinner at the appointed time, Jennifer was nowhere to be seen. This was so uncharacteristic of her, Riley automatically felt some worry. When she looked around and didn't see her, she asked for a table for two and positioned herself so that she could see the door. All the while, she was wondering absently if this had ever happened, if she had ever gotten to a place before Jen did. She couldn't recall a single time.

She ordered her usual gin and tonic and pulled out her phone to check email. Nothing of interest. She was perusing Facebook when Jennifer appeared at her table and sat down directly across from her.

"Hi, Honey," Jen said. "Sorry I'm late."

Riley shrugged. "Not like you."

Jen shrugged back. "No, it's not."

The server came, and Jen ordered her usual gin martini. The pair chatted for a while. Jennifer did not disclose why she was late, and Riley didn't ask.

After the small talk, Jen turned and looked directly into Riley's eyes.

"So? What's the deal with Edward?"

Riley chuckled softly. She detected a hint of something in Jen's voice, but wasn't exactly sure what it was. Disapproval? Jealousy?

Some combination of the two? But she was eager to share what had happened.

"Okay, here's the story. Around noon yesterday I got a call from Cameron. He was upset, really upset. And you know, Cameron just doesn't do upset."

Jen's drink came, but she didn't take her eyes off Riley. She nodded a little too solemnly for the occasion.

"And he says he'd been fired from his job, and he breaks down into tears." Riley took a sip of her drink. "And I mean big tears, like death-of-a-loved-one tears."

"And instead of being the compassionate, supportive wife that I am, I didn't say anything. I'm thinking to myself: He's in tears about losing his job? He had no reaction—and I mean zero emotional reaction—when I told him I wanted to separate. All he said was something like 'If that's what you want'. I was so angry. No, not angry: furious, enraged. After all this time, I finally got it. I finally understood that Cameron's number one priority in his life is his work. He doesn't really give a crap about me or about having a family or about his friends. He only cares about his work."

Jen tilted her head, as if this were a new slant on the story.

"So after I hung up from Cameron, I was seething. Here I'd been feeling guilt for wanting out of our relationship, but I never really felt certain about the reasons I wanted out. Oh, I had reasons, even some good reasons, according to my therapist. But they were never enough to expunge the guilt I felt for insisting on a separation from poor, hard-working, nice-guy Cameron."

She took a long sip from her cocktail. Jen was quiet, listening intently, her drink untouched.

"I was so angry I couldn't work, so I left the apartment and went for a walk. I headed toward Starbucks and who do I see but creepy, shy, awkward, not-bad-looking Edward. So I walked right up to him and said, "Do you still want a date?" and he says, well, I don't really know what he said because I threw my arms around him and kissed him with a vengeance right there in the middle of the coffee shop."

A small, controlled smile was beginning to make an appearance across Jen's still-stolid face.

"And I took him to my apartment, and we spent the afternoon having angry, aggressive, screw-the-world sex for the better part of the afternoon."

Riley stopped and squinted at her friend for a moment. "TMI?"

"No, no," sputtered Jen. "It's just . . . just . . . just so not you!" Her eyes sparkled a little. "Me, yes; but you . . . I'm having a hard time picturing this."

Riley tilted herself sideways and met Jen's eyes. "I've never done anything like that in my life." She paused just a moment. "Not sober anyway. It was wonderful." She paused and took another sip of her drink. "After Edward left, I felt free: free of the guilt, free of Cameron, free of my obsessive self-critical thinking. Free in a way I'd never felt before." She chuckled softly. "Free enough to call the attorney and make an appointment to finally file for divorce. Which I did this afternoon."

"Wow!" said Jen.

"Yeah. Wow," replied Riley.

Silence descended on the pair for a few moments. Riley was still savoring her new-found freedom, and Jen was trying to wrap her mind around the changes she was seeing in her friend.

"Does this mean we can have sex now?" As soon as Jen said it, she knew she had crossed an inviolate line.

Riley's reaction took her by surprise. She didn't respond right away. She put her drink on the table and looked straight into Jen's eyes. "Who knows?"

There was a moment when that short phrase fell out of her mouth that the two women held an intimate eye-to-eye look. An ethereal silence inserted itself.

Then the moment passed.

Riley didn't want to have sex with Jen. But she was still pumped from the afternoon before—even more so, really, since meeting with her attorney this afternoon—and she so wanted to keep Jen as a friend that she couldn't close the door permanently on something she was pretty sure Jennifer wanted. She thought it was silly and impulsive when she said it, but she had this definite sense that Jen was not entirely happy with her at the moment. And the last thing she wanted was to lose her as a friend.

The two sat in what looked like amiable silence for a while, sipping their drinks and letting the stress level recede some.

Riley reached across the table and patted Jen's hand. "I am so glad you are my friend," she said, looking into Jen's eyes.

Jen turned her hand around and squeezed Riley's. "Me, too, Riley. But sometimes, sometimes, you know . . ."

"I know." Riley had no idea what Jen was talking about; in fact, she did not want to know.

Fortunately, the server came up and asked if they had any questions about the menu. The pair picked up the single-sheet menus and looked them over.

"I'll have the crab cakes," Riley said.

"The same for me," said Jen.

The server departed and the two resumed their slightly less comfortable silence.

"So, are you going to see him again? This Edward guy?"

"Jen, I don't even know his last name or where he lives or his cell phone number or anything. All I know is that he occasionally hangs out at a Starbucks near me, the door of which I will never darken again."

Jen laughed and the distinct heaviness that had been in the air between them began to evaporate a bit.

"How's your book coming?" she asked, ready to change the subject.

Riley thought for a while. "I'm not sure it's actually a book," she said. "It may be more of a . . . I don't know . . . a therapeutic exercise. I guess I could call it a memoir of sorts."

This was met by a quizzical look on her friend's face.

"I'm writing about a divorcing couple. It bears too much of a resemblance to the past year of my life." She paused and took another sip of her drink. "It's coming, but not as quickly as I would like."

"Can't wait to hear how it turns out," Jen said.

"Neither can I," replied Riley.

Jennifer smiled inwardly. She never understood Riley's approach to writing. Riley invariably described it as if she weren't in charge of the process, as if she were somehow channeling her characters out of thin air rather than deliberately creating them. This sounded a little weird and even disingenuous to her, but since she was barely a reader and not at all a writer, she just chalked it up to an area of life about which she would remain forever ignorant.

The crab cakes came, and the pair picked up their utensils as if on cue. The bond between them, having been restored, felt stronger to each of them, at least on the surface. They ate in companionable silence.

Gradually, the conversation resumed and shifted to more mundane topics. It even touched upon Jen's work, which she ordinarily never talked about. In fact, Riley wasn't exactly clear about what it was Jen did. All she knew was that she worked for a large company, travelled occasionally, and it had something to do with training other people in the company. For all her amiability and apparent openness, Jennifer was not very revealing, even with the person she regarded as her best friend. So Riley was eager to hear about her friend's workday.

"I had a bear of a day today," Jen said in between forkfuls of crab.

"Tell me about it," Riley said, expecting more details.

"Some people are just never satisfied."

Silence. Riley motioned with her fork for Jen to continue.

"Same old bullshit," said Jen with a sense of finality.

Still vague about what she does, Riley thought. She put another bite of crab into her mouth.

After a while, they finished eating, split the check, and got up to leave. As they crossed the threshold of the restaurant, Riley said, "Nice place," and casually wrapped her arm around Jen's. She could feel her friend tense slightly and then relax, as if she were taken by surprise; but Riley was just having warm feelings towards her.

At the corner where they were to go their separate ways, Riley turned to Jen and said, "Thanks for being there for me, Jen. I love you."

Now it was Jennifer's turn to bite her lower lip. She did not say anything, but she gently put her arms around Riley and pulled her close. She fought off an urge to kiss her and said, "And I you, Riley." Then she dropped her arms, stepped back, turned, and pointed herself in the direction of her apartment.

# — 8 —

Riley had vivid dreams that night. She dreamt of Jennifer, of Edward, and of Cameron. They were part of a committee together, something having to do with her, but she wasn't sure what. It wasn't a nightmare, but it felt like a serious dream, and it woke her from a deep sleep in the middle of the night, wondering what it might mean.

She got up to go to the bathroom and have a drink of water. She didn't really know what to make of the past few days, except for the fact that she knew something deep inside her had changed. It wasn't just about sex or about Cameron or Edward or about Jennifer; it was something about her. And these people she had had dealings with over the past twenty-four hours were each playing a role in her life. Significant roles, she felt for sure. She just wasn't sure what they were. And at the moment, she decided she didn't need to know.

She got back in bed and turned off the light. Tomorrow she would resume her normal routine and continue working on the book she had started.

Within minutes, she fell into a deep sleep.

The same dream picked up where it had left off. The three characters were sitting on one side of a table, as if in a tribunal of some sort. They were discussing Riley, who was watching the scene, from another chair facing the threesome. In the dream, Riley felt detached. She was wondering why they were talking about her but in her heart she knew it didn't make one bit of difference. They really didn't know her. Nobody did.

And it was with that thought in mind that she awoke to the sound of her alarm. Nobody? She ran through the principals of her life: her parents, previous boyfriends, school friends, work friends, the current set of people she knew. She wondered which of them knew her the most.

And only one person really stood out. And that was Jennifer. But Riley knew in her heart that she was careful even in her presence. True, she had been fairly open with her this past evening, but not entirely. And she was aware that cracking the door open just a bit on the prospect of having a sexual dalliance with her friend was dangerous territory. It was something she had never seriously considered before and in fact wasn't considering now. She had no idea why she had done it, other than she had some apprehension that Jen might leave her if she was too definitively closed to such an arrangement.

This is crazy, she thought. I've got to get to work.

And she did. After her morning ritual of showering, make-up, coffee and toast, she ambled over to her computer and powered it up. Without pausing for a moment, she started typing as soon as the Word document reopened.

*The next morning Adam woke up at his usual time, 6:30, to find the bed empty. He sat up and wondered groggily if Suzanne had just gotten up before him, but her side of the bed had been untouched. He went straight to the bathroom, threw on some clothes, and walked into the living room. Empty.*

*Adam stood motionless for a moment. Where could she be? He looked around the house, which wasn't large. He even checked the basement. Finally, he looked out the window and noticed her car was gone.*

*She left?*

*Adam was beginning to feel a little unhinged: mentally he could feel himself split a bit, as if his grasp of reality was shaky. He went into the kitchen to make coffee and found a note on the door of the refrigerator.*

*Adam,*
*I couldn't bear staying here for the night,*

*so I went to a hotel. I'll contact you tomorrow.*
*Suzanne*

*Jesus! Adam thought.* He dropped the note on the counter and continued making coffee, glancing at it every few seconds. He was angry, he was scared. He felt tears rolling down his cheek and fury inside his gut. *She's really serious about this.* And he was just getting a glimpse of how little he knew the woman he was married to.

Adam went about his morning as he always did, minus the casual conversation with his wife that ordinarily began their day together. She usually left around 8:30, and he didn't start work until around 9:00. He glanced at his watch: 7:45. *Time to kill.*

Ignoring the feelings wracking is body, he pushed the speed dial button on his phone to call Suzanne. He had no idea what he was going to say or why he did it. It just didn't seem right for him to start the day without touching base.

The call went straight to voice mail.

*Her phone's off? She never turns her phone off.*

*Maybe she was on another call.*

That thought made him even angrier, as the only person he could imagine her being on the phone with was Ellie. He threw his phone down on the table.

*I'll be damned if . . .*

But there was nothing to follow the 'if'. All Adam knew at that moment was that he hated and feared his wife and would never show weakness in her presence again.

"I understand," Riley said aloud to her computer screen.

Adam forced himself to focus on his routine. He powered up his computer to get the daily instructions from his supervisor at work. As he downloaded the file, his face did not waver from the screen. He just wanted to think about work; he didn't want to think about Suzanne. He knew he was too angry, too sad, too jumbled up inside to make sense out of that situation just now. And, truth be told, he felt he was still in shock. The irony of his wife being the one to throw down the gauntlet on the very same day when he had been wrestling with a similar desire arose every time Suzanne flashed in his mind.

*But it was the news that she had cheated that kept going through his mind. He kept repeating it in his mind: she cheated; I didn't. And the fact that it was with another woman . . . well, he had no idea of what to make of that.*

*After forcing himself to work for a couple hours, he pushed back from the computer and took a deep breath. Why didn't I cheat? It's true, there weren't many opportunities these last few years as his job became pretty much telecommuting, but he could have hooked up with someone.*

*The fact was he never wanted to. Suzanne was a lovely woman and, at least in the beginning, a willing sex partner. He had an old-fashioned sense of loyalty that formed a natural boundary to what he would and would not allow himself. It was probably easier since he had so few contacts with women, but he thought that, even if he had spent time at an office, he still would not have gotten involved with another woman. In addition to whatever loyalty he had to Suzanne, the prospect of another sexual relationship just seemed too damned complicated.*

*Now all that felt foolish. Now he just felt like a cuckolded husband, a naïf whose 'virtue' seemed just an excuse for inaction. He knew he'd been unhappy for a long time. And his sex life with Suzanne was more historical than recent. It had fallen off precipitously this past year. His chalking that up to getting older, even at the tender age of twenty-eight, now felt like willful blindness.*

*Adam looked back at the computer. He figured he had about another hour and a half to complete his daily assignment, so he began powering through it just to rid himself of the thoughts that refused to leave his consciousness alone. I can do this, he thought. And he could.*

*Approaching noon, he was wrapping up his work when his cell phone rang. Suzanne!*

*"Yes?"*

*"Adam it's me," Suzanne said unnecessarily. I . . . I'm sorry I left last night, but I just couldn't bear being there."*

*Silence on the phone. Adam had no idea what to say.*

*"Do you want me to come home tonight?"*

*No response.*

*"Adam?"*

*"I don't know what to tell you, Suzanne. If you want to come home, come home. If you don't, don't."* It was all his hatred would allow.

*After a pause, Suzanne said, "Well, I guess we'll see how I feel later today." The line went dead.*

*This is marriage? Adam thought.*

*It's how it ends, came a voice inside his head.*

# — 9 —

The day following her intriguing dinner with Riley, Jennifer Stokowski left her office at noon. She had gone to work in the morning as usual, but there wasn't much for her to do, and she was still churning about Riley's seductive behavior with her the evening before. She couldn't get it out of her mind. Jennifer knew how she was: she knew she relished the thought of a tryst with Riley, but she also knew that it would be short term and would likely end their relationship. The fact that Riley and she had been friends without sexual intimacy for so long was unusual for Jennifer. She had some friends, even some good ones, but they were mostly old college buddies who lived out of town. There was no one she felt so close to as Riley, and she always felt lucky that they had gotten together.

And even though there was a distinct sexual undercurrent on her part, she intentionally kept it in check. Riley always intimated that she was straight, whatever that meant. In addition, it was privately a matter of pride for Jennifer: it wasn't often she kept her sexual feelings under wraps. In fact, she could barely remember being attracted to another woman and not using whatever wiles she had at her disposal to land in bed together. She was pretty good at it.

But Riley was different. When they met almost two years ago, her attraction to Riley was immediate. Jennifer was always very attuned to her sexual responses. But Riley made it clear from the get-go that she wasn't interested in sex. Not that she had to say anything; she just had a defensive perimeter around her that extinguished unwanted advances as soon as they appeared. And Jennifer was too attuned to those sorts of signals to miss them.

But she liked Riley immediately. They met at a conference, a writers' conference as it turned out, and Riley was wandering from booth to booth seeing what each had to offer. Jen was there for her company, where she was involved in marketing. Her company sold marketing packages to authors and do-it-yourself publishers. Jen remembered it as if it were yesterday.

Riley walked up to the exhibit about ten minutes before closing, glanced at the sign and said, "I could use some marketing help. I hate to do it!" And then she laughed nervously.

Jennifer, her systems alerted by this attractive woman drifting casually into her orbit, responded immediately with "That's okay, because I love to do it."

The two started talking and ended up getting a drink that evening. Riley was not only attractive; she was smart, quick-witted, and curious. Just the kind of woman Jen was drawn to. At the end of that first evening, they each expressed a desire to stay in touch. They exchanged business cards.

And they did get together a couple days later. Jen called Riley to see how she was doing and if she remembered her.

"Of course, I do, Jen. You're the only person I've ever met who's said she likes marketing."

"You don't get out enough, Riley," Jen replied. "In my circles, everyone likes marketing. Or at least they do a good job of pretending to like it."

The two had dinner that evening and regularly ever since.

In the early weeks of their relationship, Jen would make oblique references to sex in order to test the water. Riley almost never responded, or if she did it was to say some bland thing about how great her sex life with her husband was. Jen didn't think that sounded so genuine as it did defensive, but, according to Riley, sex was one of the highlights of her marriage, or so Jen understood it. Riley never said anything else about her husband.

Jennifer was usually undaunted by women, even women who were married to men, who often protested their heterosexuality a little too much. She had slept with plenty women in similar circumstances. But she got nowhere with Riley.

And then finally, one day about a year later, she flat out asked Riley. "You know I'm gay, right?"

Riley responded with a mix of a nod and a head shake, which Jen interpreted to mean that maybe she had an idea but wasn't sure and it didn't really matter anyway and it was all right with her no matter which way she was oriented.

And she was right about that interpretation.

Ever since then, Jen kept her attraction under wraps for the most part. She still was drawn to Riley, and she still held out the prospect that maybe it would be more than friendship, but she didn't push it. It was something of a personal challenge, but the fact was she just liked Riley the way she was, sex or no sex.

But yesterday was different. For the first time there was a breach in Riley's armor. Jen scolded herself, albeit mildly, for having broached the issue of sleeping with her, but she was shocked at her friend's response.

Do I or don't I want to sleep with her? she kept asking herself. And what's with Riley, screwing a guy all afternoon and then telling me about it? And then flirting with me?

That word 'flirting' kept popping up in her mind. What's up with that? Was she really flirting, or what that just me getting turned on by her story?

She found herself obsessing about this so much that she decided to take the afternoon off and do . . . she didn't know what. Go to the gym? Masturbate? Call an old flame? All of those seemed like equally unappealing paths.

So what she did was stop at a restaurant not far from her apartment and ordered lunch. Along with a nice glass of chardonnay. Jen didn't usually drink during the day; nor did she drink alone. But today seemed like the day to do something different. She didn't feel alone. She felt she was being accompanied by a large presence of big thoughts. And she was so keyed up she thought maybe a glass of wine would help.

And the wine did help her calm down a bit, so she ordered another. It's just wine, she thought.

A couple hours later, an inebriated woman attempted to stand up after paying her check in a mostly deserted restaurant that was about to close. She would have succeeded in standing, save for the fact that she was wearing shoes that slipped off very easily, and one of them slipped right off her left foot as she was attempting the standing maneuver. Her ankle twisted, and she thought she heard a pop.

"Son of a bitch!" she said not quietly.

The remaining serving staff, who were cleaning up from the lunch crowd, stared at her in the middle of the empty restaurant. Her server came up and asked if she was all right.

Jen looked at her as if she couldn't quite place her. "Do I know you?" she said, slurring her words. "Have we slept together?"

The server took a step back at the last comment. "Maybe you'd better sit back down," she said firmly.

Jen couldn't get the idea out of her head that somehow she knew this woman. Maybe she'd slept with her, but she couldn't recall when. Then again, maybe not. This fuzzy line of thought was interrupted by her suddenly throwing up on the white tablecloth. God my foot hurts.

Jesus! thought the server. She was so focused on her drunk guest that she didn't notice the day manager walk up behind her.

"Are you all right, Maggie?" he said. Maggie jumped. Then he looked down at the mess on the table and the smelly woman leaning sideways in the chair. He paled a little and then motioned for some of the other wait staff to come over and help.

"Let's get this woman into my office," he said.

Jennifer was largely impervious to what was going on around her. The room was spinning, and she felt she might vomit again. She had a terrible taste in her mouth. She was still wondering vaguely about her server and her foot when strong arms on either side of her lifted her up by the armpits and took her to the manager's office, where she was deposited on a worn sofa. It was a relief to be on a couch.

She fell asleep.

## 10

Riley got a call a little while later from the manager of the restaurant.

"Is this Riley Cotswald?" came a young male voice over the phone.

"Yes."

"Ms. Cotswald, I'm the manager of Caldwell's restaurant. We have a woman here who unfortunately got sick after lunch. She may have hurt her ankle. She is asleep in my office. We found her phone that she left on the table and took the liberty of checking it. Your number came up the most frequently."

It can only be Jennifer, Riley thought. But what was she doing in a restaurant on a workday afternoon? "What is her name?"

"Jennifer Stokowski," replied the manager, reading from Jen's driver's license.

"If she's sick, why don't you call an ambulance?"

The manager paused a moment. "Well, she isn't exactly sick. She's, um, drunk."

Jen? Drunk in the middle of the day?

"Are you sure?"

"Yes, quite sure. She threw up all over the table where she'd been sitting."

"I'll be right over."

She wasn't sure why she was going to the restaurant. What was she going to do? Carry Jennifer home? To her apartment?

She decided all she really had to do was check on her and see if she was okay. If, in fact, she needed an ambulance, she could call one. But Riley had a hunch she probably didn't need it.

Caldwell's Restaurant wasn't far from Riley's apartment, about a ten-minute walk. She couldn't decide if she should be worried or not. She was inclined not to be; she had a lot of confidence in Jennifer's ability to navigate difficult situations, even ones like this. So she didn't rush. Mostly she was surprised: no, not really surprised, just curious. How could she have done this?

She sauntered along the street taking in the welcome fresh air. It felt good to walk. She kept wondering what had happened to trigger this situation. She could not really fathom that her best friend would get drunk in the middle of the day when she should be working. Especially without telling her.

Riley knew she didn't really understand the details of what Jen did beyond what she learned when they first met and some throw-away references thereafter, but she assumed she had a regular job. She seemed to live well, and money was never a problem. But then she thought that maybe she didn't know Jen so well after all. What if she has a serious drinking problem? Riley had never seen her drunk, but she did love her martinis . . .

This thinking was going nowhere. She turned the corner to the street to where the restaurant was located. She noticed it was closed, probably between the lunch and dinner times; but lights were on inside.

She approached the closed door and pushed. It opened. She stuck her head in to look around and spotted a young man, no doubt the manager, heading right towards her.

"Are you Ms. Cotswald?"

"Yes. Call me Riley."

"This way, er, Riley."

He ushered Riley into his small office, where Jen was snoring on the couch.

The sight of her disheveled sleeping friend struck Riley as hilarious. She burst out laughing.

The manager was fidgeting. "Uh, does this happen often?" He was trying to be serious.

Riley managed to stop laughing and turned to the pale young man.

"No, it doesn't. As far as I know, it's never happened. What was she drinking?"

"Wine. White wine. She had five glasses of it over a two hour period."

That would do it, Riley thought. She sniffed the air. The vague smell of vomit was evident, and the clothes Jen was wearing were rumpled. Riley had never seen her like this.

"If we can wake her up, I'll get her home."

The manager let out a long sigh of relief. "Let me help you."

Riley bent over and shook Jen's arm. "Jen, it's Riley. Wake up, Honey."

Jen did not stir at first. Riley shook her a little harder.

"Jen . . ."

Jen's eyes opened. "Riley?" she said. Her eyes searched the room, trying to make sense of where she was and what she was doing. "Where am I?"

"You're at Cardwell's Restaurant. Evidently you got sick over lunch."

Jen crinkled up her face as she sniffed the air. "It smells in here."

"Yes, it does, Honey. Let's get you home."

Riley took Jen's arms and with the manager's help gently helped her sit up. "Can you stand?"

Jen nodded. "I think so." But she didn't move.

"Give me a minute."

Riley and the manager stood motionless, watching Jen trying to reconnect with the normal powers of locomotion, ready to catch her if she did not succeed. Jen looked up at them, a look of embarrassment on her face. "Okay," she said. "Here we go."

She got up unsteadily, grabbing waiting arms of the other two adults in the room. Once upright, she sighed. "Okay, then." And she started walking. After two steps, she let out a loud yelp. "My foot: I think I sprained it."

Everyone slowed down to give Jennifer time to think of what to do. Riley didn't have a car, and, if Jen's foot was sprained, it probably needed medical attention.

"Look," she said, turning to the manager. "I didn't drive here. In fact, I don't have a car. We need to get her to the hospital."

The manager, who was dreading this very situation, visibly surrendered. "Okay," he said. "I can call you a cab."

After helping Jen to the door of the restaurant, the manager left to make the phone call.

"I'm so sorry about this, Riley," Jen said.

Riley just nodded. "We'll talk about it later," she said. "Let's get you to a doctor."

A few minutes later, a taxi showed up, and Riley and the manager helped Jen into the back seat. Riley slid in beside her and took her hand. "St. Mary's Hospital," she said to the driver.

## 11

Hospitals are terrible places, Riley thought as she helped Jen out of the taxi and into the emergency room. Fortunately, there were not a lot of people around. It was late afternoon, not an especially busy time in the ER.

She deposited Jennifer in a chair and explained the situation to the intake attendant. Then she sat down next to her friend.

"How are you doing, Jen?"

Jennifer looked at Riley askance. Her face reddened. "Terrible," she said. "I am so embarrassed." A tear rolled down her cheek.

"Don't worry about this," Riley said. "We'll talk about it later, once you get that foot looked at."

The attendant announced Jennifer's name, and she hobbled to the door of the examining room with Riley's assistance. A nurse came in and took her vital signs. Otherwise, there was silence. The smell of alcohol was apparent.

And then the questions started. "How much did you have to drink? How often do you drink? How often does this happen?"

Jennifer looked at the nurse with squinted eyes. "I'm here for my foot. Otherwise, I never drink during the day. I took the day off. I wanted to relax. This has never happened before. Ordinarily I just drink socially."

"How much and how often?"

"A martini before dinner a couple times a week."

The nurse was writing. Riley was thinking this sounded about right.

"Have you ever been treated for alcoholism?"

Jen was shocked. "No, of course not."

"The doctor will see you shortly." She gathered up her things and left the room.

Jen looked at Riley. "Treatment for alcoholism?"

Riley just shrugged.

An x-ray tech walked in pushing an ungainly machine. "Gonna take pictures of that foot," said the earnest young man pushing it. He set about arranging it over Jen's shoeless foot.

After a few minutes, the young man looked up and said, "All finished." He pulled his equipment out of the room. Silence.

Jennifer closed her eyes for a moment. Here I am with my best friend in a terrible situation. She probably thinks I'm a drunk.

"Riley," she began. "You understand . . ."

Her words were cut off by the entrance of the doctor, who was carrying a chart. A heavy-set woman, about fifty, with reading glasses on her nose. She looked up from the paper. "I'm Dr. Sanders," she said, extending her hand to Jennifer.

"Hi, Dr. Sanders. This is my friend Riley."

The doctor nodded to Riley but quickly returned her attention to Jennifer. "Looks like you sprained your ankle. Nothing broken. We're going to wrap it and send you home."

Relief was palpable on Jen's face. The doctor continued.

"However, we understand this happened after you drank a lot of wine at lunch today." She gazed at Jen over her readers.

"Yes," Jen said. "That's correct."

Nobody spoke for a few minutes. Dr. Sanders turned to Riley. "Could you leave us alone a bit?"

Riley glanced at Jen, whose turn it was to shrug. Taking that as assent, she left the small examining room.

Riley waited at the nurses' station until Jen was finished. It didn't take long. She saw Dr. Sanders walk out the door of the examining room about ten minutes later, leaving it open and motioning with her head that it was okay for Riley go to back in.

She hesitated just a moment; then walked into the room.

She found Jen lying back on the examining table staring at the ceiling.

"What happened, Jen?"

"I got my first lecture on the evils of alcoholism," she said softly. "It wasn't pretty."

"What did she say?"

"She said this was how it starts: taking a drink to feel better because something bad happened. Then you start drinking more and more frequently until pretty soon you find you can't do without it." She lifted her head to face Riley. "A standard routine."

Riley didn't say anything.

"She also said that she didn't have enough data to suggest outright alcoholism, but that I should watch it and if it gets worse stop drinking and start going to AA meetings." She raised her hand, which contained a leaflet. "This is a list of available meetings in the area."

"I've never been so humiliated in my whole life."

"Let's get you home, Jen."

# — 12 —

The pair took a taxi to Jen's apartment, neither saying a word. When they got to the building, Riley spoke up.

"Do you need help up to your place, Jen?"

"No, thanks, Riley. I think I can make it."

Nothing further was said. Riley waited until Jen got through the main door of her apartment building before giving the driver her address to her own. She noticed that Jen did not turn and wave; she just limped up to the front door.

More silence during the short ride to her place. What's going on here? Riley wondered. Jen said that she wanted to take the afternoon off and relax. Why? While Riley wasn't sure of the details, she always thought that Jen was a consistent, reliable worker. And what's up with all the interest in her drinking? Riley never thought for a moment that Jennifer had a problem with alcohol, but she realized she might not know. From what she did know, alcoholics are known for keeping secrets.

And she did hurt herself in the process. But the question that kept coming back to Riley's mind was, What happened to trigger all this? There was obviously a big missing piece to the story. She had just seen Jen the day before, and nothing seemed wrong then.

As the taxi pulled onto her street, she found herself blushing over the mild flirtation she had done with Jen the previous evening. That can't be it, she thought.

As they neared her building, Riley spotted Edward standing in front of it. Waiting for me, no doubt. She leaned toward the driver.

"On second thought, don't stop here," she said.

The driver shrugged. "Okay, lady, where to then?"

"Um, just keep going down this street. Turn left at the next corner."

What am I going to do? Not go home? What is Edward doing there? It really wasn't too hard to figure out why shy, creepy Edward was standing in front of her building. After all, that was the place where he probably had the most intense sexual experience of his life.

So what do I do? Am I just going to just hide from him? The more she thought about this, the more irritated she got. Best to nip this in the bud.

"Okay, turn left again. Go around the block. Back to the same address."

As the taxi pulled up in front of her building, Riley reached into her purse to pay the driver. She gave him a twenty-dollar tip. "Please watch me until I am inside the building. Alone."

The driver nodded as if this were routine. "Sure, lady."

Riley got out of the car and walked straight up to Edward, who was smiling goofily.

"What are you doing here?" Her tone was not friendly.

"I was waiting for you to come home."

"I'm home."

Edward looked at the ground. "I didn't have any other way to contact you," he said. "I don't even know your last name." He grinned stupidly.

"You know what, Edward? That's fine for now. I don't know yours either. Let's keep it that way. If I want you to contact me, I'll let you know."

Edward tried to say something, but before he could, Riley turned away and stuck the key into the lock and opened the door without another word.

She was relieved when the door clicked shut and she was out of range of Edward. She wasn't really afraid of him; she just didn't want anything further to do with him just now. Maybe ever. She turned just in time to see the taxi driver pull away. She hurried up the stairs to her apartment.

Once inside, she locked the door and threw her purse on the table. What's going on here? Jen is acting strange. Edward, to no one's surprise, is also acting strange. Cameron is off the deep end for no good reason. Edward was the most immediate bit of strangeness, and she wondered if she *should* be scared.

She went over to a window that gave out to the street and peered through it. She was tempted to stick her head out to see if Edward was still there, but she thought that was a little too paranoid even for her, so she didn't.

But after a while she couldn't stand it any more. She slowly opened the window as soundlessly as she could and gingerly stuck her head out, all the while scanning as far as she could see. She sighed with relief that he was nowhere to be seen. She shut the window as silently as she had opened it and leaned against the wall, staring down at the floor.

What is going on?

# — 13 —

Jennifer didn't find any mystery in what was going on. She knew she got herself tied up in knots all because of a few throwaway comments she made to Riley and a similarly innocuous response from her. Of course, it wasn't innocuous to Jen. Nothing sexual ever really was.

*This has to stop. Riley is off limits.* But she certainly felt grateful that her friend had come to rescue her earlier in the day.

She took off her clothes and got ready to take a shower. Limping into the bathroom, she stopped in front of the full-length mirror on the door and looked at herself nude. *You still look good, girl,* she thought, contrasting what she saw in the mirror with the embarrassing spot she was in midway through the twenty-eighth year of life.

She was thinking about sex, a topic never too far from her mind. Sex was her go-to experience when there was stress or if she wanted a pick-me-up or if she just wanted to pass time in a pleasurable way. The most pleasurable way she could imagine. She loved it. She had absolutely no interest in children and a great deal of interest in engaging in the activity that was designed to produce them, although, to be clear in her case, not the kind that was ever going to result in an accidental birth. Just thinking about sex aroused her. And arousal seemed far preferable to the humiliation she had felt earlier. She stepped gingerly into the shower and was washing her hair when she tried to think of somebody she could hook up with.

There were some acquaintances of Jennifer's who were basically occasional sex partners. Very occasional: she much preferred the roller coaster of meeting someone new, falling in love—by which she meant falling into major attraction—and being wrapped up in the whole experience of romance, novelty, excitement that only falling in love provided. She was reconciled to taking the sexual part of the relationship as far as it would take her. That usually took a couple months. If she was fortunate three months. But then she would lose interest and . . .

She shook her head. She didn't want to focus on that part; she never did. She wanted to focus on the joy, the excitement, and the thrill of encountering another woman sexually. Just thinking about it heightened her arousal.

She knew how to take care of that for the moment.

After toweling herself off, she lay down in bed and reached for her vibrator. This was the only sensible way to put this day behind her. She fell asleep to mental images of an undressed Riley Cotswald.

When Jen woke up a couple hours later, her mood was greatly improved. She pulled the bed sheet over her still-nude body, reached for the remote, and flipped on the television. She no longer felt the residual effects of the wine she had had for lunch. She no longer felt a compulsion to hook up with someone. She took in deep breaths and felt her body. A flood of relief washed over her. I can handle this. She turned the television off.

After an uneventful, dreamless night, Jennifer woke up and immediately went about her morning ritual: another shower, careful application of makeup, a light breakfast of toast and coffee, and the gathering together of what she needed for work that day. She was grateful to have a job and a focus to her day. She did not want a replay of the previous one.

Walking to work as she ordinarily did seem a little too daunting because of her ankle, so she hailed a taxi. On her way to work, she wondered if she should contact Riley. Maybe give it a few days. I think I need this day to just get back on track.

She entered her office building with a renewed sense of purpose. She greeted the building receptionist warmly. There was another man in the elevator with her, but she didn't recognize him. He smiled at her. She smiled back. This guy has no idea, she thought, smiling inwardly. They got off at the same floor.

Jennifer greeted the office receptionist with even more warmth. She was just glad to be at work.

As she was settling in for the day, making a list of things to do, her office phone rang. It was her boss.

"Jennifer," Matt Macon said, "Could you come to my office?"

"Sure, Matt. Be there right away."

It wasn't unusual for Matt to call her in. It was usually about a new project or some other work-related thing. In general, she thought he approved of her work and was satisfied. But their relationship was strictly professional, so she really wasn't sure what his personal thoughts were. He had given her several solid performance evaluations.

She knocked lightly on his door. "Come in."

"Morning, Jen. Please come in. Have a seat."

"Good Morning, Matt," Jen replied, sitting on the seat directly across from her boss.

"Jennifer, I got a request from headquarters yesterday afternoon asking if there was someone on my staff who could work a major convention in New York. It's short notice: the convention starts tomorrow."

Jen nodded but didn't say anything.

"Apparently the person who was going to be running the show left the company suddenly for reasons that were not shared with me. I told him that you were the best we got. Would you be open to doing this?"

Would I ever, Jen thought. She nodded.

"That doesn't give me much time," she said. "Did the other person take care of any of the prep work?"

"I believe so," Matt said. "If you're open to this, Jim Kranke wants you to call him. He's in charge of communication at the main office." He paused for a moment. "I told him you would call him this morning."

"I'd be happy to talk to him, Matt."

"Great! Here's his number."

"I'll call him and get back to you right away." Jennifer stood up, a little wobbly from her ankle.

"Are you all right?" said Matt.

Jennifer nodded. "Yeah. I sprained my ankle yesterday. No big deal."

Jennifer left Matt's office with even more of a sense of relief. Getting out of town was exactly what she needed to get away from the recent unpleasantness. She went to her office and called Kranke.

# — 14 —

As the day went on, Adam became more and more fidgety. He fulminated about Suzanne, but what else could he do? She was the one who dropped the divorce bomb on him. She was the one who wanted out. And she was the one who was involved with someone else.

That should have been his guilt-free card, but it didn't feel that way.

Why am I feeling guilty? He didn't know. None of it made sense to him, and the more he thought about it the more tangled his thoughts became. Tangled and useless. Worse than useless: they fed his growing anxiety and irritation.

After wrapping up his work around noon and forcing down something to quell his meager hunger, Adam went for a walk to clear his head. He walked out the front door and stood there for a moment, trying to think of what to do. He began walking aimlessly. It was not helping with the agitation that rumbled throughout his body.

He realized his breathing was shallow, so he began to take deep breaths. After a few moments of that, he began to jog. It had been some time since he exercised regularly, but he had been a jogger/runner for years prior to his marriage. Another thing he gave up for his marriage, he realized darkly. He picked up speed.

It took Adam only a couple of city blocks running at a jogging pace to find himself winded. He slowed down and gasped for air, forcing himself to expand his lungs. He bent over and beheld his out of shape self, furious that he had let himself go.

After a few moments, he stood upright and turned to go back home. Even calling it that, the address where he had spent the last *few years, was a source of uncertainty. He hated uncertainty. At the moment, he hated a lot of things about his life.*

Angry guy, thought Riley as her fingers paused over the keyboard.

She was writing because she wasn't sure what else to do. After she left Jennifer, she found herself more worried and concerned than she had been the day before. Does Jen really have a problem with alcohol? That did not feel right, but Riley had to admit that Jen was more intoxicated than she had ever seen her at the restaurant yesterday. She also knew that, if Jen had to give up drinking completely, Riley would miss their evening cocktails together, so she had sort of a stake in Jen's ability to enjoy alcohol. But really it was something she could talk to Jen about the next time she saw her.

That thought led her to pick up the phone to check on her, as she had not heard anything from her since she left her at her apartment last evening.

The call went straight to voicemail.

Riley wondered idly if she had gone to work today or if she took the day off to recuperate. She was sure she would hear from her later in the day. She went back to work.

*Adam was in the shower when he heard the phone ring outside the bathroom. He was tempted to stop what he was doing and answer, but shook his head, castigating himself for being so desperate. He knew it was Suzanne because her number was programmed with a unique ring. He would call her back.*

*And after finishing his shower and putting on some clothes, he picked up his phone and listened to the voicemail he assumed she had left. Only she hadn't.*

*Heh. Adam threw his phone onto his bed. Why didn't she leave me a message? He was irritated. Is she playing games? Not finding any answers there, he picked up his phone and hit her number.*

*She answered on the second ring.*

*"You called me, Suzanne."*

*"Yes, I was just getting back to you about this evening. Um, um, if it's okay with you, I'd like to come over and spend the night."*

The fact that this sounded something like a sexual proposition cooled Adam's irritation a bit. He wasn't sure it was a proposition; after all, it was her home, too. "Sure, Suzanne," he said. "Come over any time."

"I'll be there right after work," Suzanne said.

After hanging up, Adam realized how pleased and relieved he was that she was coming over, sexual proposition or not. He fell onto the bed and found that his head was clearing. It felt like a return to something close to normal.

— 15 —

Edward McAlister couldn't stop thinking about what was happening. One day, Riley ravishes him in a way that was inexpressibly primitive, passionate, and head-spinning. The next day, she studiously and deliberately avoids him, apparently having a taxi driver go around the block to do so. Then, when she decides to finally come within touching distance, she tells him in no uncertain terms that she does not want him to contact her, that she would contact him if she wanted to. What? Why?

If sex the day before had been just a little less engaging, or if he were less believing of a future with Riley, he might have chalked it up to personal insecurity: I'm not good enough; I disappointed her somehow. But he was pretty sure that wasn't it. It was a dizzying sexual ride for both of them: that much stood on its own.

He could not get the day before out of his mind. He had been thinking of nothing else since the pair spent the afternoon in bed together. He had never, ever in his life felt so sexually charged, so attracted, so turned on. His body heated up just thinking about it. He knew he couldn't just let it go.

He wanted to talk to Riley about it. He needed to talk to Riley about it. He was so worked up he went directly to her apartment building after school, hoping he would find her. When she didn't answer her door buzzer, he had even gotten himself buzzed into the building by posing as a repairman. But when he went to her apartment and knocked on the door, there was no response. He decided to wait in front until she got home. He didn't want her to think he was stalking her.

That's where he was standing when he spotted her in the taxi when it first pulled up in front of the building. Initially, he was confused when it sped up again and turned at the next corner. He was still wondering what happened when it reappeared a few minutes later, this time stopping and letting Riley out.

The first sign of trouble was the look on her face. She didn't look happy. And when he tried to explain what he was doing there in front of her building, she looked even less happy. She did not give him a chance to explain himself or tell her how important it was to talk to her. It happened so fast. She just turned and walked away, not even giving him a chance to say anything. He was humiliated. No, that wasn't it exactly. Truth be told, he was accustomed to being humiliated by women. It was more that he was frustrated. Acutely frustrated.

He would have been angry if he weren't so tied up in knots by his attraction to this woman he'd been watching for months. He felt guilty; he felt turned on; he felt embarrassed. How can I explain myself to her if she won't even talk to me?

Edward replayed the encounter in his mind. After Riley got into her building and walked up the stairs, he figured there was nothing he could do at the moment. He turned and slowly started walking away. At the corner, he crossed the street and positioned himself on the other side of the corner building so she couldn't see him. He stopped and leaned against the stone facing of the high-rise. He took out his smartphone and turned on the video camera. He slowly edged it over the corner enough for the tiny lens to get an image of her building, but not so far that she would notice, aiming it to where he thought Riley's apartment was. He managed to catch her opening and then closing the window. He was sure she was looking for him. That made him smile. He looked at Riley's image on his phone for as long as she was looking out her window. Maybe she had changed her mind. Maybe she would come out and look for him. To apologize. To arrange another tryst. That was all Edward wanted; it was all he could think about.

He waited for a good ten minutes, but no Riley. He debated what to do next. Go back in front of the building and wait? Something in the back of his mind told him that wouldn't be a good idea, so he decided he'd done enough for the day. He turned and headed back to his own apartment.

On the way home, he couldn't stop thinking about the day before. Riley was an animal. And he rode that animal and matched her intensity every step of the way. He had never felt so free, so sensuous, so male. He felt his body in a whole new way: it was stronger, more capable. Certainly a more experienced one.

Edward blushed as he realized he was getting aroused walking down the street. This can get me arrested, he thought, so he tried to think of something else. It wasn't easy.

It took him about twenty minutes to get home, and he unlocked the door to his building and walked up the steps to his apartment. After closing and locking the door, he emptied his pockets on the small hall table in the small hall of his small home.

He walked into his small kitchen and took a glass out of the cabinet for water. He drank it eagerly. All this excitement had made him thirsty.

Edward was anxious to be sure, but he wasn't stupid. The first casual encounter he initiated wasn't exactly a spontaneous event; it was something he had been planning for some time. He had been interested in Riley ever since he had noticed her in the coffee shop about two months before. He had followed her discreetly every chance he could get, but it took him weeks to figure out her routine. Sometimes he would order coffee in the same shop, but other times, he would pretend to be interested in some of the other shops along the street, where he could watch from a safe distance. It was obvious that she didn't have a regular job. She seemed solitary; she seldom spoke. Probably a writer or somebody who worked from home.

He set about doing a little low-level sleuthing to find out more about her. One day he noticed that she had left a receipt at the register where she purchased a cup of coffee. She left the shop immediately, and Edward took the opportunity to go up and divert the cashier's attention by asking him some inane question. He picked up the receipt as discreetly as he could and slipped it into his pocket. It had her full name. After that, all it took was a Google search to learn that she was in fact a published author. She even had a Wikipedia page, which indicated that she and her husband had recently been separated. He bought her book and read it. He learned everything he could about her. Despite what he told her yesterday about not knowing her last name, he knew as much as anyone about her work, her life, and her achievements.

He had to admit that, after he first approached her two days ago, he was disappointed; but after thinking about it gave himself a C+ for a first attempt at conversation. Plus, he had heard that some women take to men who are a little shy and uncertain. It's true that he did not get the date he wanted, but he did manage to spend some time with Riley and introduce himself.

And when she came back the next day and threw herself at him, he was sure that all his patience had paid off. And then the high-flying sex confirmed his suspicion that she was the one for him. God, it was great. Better than he could have imagined. It more than validated what he had been looking for in sex all his life.

But now she was acting cold, and he wasn't quite sure what to do. He was even less sure what it meant.

Edward walked over to the desk and flipped on his computer. He noticed his hands were trembling as he waited for the machine to boot up, and he realized that he was still aroused. Sure, he thought, you want to talk to Riley, but you really want to fuck her. Again.

Yes, I do.

So, how you going to make that happen?

I'm working on it.

The home screen came up, and he started flipping through routine chores: checking email and messages, a couple news sites, and social media. The last was typically disappointing because he didn't have a lot of friends on Facebook or otherwise. In general, that didn't bother him, but it left him with a lot of time on his hands.

Now that he was by himself, Edward could not contain his arousal. He shot up from his chair and walked around a bit. He had never felt this way before about anyone. Sure, he had dated some, but he had never had the kind of liberating experience he had yesterday with Riley, and he could not even fathom the thought that it was just a one-time thing.

Be reasonable, he tried to lecture himself.

I am being reasonable, he replied. Isn't it reasonable to want to do something that was no doubt the most exciting thing I'd ever done in my life?

Silence from his inner voices.

He sat back down. Sure it is.

## — 16 —

Edward made it through the night and went to school the next day as he always did. Teaching middle school kids was not the most interesting work on the planet, but he liked it well enough to keep at it, even after ten years.

Throughout the day, he would look at his charges, especially the young girls who were on the cusp of adolescence and wonder how they would turn out. How would they look? How would they act? It was an idle curiosity, but it took up some of the mental slack in his workday. He sometimes fantasized about some of the more rapidly developing girls in his class, but he hid that part of his experience with all his might. He did not want anyone to have any indication that he had an untoward thought about the children he taught.

Otherwise, he enjoyed teaching the kids social studies. He felt it was important work to mold these young humans into responsible citizens. It felt like a solid vocation.

What was not so solid was his personal life. Mostly a loner, Edward most often preferred being by himself rather than with others. He had developed what he thought of as an acceptable life style. He worked; he read a great deal; he was fastidious about exercise. In the summers, he typically got a short-term job as much for something to do as to increase his income as a teacher. And to meet people. Edward never regarded himself as a complete isolate: he encountered people he liked from time to time, but he rarely met someone he understood or who understood him. People seemed so opaque in their decisions, in what they said, in their choices, in their life partners. They were mysterious.

What he did understand was sex. On those occasions before Riley when he dated someone with whom he had sex, he found that part unmistakably positive and comprehensible. It was pure pleasure. Even if the rest of the relationship fell back into the treacherously ambiguous, sex itself seemed easy to understand. But, then again, he had never had the kind of intense experience he had with Riley yesterday. That only confirmed in his mind that sex was perhaps the highest good, the best he could hope for in the human interaction department.

There were caveats. Not every woman he dated was equally open to the experience; in fact, some refused outright; some seemed to do it out of a kind of obligation, as if it were expected of them. That made no sense to Edward, who had had sufficient sexual experience to know when a woman was a willing participant versus one who seemed to have her mind elsewhere.

He always hoped for more. He hoped to have a regular sex life, and he now fervently hoped that would be with Riley. He could not even fathom the possibility that he and Riley wouldn't be together again. He just knew it would happen, and sooner rather than later.

He began to think that maybe something else was going on with her yesterday, something that upset her or that she was concerned about. And she took it out on him. It's like kicking the dog after a bad day at work. Happens all the time.

This explanation seemed lame even to him. Truthfully, he had no idea why she treated him so magnificently one day and abysmally the next. He was pretty sure neither had to do with him so much; after all, she barely knew him. But the fact that he was on the receiving end made all the difference in his mind. Whether he wanted it to be this way or not, and no matter what Riley wanted, he and she were destined to be together. That's all there was to it.

But there were details to figure out.

That night, as Edward lay in bed pondering this new situation, he began to think back to his early years, to his time growing up. He thought about his hard-working father and his somewhat erratic mother. He thought about the unsmiling Lutheran upbringing that they insisted upon. 'Starchy' was how Edward came to think of it, even early on: the starched collars in church; the starched robes worn by the minister. Even the doctrine seemed stiff and unyielding, as was what passed for discipline in his home. It was the kind of approach to child-rearing that traded in unsmiling rigor. Or pain, he thought grimly; although, mostly, it seemed to emphasize tedium above all else. He never thought he had a bad childhood so much as an empty and unhappy one.

His parents were decent people, by all accounts. They did not abuse him, they didn't drink to excess, they didn't smoke. They never, ever got in trouble with the law. They paid their taxes and observed all traffic rules. He could not recall a single time when either of his parents had even gotten a traffic ticket. Nor, he realized, had he. Edward's parents did not demand much from him, but then again he wasn't much trouble. He was a decent, or at least, a conscientious student, had a few friends growing up, and in general never made a mess of things. But he did not feel especially attached to his parents. When he went off to the university, he rarely contacted them; nor did they contact him very often. He dutifully went home for major holidays for the first year or so of college, but after that even those dutiful things became less and less frequent.

When his parents were alive, he would call them on their birthdays, their anniversary; he would make a point of returning home for a holiday, usually Christmas, once a year. But the conversations got so strained, the bonhomie so superficial, that it was becoming a chore. When he got the call from his mother about his father's death, he was befuddled at first: the news felt a little too personal, coming as it did from a woman who never shared her personal feelings with him. He heard her voice tremble a little and felt as if he had happened into a sacred realm to which he was not entitled. Then, there was the fact that his father, who was only in his late fifties, was no longer among the living, a concept he could barely comprehend.

In spite of the distance, the starchiness, the vacuity of this familial connection, Edward felt tears come to his eyes for the first time for another person. He had no idea why. That was the first time he ever shed tears for one of his parents.

When he learned from a distant cousin a few months later that his mother died, the bottom unexpectedly fell out of his life. Again, he had no idea why. He hadn't thought prior to that time that his parents were so important to him. He just thought of them as taskmasters, people whose (perhaps somewhat resented) job it was to raise him. Once he was on his own, their job was over. Mostly, he thought of himself as something of a burden to them, someone they had to take care of because he showed up at a time he couldn't recall. He never had a sibling with whom he could discuss these matters. In fact, he never knew why he was an only child. The lack of information was stunning when he thought about it. He tried not to.

The memories of how devastated he was when both his parents died within a year of each other still haunted him from time to time. He tried not to think of the months of sorrow that would not recede, the lack of sleep, the weight loss: all the classic signs of depression. At first, as an only child, he had things to do: take care about the funeral, sell the house his parents had lived in, and liquidate their estate.

He did not mind those tasks really. They gave him a focus and something to do with himself and his grief. It was emotionally wrought to be sure, but it was clearly his responsibility and his alone. In the process, he met a few people who, like the cousin who called him, were related distantly, both emotionally and geographically.

It was when he completed those end-of-life tasks that the full weight of unexpected grief made itself felt. In his rare moments of lucidity, he was just surprised how terrible and enduring the grief was. He was never unable to function—teaching was helpful that way—but he would often weep uncontrollably for hours at a time when no one was around. And beyond the obvious loss, he didn't have a clue why the feelings were so intense.

That year his parents died cast a long shadow. He thought of talking to his physician about his mental state, but all he could think about were reasons not to. He was torn about it. What would he say? That he was sad? Of course, he's sad: his parents died. Plus, for him to admit feeling so dismal seemed to be an acknowledgement that he was mentally ill. No normal person could possibly hurt this much and still go on day to day. But mostly, he thought and hoped that the emotional abyss into which he had fallen might not last forever, even though it felt bottomless most of the time. If only he could hold on.

Conflicted to the point of inaction, Edward simply suffered through, putting one foot in front of the other, doing what he was doing, forcing himself to keep his feelings to himself. He had few friends during this time, with the exception of a couple other teachers. But they, like his parents, were not really close.

He made it through. After several months of undisturbed anguish, he began to feel a little better. Not great, but the intensity of the grief seemed to have abated somewhat. It was a little easier to get out of bed in the morning, his appetite was returning a little. He resumed an exercise routine, which he had let go. Also, because there was a small but not insignificant inheritance, he felt less financial pressure in his life. As spring flowed into summer, the sunshine and the warmer weather lifted his spirits. He noticed the change and was grateful for it.

It was during that time that he decided to start dating again. Fortunately, the Internet made that much easier for someone so introverted as he, and he found himself seeking out similarly oriented women. Those who did not seem to be so outgoing, or loud, or interested in just getting ahead. Women who were at least temperamentally like him.

Rita was the first woman he dated, and, much to his surprise, she turned out to like him pretty much. She was a little reserved but agreeable. She was neither pushy, nor demanding. Not at first.

It was on their third or fourth date that they were saying goodnight in front of her apartment building, holding hands and kissing gently, that Rita invited him into her apartment. Secretly, this thrilled Edward, who had been wondering since their second date how and when to bring up the topic of sex. He took the invitation as a step in the right direction.

This was not Rita's agenda. In fact, she used that time in her personal space to explain that she had never had sex and would never engage in it before marriage: it was against her religious views, her personal feelings, and her value system. And if she and Edward got to the point where they were serious, meaning marriage was in the cards, she would perhaps allow him to touch her a little more but would definitely not have intercourse until the night of their wedding.

Edward listened in what he hoped was a polite and sympathetic way that revealed nothing of his actual reactions. Internally, he was wide-eyed and uncomprehending. He felt a kind of tightness in his chest and had some trouble breathing that he hoped was not visible to the pious Rita.

He nodded and looked solemn as Rita preached on about the virtues of abstinence prior to marriage and how important her religion was to her. As his initial shock began to recede, he heard himself thinking in the back of his head, "How could she possibly be so sure of all this; she is only twenty-four." But then, he figured perhaps she had had a starchier upbringing than he, the difference being that it seemed to have made more of an impression in her life.

When Rita stopped talking, she looked at Edward. "What do you think?"

"What you are saying makes a lot of sense, Rita."

There was a pause. Rita looked at him in a way Edward thought coquettish; but he realized it probably wasn't in light of her fervent and pious monologue. "I am so glad you think so, Edward. I like you a lot."

After agreeing with everything she said for a little while longer, Edward glanced at his watch and politely said he had to be going. She walked him to the door, where he gave her a peck on the cheek, turned, and left, never to have any further contact with pious, starchy Rita.

After that, Edward thought that perhaps he had been vetting prospective dates a little too rigidly. Maybe a more outgoing woman would be a better complement for someone as solitary as himself.

He set about compiling a dating life with statistical precision. He worked hard to figure out the signs of a woman being outgoing but not too much. Enjoying ball games was okay, but clubbing was beyond the pale. Women who drank too much scared him almost as much as women who did not drink at all.

This turned out to be more fun overall, but also involved a new set of threats. Because he was around thirty at this time, he began to think that maybe he should be more accomplished in the relationship department than he was, so he tried posturing maturity, which, he learned, is almost always a recipe for disaster in personal relationships.

His ersatz education came when a pleasant young woman asked him a question: What do you think about the AHA? she asked. Edward had no clue what she meant. The American Something that Begins with an A. American Hospital Association? American Heart Association? Unknowing but undaunted, but he could not bring himself to admit ignorance. He hemmed and hawed a bit and finally asked how she meant that. What do you mean, how do I mean it? Do you think it's a viable option for activism or not? It was only then that he was forced to admit that he did not know what it was and, when he learned the letters stood for The American Humanist Association, he had only the dimmest idea of what might be. Another single date, but not exactly of his choosing.

Edward tried not to think of the downside of a regimen of dating: he had some hits and misses, but in the end he was able to have sex with several women, during which he determined that that intimate activity was probably the most pleasurable experience he could expect in life. He was a conscientious and dogged lover. As for the rest of it, the norms remained opaque to him. How often to make contact, text or call, take the initiative or leave some room for the other person to do so, etc. Choices with no clear answer, choices that fell into the ambiguity of human life about which Edward was so permanently unschooled.

Sometime Edward's desire to manage his relational life lapsed into fastidiousness, which is difficult to sustain in the throes of passion and is often a tipoff at the start of a dating relationship. He learned not to ask a lot of questions, which made him appear less neurotic, but then he was beset by ignorance as to the proper way to act. It was all befuddling.

This is one of the reasons his experience with Riley was so redeeming: there was no befuddlement, no confusion, no mystery. Until the day after they slept together. Still. Edward did not think the situation was insurmountable. He would try again.

# — 18 —

Adam was nervous. In an effort to quell his anxiety, as well as prepare for Suzanne's arrival, he began frenetically cleaning up their house. It did not seem dirty or anything, but he had to do something. His feelings were all over the place: he was mad at his wife for dumping too much information on him, but he admired her candor and her willingness to be honest about such a touchy subject. He was mad at her for having an affair but honestly did not in his heart begrudge her that. If he had had an opportunity or if he were a little less duty-bound, he might have considered it for himself. The short but intense conversation they had the day before stoked something he had thought long dead: a basic attraction to the woman to whom he was married.

He did not even know what his feelings were about her sleeping with another woman. He was conflicted: is it any worse than sleeping with another man? No, he thought; it was actually preferable. Less male competition. And, in truth, it was a little arousing to think about. He tried to put that out of his mind.

True to her word, Suzanne showed up at precisely the time she normally returned home from work. She walked in the same door she always used, threw her keys on the same table used for that purpose, and walked into the kitchen, which she always did, and poured herself a glass of water.

Adam watched all this in silence. He wordlessly followed her into the kitchen, and when she turned away from the sink with her glass of water in her hand, he said, "Hi."

"Hi," said Suzanne, holding her glass tightly.

*Not knowing what to say but thinking it was better to speak than not, Adam said "I'm glad you decided to come home tonight, Suzanne." And in a burst of uncharacteristic self-disclosure, he said, "I missed you last night." He braced himself for a bad response to that.*

*Instead, Suzanne took a couple steps toward the table and sat down. Adam followed. In a soft voice that Adam had never encountered in his wife, she said, "This is all confusing and hard for me, Adam." She paused and took another sip of water. "I thought I was clear about it, but the fact is I'm torn." She looked at him with big, sad eyes. "Last night I didn't go to a hotel. I went to Ellie's apartment."*

*That statement hung in the air. Adam closed his eyes. "So you . . ."*

*"Shhhh," said Suzanne, reaching across the small table and putting a finger on his lips. "It's not about that. I could not bear being here, and I could not bear being alone. That was all."*

*The couple sat in silence for a few moments. Both felt tears well up in their eyes; both tried to keep them from overflowing their banks. Deep breaths across the table.*

*"So . . ." Adam started.*

*"So . . ." Suzanne echoed.*

*The lengthy pause that followed was a mixture of tension, uncertain animosity, forbidding sorrow, and complete ignorance about where the conversation would go next.*

*Then, Suzanne burst out laughing through her tears. "This is so pathetic," she said. "What a mess I've made."*

*The laughter was not exactly contagious, but neither was it unwelcome on Adam's part. "I think we both made a mess, Honey," he said. "It was just a mess I couldn't imagine. And wasn't prepared for."*

*Adam put his hand over Suzanne's on the tabletop. "I don't really know what to say. I'm just glad you're here."*

*"So am I," replied Suzanne. But she shook her head slightly from side to side as she said it.*

So am I, Riley thought, letting herself breathe more freely. This is work. Her fingers went back to the keys.

*Of all the things Adam thought about Suzanne, it never occurred to him that she might be indecisive. Or regretful. She was always the one filled with purpose. She rarely acknowledged a mistake, primarily because she seldom made mistakes. If she did, she rectified it immediately and went about her business without any apparent fuss. It was just stuff, just life. Nothing ruffled her.*

*So watching her being unsure and admitting she made a mess got Adam's attention. He was beginning to see her in a different light. Maybe there was something here to save.*

*He wasn't sure. It was just a maybe.*

That's not nothing, Riley thought, removing her hands from the keyboard. She was done for the day.

She checked her phone and saw a text message from Jen telling her that she had to go to New York for business and would catch up when she got back. Riley noticed that Jennifer did not specify when she would be back, just that she would contact her at some later day. It felt a little bit like the kind of blow-off line, 'I'll call you,' that men often say when they have no intention of doing so.

She did not like that one bit, especially after her efforts to be helpful to Jen when she drank herself sick at lunch.

# — 19 —

Jennifer texted Riley when she knew she would be working, so as not to disturb her or to give her too much information about her predicament. And to give herself some distance. She told her she had to be in New York for a few days, and purposely omitted a return date.

This felt liberating for Jen, as she had so many conflicted feelings about Riley, she could barely hold them all in her body. Especially when her body was in the same city as Riley's.

She took the train to New York the next morning after she learned that much of the prep work for the convention had mostly been done, and pretty much all she had to do was stand around looking pretty and smiling broadly. She could use the time on the train to get up to speed about the account and allow herself to decompress a bit after a too-exciting few days. Her sprained foot was troublesome, but not in an unmanageable way. She was so relieved to be going out of town she didn't really care about it too much.

Once she got to New York and found the convention hotel, she checked into her room, made her way to the exhibit hall, and set up her materials without too much difficulty. Her basic job was to staff the exhibit in a hall along with other exhibitors and make as many contacts as she could. She leaned tentatively against the table to see if it would support her with her wounded ankle. Both seemed to hold up.

Once she was set up, all she really had to do was smile and nod and welcome conversation with anyone within earshot. It was a natural thing for her.

The first day went smoothly, and she was tired as the conventioneers trickled away. She thought she might go to the bar for a while to network with anyone who might be there. Plus, she thought it would be nice to relax with a martini. But the more she thought about it, the more hesitant she became. For the first time in her life, she questioned that simple practice, which, until a few days ago, would have been an innocuous but welcome idea. She decided to go to her room instead and maybe save the networking and drinking for tomorrow.

Plus her ankle still hurt.

When she got to her room, she stripped and filled the bathtub with water as hot as she could tolerate. While it was filling, she removed her makeup, examining herself closely in the mirror. Being in marketing gave her and all of her colleagues a pass on excessive vanity, as how one looked mattered a lot to one's job. For Jennifer, as for many of her peers, it was a convenient excuse to let her vanity run wild. No one ever saw her sartorially unprepared in public.

But she was alone now and was actually savoring the time by herself. As she slipped into the steaming tub, she felt the tension slowly depart her body. She lay there without moving a muscle for some time. This is a better idea than hanging out in a bar.

But then a new thought: Why one or the other? Why not both? After lying in the water for a while without another thought in her head, she noticed that the water was becoming tepid. Enough of this. She soaped herself off, stood up to shower, and dried herself with a renewed sense of purpose.

After reapplying her makeup, she grabbed her phone, her room key, and a clutch and went down to the bar. Even her ankle felt better.

It was crowded. Even though the displays had closed over an hour before, a lot of people apparently had the same idea Jennifer had. She found a standing spot at the bar and ordered a martini.

As she waited, she surveyed the crowd and nodded to a few people who looked vaguely familiar to her. Then she felt eyes on her from behind.

It was a man sitting on a bar stool next to her spot, although she was facing the other direction. "Excuse me," he finally said. "Here, take my seat." He glanced down at her taped foot. "I've had ankle sprains," he said. "They are no picnic." He slid off his stool and kept one hand on the back of it to make sure no one else would grab it. He positioned his body in a semi-circle so that it was hard for Jennifer to do anything but comply.

"Thank you so much," she said, sliding onto the stool and instantly feeling grateful to take her weight off her offending ankle. "A true gentleman." She smiled a genteel smile.

The man returned his own self-deprecating smile and moved into what had just been Jennifer's spot. "I wasn't kidding about ankles," he said. "I've had my share."

"Sports?" asked Jen, feeling some obligation to be nice.

"Serious ones," came the reply. "By the way, my name is Matthew." He held out his hand.

Jennifer shook his hand and smiled, feeling appreciative for Matthew's gallantry. This was an experience she had rarely had with men or perhaps never had. "Jennifer," she said as she shook Matthew's hand, noticing how pleasingly firm his grip was.

They began talking in a normal, mostly professional way that seeped over the course of twenty minutes or so into a personal but not too personal domain. What brings you here? What do you do? Where do you do it? Do you travel often? How do you like your job? Where do you see yourself going in a few years?

In this process, Jennifer learned that Matthew came here from Chicago under circumstances similar to her own; that is, unexpectedly. He worked for a company she had heard of; he traveled about once a month; he liked his job pretty much; and in a few years, maybe ten, he wanted to have his own company.

Matthew learned considerably less about Jennifer, who was vague about where she lived ("not far"); her job ("marketing"); her travels ("occasionally"); and her future ("not sure"). It was second nature for her to keep other people, men especially, at bay.

Matthew wasn't pushy or in any way inappropriate. In fact, Jennifer found herself oddly intrigued by him. She had not had such a personal conversation with a man in so long she had almost forgotten how it felt. She had to admit, it did not feel so bad as she had come to think of it. And she knew that her damaged foot significantly lowered the possibility of Matthew getting any ideas that this casual contact would go any further. At least this evening.

It helped considerably that Matthew came off as a straight shooter, a trait less common in people than Jennifer would prefer. Especially but not exclusively, she believed, in men.

Jennifer did not hate men. She saw herself as lesbian because her experiences with women were more satisfying physically, emotionally, and even spiritually. As a teenager, she had had some sexual contact with male peers, but they had never seemed to have the same kind of intensity or intimacy than she had with her female partners. There was often, perhaps always, a competitive edge to it; not with her so much as with other males or even with themselves. And it was almost always about performance, a feature she found to be a veritable guarantee to ruin a pleasing sexual experience. As she and Matthew were getting to know one another, it occurred to her in the back of her mind how she had based a lot of her beliefs about men on a sample of high school boys, which may not be fair to the adult members of the other sex.

After a little over an hour, the bar remained crowded, but Matthew glanced at his watch and said he had to be going and what a pleasure it was to talk with her. At the same time, he motioned for the check from the bartender, who brought it within a minute. He signed it, gave it back, and turned his attention back to Jennifer.

"I hope to see you again tomorrow," he said.

Jennifer was struck by how simple and straightforward this comment was. Not demanding, not desperate; simply a statement of fact. It was so disarming, she responded in kind. "Me too, Matthew. It's been a pleasure."

Instead of shaking hands, Matthew bowed slightly, turned, and left. Jennifer motioned to the same bartender for her check but was advised that the gentlemen with whom she had been talking had taken care of it. Smooth, she thought with a tad of jealousy cum admiration.

# — 20 —

Back in her hotel room, Jennifer lay in bed wondering about her life. She thought of Riley and their relationship and her attraction to her; the difference between friendship and sex. She thought of Matthew with an odd, novel sense of possibility. This made her grimace: Really, Jen, after all this time, all those women, you find yourself interested in a man?!

No, that's not quite right. I would not call myself 'interested.' I simply note that it was not unpleasurable time spent with him.

The grimace evaporated, and Jennifer smiled, recalling their conversation. In the middle of this line of thinking, she shot up in bed.

What am I doing? Trying to talk myself into sex with a man?

No. I don't want that. And, even if I did want it once just to see how it was, I wouldn't do that to a nice guy like Matthew. "Jesus, Jen! Stop!"

She remained upright in her comfortable bed for some time piecing together this particular puzzle. Okay, so I've had this mostly subterranean thing for my good friend Riley. And pretty much I thought I could be happy with a friendship with her. But—and this was a big 'but'—when she opened that door the last time I saw her, it threw me for a loop. I got drunk and sprained my ankle, and now I'm thinking about bedding a person I would never have considered sleeping with if that hadn't happened.

She almost laughed at herself. Jen did not think of herself as flighty. Adventuresome, yes; flighty, no.

All this was beginning to make more immediate sense to her. It was nothing she did not suspect, but her reactions to Matthew were clearly a signal that she was way off base. She would fix that immediately.

How are you going to fix that?

I'm going to put Matthew out of my mind and treat him like the gazillion other men who've come onto me in the past. Nice but not open. Not really.

Instead of thinking any more about Matthew, she revisited the life she knew and loved: always being on the lookout for attractive, available women, deliberately charming them, seducing them into their bed or hers. It was most often an intoxicating ride. No matter that the charm and wonder—and sense of victory?—wore off after a few weeks or months, it was exhilarating to feel in control, to have another person submit to her wishes, to her passions.

She flashed once more on Matthew and realized she wasn't even tempted to take the lead. She knew in her heart that sex with men was a closed file she did not want to reopen. Not now; maybe—probably—not ever. Her life, as it was, fit her: she knew it, she enjoyed it, and she was willing to deal with the downside as well as the upside. And that is where things will stay.

Jennifer turned the light off by her bed and rolled over to go to sleep, secure in knowing who she was and what she wanted. Her last thought before dozing off was: that counts for a lot.

The next morning played out pretty much the same as the day before. Jennifer took up a position in front of her display, half leaning on the table because of her ankle, and started her smiling and nodding and signaling in every way she knew that people walking by were welcome to interact with her.

Around lunchtime, she saw the face she fully expected to see walk up to her.

"Morning, Jennifer," Matthew said, smiling broadly. "Hungry?"

Jennifer smiled back. "Yes, as a matter of fact I am. But, unfortunately, I have lunch appointments." She pursed her lips to underscore a dismay she did not feel.

"I'm crushed," Matthew said. It was clear to Jen that he had intended it to be a joke, but it had more heft to it than the throwaway line should have had. "Maybe some other time," he said.

Jennifer nodded. "Thanks for buying my drink last night," she said warmly.

Matthew shrugged. "It's not every day I come across such a compelling woman." That weightiness was still there.

The charm of his simple candor did not go unnoticed by Jennifer. "Listen," she said. "Here's my number. Call me sometime." She handed him a business card, which had her work number.

Matthew's cheeks reddened a bit as he dug into his pocket for his business cards. "Will do, Jen. Here's my card." He bowed slightly, turned, and walked away.

Jennifer watched him walk the length of the exhibit hall without once turning back to look at her.

She closed her yes. A good man, she thought. And a good sign he had the grace not to turn back around.

— 22 —

*Adam and Suzanne slept together in the same bed that evening. They had sex, but in a way different from how they had ever done it before. It was tentative at first, tender, new. It reflected a different mode of intimacy from what they had ever had before this night.*

*The next morning, Adam awoke to Suzanne, fully dressed, sitting on the bed staring at him. "Thanks for last night," she whispered. "I am not sure what it means, but I will be home this evening. Perhaps we can talk about it some more." She kissed him lightly on the forehead.*

*Adam simply nodded and half-smiled. He felt grateful; he felt closer to Suzanne than he had in years. At the same time, he was wary. He knew there were a lot of feelings he had been having for a long time that would not just disappear on the strength of a single intimate contact. Nonetheless, he reached for Suzanne's hand and kissed it before she got up to leave.*

*After she left, he stayed in bed awhile. He tried to make sense out of things, but really he did not want to relinquish the feelings he was having at the moment. He half-dozed to images of Suzanne from the evening before.*

Hmm, Riley thought. Now what?

*When he got up thirty minutes later, Adam was still feeling mellow. He showered, dressed, and got ready for the day. He had no idea where his relationship with Suzanne might be headed, or even if the two would continue to have a relationship, but he loved the emotional connection that he had with her last night and did not want that to go away. He went about his day with a sense of calm and energy that had been absent in his life for a long, long time.*

Something was sticking in Riley's craw. She wasn't sure if it was about the fictional characters whose lives were unfolding in front of her or it if was about her and Cameron or her and Jennifer or her and Edward or maybe just her. She needed some air.

She was hesitant to go out before she was done writing for the day, as that signaled an end to her daily productive routine. So, she contented herself with wandering around her apartment as much as possible before opening a window and sitting down again at the computer.

*Adam could not stop himself from thinking about what was possible for him and Suzanne. Would they really get through this? How do I feel about her infidelity? Can we get past that? Does Suzanne even want to? She was sweet this morning, but that could be a one-off thing. He just didn't know.*

*As the afternoon stretched out, he busied himself doing household chores that he generally did when he had free time: make simple meals, clean up after himself. He put some extra effort in making the house more presentable, as if he had to impress a woman he was just getting to know. He kept one eye on the clock.*

*At around 5:00 p.m., Adam's anxiety began to peak. He took deep breaths in an effort to calm himself. What is this about? How will Suzanne be when she comes home? And, oh, by the way, what do I want in all this?*

*He wasn't sure.*

*He closed his eyes and allowed a more reflective, calming voice from inside his head: take it slow, allow whatever is going to happen to unfold naturally. It was fine last evening, although it was hard at first. It may be hard again, but avoiding trouble was one of the reasons things got to this point.*

*Adam opened his eyes. I guess that's true. It was something of a revelation.*

*This way he talked to himself to soothe his anxiety was something he had picked up in college when a visiting speaker gave a presentation on meditation and self-talk. He found it helpful then and periodically throughout his life. It felt helpful now.*

*In the middle of these thoughts, he heard a car pull up into the driveway and a car door open and close. She was here.*

*Adam was a little discombobulated. Was she early? He glanced at his watch and realized it was the ordinary time she used to come home, unless work—or something—intervened. He had planned to clean himself up before she arrived, but that would have to wait.*

*He walked to the front hall to greet his wife, who was coming in the front door.*

*"Hi, Suzanne."*

*"Hi, Adam," Suzanne said, touching him lightly on the sleeve on her way to the kitchen. She seemed distracted.*

*Adam followed her into the kitchen where she took her ritual glass of water from the sink. Neither spoke.*

*"Are you okay?" Adam finally asked.*

*Suzanne looked at him with a look he couldn't quite interpret. "I don't think so," she said quietly.*

*As Adam had not a single clue what that might mean, he stood there silently.*

*Then, as tenderly as he could, he said in a soft voice, "What do you mean, Honey?"*

*Suzanne put her glass down and sat at the kitchen table. Tears began to roll down her cheeks. "I don't know what to do. I don't feel like myself. I have to force myself to concentrate. I'm not sure what I want."*

*Not knowing what to do is probably pretty standard in this situation, Adam thought. But perhaps not for Suzanne, who prized control over almost all things. He waited.*

*Since he felt silly standing over his wife, he also took a seat at the same table; the same seat, in fact, that he had taken the evening before. He reached for her hand, in another minor re-enactment.*

*"Look, Suzanne," he said softly. "We don't need to figure out everything right now. We've both been through a lot. Let's give it some time, and . . ."*

*"And what?!" Suzanne said in a loud voice.*

*Adam surprised himself with a quick response: "And see what is possible for us, if anything." Even he could feel the edge in his voice.*

*That edge got Suzanne's attention. "So this is all a test?"*

*A test? What was she talking about? "No, it's not a test. It's what people do when they aren't sure what to do next. They work through it. They think." He paused a bit. "They talk. A lot."*

*And what about Ellie? Suzanne thought. What about the woman who helped me the most these last few months?*

Riley pulled her fingers off the keyboard before saving the file and closing down her computer. Enough for one day.

## — 23 —

Edward spent the day at school in a state of masked agitation. He was clear about what he wanted from Riley, but he was utterly uncertain how to go about getting it. He only half-listened to his students or even himself as the day wore on. He wasn't thinking exactly; he was ruminating, flashing images through his mind of what might be possible, reliving the past few days, trying to latch on to a reasonable plan of action.

It was exhausting.

When the school day finished, he went home and plopped down on the couch in his small living room. What to do?

As much as he knew about Riley professionally, he did not have a phone number for her, so he couldn't call her. He did have a contact form on her author website, now *de rigeur* for any writer. That seemed impersonal, but it was all he had. With deeply ambivalent feelings, he went over to his computer, booted it up, and surfed to her site and the Contact Me page. He wondered if she really got these messages or if someone else took care of responding. He was even more uncertain.

He shut down the computer without writing a word. Instead, he grabbed his keys and phone, and went for a walk. He knew when he left where he was going, and he was aware of the dangers of showing up at Riley's apartment uninvited, but he could not think of a single alternative. His entire life—all his experiences, all his desires, all his inclinations—seemed to have led him to this point. He wanted Riley. Again. Now.

He knew he had to be careful. He did not want to scare her; nor did he want to piss her off. Based on his recent encounters with her, he judged her to be a force to contend with. He did not want a repeat of the last scene in front of her building.

On his way, he tried to formulate a plan that would give him something to hold on to, some strategy to re-connect with her without pushing her away. It did occur to him that she was awfully aggressive with him when she hooked up with him in the coffee shop. Maybe she wanted me to be more that way.

For quiet, lonesome, passive Edward, this was a shocking but not untantalizing prospect. He could do for her what she did for him. He could be someone he never allowed himself to be. He could be strong, male, aggressive. He got excited, even a little light-headed, just thinking about it.

When he got to the coffee shop where he had first met Riley, he stopped and went in for a coffee, as much to calm himself as to give himself a place to go. He was intrigued by his thinking about being aggressive, but he also knew that he had almost never, ever been that way. He wondered if it was in him.

So what is in you?

Deep conviction.

And that would be?

That Riley and I are meant for each other. My shy side and her aggressive side. A nice complement.

He started thinking of having sex with Riley again. It gave him strength.

He finished his coffee and resumed his walk to her apartment. Instead of hiding, he leaned against the wall of the building directly across the street, as if daring her to come out. His feelings were jumbled. For a man with deep conviction, he was notably short of ideas as to act on it.

Then he started having second thoughts. What if she sees me? What if she thinks I'm stalking her? He shook his head, turned, and started walking back home. For today, it was enough to walk by her place. On another day, even if he did not know how or when or where, he and Riley would hook up again. He was sure of that.

Edward went home to his apartment and flipped on the television. The evening news was just beginning.

## — 24 —

Meanwhile, Riley was staring at her dark computer screen. She was done for the day, but she wasn't sure what she wanted to do next. Stay in and read? If Jen were in town, she would call her to meet up somewhere for a drink or dinner, but so far as Riley knew, Jen was still in New York. She had some other, more casual friends and acquaintances, but no one quite so close as Jennifer, so she didn't really feel comfortable calling them.

So, why not just call her now and check in? They did not have to go out to dinner. Without another thought, she dialed the number.

"Hi, Riley," Jen said.

Riley was momentarily surprised that Jen had answered the phone and hesitated a bit. "Hi, Jen," she said finally. "Just wondering what's up with you." This sounded very stupid to Riley's ears, but she hadn't given this call much thought. Since when do I give a call to Jen serious thought?

"Riley, did you pocket dial me?"

"No, no. I'm sorry. I just called you impulsively. I haven't heard from you in a few days and was wondering when you were coming back." The stupid feeling did not recede much.

"I'll be back tomorrow, Honey," Jen replied, wondering if the term of endearment was a little over the top. She had never called her 'honey' before.

It was not over the top to Riley's ears. She felt oddly reassured by Jen calling her 'honey'. Humans are so weird, she thought.

"Oh, good," Riley said. "I can't wait to see you again."

This brief conversation reminded Jen how conflicted she was about Riley. It felt good that her friend was welcoming her back, but it also stirred strong feelings of conflicted desire that were still hanging. She did not know how to proceed. She hated being in this position.

"Me too," she said simply. "I'll call you when I get home."

After clicking off, Jen stared at her phone for a moment. True, this was a conversation that stirred up desire and fear. But those feelings were suddenly muted because of a chance encounter with a man to whom she was, if not attracted, at least drawn. The world is an odd place, she thought.

From the moment Cameron clicked off from his brief conversation with Riley, he could not stop berating himself. How could I have been such a fool? How could I have allowed myself to lose all control in the presence of another person? Especially a woman. Especially the woman I say I want to stay married to? It was a loathsome lapse.

No matter that he was still sniffling from the tears that momentarily overrode his normally placid, even sunny self. He fought them back with all he had, which was admittedly not much at this moment. And to his relief, his store of tears was never deep, even when intense. They came, they flowed, they disappeared. But until today that all happened when he was by himself. He had vowed early in his life never ever to allow anyone to see him lose control. To break down in someone's presence would be humiliating, shameful; it was never to happen.

Yet it did.

Never again, he vowed. Not with Riley, not with anyone. Ever.

Alas, this was not the only time he had made this vow, and he could not be in this spot without mentally revisiting the first time he did it. He was twelve years old.

As much as he abhorred it, the original scene played itself out against the theater of his frontal lobe: his father yelling at his mother, from whom he had just drawn blood; his mother whimpering, clueless as to how to contain her husband's fury. Cameron tried to intervene: he shouted at his father to stop, even though he knew from previous episodes that he would likely not stop until he left the house. He tried to stand as tall as he could so that he might seem genuinely threatening, but he had not grown sufficiently to muster much of a threat to a fully-grown adult. He tried to staunch his own tears, although they were already running down his face, so filled was he with fear and rage. The scene was all so tragically predictable. But on this occasion, the tears of rage and sorrow that flowed from his pubescent self were interrupted abruptly by his father's closed fist. It was the first and only time his father hit him.

The blow landed him on the floor, as much confused as he was hurt. He had seen his father hit his mother before and, while he abhorred it, he never felt that the rage was directed at him. Until this day. The last day he saw his father alive.

His father, stunned by his own actions, looked at Cameron for a moment unknowingly, as if wondering how this could have happened. Then he turned and fled the house in an angry, inebriated state, got into his trusty Buick and roared away. His mother ran over to Cameron to see if he was okay, the blood still streaming from her nose and mouth. She saw her own blood mirrored on her only son's face and let out a scream that neither of them had ever heard before: a deep to high-pitched arpeggio of a wail that testified before the universe that a final outrage had been done. No longer was she the sole target of her violent husband's wrath, but their only child, their only innocent, nonviolent boy had found himself in the same predicament. This was too much for even a martyr like her to bear.

She did her best to console her young son. She hugged him and began wiping the blood from his face. She cooed and clucked as if he were an infant. She repeated feckless apologies and swore that this would never happen again. She led him to the kitchen sink, where she turned on the hot water to wash his wounds, impervious to her own.

She was met by silence. An enraged, sullen silence to be sure, one that silently broadcast the contempt the young Cameron felt for both his inept parents: his father too drunk and too detached to be much more than a vague presence until violent; his mother a helpless victim forever picking up the pieces that were not rightly hers to begin with. It did not occur to him that she had been absorbing Cameron's father's violence, partly at least, to shield him.

It had been left to Cameron to make sense out of it. The rage episodes were seldom revisited in a sober light. Actually, they were never discussed. They happened; life went on; nothing changed. Ever.

But on this particular night, about an hour after the domestic altercation, there was a knock on the door. His mother looked up, startled, frightened. She seemed uncertain about answering the door. She glanced at Cameron, who she was still trying unsuccessfully to console. He nodded: he was tired of his mother's vapid efforts at consolation. She slowly walked to the door and looked through the peep-hole. She opened the door and stepped outside. A few moments later, she came back inside and closed the door. Before re-entering the room, she leaned against the door and stared at the floor for a few moments.

Then she walked over to where she had left Cameron and sat down beside him. "That was the police. Your father was in an accident." She looked off into the distance in a way Cameron had never seen before. Slowly, she turned her head back to him and looked him straight in the eyes. "He's dead."

Cameron's eyes widened and then filled with tears. Dead?!

But just as quickly, a flood of relief poured over Cameron's young body: Freedom! He instantly grasped that there would be no more beatings, no more drunken rages, no more gratuitous violence. No one would ever wait with dread for him to come home again. That man would never again strike his mother or him. It would be a new world.

True, he would no longer have a father, but even his twelve-year-old self knew that man who died was never a father. Not a real one.

He could not keep the smile from creeping across his face.

In an effort to hide it, he threw his head into his mother's lap, who again seemed to want to console him. But this time it felt different. He did not need consolation. He wondered if she was also smiling, but he dared not look up to check. He was happy for one of the few times of his childhood.

And he could not ignore what seemed to him to be the obvious life lessons: Tears are ineffectual; rage is dangerous but potent in a messy kind of way; simple facts—fast moving car, immovable object—trump any puny human emotion. No more tears. No more anger. Just facts. Facts count. I will never show weakness to anyone again. That was the first vow.

Cameron did not actually remember what followed his father's death. He had vague memories of a funeral, a gathering of some neighbors and acquaintances at their home. He did have an image of his mother, who had been something of an intimidated wall-flower for as long as Cameron could remember, acting differently, as if she were coming to life. She was a gracious host at a household gathering after the funeral. She welcomed people warmly into their home; she even smiled, but not so much as to violate the role of a grieving widow. Cameron understood by seeing her in action that he was not the only one who was relieved.

In the weeks that followed, Cameron's mother's behavior contin-ued to replicate what he thought of as a normal adult: she talked, she checked on his school work, she asked questions about his friends, whom he had never brought home before. She even repri-manded him a few times. But she never mentioned his deceased father, except to ask on a single occasion how he was doing with his death.

"Okay," Cameron replied, trying hard to pretend that he was not 100 percent pleased with it. Even his young self thought it was unwise to be too revealing about how happy he was that the man who was supposed to be his father had died.

His mother simply nodded and never brought up the matter again.

As it turned out, Cameron's father, for all his unpredictable drunkenness and violence, had been oddly responsible about planning for his demise, having purchased a substantial insurance policy that ensured that his mother and he would be taken care of financially in case of his death. Of course, there was the possibility of suicide, which would have invalidated the policy, but the police investigation determined that the crash was accidental, thereby allowing the payment to be made.

This changed the life of a woman and her son dramatically. As Cameron had foreseen the night his father's death occurred, their life was free of violence, drunkenness. It was as if the Devil himself had abandoned the field, leaving Cameron and his mother free to live a normal life. It took some getting used to.

Eventually, his mother went back to work, not because she had to but because she needed something to do. This freed up time for Cameron, who often had the run of the house. He found it easy to manage. He had some friends, but he did not change his habit of socializing at their houses rather than his. Having been raised in a home where relationships were supposed to be supportive but were not made him wary of getting too close to anyone. He liked distance. It fit him.

Another of the benefits of the financial windfall was that, when it came time for Cameron to go on to college, he was able to pick his school without worrying about money. He went to a solid private school where he majored in math and science.

Computer science in particular was made for him. It was cerebral, free of the influence of emotions, and as clear-cut as a field of study could be. Fortunately, computers were well established during this period, and the need for educated technicians was ongoing. Cameron poured all of his energy into understanding the machines that had become so important to him, to the nation, to the world. It was a safe, emotion-free zone that allowed him to feel useful, intelligent, and esteemed. It was a life; it was his life.

It was also how he met Riley. As an author starting out, she needed an online presence: website, social media, digital communication. All the tools modern authors required to build their brand. And she found all of the technology involved bewildering. Her knowledge of computers began and ended with word processing; in short, the specific skills needed to actually make words and sentences appear on a screen and then on paper. Otherwise, she was a naïve in the digital world. Cameron met her at a conference of writers when he was working for a company that helped aspiring writers build that online presence. He found himself very attracted to her. She was not only physically attractive, but she also seemed able to have feelings without a problem. When she was frustrated, she said so; when she was happy, she said so; when she was sad or angry, she said so. All without bluster, without violence, without losing control. Cameron really did not understand this, but he was drawn to it, probably because he was so mistrustful of his own emotional life.

This balance between Riley, who was emotional and outgoing, and Cameron, who was cerebral and reserved, seemed to him to be a perfect, complementary relationship.

And for a while, it was. In the early days, Cameron delighted in Riley's emotional openness. It seemed as if she had mastered how to have warm, excited, even passionate feelings without losing control, without getting drunk, without falling into pointless self-pity or assured self-destruction. He did not really understand it, nor did he fully trust it; but he found it attractive.

When he asked Riley to marry him, she seemed surprised, shocked even. She was young at the time, in her middle twenties, but certainly not too young to marry. It seemed logical to Cameron that the two should wed: they had been dating each other exclusively for over a year; they were both working; they had talked about moving in together for some time. He could not think of a solid reason why it wouldn't work.

Riley asked for time to think about it. Even though this hurt Cameron, he assented instantly, as much in an effort to mask his disquiet as a reasoned response to her request. She wanted to take a week to think about it.

It was a rough week for Cameron. He was nursing hurt feelings, but beyond that he could not understand what the problem might be. They seemed to enjoy each other's company; their sex life was good; they socialized together without embarrassing each other. It all seemed to add up to a project that would work.

When Riley finally consented a week later, to the day, he was enormously relieved. They hadn't spoken for much of the week, and Cameron did not really know what her response would be. He had begun making plans in the event that she would refuse. He supposed—again, it was logical—that they would break up and move on to other relationships. He did not want to do that, but he would be prepared for it if that was what Riley wanted.

So, the night Riley told him, Cameron threw his arms around her and kissed her deeply. "Let's do it soon!" he said.

And they did. It wasn't a large wedding, but it was nice. They honeymooned in Aruba.

And then they settled into a new apartment for the two of them. Everything seemed to be going well, until the day Riley announced that she wanted to leave.

## — 26 —

That day was tough. Cameron had no idea Riley was so unhappy. They hadn't been married but a few years, and he saw no reason why the rest of their lives would not be smooth sailing.

So when Riley—casually, it seemed to him—said she wanted to separate, he was more than surprised. Shocked, horrified even. But he held to his persona and did not, he thought, leak a bit about his deeply emotional reactions. At that point, all his defenses held up pretty well in his estimation.

The main reason, he now realized, that he was able to do that was because he just did not believe he and Riley would divorce. Maybe separate for a while, but they would get back together at some point and resume their marriage. No other option made sense to him, so he discounted any variation from this scenario. That went some distance in assuaging the fear, apprehension, and anger he felt in the wake of her announcement.

He promised himself he would carry on pretty much the way he had before, allowing for the physical separation that occurred fairly soon after Riley's announcement. It surprised him how quickly she moved out, but he chalked that up to the typical drama in matters like this. He was sure that, after these disquieting steps were complete, he and Riley would ultimately resume a happy and even stronger union.

As mortified as he was to have called Riley despondent when he lost his job and reveal parts of himself that he showed no one, he was quick to recommit himself to his childhood vow. After all, one lapse in a couple decades was not the end of the world. Riley would probably forget about it. She might even find it welcome, given that she would complain from time to time about what she saw as his excessively sunny disposition.

Secretly, Cameron was proud that Riley saw him that way. It signaled success in masking his sometimes tortured feelings. He regarded it as testimony to the success of his efforts to clamp down that unruly side of life on Earth.

He was savoring this all the more since he had found another job the very next day after he was fired. It turned out some of his co-workers had moved on in the months before and had offered him solid leads on where to look for a job in his field. He would actually be making a little more money for essentially the same work. Plus, he had a few days of free time before that job started, and he determined to use that time to relax and enjoy himself as much as possible.

He was in this self-possessed, even euphoric state of mind when there came an unexpected knock on his door. Unconcerned, he opened the door to find a man of late middle-age holding a piece of paper and a clipboard. "Are you Cameron Cotswald?" the man said evenly. No rancor, no enthusiasm; just business.

"Yes."

The man handed him an official looking document and turned the clipboard in Cameron's direction, handing him a pen. "Please sign here."

Cameron had no idea what he was doing. He looked at the document. It read "Summons".

"What is this?" he asked before signing the clipboard.

The man's demeanor softened. "It says what it is right here," he said, helping Cameron turn the paper over. "Final Dissolution of Marriage," he read aloud.

Cameron just stood there. He could feel his limbs begin to tremble and his legs start to weaken.

"What?!"

"I'm sorry, son," said the sheriff with practiced compassion. "It's just an announcement that divorce papers have been filed by your spouse. Your signing this just means you received the papers." While the sheriff was kind, he was also clearly insisting that Cameron sign the clipboard.

Unsure of how to respond and unable to do otherwise, Cameron signed the paper.

"Thank you," said the sheriff. He turned to leave with Cameron standing immobile in his open doorway.

He watched the sheriff get into the elevator and disappear.

After a few minutes, Cameron closed the door and went inside. He sat down on the couch as he observed internally how incorrect his calculations about his marriage were. She is not coming back, he realized. She is not coming back.

He sat there until the sun went down.

— 27 —

There was not much conversation in the Wilkerson house that evening. Despite Adam's direction about the importance of talking and 'working on' things, Suzanne could not bring herself to bring up the conflict that was at the base of her ambivalence.

On the one hand, she did not hate Adam. In fact, she appreciated many things about him. But compared to the intense personal joy she felt with Ellie, her relationship with him simply paled. No, more than paled: it receded into the realm of a tepid 'That's nice.'

The fact was she would rather be with Ellie now than trying to work out things with Adam. This was so self-evident she did not quite understand how Adam could miss it. She was just not ready to let go of her. She did not really understand all the reasons; she just knew that, for all her history with Adam and for all his good qualities, she did not even want to try to succeed at fixing their relationship.

Besides, she mused, relationships aren't cars or refrigerators. They don't get 'fixed.' They become tolerable or not; they become better or not. Like plants, they either thrive or they whither. And she was sure this one had withered, despite the warmth and affection they found in each other's arms the night before.

Despite the clarity she had internally, Suzanne still felt some confusion. Or perhaps she thought she should be more confused than she was. In either case, she did not know what to say. So, she said nothing.

This was, of course, frustrating for Adam, who kept staring at her expectantly, hoping to rekindle some of what the couple had *experienced the night before. He was tapping his fingers on the table, waiting for Suzanne to say something.*

*Finally Suzanne looked up and said, "I don't know what to say, Adam." She looked at him with sorrow in her eyes.*

*Adam didn't say anything, but the look on his face shifted from frustration bordering on anger, to something distinctly softer or perhaps more sober. It was occurring to him that yesterday may have been an end point rather than a beginning. It struck him that Suzanne did not really want to work on their relationship. This thought filled him with sadness, and tears fell from his eyes, seemingly without his consent.*

*"You don't want this, do you?" he said calmly.*

*Suzanne looked at him with similar tears. "No," she whispered. "I don't."*

*Heavy sighs on both sides. An unmistakable signal about the future had arrived; a future that, for all its inexorability, was something both had mixed feelings about. Neither spoke for some time, but both understood what they were looking at.*

*"I will miss you, Suzanne," said Adam quietly.*

*"And I you," replied Suzanne.*

Riley fought back sniffles as she removed her fingers from the keyboard. I'm so sorry, she whispered to herself. I thought maybe . . .

Then she considered that she was projecting her own situation onto her fictional characters. This is a little over the top, she thought, shaking her head.

But thinking about her own situation could not be avoided. Her lawyer had told her that Cameron would be served within forty-eight hours of her filing the papers for divorce. She could not guarantee that, but it was typical. It was as if the sheriff's office wanted to get the unpleasantness out of the way as quickly as possible.

If that's the case, Riley thought, it would be happening today at the latest. She wondered if it had already happened. She was uncertain whether Cameron would contact her or not. She was too nervous to contact him.

But she did have mixed feelings. Not unlike her characters, she surmised, although she did not want to go down the path of overanalyzing anyone's feelings, real or not. She just wanted to let herself feel whatever it was she was feeling.

And she had to admit that there was an unmistakable sadness about her divorce. She did not hate Cameron. She pitied him. He was so closed, so clueless about his emotions or even his motives. He seemed to really believe that pretending to be happy all the time was the same as being happy, and that this was an acceptable, viable way to live. It just isn't, she insisted to herself. Not in her life. Not in the life of anyone she had ever known, except Cameron.

She slowly went through the end-of-the-day ritual, saving her work and shutting down her computer. She felt tears in her eyes, not enough to break down and cry, but enough to affirm that her decision to finalize the divorce, though born in anger, was the right choice for her. It was harder than she perhaps thought, but it was nonetheless real. And right.

Riley did not move from her seat. She looked out the window, but she wasn't seeing anything outside. While her eyes were gazing outward, her attention was directed inward, mulling over the seriousness of her situation. "I hope Cameron is okay," she whispered.

She thought again of calling him. She had not even alerted him to the fact that she had officially filed for divorce. A sense of guilt inserted itself into her mind. That's not fair.

She picked up the phone and held it in her hand for a while, weighing the decision to call him or not. I should. I don't want to. I ought to. I am afraid.

Afraid of what? Would he get angry? Would he hurt himself?

None of that seemed likely. She realized she was just afraid of the confrontation, of tackling a painful thing head-on. That's what got me into this mess, she mused. And with that thought she dialed Cameron's number.

It went straight to voicemail. He had his phone off. Or he shunted it to voicemail deliberately. Either way, she had made the call. Now, as she listened to his outgoing message, she had to decide whether to leave a message or not and, if so, what to say. She made it this far. She cleared her throat.

"Hi, Cameron. It's me. I just want to let you know that I went ahead and filed for divorce the other day and that you would be served with papers sometime this week." She paused, unsure of what to say next. "I'm sorry." She hesitated again. "If you want to discuss this, give me a call."

Done.

# — 28 —

Cameron heard his phone ring and pulled it from his pocket without moving from the couch. He saw that it was Riley and sent it directly to voicemail. He stared at the phone for a while, pondering his next move. He wasn't sure he was ready to talk to her without giving vent to the rage he felt inside. After a few moments, the phone beeped, indicating that she had left a message. Cameron continued to stare at the phone.

He debated listening to the message. He was angry and knew it, but he would not let those feelings get the best of him. He realized it was rare for Riley to call him: he almost always was the one to initiate communication. In the end, he knew he couldn't resist hearing what she had to say, so he pushed the appropriate buttons and listened intently.

A little late, he mused humorously, clicking his phone off. Then, he turned it back on and listened to the message again. And then again. And then again. As he listened, his anger subsided slightly, something he noticed and was pleased about. After a while, he decided he was no longer angry. At least, not exactly. In fact, he didn't feel much of anything. Emptiness maybe, or a certain aridity or dryness. He felt how shallow his breathing was, how he did not feel the slightest bit hungry, how he was simply engulfed in a moment he had not expected. He felt no impulse or desire to move.

He just wanted to sit there. On the horizon of his mind, he glimpsed an alternative path for him. He thought there might come a day when he would get on with his life, when he might even explore other relationships with women. But that day was not close. At the moment, he did not wish to see anyone or talk to anyone, especially Riley; he just wanted to be in this miserable, arid moment, feeling nothing at all.

Bizarre, forbidden thoughts drifted through his mind. I could get back at her. I could hurt her somehow, even kill her. No. I could kill myself to show her how wrong her decision is. No. I could take up drinking, the way my father did and throw away my life because a woman I thought I trusted did me wrong. No.

After a while, less destructive thoughts began to arrive: I could move to another city. Maybe. He wondered absently if his new company had offices in other places. Perhaps out of the country. Again, maybe.

Cameron understood in a vague sort of way that what he did with his feelings was not what most people did or what most self-help gurus recommended. Most people did not have the strength to shove their feelings down so thoroughly. He had seen people get angry, cry, tremble, or otherwise give in to overwhelming feelings. He did not wish to count himself among people like that, but he knew his approach was one most people would not do. Could not do. Even in this dark hour, he prided himself on not letting his feelings get the better of him, as if he were in a standoff with his limbic system.

Maybe I am, he thought darkly. But that is the way I will stay.

When he noticed that night was falling, he lay down on the couch and willed himself to sleep. He did not bother with his usual nightly hygiene rituals. He was free and, since work wouldn't start for a few more days, he had no one to clean up for.

## — 29 —

Jennifer called Riley the afternoon she returned from New York.

"Hi, Honey," she said when Riley answered. "I'm back in D.C."

"I'm so glad you're back, Jen," Riley replied. "It's been quite a few days."

"What's up?"

"Well, I talked to my lawyer the other day and filed for divorce. It occurred to me this afternoon to let Cameron know, but he did not take my call. I'm thinking maybe he had already been served."

"Mmm. Tough stuff."

"Yeah. And on top of that, it looks as if Adam and Suzanne are heading toward divorce, too."

Jen was sure she missed something. "Um, who are Adam and Suzanne?"

"The characters in the book I'm working on," she said, as if it were self-evident.

Since Jen had no idea what Riley was talking about, she half grunted: "Huh?"

Riley chuckled. "You know, the book I'm currently working on is about a separating couple. Well, they were still in process until today, when I think they both determined that the relationship was over."

"Riley, are you all right?"

Riley chuckled again. "Yes, I'm fine, Jen. Actually, I'm more than fine. I am so glad I went ahead and signed the papers. I feel relieved. I am sure my marriage to Cameron is over. I think it will be better for him in the long run and am certain it will be better for me."

Jen took that reassurance at face value and changed the subject. "Are you free for dinner tonight or tomorrow evening?"

Riley thought for a moment. "How about tomorrow, Jen. I'm still digesting everything that's happened."

Jen consented immediately. She did not want to get into Riley's relationships with her fictional characters any more deeply. "Carter's around seven?"

"Great. Thanks. See you then."

Riley was so happy to have touched base with Jennifer that she completely forgot to ask her about her ankle. She called her back.

"Jen, I forgot to ask about your ankle. How is it?

"A lot better, Riley. Thanks for asking. Honestly, it could have waited until tomorrow."

"I know. But I realized after we hung up that I was so taken up with my own stuff I forgot to ask you. And I know it was a bad sprain."

"Thanks for checking, Honey. See you tomorrow."

Riley felt better for following this up. She hoped Jen was telling the truth about her ankle.

She spent the rest of her evening focusing on her relationship with Cameron. For all the recent drama, it occurred to her how little she thought about it when they were living together. She got into a rut, one not of her liking. She shook her head in dismay as she realized how extensively she just abandoned herself to routine, to not rocking the boat, to going along with whatever Cameron wanted, even though that wasn't much.

It wasn't much, was it? Came a thought in her head.

No, it wasn't. In the months before the separation, we barely spoke beyond planning for dinner or an event. Sex was fairly joyless, routine, but rare.

Riley walked through an evening routine of fixing herself something to eat, reading a little, watching TV a little, just staring out the window, and then getting herself ready for bed; but she did all these things under a spirit engendered by this stark and sobering awareness. Thank God it's over, she thought before she fell asleep.

The next day was a normal work day. Feeling more solid for having taken action with the divorce, Riley went about her morning rituals in greater possession of herself than she had felt in some time. Her life now seemed more serious, more her own, more grown up; such was the result, she was sure, of making a difficult decision.

She did not dwell on that choice and had few feelings about it. The decision itself was simply a piece of information, a datum. She wanted to focus on the direction of her life: on her writing, on her relationships, on her life alone.

She was looking forward to getting together with Jennifer for dinner in the evening, but she was glad to have spent time with herself in the meantime. She could not recall feeling quite so grounded, so mature. I am almost thirty-one, she reminded herself. And this time, it did not feel like self-pity; it was just another piece of information.

Cameron had not called her back. She could not honestly assess what he was feeling or thinking or wanting at this point. The fact that he had not returned her call confirmed in her mind that he had already been served and was dealing with whatever feelings or thoughts he had about that. She imagined those were not favorable to her, but she really did not know. And truthfully, she was pretty sure she didn't care that much.

That was part of the problem, she realized. As time went on, I cared less and less about the relationship. It felt as if there was really nothing I could do to change the course of it. I never really knew what Cameron's thoughts or feelings were about most things; anything, in fact, that had to do with any kind of unpleasantness or conflict. She realized that what she was actually saying was that she did not really know him very well. That seemed like an incontrovertibly true statement.

But mostly she was eager to get back to her work.

## — 30 —

Neither Suzanne nor Adam moved. It's not that they weren't communicating after a fashion. Both continued to have tears running down their faces; both looked at each other from time to time, when they looked up from whatever faraway focus they had to get themselves through this peculiar moment. A moment that seemed to stretch out indefinitely.

"How do you want to proceed?" Adam finally said.

Suzanne let out a long stream of air. "I'm not sure, Adam," she said. "I guess one of us will have to file for divorce, but it shouldn't be complicated." She realized as she said this that putting it that way revealed that she had given it some thought. That was not lost on Adam, who wanted to get angry but did not want to push Suzanne further away than she already was.

"I don't imagine that it will be," he said with a chill in his voice. "Would you like to stay here or find another place?"

Suzanne pretended to think for a while. "I think I'll find my own place."

Adam knew two things: #1 She was pretending to think. #2. She had already made decisions about these things. Separating was clearly not a new idea for her.

Adam was feeling as if he were the last to know what had been going on with his wife—a situation he found surprising, odd, and unacceptable.

"Have you made any other plans?"

Suzanne shook her head.

"Well," said Adam. "I guess that's it. If you'd prefer, I'll file." He looked askance at her. "Unless you want to, of course."

Suzanne shook her head quickly.

I guess she had decided that I would be the one to file, he thought.

I guess so, thought Riley. You can always count on an overly responsible guy to take care of business.

Adam thought a little longer. "Have you already found a place?"

Suzanne shook her head. "No. I haven't even looked."

There was something about the way she said it that made Adam not quite believe her. But he had learned so much in the last hours about his wife that he thought maybe he could never really believe her. She had, after all, carried on an affair in secret, which she hid with airtight effectiveness.

"Is there anything else I need to know about, Suzanne?"

"What do you mean, Adam? Like what?"

"Like: Was your affair with Ellie the first time you cheated on me?" He wasn't sure why he asked that. He just wanted to know more.

Suzanne blushed. "Of course," she said with a complete absence of candor.

Adam did not think he could be any more shocked than he was when he heard about Ellie or when he realized moments ago that his marriage to a woman he thought he knew was ending for sure. But he was.

He stood up to move and force his body to take in some air. "Jesus Christ!" He looked down at her sternly. "Are you ever going to tell me the truth?"

Suzanne shook her head slightly without meaning to. She was silent.

"I think it best that you not stay here," said Adam, feeling the fury rise inside him.

Suzanne was silent.

"I think it best that you leave now."

Suzanne's eyebrows arched, as if this were a completely unexpected development, which in fact it was. She wondered for a moment if *she were in physical danger, something she had never ever felt from Adam. She quickly concluded that she could not rule that out.*

*She stood up to face him and get ready to leave, posturing more fearlessness than she felt. "I'll pack some clothes and leave. I'll be back for other stuff later." She turned and walked into their bedroom to start packing.*

*Adam almost grabbed her to throttle the truth out of her, but he knew that was highly inadvisable. Instead he stood at the table taking deep breaths. After a few minutes, he walked outside to get some air. He located himself outside of Suzanne's probable path of departure. He did not even want to look at her.*

*After a while, he heard the door open and close behind him; then a car door open. He looked up to see Suzanne watching him.*

*"What do you want?"*

*"I just wanted to say good-bye."*

*"Good-bye, Suzanne," he spit out.*

*"Good-bye, Adam," she said gently. She got into the car and drove off.*

Jesus! thought Riley. That was quick. What a mess.

She couldn't stop.

*Suzanne got into her car stony-faced, a kind of steely calm that she often used in tense situations. She felt exposed, caught. She did not like it one bit. As she got far enough from the house so as not to be visible, she felt a tear drop from her eye. It was not, however, a tear of sadness; it was evidence of the shame, humiliation, and rage she felt at being exposed.*

*She lied to Adam and he knew it. She knew he knew it. She did not expect the question about other affairs and wasn't ready when he asked. She could not control the blush; it was a dead giveaway. How could I have been so stupid?*

Riley sat wide-eyed staring at the screen.

*She drove until the rage receded. She needed to think. She found herself on the interstate and decided to stop at the first rest area she came to. She pulled off the freeway and found a parking spot in the mostly deserted rest area. She killed the engine and stared straight into space.*

*So what? So what if Adam knows that I have not been the faithful, dutiful little wife? Our relationship was okay, but it wasn't as if it were high-powered. It was okay. Just okay. I am better off free of it. Free of him.*

*She took a deep breath. Not the best resolution, she allowed, but a resolution nonetheless. She thought back to when she longed to be with someone else, almost anyone else but Adam. She remembered the months they spent faithfully together. That was nice at first. It was warm, erotic even, close. It was sometime after the first full year of marriage that she felt things go south. The passion receded; the conversation cooled. Life became ordinary. Humdrum. Stifling.*

*She kept up her public persona as best she could, but it did not hold in every circumstance. She found herself longing for something more intense, some of the passion she and Adam had at one time but seemed to have lost. The kind of no-holds-barred sexual encounters that she had had with several partners prior to her marriage. She not only longed for them; she went looking.*

*It was tricky at first. She did not like lying to Adam. He was a solid citizen, not a dishonest bone in his body. But lie she did. It was tricky but not hard. After a while it almost seemed like second nature.*

*She wanted to be careful, but she wasn't too choosy about her selection of partners at first. Fortunately, she travelled sometimes for work, and this allowed her to pick up other people at a distance: either men or women, mostly men at the beginning. They were the most obviously available people. But the occasional woman.*

*Ellie was the last person she was with, but that was different. It was not just a fling. She wasn't looking to get involved with her sexually. It was definitely not a one-night stand or a passing inter-est. Ellie actually seemed to care for Suzanne, something she deeply appreciated, especially as she felt her marriage fall to pieces. Ellie was a little older and took an interest in Suzanne's career, as well as her personal life. She offered advice and guidance when asked, but mostly trusted Suzanne to make her own way.*

*She lied to Adam about the night she spent with Ellie after she announced the end of their marriage. She not only went to her house to be with her, but to also submerge herself in the physicality of their relationship, the sensuousness of her embrace, the stimulation of her sexual moves. It was welcome bliss after the difficult conversation with Adam.*

*She wasn't sure why she slept with Adam the next night. It seemed appropriate at the time; it also felt as if their marriage deserved one more time. It did not hold nearly the intensity of her night with Ellie, or of any other sexual experience she had had with her, for that matter. It was something of a duty. At the same time, there was the warmth and familiarity of having sex with someone with whom you have a history. It felt okay. And then it was over. All over.*

*Her plan, though not very specific, was to make the divorce as painless as she could make it. There wasn't a lot to split up, but she liked the idea of ending relationships on decent terms. She knew it wasn't always possible, but it was always preferable to high-drama break-ups.*

*But she failed to avoid the drama in this case. That was a tough thing to swallow, but at least it was finished. It was clear from Adam's behavior this evening that he was angrier than she had ever seen him. She might have one or two other contacts with him for practical reasons, but mostly likely she would never see him again. That thought did not even register as a serious loss.*

*So, now it was done. In fact, she was certain that the entire marriage, relationship, and time with Adam had come to a close. I suppose that's one of the good things to come out of being exposed like this. She wondered idly if there was some arcane psychological purpose in her disclosure, something that prompted her to throw the biggest wrench she could into the mechanism of their relating. Something to destroy it forever.*

*If so, it worked. Beautifully, she thought. As these thoughts ran through her head, she began to feel better, to calm down. What's the worst thing that can happen? Is he going to tell people? I doubt it. He would be too embarrassed by the whole thing. What will he tell their friends? Who knows? Who cares? They were formulary friends for the most part, couples with whom they socialized but nothing too close or intimate. More like work friends. From another department.*

*With the exception of my friend Ellie, she thought. And a smile broke out onto her face.*

*All the same, for a liar to admit lying always felt dangerous. She shook her head and restarted the car engine. Before she pulled away, she dialed Ellie's number.*

## 31

Riley was looking forward to meeting up with Jen for dinner. As it happened, they both got to Carter's at the same time and walked into the bar together, found a table, and ordered a pre-prandial cocktail.

Settling in, Jen said, "So, tell me, Riley: What's going on?"

Riley shook her head, as if it could not contain the thoughts, feelings, and experiences she had. "I guess the biggest thing was filing for divorce," she said. "I can't believe what a relief it is. I don't know why I didn't do it sooner. I guess I wasn't ready." She smiled at her friend. "But boy, am I ready now."

Jen smiled. "Have you heard from Cameron?"

"No. I left him a message—somewhat belatedly perhaps—telling him that I had filed. He didn't pick up." She shook her head. "He always picks up when I call."

"Well, either he did not like what you had to say or he had already been served."

"That's what I think. The lawyer told me it would just be a few days, even though I think the court has, like, thirty days to execute. But they like to get it out of the way. Honestly, it did not occur to me until yesterday to alert him." She winced. "I think I was too late."

"Happens," said Jen.

"What about you, Jen? How was your trip? I couldn't believe I almost did not ask you about your ankle. Is it really all right?

"It's better," she said. "But it was annoying standing around on it all day. Fortunately, I was able to half-sit on the display table, so it wasn't too bad." She was eager to get off the topic of her. "You know, this was a last-minute thing my boss dropped on me the day before the conference was starting. Fortunately, the guy who was going to go had done almost all of the prep work, so pretty much all I had to do was stand around and talk to people." She took a sip of her cocktail that had just arrived. "It was work."

"And basically, it was considerably less interesting than your time here in old D.C." She smiled.

Riley looked at Jen for a moment as she sipped her drink. "I'm glad you're back."

"Me too, Riley. Me too."

They ordered dinner and sank into the same kind of easy silence that they often had together. Each feeling connected to the other; neither wanting to just fill up the air with words.

Jen was somewhat bothered in her mind, even a little nervous. Beneath her companionable self, she debated whether to tell Riley about Matthew. She felt her insides rebel at the thought, however, and decided now was not the time. She wasn't sure when the 'time' was, or even if there was anything to talk about. If it hadn't been at least indirectly about Riley, she would not have hesitated to bring it up. As it was, it was still too fresh from the issue between them. She decided to lay low about that for now.

"Are you going to talk to Cameron about the divorce?"

Riley shook her head. She was a little surprised at the question but acknowledged that she hadn't thought about it. "I don't know." She thought for a few moments.

"On the one hand, I can't imagine I won't. It seems like something I should do, if for no other reason than we spent years together trying to build a marriage." She took a sip of her drink. "But truthfully, I don't know what I would say to him that wouldn't sound, I don't know, patronizing, critical, negative." Another sip. "I don't think he needs that. Or deserves it."

Good points all is what Jen thought. What she said was, "Have you talked to your lawyer about it?"

Riley shook her head. "No, she pretty much limits her contributions to the legal side of things. I think she is one of those psych-adverse people who has zero desire to understand people's feelings. From her perspective, it's just wasted, non-billable time." She chuckled before attempting an imitation of her no-bullshit attorney: "If you want to feel good, talk to a shrink. Or get drunk."

Jen chuckled but did not say anything.

Then Riley realized she may have broached a delicate topic. "I'm sorry, Jen. I didn't mean to imply . . ."

Jen waived her off. "No problem, Honey," she said. "Water under the bridge." Then, with a gleam in her eye she said, "It was a learning experience."

The silence returned, but each member of this couple had things they separately realized they were not talking about. Maybe could not talk about. This made Riley sad, but she did not say anything about it. What could she say? She was the one who had just made a gaffe.

Talk turned to other things. Riley talked about her book, something Jen had almost no interest in, and Jennifer talked about the trials and tribulations of being handed an assignment at the last minute and doing her injured best to make it all work out. It was as if they were having separate conversations with other people, people who might have had an interest in what each of them was talking about.

Dinner came, and the silence descended once again as they began eating. Riley began feeling kind of edgy; Jen wasn't sure what to think. Or say. Or do. So she did nothing.

Finally, they finished dinner and asked for the check. Both women glanced at their watches at the same time. "Must be time," Jen said. "I've got an early call tomorrow."

Riley nodded, then looked away. Then she turned back to face her friend. "It's so good to see you, Jen," she said. "I missed you."

Jennifer nodded. "And I you," she said, wondering for the first time if it were true.

At the door, Riley put her arms around Jennifer. "Thanks for being my friend," she said.

Jennifer nodded. The pair split up in the exact reverse of how they arrived.

As they parted, Riley's head was full of questions. What is going on with Jennifer? Why do I feel uncomfortable with my best friend? Something did not add up, but she had no idea what it was. She had nearly forgotten the drunken episode at the restaurant; nor did she know what triggered it. Gaps, she thought to herself. Big gaps.

## 32

For her part, Jen could not help thinking about Riley as she walked back to her apartment. She felt an unwelcome shift in that relationship and did not know what to make of it. It seemed to her that Riley still seemed to want a closer connection, something that had thrown Jennifer into a tailspin the week before. She frowned a bit as she thought that connection would probably not include sex. After all, she and Riley have been friends for some time now, and, even though sex with her had always been something of a fantasy in the background, she always thought that sex would cost her the friendship they had. But if that friendship were in jeopardy anyway? Then having sex with her would provide both a climax and a resolution. And that would be that for the friendship.

She frowned again. That wasn't something she wanted, not at this point. Yes, she was attracted to Riley, but just now she was going to continue their friendship and put everything else on hold. She hated being unsure what to do. So she decided she would not be unsure. She would definitely let their friendship be what it was.

But she could not help thinking about her life. As she entered her apartment, she thought back to her teenage years, when she first started exploring her sexuality. She had been raised in a fairly open home: her parents were neither too rigid nor too lax. They gave her the space she needed and provided support and correction when called for. None of this was overbearing. She was an only child, and she had always had what she regarded as a solid if less than forthcoming relationship with her parents. Even though they lived a thousand miles away, she kept in touch with them periodically.

At the same time, she had never 'come out' to them as a gay woman. In fact, she had never come out to anyone as a gay woman. One of the main reasons for this was that, despite her dalliances with other females, she never really considered herself exclusively lesbian. Until now. She thought—when she thought about it, which wasn't often—that she was probably bisexual, but closer to the gay rather than straight end of the continuum. Sex was something she never discussed with her parents. She had no idea how they might respond to her about it. Probably pretty well, she believed.

Her vibrant sexual life was always something she chalked up to the fact that she found sex to be one of the major pleasures of life. Even though it was complicated at times, it was most often a highly pleasurable experience to find herself engaged in an intimate setting with another person. In recent years that meant women, but she never deliberately ruled out becoming involved with a man. She thought from time to time that there would come a moment when she would perhaps abandon her extravagant sexual life for a more stable, maybe even a marital, relationship. But she also thought that this was a prospect that would probably never escape the future. The fact was she liked her life the way it was: freewheeling, sensuous, alive. It was hard for her to picture anything else.

This was a conclusion she always came to. It was the way she preferred things. "Who am I kidding," fell out of her mouth. "I'm a lesbian." And for the first time in her life, that felt completely right.

So what about Riley? In the back of her mind, Jennifer knew that she had always held a special place for Riley in her heart. She actually enjoyed the time she spent with her—with the possible exception of this evening, when it seemed kind of weird and complicated—and liked the fact that Riley was more friend than lover, despite her obvious attractiveness. But a lot of that had to do with the fact that they talked about their lives openly, even though they moved in distinctly separate orbits. That was something

Jennifer valued. This evening, however, it bordered on the tedious. No, it actually crossed the border into tedium.

Jennifer was not accustomed to being conflicted about relationships. They fit into neat baskets: there were business associates (some), lovers (lots), friends (fewer), relatives (even fewer), and confidants, a crossover category that had variously included friends and lovers but never relatives or business associates. Just now, Riley was her only confidant. And she had to admit, realizing she had not mentioned Matthew to Riley, that she was not one hundred percent forthcoming with Riley or anyone.

Is this a problem? Not really being upfront with the one person to whom I feel closest?

She sat down on her bed and massaged her ankle. It throbbed a little, which did not bother her so much, but the massage felt good to her. It was good to take care of your body, she thought.

I don't know what to do about Riley, she concluded. I don't know why things were weird this evening. I'll figure it out in due course. Right now all I want to do it sleep. And so she did.

— 33 —

Cameron was still reeling in his own way from being served with divorce papers and the matter-of-fact tone of Riley's voicemail. He knew he was seething, and he was working hard to contain it. But he also indulged various revenge fantasies against her for having the nerve to leave him so easily. All of this happened, of course, as he strove mightily to maintain a light-hearted, positive air.

The problem was he was angrier than he could ever recall being, and his generally intact defenses against it were leaking.

He had snapped at someone at his new job the day after he started, an administrative person who hadn't really done anything major. After he snapped, she just looked at him with a shocked, hurt, and surprised expression on her face. He quickly apologized and tried to explain it away because he was nervous about his new duties. He did not know if she bought it or not.

He got through the first day on his new job without any other incidents, but it left him feeling more vulnerable than he was used to feeling. He knew he was furious with Riley, but he did not know what to do about it that wasn't destructive. There wasn't much leverage: they did not have much common property, so he imagined that a divorce would simply be a legal parting of ways. In theory that was okay with him, but the reality meant that he would be alone, without someone to talk to, to be with, to be intimate with, to have as a friend. His anger did not seem to want to go anywhere.

The other thing was that he missed her. Even though he was angry, her leaving left him with few connections to other people.

Most of their friends had been just that: their friends. Not his or hers but social connections they hung out with from time to time. Nothing really deep there.

Cameron realized that he had let personal friendships lapse over the course of recent years. He no longer kept up with high school or college buddies, apart from Facebook contact, which most often amounted to almost no actual contact at all. He tried to think of someone he could talk to about what was going on, but he could not think of a single person. He did not even know of a lawyer to call. He did not even know if he needed a lawyer. Shit.

On his way home from work, he wondered what he could do to remedy this. I am sure there are legal referral services, he thought, and I can check those out online. As for talking about his feelings with a stranger: that was something he was loath to do, even if someone were available. The thought of seeing a therapist was so far-fetched to his way of thinking, he could not focus clearly on the possibility, much less give it serious consideration. Talking about your private life and thoughts with a stranger? Abandoning the skills he developed to survive for all these years? It just did not compute as an option.

So he did the part that seemed reasonable. When he got home, he searched the Internet for legal referrals and compiled a list of potential lawyers. He then Googled their ratings and excluded the ones with really negative comments. He ended up with a list of five people, all men.

The last thing I need is a female attorney, he thought. He resolved to begin calling them tomorrow during breaks and lunch at work. He was sure he would find someone. Even if he was unsure of whether or not he needed one.

'Why spend money if you don't have to' was the thought that kept floating through his mind. Obviously, Riley has retained an attorney; let her pay for that. There isn't really much to split up. He could not think of a single thing he could not part with, although he bristled at the thought of giving her anything beyond what she had already taken.

But then he began to think that maybe Riley would want more from him than he was willing to give. What if she wanted support, maintenance, alimony? He had no idea what was normal for all that stuff. After all, this was the closest he ever got to divorce. His parents never divorced even though he often wished they would. They were spared that ordeal by a different one. And he could not think of even distant relatives who went through the process.

He decided to spend more time online to find out some of the steps and pitfalls of divorcing. It turned out there was a great deal of information available. It was nearly midnight by the time he felt he had some idea of what to expect. It did not look bad. He wasn't sure exactly of how much money Riley had, but he knew she had gotten paid from her first book and felt it was sufficient to keep writing. But he kept thinking of how little he actually knew of the details.

He went to bed that night feeling fairly certain that the legal situation would not be a threat to his economic well-being. This did little to assuage the rage he felt inside, but it was enough to allow him to drift off to sleep with the same fantasies of revenge he had been having in the back of his mind all day long.

Across town that very evening, Edward was planning. He had tried setting up a situation where he would just run into Riley, but that had not worked out so well. When he tried to think of alternative plans, he kept coming up empty handed. There was really only one thing to do, and that was to resume surveillance. But surreptitiously so, in order for her not to notice him.

He wondered what Riley thought when she thought of him. He wondered if she did think of him. Surely she did, he insisted to himself. After that afternoon, how could she not? But, as with most things, he wasn't certain. Maybe she was like that with other men. Maybe she was just—what can I call it? Loose.

That souring thought did nothing to assuage his eagerness to reconnect with her. If she was just some sort of sick sex addict, it was accompanied by a perfectly respectable career. The thought of her being a serious writer publicly and a sexual savage privately just turned him on more.

All roads lead back to her.

So he set about planning. He knew where she lived. Surely she must go out to other places besides the coffee shop where they met. His evenings were mostly free, so he could follow her for a week or so to determine if there was a regular pattern and then decide what to do from there once it was clear.

This was a satisfying idea for Edward: it gave him a direction and a sense of purpose. And he just knew that the end result of any investment of time and energy would result in a happy reunion.

He began immediately. He thought about what he needed. His phone, of course; but also a pair of decent binoculars so he did not have to get too close. Maybe a better camera than his smartphone provided, but he was unsure of that. Fortunately, he had a good pair of binoculars that he had purchased while in a bird-watching phase. They would be perfect. He gathered up his things and set out for Riley's neighborhood.

It was later than he would have preferred, about 8:30 p.m.; but he was so eager to start he just could not contain himself. When he got to the street where Riley's apartment was located, he slowed down at the corner and looked around carefully. He wanted to make sure he did not run into her by accident. This was an observation mission, not a contact one.

He scanned left and right and even turned around to see if she was behind him. Finally, he got to the corner and looked up to where he knew her window was.

Just then, he noticed her coming from the other direction. He slipped back behind the corner building and waited. Much as he did the last time he was in this very spot, he took out his phone and used it to watch her walking toward the front door of her apartment building. He noticed that she seemed preoccupied, for which he was grateful. She was not looking around; she was looking down at the pavement in front of her, apparently lost in thought.

Edward wasn't sure what to do if she passed by her door and kept walking, which would increase the odds of her seeing him. Cautiously, he withdrew his phone and turned to walk away before she could see him.

Then he stopped. It was very unlikely that she would miss the door to her own apartment, he reasoned, so he quietly walked around the block and peered around a different corner. Sure enough, he caught a glimpse of her entering her building.

Relieved, he waited for her to get to her apartment. He noted the time: 8:52 p.m. She must be coming from dinner out, probably with a friend. A date? Could be, but he had no way of knowing. Edward reminded himself that he was just doing surveillance; he could draw conclusions later, after he gathered more information.

When he saw the light in her apartment go on, he waited a moment to see if she would open the window. She didn't. He waited a few more minutes, and then turned to the direction from which she had come, thinking that maybe there was a restaurant close by that she frequented. He walked several blocks, where he found a number of bars and restaurants that were still open. He wrote down the names and decided he could check them out online to see if he thought they would appeal to her. He recognized that this was a long shot, but this was, after all, a surveillance mission.

Satisfied that he had collected enough data for now and had also gotten to catch a glimpse of Riley herself, he decided to return home. He would resume his data gathering tomorrow evening and every evening thereafter until he felt he had sufficient information about her habits. Then he would formulate a plan.

He got to his own apartment, certain he had made a good start. He had a plan, a purpose. He wasted no time. He went to bed early, eager to get up and start another day.

— 35 —

Riley did not know what to do with herself after dinner with Jennifer. As she walked home from Carter's, she found herself getting more and more upset. What is going on here? she wondered. Am I losing my best friend?

That's what it felt like. She thought of calling Jen, but she did not know what she would say. She tried to journal a bit when she got home but was equally clueless about where to look for the source of any problem that could explain the unusual experience she had with her this evening. Maybe something happened in New York, she thought; or maybe that episode at the restaurant was more serious than Riley knew about. Jen obviously did not overdrink this evening. She had one cocktail and a glass of wine with dinner, a pattern Riley naturally labeled social drinking, especially because she had precisely the same amount. She did not feel drunk, and she couldn't imagine that Jen did either.

She turned out the lights in her apartment and went to sit by her window and gaze out at the city below. It was something that often helped her calm down and think through things. She thought wistfully about the end of her marriage to Cameron, and it occurred to her that this would be a bad time to lose her relationship with her best friend.

Is that what's happening? It couldn't be. Then, why was this evening so . . . awkward? She didn't know. She just knew that she did not want to lose her friendship with Jennifer. Maybe she could talk to her about it, but the truth was they had just started getting more affectionate with each other recently. They had always been buddies and talked about the things friends talk about: other people, clothes, work, odd occurrences.

There have certainly been some of those between us lately, she thought grimly. But she could not shake the nagging feeling that there were elements at play in this story to which she was not privy, so she could not come to any plausible or realistic conclusion.

The city outside her window was quieting down. There were fewer people on the streets, and the streetlights had come on. Faces ran through her mind: Jennifer, Cameron, even Edward, whom she had not really thought about since the day he showed up at her apartment building waiting for her. That gave her a chill. It was just too weird. He was just too weird.

Then, she noticed a man across the street looking up at her apartment building, as if looking directly at her window. She stared a bit, but it was only a glimpse before the figure turned and walked in the other direction, towards Carter's. She could not be sure if what she felt in her gut to be true was in fact the case. Could it really be Edward? She squinted at the figure as he became smaller and smaller. She thought of running down to the street to him, but by the time she got there he would most likely have disappeared. He knew where she lived; he even knew which apartment was hers.

She shook her head. She knew she could not be certain if it was Edward or not, but her gut told her it was, and that mystical organ often trumped reason in situations like this.

What a mess. And I brought this on myself. She could not help thinking that she was playing some role in Jennifer's modified attitude towards her, even though reason (again) indicated that she had no evidence to confirm that. And she was absolutely certain that her impulsive and over-the-top indiscretion with Edward was completely her own doing. Even Cameron, who appeared not to be speaking to her—angry at her, no doubt, or so her gut told her—was doing so because she blew off simple civility by filing for divorce without even telling him.

She had a sinking feeling her life was about to get more complicated. And she had no one to blame but herself.

She got up from the chair by the window and prepared to turn in. Let this day be over, she sighed as she slipped into bed.

## 36

*Ellie did not answer. Suzanne cursed and drove to a nearby hotel. The truth was she did not care much where she was; all she wanted was to be with her. And if she couldn't, any hotel would be a satisfactory if temporary alternative. Tomorrow she would have to find another place to live.*

*She called Ellie's number a couple more times before she gave up and spotted a Hampton Inn. She pulled in and paid for the night. She took her suitcase up to her room and plopped down on the bed.*

*Now what? Though she longed for Ellie to be there—perhaps to see that she called and call her back—she did not know where that relationship was going. Did she want to marry Ellie? No, not really. She did not want to marry anyone, especially just coming out of a difficult situation with Adam. But she longed to be close to someone. She did not like being alone.*

*So go find someone, came a familiar voice in her head. She checked the time: 6:30 p.m. Plenty of time.*

*She got up from the bed and looked herself over in the mirror. A little make-up repair and maybe a change of clothes would do before she set out to seek some company. She recalled that there was a tavern about a mile from the hotel, and she thought that would be a decent place to start.*

*After making appropriate modifications to herself, Suzanne climbed back into her car in search of the tavern. She spotted it exactly where she thought it was, pulled her car into the lot, and entered the squat but nicely landscaped building.*

*It was not exactly the Ritz. It may not even have been Ramada Inn level quality. But it seemed clean and friendly enough. There were a number of people inside who looked to be commuters from the District. She realized she was not exactly certain where she was, but a glance out the window indicated she was somewhere in Maryland; every one of the cars that filled the small lot save hers had Maryland plates.*

*It doesn't matter where I am. People are pretty much the same everywhere. Over the past several years, she had good practice spotting people who were looking to hook up and sizing them up rapidly. She dismissed the ones who were making their first foray into the world of illicit hook-ups on the one hand and the ones who were way too practiced on the other. It was the middle that interested her: people with some experience but not too much. Someone who still dreamed that meeting someone in a bar for a night might actually lead to a solid relationship. A young-ish person. She slipped into the only remaining stool at the bar.*

*There was a man three stools down who looked the type. Nice looking but not movie-star handsome. Clean, well-groomed with appropriately stylish facial hair. Clothes from a larger department store and not a thrift shop; clean enough to have washed up before he got here. Not a smoker. He was nursing something that looked a lot like a Bud Light.*

*As the bartender came to take her order, she flashed a smile in the other man's direction before turning her attention back to the bartender, who seemed like a nice guy. Young, eager; probably his first full-time bartending job. Maybe a student.*

*"Been here long?" she asked him.*

*"Two weeks," he said with a smile.*

*"So, still learning the ropes."*

*"Sort of. I've done this before." He smiled again. "You from around here?"*

*"D.C.," Suzanne said candidly. "Had some projects out this way."*

*"Love D.C.," the bartender said. Then, he handed her a beer and extended his hand. "I'm Luke."*

*Of course you are*, thought Suzanne. *All young, good-looking bartenders are named Luke.* "Roseanne," she replied, in no mood for this relationship to go much further.

In the meantime, the target three stools away was surreptitiously watching this interchange and seemed to understand that Suzanne was surreptitiously watching him. Their eyes met very, very briefly before looking toward the back of the bar.

When Luke went off to take care of other customers, the person sitting at the stool next to her got up to leave. Third Stool got up and sauntered over to the now vacant seat next to her and sat down. "Can I buy you a drink?"

Third Stool extended his hand to her. "Name's Crowley," he said. "Justin Crowley."

"Roseanne," replied Suzanne.

A momentary silence descended on the side-by-side stools, as each was waiting for the other to say something. It was a control thing common among the pick-up crowd. The first one to speak was automatically, if often unconsciously, labeled the more desperate of the two. Or perhaps the needier.

Suzanne didn't care. "You from around here?" she said.

"No," Justin replied. "Just driving through. From Ohio. Dayton."

*The middle of nowhere,* thought Suzanne. She wondered vaguely what brought him to Maryland, but she waited for him to speak.

"And you?" he said after a pause.

"D.C."

"This is pretty far from the District. What brings you out to the badlands of Maryland?"

*Good question,* thought Suzanne. *Waiting for my same-sex lover* was what flashed through her mind, but she had a ready answer. "Some projects out this way. I work for a consultant firm."

Justin nodded and looked into the distance as if he did not really believe her, something Suzanne picked up on immediately.

"So, you don't believe me," she teased.

He looked at her for a moment. "It's your life and your story, Roseanne. I'm just here to listen."

*Whatever interest Suzanne had in this man, whose name may or may not be Justin Crowley, evaporated. A manipulative listener, she thought. She was not about to tell him a single honest detail of her life, except perhaps that she might have been willing to have sex with him up till this last moment. Even if he is telling the truth, she thought, she could not find a single piece of the picture beyond his kempt appearance that interested her, physically or otherwise.*

*The conversation re-started slowly, each person parroting things they had said many times in many similar bars on similar stools. It was almost comical, and at one point Suzanne actually chuckled.*

*"You've done this before?" she said, violating a cardinal rule of hooking up.*

*"What?" said Justin, as if offended.*

*"Nothing," she said. "You just seem very smooth." She hoped he would take that as a compliment.*

*He appeared to. He actually smiled. "A time or two," he said.*

*Suzanne considered her options. Zero contact and a soft-ish landing for 'Justin;' some low-level physical contact either outside or in the hall that leads to the bathroom; actually hooking up in his or her car or his or her hotel room. There was no doubt in her mind that she would take the first option.*

*She slowed the conversation and then looked at her watch. "Well, Justin. It's been nice talking with you. I've got an early appointment, so I'll be needing to turn in."*

*Justin's face was expressionless, except for a slight tic under his left eye. She surmised that he had been rejected before, and it was perhaps no big deal for him. On the other hand, he could be pissed. She motioned for the check from the bartender.*

*"I'll get this," Justin said. "After all, I offered."*

*This was Suzanne's opportunity to give Justin a second chance. Suddenly, a weird feeling of apprehension swept over her, something that was not common. "Thank you so much," she said and slipped off the stool.*

*She walked to the end of the bar and got Luke's attention. She thought it would look as if she were directing him to bill Justin for her*

*drink. In fact, she did that, and then whispered to him, "Please make
sure he doesn't follow me out." Since she had pointed to Justin, who
was watching her, she waved good-naturedly and smiled a phony
smile before turning and leaving the bar.*

*It took all her strength not to break into a run. She hoped Luke
was the watchful, honest sort he seemed to be. She glanced around
and got into her car, started it, and sped off.*

*Relieved, she drove to her hotel, where she parked as close to the
door as possible. Again, she scanned the parking lot and the street she
had just come up to see if she had been followed. Not seeing anyone,
she walked carefully into the hotel, relieved to see someone on duty,
and then proceeded to her room, unlocked and relocked the door,
and fell into bed.*

*She realized her heart was beating fast. I can't recall ever being
this paranoid, she thought, or even this frightened. She listened for
noises outside her room but did not hear anything. She wished Ellie
would call her, but she was wary of her phone ringing. She pulled it
from her pocket and turned off the volume, leaving only the vibrate
function on. That will be enough.*

Riley removed her hands from the keyboard and sat back in
her chair. Now what? she wondered. Just what kind of woman was
Suzanne?

Complicated.

*Suzanne switched on the television and surfed the channels until
she found some innocuous series that often put her to sleep. She kept
the TV on as she performed her nightly ministrations, removed her
clothes, and climbed into bed.*

*She wanted to put 'Justin' out of her mind. Despite his practiced
Midwestern demeanor, he just seemed up close to be creepy—if not a
serial killer type, some kind of serious oddball. She wasn't sure what it
was exactly: maybe it was a certain overly prepared self-presentation,
a certain hardness in his eyes, a hardness that belied the superficial
congeniality. Not at all the clean-cut guy he postured himself to be.
She could not be sure of the serial killer business; it was something
people said almost casually. In fact, she had no idea what a real serial*

*killer was like. She only knew what she saw on television. Maybe she watched too many cop shows.*

*Instead, she forced herself to think of Adam. In her original plan, their separation and divorce was supposed to be a smooth, even caring, kind of thing. But she just couldn't do it. The truth was, there was so much resentment, frustration, and even rage built up over the years of their marriage that she could not help but stick the knife in psychologically and let it hang there. She realized she was glad he knew that she had cheated on him, even multiple times. Did she feel some shame about that disclosure? Sure, but not nearly enough to outweigh the bitter disappointment she felt about the whole relationship: the whole soulless, passion-less, dreary relationship that propelled her to look for stimulation elsewhere. It was, on balance, a pathetic waste of time.*

Some honesty in this woman, Riley noted with a certain grim sense of satisfaction.

She glanced up at the time on her computer screen. It was nearly noon, time for a break and for lunch. She was hungry, but not for food. She wanted to begin to repair some of the mess she had made in her life. And she thought she would start with what may have been the worst.

She did not know how to contact Edward, but she had a distinct sense that it was he whom she saw the night before looking up at her apartment window. This fit with her mental image of him as a kind of lonesome soul whose world would be forever changed by the passionate escapade of the type Riley visited upon him. She could imagine he was probably obsessed with her. She realized she had not taken that obvious consequence into account when she . . . what? . . . took advantage of him?

Sort of. She really did not know what to call what she did with Edward, except to note that it did remind her that she had sexual, um, needs. When she surveyed all she knew and thought about him, she thought he would not be that far away from the needy, at least slightly pathetic loner type.

She made a decision to return to the Starbucks they had both frequented in the hope that she would run into him there. If she did it daily after normal school hours, she might get lucky. But that would have to wait until later this afternoon. She decided to tackle the second mess first: Cameron.

She picked up the phone and dialed his number. He was probably at work, but in most of his jobs he had sufficient flexibility to answer the phone.

Somewhat to her surprise, he did. "Cameron," he said simply.

Ignoring the forced formality, Riley got straight to the point. "Cameron, it's me. I am calling to say that I owe you an apology. I should have spoken to you before filing divorce the papers and I didn't. I'm sorry."

Cameron sat back in his chair in front of his computer and considered this. He glanced around to see if there was anyone in earshot, and decided there wasn't, as his office was behind glass walls. When he had seen Riley's name on the screen before answering, he felt an immediate surge of anger and wanted to say something hostile, but she spoke first, and her voice was even and her tone sincere. His anger was defused by a deserved apology. Now, he was uncertain what to say.

"Cameron, are you there?" said Riley.

"Yeah, I'm here, Riley," he replied. "I'm just not sure what to say."

"Well, I know you're at work and probably busy, but if you would like to talk sometime, please give me a call. I'm ready now."

Cameron was feeling so many conflicting things he began to feel a little light-headed. "I will, Riley." And then he added, "Thanks for calling." Then he hung up.

Riley felt relief wash over her. He took her call; he responded reasonably; he committed himself to continuing the conversation. She did not think she could ask more of him, especially, as she learned, when he was at work. She was so relieved she realized she was actually hungry.

As she was munching on a microwave meal that she had popped into the oven, she thought of the third leg of her agenda, Jennifer. She was unsure how to approach this because she did not think or feel that she was in possession of all the facts. She felt she and Jennifer needed to have a truth-light conversation, but she was afraid of what the consequences of such a conversation might be. Ugh.

What could I say to her? That something seems to have come between us and I don't know if it has or what it is? If so, is it about me or something I did?

That's precisely what you should say to her, came a voice from deep inside her.

I guess so, she thought. It did not seem so undoable.

## 37

Later that afternoon, Riley went to the coffee shop/scene of the crime. She was a little nervous and did not know whether to expect to see Edward or not. She was pretty clear about what she wanted to say to him. She wanted to be gentle about it, but it came down to a single, one-syllable word: STOP. And then to specify: I do not want to have any kind of relationship with you. I understand I crossed a line, but that was then, and I no longer wish to have any contact. I am sorry.

That seemed easy to do in the confines of her own mind and alone in her own apartment. She wasn't sure how much of it she would be able to say to him in person. She felt butterflies in her stomach just thinking about it. But she had to try.

In the end, at least on this day, it did not seem to matter. Edward was nowhere to be seen, and Riley figured if he were to visit this shop it would be during this time. She went to the counter and ordered a coffee; then she went to find an open table. It wasn't hard, as customers were few in the hours between lunch and the end of the business day.

She pondered her next move. Time to call Jennifer? She glanced at her watch. No, she concluded, Jen would still be at work, and she did not want to disturb her there.

Why not? she thought. I am on a roll.

Without thinking any further, she pulled out her phone and dialed Jen's number. It rang and rang and went to voicemail.

"Hi, Jen. It's me. Give me a call when you have a chance."

That seems innocuous enough.

She spent the next minutes feeling pretty good, congratulating herself for taking care of personal business in a way she had avoided for what felt like a long time. She felt freer. And happier.

And then Edward walked into the coffee shop.

She wasn't sure he saw her when he went up to the counter, but she spotted him, and her heart began to pound in her chest. 'Oh, shit' was all she could think.

When Edward turned around to find a place to sit, it was immediately obvious that he had not seen her, given the genuinely shocked look on his face, and the fact that he froze in place when he spotted her. They stared at each other for some moments before Riley took a deep breath and motioned for him to join her.

This was not at all in Edward's plan, although as he began to breathe again he had to admit he felt a mixture of pleasure along with the shock of seeing her in a place he had come to least suspect. He walked over and sat down across from Riley.

"Hi," he said stiffly.

"Hi," she replied.

Mustering all the courage she could, assisted by as deep a breath as she could manage, Riley looked Edward right in the eye. "I am glad you are here. I was wanting to talk to you."

Edward nodded. Hope stirred inside him.

"When we first met, I was having a difficult time. And I took advantage of you in a highly inappropriate way," she began.

Edward felt the hope that stirred inside him begin to weaken. He started to pale.

"I want to apologize to you personally for that."

Riley looked at him. She noticed that his face had lost color, and the small muscles around his eyes and mouth had started to quiver a bit. He looked as anxious as she felt, but, as she spoke, she could feel resolve coalescing within her.

She leaned towards him, and spoke in a small, gentle voice. "I think you believe that it is possible for us to have some kind of relationship, Edward. I want to tell you it is not."

A heavy silence hung over the pair as they sat in the nearly deserted coffee shop. Edward's face made more odd movements. Tics, Riley thought, or just anxiety. Or both.

"Am I clear?"

Edward shook his head, as if to say 'no.' Do you understand what I just said?"

He was still shaking his head.

"Edward, look . . . " she began. But she stopped when Edward sprang from his seat and ran out of the coffee shop, leaving his coffee and Danish at the table in front of Riley.

"Jesus Christ!" she said aloud. Now what?

At first her mind was blank. But then she began to question what happened. What did this mean? It definitely seemed like a bad sign. Is Edward so fragile that he can't talk about what happened between them? Apparently. Did he understand what I said to him? Probably; that must have been what he was responding to.

She took a while to calm herself down. She had actually delivered the message she wanted to deliver, and, even though she was surprised, and more than a little anxious about Edward's reaction, Riley felt that she had accomplished her goal.

She sat there for a while, sipping her coffee and wondering if this was really the end of the matter. Edward's panic reaction suggested that perhaps it wasn't.

Riley hoped she was wrong about that. She felt a chill pass through her body.

# — 38 —

*The days were rough for Adam. He was beyond shocked to learn that his wife—who, for all the challenges of their relationship, was someone he loved—had cheated on him on more than one occasion. It seemed to him that she inferred, although did not specifically say, that she had had a number of affairs. He had a lot of trouble wrapping his mind around that fact. The logistics involved seemed daunting to him. How did she pull that off? How is that even possible? These were the befuddling, infuriating, and sad thoughts that kept running through his mind.*

*Beyond the attention required for work, which he dutifully continued to do, Adam spent his days sitting around wondering, crying, getting angry, getting bored, and in the evenings getting loaded. The anger and sorrow came out more readily with the assistance of alcohol.*

*He hadn't bothered to shower since Suzanne left. He thought maybe he smelled funny, but it's hard to tell how one smells unless other people are around. And he had seen no one since Suzanne. He woke up, drank some water, took some aspirin for his hangover from the night before, and got to work. He was grateful to have something to distract himself from his misery and began to see his daily work ritual as something of greater value than he had previously thought. At the end of work, around noon, he did his most serious sitting around wondering and being depressed. He thought maybe he should change his clothes, but again he did not really give a damn. He was beginning to wonder why people changed their clothes ever, even to sleep.*

*It was a surprise when the phone rang, and Suzanne was on the other end of the line. Even in this short time that seemed to stretch out into eternity, she had become in his mind something of a mythical figure, someone he was sure he knew but really did not. At times throughout the day, he wondered if she really existed or if his relationship with that person, his marriage to her, was some kind of dream event, something his unconscious mind had conjured up to build out his life in a way that made sense but that was disconnected from reality. The world around him began to feel like the one in* The Matrix, *one that appeared real but in fact wasn't. He was hoping for the blue pill.*

*The last time he saw Suzanne shattered years of what he thought was true. He was adrift. He kept going to the refrigerator for another beer.*

*He did not answer his phone. He was pretty sure that, even though he felt lonely and cut off from humanity, she was the last person he wanted to talk to. Nor did he check his voicemail to see if she left a message. He did not want to validate that Suzanne was an actual person to whom he was married who defeated him so completely, sabotaging their marriage and perhaps his life in the process. He just sank more deeply into depression.*

*For her part, Suzanne listened to the announcement on Adam's phone and debated about leaving a message. It took her until the end of the announcement to decide that she did not have anything to say to him. She hung up.*

*After the frightful night in Maryland, Suzanne had returned to D.C. and found a residence hotel; she signed up for a week, thinking that would give her sufficient time to find an apartment. She went to work and noticed Ellie was not in her office. In fact, her office looked different, as if no one worked there: no personal items, photographs, or coffee mugs sitting around. She felt an uptick in anxiety and went to see Gail, another colleague she worked with regularly.*

*"Where's Ellie?"*

*"Oh, you haven't heard? She was transferred out of this office all of a sudden."*

*"What?! When did this happen?"*

"Yesterday," Gail said. "It was some kind of emergency situation in the Dayton office. She left work early to pack and get on the road." She paused. "Beyond that, I don't have any details." She paused a bit. "No one does."

"Who's taking her place?"

"TBD so far as I know. To be determined."

Suzanne could not understand why Ellie would not have called her to let her know this major event was happening. *She cared for me,* she kept thinking. *She loved me. She could have called me from the road.*

*Is this some kind of cosmic payback? Bad karma? For what I did to Adam?* Suzanne's thoughts erupted in irrational ways she had not had since she was in middle school. Suddenly, her world, which had had clear if problematic parameters just minutes before, was seriously askew. She went to her cubicle in a daze and tried to get organized for the workday. Her heart was not in it; in a moment of what had become uncharacteristic candor, she realized her heart was broken. And she was not happy about it.

*Jesus Christ! Now what?*

*Get to work,* commanded an internal voice. *Stop thinking of this for now.*

That sounded like a good idea to Suzanne, whose feelings were so mixed up she could imagine no way to disentangle them. She forced herself to focus on nothing but work, and after a while fell into a familiar cycle of being productive, collaborating with colleagues, sending memos and emails, and in general carrying on the work she was hired to do. Around noon, she pushed back from her desk and allowed herself to think for a few moments about her situation. Options did not immediately come to her except for the necessity of finding a place to live. Then she thought about Adam. *Maybe I should call him.* She was not sure why. She had not spoken to him since she left at his demand the day before; and, even though her behavior with him was well-rationalized if hostile in her mind, it still felt like a big loose end. She decided to wait until later in the day, preferably after she left the office.

*She also allowed herself to think of Ellie. She did not want to think of the obvious meaning of her former boss's behavior: that whatever happened between the two of them was something other than what Suzanne had come to believe. Was Ellie using her? For sex? For companionship? For both? It was all still muddled in her mind, and she found herself unwilling to get into the messy feelings she had about it, so she grabbed a bite to eat from a vending machine and forced herself back to work. I'll have time to think of this later.*

*She left the office at the usual time with no more insight or information into her situation with Ellie, or her situation with Adam, for that matter. When she got to her hotel, she threw her things down, pulled a chair up to the small desk, and dialed Adam's number. It was half intentional, half impulsive.*

*He did not pick up—she really couldn't blame him for that—so, she left an uncharacteristically candid voicemail. "Hi, it's me. Yesterday was tough. Call me."*

*And then she threw her phone on the bed and went to find something for dinner.*

## 39

Jennifer listened to Riley's voicemail twice. It was not so unusual to receive a message from her, although it was a little odd getting it in the middle of a workday. She decided to call her when she was finished working for the day.

She called her as she was leaving the office, and Riley picked up after a single ring.

"Hi, Honey. Returning your call."

"Jennifer, I need to talk to you."

"Sure, Riley, where and when would you like to meet."

"How about your place or mine?"

An unusual but not outlandish request. Jennifer could hear anguish in Riley's voice. "Sure, Honey. I can be at your place in twenty minutes."

"Great. See you then." Riley clicked off.

As Jennifer put her phone away, she wondered what was going on with Riley. She seemed upset and urgent about getting together, and it wasn't just another 'let's-have-dinner' kind of thing. She had no idea what was so urgent, but she had that feeling of level-headedness that comes from a productive day of working. She felt ready for whatever it was.

When she rang the bell to Riley's apartment, the door buzzed open immediately. Jennifer got on the elevator and was at Riley's door in a few minutes.

When Riley opened the door, Jennifer's eyes widened. "Riley, what's the matter?" she said when she saw her friend's tear-streaked face.

"I just. . . I just . . . I just had something of a meltdown," Riley said. "I needed to talk to someone."

"I'm here, Honey," Jennifer said soothingly, and she walked into the apartment and closed the door after her. "Talk to me."

The pair sat down on the couch next to each other, knees touching.

Riley tried to collect herself before launching into the story. "I realized the other day, yesterday, really, that I had made of mess of several big things in my life. I treated Cameron poorly; I crossed the line big time with Edward; and I . . . " She looked at Jennifer cautiously, wondering about the wisdom of this next piece. "I thought our last visit was awkward, and you are so important to me I got afraid of losing you and . . . " And she did not know what to say next.

Jennifer reached out and took Riley's hand. "Whatever that last thing is, Riley, we'll get through it. I'm your friend." She felt truth in those words.

Riley broke down and cried, and Jennifer reached over and cradled her in her arms. "It's okay, Sweetie. It's okay."

After a few minutes, Riley was able to resume her end of the conversation. "I'm sorry. Something just happened with Edward. I decided to clear the air with him, so I went to the Starbucks where I first met him. I didn't really think I'd see him. I mean, I thought it was a long shot. Plus, it was the first time I'd been there since we had our . . . dalliance." She picked up the glass of water next to her and took a big gulp. "He came in when I was there. He didn't see me at first. When he turned and saw me, he came over. I invited him to join me. I wanted to put an end to whatever he was doing."

Then, she thought for a moment. "Let me back up. Last night, I was looking out my window just thinking about things, and I was sure I spotted him looking up at my apartment window. And then he walked back toward Carter's, where you and I had had dinner." She paused and looked at Jennifer, who was paying rapt attention. "That's when I decided he was up to something—I think he may be stalking me—and I needed to put an end to it or to whatever he's doing. I got scared."

Jennifer was still holding Riley's hand. She squeezed it lightly.

"So when we met, I told him that I did not want to have a relationship with him. I asked him if he understood. He kept shaking his head as if he didn't. When I tried to clarify, he got up and ran out of the shop without a word."

Jennifer's eyebrows raised. "Ran? Without a word?"

Riley nodded.

"Jesus Christ," said Jennifer.

"That's what I said. So I came home. At first I was just unclear about what happened and unsure of how to proceed. But the more I thought about it, the more frightened I became. Almost a panic attack. No. Definitely a panic attack." Her eyes widened as she proceeded. "He was or is stalking me; he wants a relationship. He obviously has trouble taking no for an answer. Or maybe in his mind . . . I don't know what's possible. Here's a weird, weird man, Jen. I don't know what he's capable of. If he were a love-sick teenager or something, that would be one thing, but he's, like, in his thirties." She sat there in silence with tears running down her face.

Jennifer did not say anything. She just kept holding Riley's hand. Minutes ticked by.

After a while, she said, "Riley, this would freak out most women."

Riley looked at her. "Really?" She felt like a child.

"Really." She held her hand more tightly. "Look, when ordinary guys get the brush off, they may not like it—okay, they never, ever like it. But they go on: they find someone else, they drink too much for a couple days, they go out with their buddies and whine. But stalking? That is a whole other thing. It's not normal." She paused a moment as an idea struck her. "And I think you should call the police."

That last thought hit Riley like a thunderclap. The police? She looked at Jennifer askance. "I can't," she said. "I don't even know his last name. Or where he lives. Or anything else about him."

Jennifer bit her lower lip. "Honey, you are so not up to date on your media training. We can find that stuff out about anybody in no time."

"Really?"

"Really."

A mildly conspiratorial smile crept across Jennifer's face, who was amused by Riley's naiveté. Riley, on the other hand, was befuddled but tempted to feel relieved that the things she had felt limited by might not be limiting at all. According to her friend, whom she trusted, they could be readily discovered.

"Can I use your computer?" asked Jen.

"Sure." Riley went over and turned it on, entered her password, and waited for it to boot up. While they were waiting, Jennifer asked Riley to tell her everything she did know about Edward. She did; it wasn't much. Mid-thirties, a teacher of, she thought, middle school students. Taught social studies.

Jennifer got to work. Riley had never seen Jen use a computer, and she was a little awed by the speed and efficiency of her command of the machine that Riley saw as basically an elaborate typewriter. For Jen's part, it would have taken too much time to explain each step of a complicated process to Riley, so she just thought and talked herself through public sources until she whittled down the number of possible people to five.

She pulled the chair away from the computer and said to Riley: "Does he look like any of these?"

She looked at the screen, where five thumbnail images of teachers who were members of a Social Studies association of some sort stared back at her. He looked like the top picture. She read the attached information: Edward McAllister, Social Studies Teacher, Wittington Middle School. She pointed limply to the screen and said, "That's him."

"Great," said Jen. "Let's hold off on the police just now. You have a lawyer, right? The woman you told me about who filed the papers?"

Riley nodded. She was still in something of a daze.

"Call her first thing in the morning and tell her everything that's happened. Don't hold back anything. Don't feel guilty or bad or responsible or anything but thorough. Ask her if she thinks it would be advisable to file for a restraining order against . . ." she glanced at the screen, "Mr. McAlister."

She looked at Riley, who was not responding. "Riley, Honey. Do you understand?"

Riley turned slowly toward her friend. Now it was her turn to bite her lip. "I understand, Jen. Thank you so, so much." She dropped to her knees and threw her arms about Jen, who was still sitting in the desk chair.

"It's okay, Sweetie," she said. "It's okay."

## 40

Edward ran until he could not run any more. He leaned against a building to catch his breath. His heart was pumping hard from the exertion, and he would have been grateful for the exercise had he not been so overtaken with rage. His feelings had clearly gotten the best of him.

She doesn't want me. She does not want to have sex with me. She does not want a relationship with me. These phrases burned in his head like incendiary sky banners. And they pointed to the one truth he did not think he could ever abide: to live the rest of his life without a relationship with Riley. He was sick with anxiety, grief, panic. And rage.

He straightened up and continued walking towards his apartment. He tried to think his way through things, to be reasonable; but his mind was too jumbled in the face of a message that was too clear. What do I do now? What can I do?

By the time he let himself into his apartment, other thoughts appeared. She used me. This is the one that came, slowly at first, but then grew larger and larger in his mind. She used me. She used me. He had dedicated the last months of his life to learning about her, pursuing her, following her. And just when he felt the triumph—when it was she, herself, who raised him up to the triumphant climax of his efforts—she drops him like . . . like . . . like . . . like a nobody.

It was all a sham. What he thought was the highlight of his life, the pinnacle of his ability to derive joy, satisfaction, and pleasure from being on the planet, evaporated like so much dissipated smoke.

Edward did not know the reason for this, but he figured Riley surely knew. For his part, he could not imagine anything he might have done or said that could possibly have offended her. He was not unkind; he was not dishonest much. True, he did not tell her he knew who she was; nor did he tell her he had scoped out her apartment while waiting for her. But lovers often tell fibs. They don't really count. Other than those few dissimulations, he was frank with her. And nothing but polite.

And this is how she repays me. She came looking for me today; he was sure of that. She came looking for me so she could blow me off in person, so there would be no doubt about her intentions. Or lack of them.

Edward just did not understand why. His mind could not fathom why this woman, to whom he was so drawn and with whom he was so intensely intimate, could flush him down the toilet so quickly, so bloodlessly, so definitively. It did not make any kind of sense in his head.

I thought our relationship was bliss, but maybe it was just Riley getting herself off on my dime, so to speak. For reasons I do not know. I may never know.

These powerful feelings and the enormous gaps in his understanding were too much for Edward, who had always prided himself for being simple, good, honest. He tried to think: had I ever seen my parents this angry? Had I ever been this taken advantage of? In fact, had I ever seen anyone in real life go through what I'm going through? He was sure he hadn't.

He could feel the rage percolating, taking over his entire brain space. In an effort to stop resisting, he plopped down on his bed and stared at the ceiling with nothing but bitterness in his soul.

Then an odd thing happened. An idea the likes of which he had never entertained appeared just on the horizon of his mind. It had to do with how he felt and how he could stop feeling what he was feeling. He realized, slowly at first, but then more clearly, that he had options. He could strike back. He could hurt Riley the way she hurt him.

But he was torn. He sat up in his bed. "I'm not like that," he said aloud. "I don't hurt people."

He turned toward the window of his small bedroom. Instead of seeing a blue sky, he saw his life in a new way. He saw his arid childhood and his distant parents. He saw his efforts to be good and to do well. He saw how his shyness and fear of people was always a struggle. He saw his one magnificent opportunity for love vanish before his eyes for reasons he could not know.

Is this all there is?

An ancient memory made itself felt in his mind. Though his parents weren't seriously religious, they did take him to church a few times in an effort, he supposed, to check that item off the list of Responsible Things Parents Do. And he remembered a preacher who scared him half to death talking about God's vengeance. How the wicked would be killed and scattered and deprived of all their earthly possessions. How the burning fires of hell were forever, not just an endurable period of time justified by the extent of the misdeed. With God it was apparently all or nothing.

He even now could visualize the preacher holding up his Bible, his hands trembling, his voice shaking, spittle shooting from his frothy mouth, and shouting a quote: "Revenge is mine, sayeth the Lord."

He blinked and began to notice the blue sky out his window. Not anymore it's not. Vengeance is mine. Now I am the Lord.

## — 41 —

The next morning Riley called her attorney. She was not looking forward to it, but she did not know what else to do. What Jennifer said made all the sense in the world. They had spent the rest of the evening talking more about it, consolidating a plan, and talking about sensible safeguards.

They talked about calling the police, but they both thought upon closer examination that the cause for doing so was not sufficiently substantial. They decided that Riley should first talk to the attorney and, if possible, get a restraining order. Then, if he violates it, call the police. That made good sense to Riley.

Still, she was nervous about calling Lauren. She had never actually met her in person but had talked to her on the phone several times, a few times at length. She struck Riley as a no-nonsense woman who was a capable attorney. She felt safe with her.

She took Jen's advice and told Lauren everything: how she and Edward had met; how she invited him into her apartment to have sex with her; how he showed up at her apartment building the next day; and how she was sure he was stalking her yesterday. It was not easy sharing this with someone she'd never met in person. After spewing all the relevant details, she waited for Lauren's response.

She did not have to wait long. "Yes, it appears that he has been stalking you. But no threats have been made and no incidents of abuse have occurred. You may have seen him outside your building, but there is no photograph or other evidence that this actually occurred. And there is no law against standing on the street. It is basically your word against his." She went on to explain how a judge had to determine whether an order of protection was warranted, and she assured Riley that no judge would do so on the basis of zero evidence.

Her lawyer was completely noncommittal about the parts of the story that Riley wasn't proud of. That is to say, she did not seem to care about the sex part, and that attitude went some way towards helping her get over a psychological hump. She did advise Riley to be watchful. "If he shows up again, keep a camera handy. Use your cell phone. Document any contact you might have with him, especially anything he does that is threatening or hurtful. And keep in touch with me about this. I do not take these things lightly."

It was a sobering conversation, and none of it made Riley especially happy, but she thanked Lauren and ended the conversation. Even though she did not get an easy solution, she felt it was not a waste of time. She had taken positive action. She had done something besides fall apart and get fearful or panicky. In her own way, she, with Jen's help, faced the situation head on. She was pleased about that and was glad she pursued it. She liked taking care of business. It made her feel more grown-up.

And Riley believed Lauren's concern for her. She felt she had another ally in her life. She felt free enough to start writing.

*The next morning, Suzanne returned to work and found her coworkers on edge. She looked around. No one was really working. Some were staring at their computers. Others were whispering to each other in the corridors. She spotted Gail standing listlessly by her desk.*

*"What's up, Gail?"*

*At first, Gail avoided looking at her. Then, she turned toward Suzanne full face and said, "It's Ellie. She's dead."*

*Suzanne thought she had misheard what Gail had just said. "What?!"*

*"She's dead, Suzanne. She was killed in an automobile accident yesterday on her way to Dayton. A tractor trailer jumped lanes and plowed straight into her car." A tear fell from Gail's pale face.*

*Suzanne felt herself slipping into shock. Her vision narrowed, her breathing became labored, she felt dizzy; she began to feel unsteady on her feet. She limped over to her desk holding onto anything she* could and sat down on her work chair and forced herself to take deep breaths. *This can't be happening. This just can't be happening.*

It was immediately clear to Suzanne why Ellie had not called her. Maybe Ellie was even trying to call her when the truck crashed into her car. That thought filled Suzanne with acute but momentary guilt, but those feelings paled in comparison to the crushing grief that was descending upon her.

She put her head in her hands and cried harder than she had ever cried in her life.

*Jesus!* thought Riley, as if this development surprised her as much as Suzanne.

After some time passed, Jerome Bitworth, the general manager of the office, walked into the shared workspace and asked for everyone's attention. Suzanne wiped her eyes and adjusted her make-up as best she could. She stood up to listen, holding onto her desk chair.

"As you know, yesterday our company experienced a tragedy. We lost one of our most productive and valued employees, who had selflessly consented to help us deal with an urgent situation in another city." He paused and shook his head. He had clearly been the one who suggested the transfer to her. "She not only agreed to help, but she also saw the need to go immediately." At this point, the stolid Mr. Bitworth, as everyone thought of him, actually choked up. "Excuse me." He looked away for a few moments, then turned back to the assembled workers. "I just got off the phone with her parents, who are, as you might imagine, devastated." He paused again before continuing.

"I know many of you knew, respected, and loved Elizabeth. Our management team has decided it would be best if we cancelled our work for today and closed the office out of respect for her and so you can all deal with this in your own way." Another pause. "Please go home and pray for Elizabeth's family. And for each other."

On his way out of the large room that was everyone's office, he passed by Suzanne's desk. He saw how distraught she was. As did everyone else.

"Ms. Wilkerson, could you stop by my office before you leave? Take your time; I just want to touch base with you about something *important before you go today." He walked out of the room with his head down, not looking at any of the other two dozen employees who were still standing around as if uncertain what to do.*

*The employees looked at each other. They slowly began to comply with their boss's request and started gathering up their things and trickling out of the office. Gail looked over at Suzanne, who was still glued to her chair, pale and drawn.*

*"You okay?"*

*Suzanne shook her head. "I don't think so."*

Doubtful, Riley thought. How could she be okay?

*"Is there something I can do for you, Suzanne?"*

*Suzanne shook her head. "I don't think so."*

*Gail moved imperceptibly in Suzanne's direction, as if to give her a hug or a reassuring gesture of some sort, but then thought better of it. "Well," she said. "Feel free to call me if there is anything I can do." Then, she turned and walked out of the office.*

*Suzanne sat in the huge empty space with her mouth open. Moments passed, but she was not aware of time. Then she remembered that Bitworth had asked to see her before she left. She could not imagine why. Did he know about her and Ellie? Doubtful. And even if he did, she just didn't care. She didn't care about anything at the moment except the leaden feeling of loss in the pit of her stomach.*

*Slowly, more slowly than she thought she could move, she picked up her purse and a messenger bag that contained work material and threw them both over her shoulder. Then she decided not to carry them into Bitworth's office. That did not seem professional. That seemed like she was in a hurry to leave.*

*She dropped her bags and walked slowly to the corner office. She knocked gently on the door, mostly hoping that he wasn't there.*

*"Come in."*

*Shit. She opened the door to find Bitworth behind his large wooden desk. "You wanted to see me, Mr. Bitworth?"*

*"Yes, yes, Suzanne, please come in. Have a seat." He motioned to one of the chairs in front of his desk. When Suzanne was seated, he got up to close the door of his office.*

"I know this is a difficult time for everyone, and perhaps especially for you. You and Ellie worked a lot together and seemed to do so very well. It is my understanding you became friends."

The hair on Suzanne's neck stood up. Uh-oh. She nodded but said nothing.

"That does not matter to me, except that . . ." He looked as if he was choosing his words carefully. "Her death put us into a bind. She was the only one who was familiar with the accounts that the Dayton office handled. It was why we sent her to take over when the director there left suddenly. And now . . ."

He's not, Suzanne thought. No, he can't be.

"Now we have no one who can do the job, with the exception of you." His speech picked up speed, and he appeared to be looking at a point above Suzanne's head. "You and Elizabeth worked closely on several of these accounts; in fact, the two of you worked on most of them. And no one else in the office knows as much as you do about them."

Jesus Christ! Suzanne blinked twice. She was coming down from shock and grief and colliding with surprise and something like dismay, not so much for what she saw coming as for the incomprehensible timing of the request.

She did not say anything.

Bitworth looked at her through squinty eyes. He knew he was asking for the moon at the most difficult time imaginable. But he had—the company had—to get moving in Dayton, or those accounts could be lost. Suzanne understood that.

"We would like you to move to the Dayton office. You would be Ellie's replacement." Then, he paused a moment. "I know this is a lot to ask," he said as gently as he could.

And there it is, thought Suzanne. Distraught thought she was, she began doing the calculus of this offer in her mind. A promotion, no doubt. More money, probably. Definitely. A move to Dayton. Dayton?! Her face was placid externally but internally she was squinting. She hoped it didn't show.

"How would this actually work, Mr. Bitworth?"

"*You would move to Dayton and take up the director position. There would be a promotion with an appropriate increase in your salary. In fact, the base salary schedule would change. Personnel at that level also participate in a profit-sharing program . . .*"

Suzanne had heard whispers, resentful ones mostly, of a profit-sharing program that management had. No one really talked about it openly. The whispers were largely the result of observations about nicer cars, better clothes, moves to swankier neighborhoods. It was thought to be a generous program. But no one really knew any details.

"*Profit-sharing?*"

"*Yes. At the director level and above, employees participate in a profit-sharing program to provide both motivation to excel and reward for doing so. Look,*" he said, "*I know this is a rough time, but the truth is we are in a bind. Take today to think about it. We will do anything you need to make the transition go smoothly. That includes taking care of any apartment leases or other expenses that might be problematic.*" He looked at Suzanne with what seemed like genuine warmth. "*We'll talk again in the morning, and you can tell me your thoughts.*"

"*Of course.*" Suzanne got up to leave Bitworth's office. She headed for her desk to collect her things.

*Ellie, what have you done?*

She looked around the cavernous space. She knew there was no doubt she would take the job. She would be a fool not to. And she knew it might entail spending some time, a few years perhaps, in Ohio; but she also knew that, after that, more options would open up.

And it would get her out of D.C. and away from Adam and her marriage and the bad habits that had grown up around her these last years. It was a fresh start.

Thoughts and images percolated through her brain, but only one thought rose ascendant in her mind as the tears resumed: *Thanks, Ellie; but I'd rather have you here.*

— 42 —

As Suzanne was trying to reconcile the terrible loss and grief she felt for Ellie with the opportunity it offered her, Adam was still chewing on the new information he had gotten from her. He really did not want to replay the last day he saw her, when he was adrift among painful feelings he had not ever felt in his life before this. But at the same time, he could not ignore the catching up he knew he needed to do in order to deal with this situation in a more or less sane manner.

In his mind, he just couldn't grasp how wrong he was about the woman he was married to. He always thought of her as a pleasant, personable, capable woman whom everyone liked. Maybe their relationship was rocky, but he always assumed she was honest. She always struck him as a little tightly laced, but she seemed otherwise sensible. This now seemed painfully naïve to him, but he never considered an alternative. The image of her taking lovers without his knowledge just did not figure into this picture.

If she wanted to do that, why did she stay with me? Why be married? We had no children, so that was not a consideration. She had a job and could easily support herself. Truthfully, Adam did not know exactly how much she made, but they both contributed equally to the household expenses and money was never an issue. And it wasn't as if they didn't enjoy each other's company. They seemed to. Of course, he knew the answer to that question: She chose not to stay married. That's what this has been all about. He marveled at how quickly and thoroughly his life had changed. She had apparently come to the conclusion that marriage was not for her.

*It was hard not to take it personally, and, being the responsible sort that he was, he did. It wasn't just that she did not want to be married. She did not want to be married to me. She said that quite clearly. It still stung.*

*He poured himself a scotch over some ice after he had sent his work off to his company. 'Seemed' was the word that lingered in his mind. Yes, he allowed, their marriage 'seemed' okay on the surface, but it really wasn't. He reached back in his memory to identify a time when they had a genuine heart-to-heart conversation, whether over dinner or over the bedroom pillows. He had trouble locating one.*

*Did I just want everything to be all right? Maybe. He thought of the day he wanted to tell Suzanne that he thought the marriage had run its course, and how clear that was to him. That day seemed like ages ago; in fact, it was only a week. And he felt so aggrieved by her most recent revelations that he could not feel the clarity that he had that day, when he wanted to talk about how distant things had gotten between the two of them. He recalled how he felt at that point that the marriage was all but over if not completely finished. He was astonished now how correct his assessment was. If the day had gone as he had planned, he would have been the one initiating the talk of separation or divorce.*

*But she beat me to it. I lost my nerve, but she seemed to have plenty in reserve. I took the cowardly way out, but she addressed it head on. Adam had to admit that he admired that about his wife.*

*The revelation about her hooking up with Ellie threw him, but it was, he thought at the time, a one-time thing, a single indiscretion. It was the revelation about other liaisons that threw him into a tailspin. The thing with Ellie wasn't the one-off fling that he had assumed. She had been cheating on him for some time, maybe for years.*

*The more he thought about it, the more twisted the whole damned situation felt. Involved with a woman, but had numerous affairs with . . . whom? Only other women? Men? He didn't know. He wasn't sure he wanted to know except that, of course, he did. But he didn't feel he was in any position to ask.*

*He went back to the fateful day in his mind. What was it I was thinking and so afraid to say to her? That I was unhappy, and she did not seem any happier? That our relationship was dying?*

*Those are truer assessments than I believed at the time.*

*He glanced at the glass of scotch in front of him. He had not taken a sip. I don't even like scotch; I've had this bottle in the cupboard for over a year. A gift from someone, if he recalled correctly. He looked around. Why am I sitting around feeling terrible when what really happened, however it happened, was the best thing, even the right thing, given what I know now. For whatever reason, our marriage didn't work out. It is taking me some time to face that, and I avoided saying it out loud because . . . why? Because I was afraid of what she might say or think or do? Or of how I might feel? He really had no clue.*

*Except for the misery of the past few days, I am okay. True Thing #1: I'm shocked and hurt and sad that things did not work out and that I have to rebuild a life, but that's what people do in these situations. True Thing #2: Suzanne is gone, but if half of what she told me is true, I need to run, not walk away from this marriage.*

*The world around him shifted. The dull gray that had been hanging over his head suddenly began to lighten a little, and he began to notice colors again. He got up and poured his untouched cocktail into the sink.*

*He went to take a shower.*

# — 43 —

Jennifer left Riley's apartment sometime after 10:00 p.m. She had a lot of thoughts and feelings that she needed to sort out.

One thing that stood out to her was that this was the closest she had ever been physically with Riley. Several times over the course of the evening, she had wrapped her in her arms to console her, to ground her, to help her get through the things that people go through when they are scared. She could not recall another time when she did that with anyone outside a sexual relationship.

But what she found glaring was that it was not at all sexual or titillating. It was a different kind of connection, a friendship. It felt strong but not passionate or erotic. Suddenly, the fantasy about her and Riley becoming sexual that had plagued her seemed to break up. She knew it just wasn't in the cards. Riley didn't want it, and I don't think I want it.

That was an unusual thought for Jennifer, for whom sex had been so important for so long. This episode, more than anything else, helped her break through the awkwardness she had been feeling during these past few weeks, when she had worked herself into a tizzy over what may or may not have been signals Riley was sending about closeness. All that just seemed like . . . like she had no idea what. Just weird.

When she got to her apartment, she felt her phone vibrate. It was a text message from Riley: *Thank you for being my friend.*

Jennifer texted back immediately. *Thank for you being mine. Take care of yourself.*

She went into her kitchen and poured herself a glass of white wine. She went over to the couch and sat down with her good leg comfortably under her, thinking of Riley's situation, her vulnerability, the challenges she's facing. She was a little worried about Riley's safety, but now that they knew who Edward was, they were not without leverage.

'They' she thought to herself. A pair of friends. Together. This was a warm and precious feeling. She savored it as she savored the oaky light liquid in her glass.

Then an idea came to her. Riley had told her that she did not know anything about Edward except his first name, the fact that he was a teacher, and the fact that he frequented the Starbucks down the street from Riley. She assumed that Edward knew that Riley did not know anything else. She began to think that maybe somehow letting Edward know that facts about him were known would level the playing field a bit.

This was a tantalizing idea. Should I talk to Riley about this before I do anything? Nah, she's too upset. And I am sure she would not want to speak to Edward at this point.

But I can.

She reached over and picked up her laptop from the coffee table in front of her. It was never far away. She began reproducing some of the search protocols she had done in haste earlier in the evening. This time, she went more slowly and delved more deeply into Edward's Internet presence.

There wasn't much to it. Edward struck Jen as something of a loner, a person without a big social media profile. That sent small alarm bells off in her mind. What kind of young-ish person doesn't have an online social media presence? Isolates, sick ones, loners. Or maybe someone who preferred not to be publicly known. As if that were possible in this day and age.

She did find a contact number on an old social media site. She wondered if it still worked. She glanced at the clock. 10:30 p.m. She picked up her phone, blocked her own number and dialed his.

A man answered. Jennifer had no idea if it was Edward or not, so she said simply, "Edward?"

"Yes," came slowly out of the man's mouth.

"Edward McAllister?"

"Uh-huh. Who is this?"

"Someone who knows who you are and what you're up to."

And Jennifer clicked off.

Satisfied, Jennifer put her laptop back on the table and dropped her phone on the couch next to her. Now he knows he is not acting under a cloak of absolute secrecy, she thought in a self-satisfied way. Now he knows someone is watching.

Probably his worst nightmare. She smiled a sly smile.

# — 44 —

Edward sat staring at the phone in his hand for a long time, as if it were alive. He felt dead inside. It took him a while to have clear thoughts. Fear began to course through his body.

Finally, he put the phone down, stood up, and stretched. Then, he started walking around in the tight circles allowed by the limited space of his home. He looked out the window and forced himself to think.

What was that all about? Why would someone call me, know my name, and then say she knew what I was up to? He felt agitated. He tried to force himself to remain calm.

An old girlfriend? He tried to redial the number, but it had been blocked. So it was obviously someone who knew their way around technology; at the very least someone who knew some of the things a smartphone was capable of. He tried to think back to a woman he knew who was tech-savvy that way.

Almost all of them. Everyone knows how to do that. At least everyone I have ever known. Even I know how to do that.

This line of thinking did not help his growing agitation. He did more stretches, so his blood could start circulating normally again. He had felt his face go pale and cold and wanted it to feel normal again. He rubbed his hands together to get the feeling back there as well. He felt a slight tremor in his hands.

How could anyone know what I was up to? What did that woman even mean by that? And who was she?

As far as Edward was concerned, there was only one thing he was 'up to,' and that was wreaking havoc on the life of Riley

Cotswald. And no one, no one, could possibly know about that. He had not said anything to anyone about any of it. In fact, he had not spoken to anyone since he sat with Riley earlier in the day.

All the feelings of righteous potency that he felt in the wake of his decision to take vengeance on Riley disappeared in an instant. He did not know what he was up against. This did not translate in his mind to abandoning his plan, which he was just beginning to formulate; but it did ratchet up his level of caution. And that level was already high.

Edward lay back on his bed to try to think clearly about the position he was in.

Okay, someone knows who I am, my phone number, and no doubt where I live and work. He concluded quickly that someone had done a deep dive into the Internet to find out these things. He was pretty sure it wasn't Riley, but he could not be certain. He really did not know her friends. In fact, it was one of his ideas just yesterday to do some searching about who her friends were. Now I'll have to be more circumspect about that.

For the moment, Edward did not know what to do, so he did what he always did in this situation. He closed his eyes and hoped he would fall asleep.

But sleep did not come willingly this evening. Thoughts raced across his mind; fears, reasonable and unreasonable, crisscrossed the theater of his brain.

He finally got out of bed.

He once again paced around his small apartment. This was not much relief—there wasn't much room to move around. He thought maybe a walk outside would be better and give him greater perspective. It was late, but not so late that no one else would be out. He grabbed his wallet and keys and left.

He thought of going by Riley's apartment but decided against it. In fact, he walked in the opposite direction. But then he changed his mind. Why not? It wasn't Riley who called me; he was sure of that. But it must have been was someone who knew her, someone she talked to about me. He weighed that against the possibility that it was some kind of random prank call from a lonely teenager who was trying to get a rise out of people. Then, he dismissed that thought: the voice was from an adult, a mature woman. Not a kid. And the odds on it being a random call were near zero.

As he got nearer to Riley's apartment building, he began to calm down some. Okay, he said to himself, what has really changed? Someone, somewhere found out my name and pertinent details. They are probably not hard to find these days. It could be anyone. But the reference to 'what he was up to' would not leave his head. No one could really know that. Nobody but maybe Riley. He stopped walking.

Then the obvious occurred to him: she put somebody up to this. He shivered in the warm night air. She is still out to hurt me. She won't let me go. That was at once a delicious and repelling thought. It bolstered his resolution.

He resumed walking until he got to her building. He looked up at her window, which was lit but dimly. You are not going to get me, Riley. You are not going to hurt me again.

He turned and went back to his apartment.

## — 45 —

Suzanne met the next morning with Bitworth, who was waiting in his office.

"Go right in," said his secretary.

"Good Morning, Suzanne. Please have a seat." He looked at her expectantly.

"Mr. Bitworth, I appreciate the offer you talked about yesterday. I also appreciate your giving me time to give it some thought." She shifted slightly in her chair. "You mentioned how the position and compensation package would change. I'd like to hear those details before I make my final decision." She gave him what she hoped was a very professional look.

"Of course," Bitworth said. And he laid out precisely what her title and position would be and the salary she would receive. It was more generous than Suzanne had thought.

"And you mentioned a profit-sharing plan?"

"Yes, twice a year, profits are calculated office by office. You would receive five percent of net proceeds from each assessment." He matched Suzanne's look with a noncommittal professional one of his own. "In the Dayton office, it comes to a substantial sum."

This jived with what Suzanne expected, but she had no idea what 'a substantial sum' might actually be. Momentarily, she thought of insisting on the specific numbers, but, given her new salary level, that struck her as unprofessional in the moment—trying to take advantage of a tragedy—so she simply said, "That would be satisfactory."

The relief was visible on Bitworth's face immediately. "Thank you, Suzanne. I appreciate your willingness to do this. Now, when can you be in Dayton?"

"I can leave immediately, sir."

The uptick of Bitworth's eyebrows told her how pleased he was with this move.

"Any loose ends you need our help in typing up? Leases? Rent?"

"No. Actually, I was in the middle of relocating anyway, so in that respect this comes at a good time."

More pleased looks on Bitworth's face. He scribbled something on a piece of paper and handed it to Suzanne across the desk.

"This is the contact person in the Dayton office who will assist with the transition. Right now, he's the acting director of the office, but he will be told about your appointment right after this conversation. He will also be told to assist you in any way possible."

Keys to the corner office, Suzanne thought. She felt a flush a power, something she had longed for but was now at her doorstep. She inhaled sharply to suppress the experience. She knew she was entering a club she did not expect to attain so young. It felt almost giddy, which she knew was wildly inappropriate under the circumstances. She forced herself to breathe slowly, maintain her ramrod posture, and keep her face as neutral as possible.

"Thank you, Mr. Bitworth. I will give him a call this morning."

A little more time was spent discussing how to wrap things up in the current office, along with some other advice Bitworth gave her as she transitioned to the next step up the ladder. Then, Bitworth hesitated. "And please," he said slowly, "please drive carefully." The look on his face was sad and apprehensive.

"I will, sir. I promise." Suzanne returned his sad, serious look. "And I will do my utmost to make this work, sir. I appreciate the trust you are placing in me." She stood up, shook his hand, and left the office.

She walked back to her cubicle and started gathering up her things.

Gail looked over and said with a panicked look on her face, "Suzanne, what are you doing? Did he fire you?"

*"No, he didn't."* Suzanne kept gathering up items on her desk. *"I'm replacing Ellie in Dayton."*

*"Oh. My. God."*

*"Yeah."* She gave a look that she hoped would be interpreted as appropriately somber, given the circumstances.

To Suzanne's surprise, a tear fell from Gail's face. *"I'll miss you."*

And without missing a beat or allowing a grain of truth to seep into her expression, Suzanne said, *"I'll miss you too, Gail."*

Within an hour, Suzanne had collected her belongings, talked to the contact in Dayton, and was walking out the door. One more loose end bothered her. She knew Adam had not responded to her voicemail the other day, and she was a little hesitant to try again. But she owed it to him and to herself for this not to be a surprise. For all she knew, he might be glad.

She headed for the garage and dialed his number along the way. She fully expected another voicemail announcement. That was fine. All she really felt obligated to do was inform him that she would be moving out of town.

To her unhappy surprise, he picked up.

*"Hi, Adam,"* she said. *"Honestly I did not expect you to pick up."*

*"What do you want, Suzanne?"*

It wasn't a hostile question; more like a professional one. One she could match in style.

*"I'm calling to let you know that . . . "* Should I tell him about Ellie? *"Look, there's been a serious accident. My boss was unexpectedly assigned to the Dayton office, and on her way there she had a serious car accident."* She hesitated before the final news. *"She was killed."*

She could hear a slight but unmistakable intake of breath on the phone.

*"Ellie?"* said the shocked Adam.

*"Yeah, Ellie."*

Adam did not know what to say. It flashed through his mind that this must be a terrible loss for his soon-to-be ex-wife, but Ellie was, after all, the woman with whom Suzanne had had an affair.

*"I don't know what to say, Suzanne."* He bit his lip. *"I am sorry."*

*"Thanks,"* said Suzanne.

*There was a moment of silence, as Suzanne wondered what to say next.*

*"The reason I'm calling is that I've been chosen as the person to replace her in Dayton. So, I'll be moving there. I just wanted to let you know."*

*There was a slight delay on Adam's end of the line. In a softer voice, he said, "When, Suzanne?"*

*"Today. Right now."*

*A long stream of air on the other end of the phone. "Okay," Adam said. "Thanks for letting me know."*

*Suzanne was feeling flustered about the whole conversation, and the speed of her voice picked up. "Look, Adam. If you need anything, my cell number will be the same. I'll send you my address when I get settled. Feel free to call me."*

*"Okay."*

*"Okay." She clicked off, got into her car, and drove away.*

Sometimes I hate writing, Riley thought. Relationships are complicated. Everybody has feelings all the time. It's too much like life.

It *is* life, you silly girl, came a voice from inside her.

I am not a 'silly girl' another voice replied. Just teasing you, Luv. And she instantly recognized that last phrase as the voice of her mother. Something that made her heart feel warm at first, and then hurt a little. She felt so cut off from her family. They live in the Midwest; she lives in D.C. She knows she could call them more often but ordinarily doesn't.

There was a time when she and her mother were close; or at least in Riley's narrative of her upbringing, she believed this to be true. Riley was young. Her mother used to tease her a lot, and, as a child, Riley never interpreted it as anything but an endearing jostle. As she got older, she teased her mother back, but after a while the teasing started taking on an edge, and she saw that she hurt her mother a few times. The look on her mother's face, which she could still picture, spoke of the never-mentioned hurt feelings that Riley had inflicted on her. That made her sad. And guilty.

And it was in adolescence that she began to grow away from her parents. She did not hate them; in fact, she always knew she loved them. But as she set her sights on something beyond rural Indiana, she knew her lifestyle parted ways with the decisions of her parents and of her only sibling, who still resided in the same town. All of this made her sad. She tried to think of something else.

She glanced around her apartment, but she knew there was only one thing with sufficient strength to help her escape nostalgic and largely futile feelings. She resumed writing.

*Adam held the phone in his hand for a while. He was pleased in a distant sort of way that he had answered Suzanne's call. The thought of Ellie getting killed triggered mixed feelings. Once again, he felt the revulsion of learning that he had been betrayed and the confusion about what it meant that his wife had an affair with another woman. Her boss, no less. Still, if they were close, this was probably painful for Suzanne. He wanted not to care about that, but he couldn't help himself. I do not want to turn into a monster. It's okay to recognize pain in another, even if you and the 'other' are on opposite sides for now. It wasn't always that way between us.*

*And moving to Dayton? Suzanne was such an Eastern seaboard kind of person. He could not imagine her out in the middle of the soybean fields of Ohio. But maybe Dayton was a more sophisticated place than he thought. He recalled someone who had attended a university there. Maybe it's a college town. He really had no idea.*

*He Googled it, as much to get his mind off the complicated grief scenario as to find out about a place he never gave a thought to until this moment. Let's see. At least one of the Wright brothers was born there, but they both worked there later. It has aerospace, hospitals, the National Museum of the United States Air Force . . .*

*Why am I doing this? Who cares where she moves? As the moments sauntered by, he could feel his body getting more and more relaxed. A dull but unmistakable pain in his back that had followed him around for the past few days was lessening in intensity and was nearly gone. He found his breathing easier. Within ten minutes, he found himself limbering up, stretching muscles that he had ignored for way too long. He felt a desire to go jogging, something he had not done in years.*

*So he did. He rustled around until he found his neglected jogging clothes, put them on, and left the house, heading in no particular direction.*

*His breathing kept pace. He wasn't moving fast, but he was moving, and for the first time in recent memory he began to feel . . . what? Physical? Alive again? Yes, that's it. Alive.*

*I did not realize what that whole business cost me. 'That business' being his marriage to Suzanne. I am so glad she is not here. Dayton sounds fine. She'll at least act as if she loves soybeans. And I'm sure she'll enjoy the museum visit.*

*He actually smiled when he thought these things.*

*Freedom is a wonderful thing, he kept thinking. Freedom is a wonderful thing.*

Yes, it is, Riley thought. She was growing fond of Adam.

*When Adam got home, his body was pleasantly exhausted from running, but his mind was not at all tired. If anything, he was alert and ready to move on to the next thing. This is so different from those feelings of being beaten down that I had gotten so used to. And all this from jogging for—he glanced at his watch—twenty-five minutes. He walked around the house to cool down and then went to the fridge to find some cold water. He savored every sip.*

*He knew that this experience wasn't just about jogging. It was about catching up with himself: realizing that his marriage to Suzanne had in fact been as moribund as he thought it had been. He berated himself a little for not being the one to say the truth out loud first, but he was actually grateful that Suzanne did it. She started a conversation that was just waiting to take place.*

*And now things are coming full circle. Suzanne is, as far as he knew, on her way to Dayton and a new life. She is free to do what she wished, and so is he. He could not get over how good this made him feel.*

*After resting for a while, Adam sat at his desk and began to make a list of things he needed to do. 'Find a lawyer' was first. Then other stuff: make a budget; decide to stay in the rented house or move; stay in D.C. or move (not to Dayton, he wrote); find a new job; find a new girlfriend. He put parentheses around this last item, along with a question mark. Really? No, not really. Not yet. I'm not ready.*

No, you're not, Adam.

*But sometime in the not too distant future, I will be.*

That is no doubt true, Riley thought.

## — 47 —

Riley was hungry and, after glancing at the clock, realized it was nearing lunchtime. She hoisted herself off her desk chair and went into the kitchen looking for something to eat. The thoughts about her childhood and the sad feelings she had about her family had vanished, as she knew they would, as events between Suzanne and Adam moved forward. In the back of her mind, she wondered what would happen to them.

She found some not-yet-moldy bread and some peanut butter and jelly that would have to do for lunch. As she was munching on her sandwich, she thought of Cameron. She wondered how he was, what he was doing, what his response to the divorce has been.

She hadn't spoken with him since she called to apologize a few days ago. She recalled that she had invited him to call her if he wanted to talk, but she had not heard from him. This made her feel sad, but only a little. She could feel Cameron's presence in her life flickering, blinking more and more slowly. Soon, she was sure, it would be extinguished completely. Well, perhaps not completely—she would never forget the experience of being married to Cameron—but by then that whole relationship would just be a fact of her history, not the center of it.

These thoughts felt correct and did not make her sad. She saw the separation and divorce as inevitable and even desirable. The fact was there was not a single time since she moved out that she wished she were with Cameron. There were tinges of sadness to that, but in a sort of cerebral way. It's sad that such a thing happens to two basically nice people; but it does happen, and one hopes that both are better off for the breakup.

She lay on her couch to rest before she resumed her writing. She fell asleep to dreams of running through sunny open fields.

•  •  •

Cameron, on the other hand, was not so philosophical about his situation with Riley. After he spoke to her a few days ago, he forced himself to re-focus on work. It was hard. He understood that she was calling to apologize, but a phone call seemed like small beer after having a sheriff unexpectedly inform him of her decision to divorce. The one just did not make up for the other.

But force himself he did, and by the end of that day, when he worked late at the office, he felt stable again. Thank God for work, he thought yet again.

On his way home, thoughts of Riley returned; at first he was able to easily dismiss them. He focused on driving, on traffic, on the local scenery. He focused on anything but the woman he was so mad at.

But those mundane things could not prevent the holes in the dykes of his mind from leaking. He drove and thought of how Riley and he would take long drives together; he observed traffic and thought of how Riley would complain about D.C. traffic but he would remain silent and smile; he noted the local scenery and thought of how lovely it was and how lovely Riley was. Finally, he pulled over to the curb and closed his eyes. He tried with all his might to banish her from his mind. But as the proverbial instruction 'Don't think of an elephant' nearly always makes one think of little else, all he could think of was Riley.

He sat in his empty car beholding her face, her body, even her scent, in his mind. He noticed how attractive she was, how gifted he felt when they were first intimate, how complete he felt when she consented to marry him.

All gone, he thought. All gone. And he started to cry.

The first thought that crossed his mind when the tears began was 'I don't cry,' a belief about himself that up until this moment had been true. But suddenly that notion was being invalidated. As

Cameron sat alone in his car on a nameless street in the District, he unleashed—quite without his conscious consent—a torrent of tears the likes of which he had never previously allowed. He had always prided himself on the absence of tears in his life. He did not cry for his pathetic father or even for his feckless mother, who in her later years turned out to be an actual person. Until this moment, he had not shed a tear for the loss of the woman he married. But now he was weeping for her and for all those people in his life who were gone. And he could not stop.

He cried and cried, wiping away the tears with his hands, which resulted only in a moist steering wheel and a wet shirt. He buried his head in his arms and his entire body began to shake. He wondered if he were ill, or if he were dying. At this moment, that was as much a hope as a wonder.

Rather than recede, the emotional firestorm intensified. Cameron let out a wail so raw he thought maybe he was losing his mind. A tiny remnant of his observing self was horrified that his tears were joined by choked syllables and incoherent words. He had no idea what he was saying. But it occurred even to that tiny remnant that he, Cameron, as emotionally unpracticed as he had always been, was ejecting years of suppressed feelings on a moderately busy stretch of road somewhere in Washington, D.C. He did not remember where he was, though he had driven this way before. And he did not care.

After an incomprehensible amount of time—perhaps ten minutes, perhaps an hour; he honestly had no idea—the torrent began to slow down. He began to feel depleted, defeated, dejected, and utterly helpless to do anything. He knew he could not stay where he was, so he slowly looked around and willed his hand to reach for the start button on his car, only to realize that he had never turned it off. He shook his head, put his car in gear, and slowly resumed his ride home.

He drove towards his apartment, thinking what a curious term 'home' was. What an odd way to refer to the apartment where he lived by himself. Maybe it was something like a home when Riley was there, but he was loath to think of it that way now. It was just a place he happened to be living, much like his life before Riley, when he lived alone and barely gave a thought to anything beyond the bare necessities: a bed, some food, a table, a chair.

Of course, 'home' had always been a problematic concept in Cameron's mind. The house where he grew up was home in name only: the constant feeling of being on edge, the constant fear of violence, the absolute incapacity of either him or his mother to relax—all of these things made the house seem more like a weird danger zone rather than the safe emotional place he heard about in school.

But the fact was that just now he was so emotionally spent, none of this felt real: not the thoughts he was having, not the car he was driving, and certainly not the apartment to which he was return- ing. It wasn't because the thoughts and practical realities of his life weren't real; it was because he was beyond feeling anything or making sense out of anything. He was a store with empty shelves, useless.

When he arrived at what was now his apartment, he was on automatic pilot. He pulled his car into the parking space, collected his things, and got out of the car, locking it along the way. He wordlessly got into the elevator and took it to his floor, got out, and unlocked the apartment door.

The place felt emptier than it ever had. Even in the days just after Riley left, he could still feel her in the space. He knew where she sat and worked and what she ate and drank. He knew her habits and the way her skin felt. He could smell her. He realized something he knew but never really thought much about: I love her. That produced an ironic hint of an unhappy smile on his face.

And she is gone. Gone and not coming back. Tears returned to his eyes, but in a much less intense way than before. While the actual tears fell weakly on his face, the wrenching grief reached down into his belly, which felt nauseous and tight. He tasted bitterness in his mouth. He lay down on the couch and hoped he would die.

He did not die. He did not even fall asleep. He just lay there, blankness and pain filling his head and his body in open rebellion.

His internal voice sounded muted, even to him. It was barely his, although something solid inside himself told him it was. It was the kind of thing he would think. Things like: Why is this so hard? I've been able to keep more unpleasant things than this at a distance my whole life. I always prided myself for being able to do this. I understood most people do not act this way, but I did. It was part of me. It was who I am. It *is* who I am.

Maybe not. Look what it is doing to me now. Look at what a pathetic shell of a man I am. With the same observing distance from himself, he felt contempt for the person he was.

With those somber thoughts, sleep finally caught up to him.

# — 48 —

Jennifer went to work feeling a little smug for outing Edward and more confident about her own life. She had no clear idea where her noteworthy confidence came from. For most of her life, it's been there. She always thought of herself as a confidant, capable person. That took something of a hit a couple weeks ago after the embarrassing scene at the restaurant, but that whole scenario had rapidly slipped into the mist of history when she went to New York.

She thought about Matthew. The charming man whom she thought might try to contact her after the conference. He hadn't, and that allowed Jennifer to relax. Just like a guy, she thought without bitterness. The truth was she did not think much about him after she returned to D.C. And that's the way she planned it and liked it.

Recent, more local events were more pressing.

She kept thinking that last evening brought some clarity to her relationship with Riley; at least it resolved whatever sexual tension had been there for her. She was now certain Riley was simply a friend. A good friend, but that was it.

That's enough. Why do people say things like 'just a friend?' Jennifer did not think there was any 'just' about it. Friendships like this were on the list of most important things in life. She had to chuckle at herself, however, as she recognized that this concept came to her only yesterday. But it made her a little euphoric, or, in layman's terms, happy.

As she went about her day, she thought from time to time that she should let Riley know what she did. She even had a vague but unmistakable sense of guilt about it. Guilt was never one of Jen's close companions, so it made her noticeably uncomfortable. When she finished lunch, she picked up her phone and dialed Riley's number.

It rang five and then six times. Jennifer wondered where she might be. She answered on the seventh ring.

A groggy voice answered. "Hi, Jen."

"Did I wake you up?"

"Um, I guess so. I must have dozed off after eating lunch. What's up?"

Jennifer hesitated a bit before proceeding. "I just wanted to bring you up to date on something, Riley," she began. Pause. "I, um, I, um . . . I called Edward last night after I got home."

"What?!" said a suddenly alert Riley.

"Yeah, I wanted him to know that someone knows about him and that we know what he's up to. I blocked my number so he wouldn't know who was calling. He doesn't know my name or phone number. He just knows that someone knows." Jennifer could feel the self-justifying tone in her own voice.

Silence on the other end of the line.

"Anyway, Riley. I thought I should tell you, just so we're all on the same page."

"Uh, yeah, uh, of course. I'm just surprised. Thanks."

Jennifer waited a few moments, and then said, "Okay, listen. I'll give you a call later."

"Okay."

The conversation ended. Jennifer considered that she had perhaps had made a major faux pas, but she was uncertain as to where to lay the blame and the guilt. She was unsure if the problem was what she did or Riley's response. She did just wake her up apparently, so maybe it was all. . . she didn't know what.

She went back to work.

By mid-afternoon, she realized this business with Riley was still bothering her. Should she call her back? She did not think so; truthfully, she did not know what she could say beyond what she had already said.

But on her way home, she changed her mind. As soon as she entered her apartment, she dialed Riley's number.

"Hi, Hon," she said agreeably.

"Hi, Jen," came an equally agreeable reply.

Jennifer decided to get straight to the point. "Okay, Riley. I was a little concerned after talking with you earlier today. You sounded . . . I don't know . . . you sounded unhappy when I told you about contacting Edward." She waited and found herself breathing shallowly.

To her surprise, Riley chuckled. "I think you caught me off guard, Jen. I dozed off after lunch, and your call woke me up. I did not know how to react to your calling Edward. How did you get his number, anyway?"

"The same way I found out his last name, his place of employment, and his address," replied Jennifer. "Online."

"That was all an impressive performance."

Jennifer allowed herself to take the compliment.

Then Riley said, "What did Edward say?"

"Nothing. I checked out if he was the same Edward I'd tagged earlier, and then I told him we knew what he was up to. Then, I ended the conversation. I'm sure it took him some time to absorb what happened. I'm sure he wasn't expecting it."

"I bet not."

"So . . . you're not mad at me?"

Riley hesitated. "No, not a bit. It does seem kind of . . . I don't know . . . cloak and dagger." She paused a moment. "Why would I be mad at you?"

"No good reason," replied Jen, feeling the relief she was seeking. "Just checking."

They went on to talk about other things. After a while, Jen told her about Matthew. She described how they met, how charming she found him, and how unusual it was to have such positive feelings about a man.

"But, you know, I nearly convinced myself it was worth a try. I mean, I realized I hadn't dated a male since high school, and I thought well, why not? Maybe I would give them another chance."

She laughed. "But then I came to my senses. And really, once I got back to D.C. I didn't give him much thought."

Riley laughed.

"Let's get together soon," Jen said.

"Absolutely."

## — 49 —

*It did not take Adam long to start on his list. He searched online for lawyers in the D.C. area, which apparently has more lawyers per acre than anywhere on earth. He found that more than a little bewildering. Finally, he called some people he knew, a couple of whom had been through divorces, and asked for referrals.*

*As he went through this process, he could not stop thinking about Ellie's death, Suzanne's transfer, and all things related to his marriage to a woman now inexorably separated from his life.*

*He continued to feel the flush of freedom, but he also felt the tentativeness of a life alone. Or was it fear? He was thinking how little he and Suzanne actually depended upon each other: they kept separate bank accounts, had different jobs in different industries, and had their own circle of acquaintances. Like many busy young people, Adam had focused more on his job than his marriage or his social life, such as they were, and now he was seeing how shortsighted he had been.*

*He made a list of acquaintances and former friends that he might contact. It was from this list that he identified a few people to inquire about attorneys. He started making calls, and, to his great relief, no one seemed surprised or unhappy to hear from him. I guess we are all too busy to keep up, he thought.*

*This whole process felt as if he were using muscles that had long lay dormant. Rather like his jog the other day: the muscles were a little stiff, even creaky, but once engaged they worked okay. He was self-conscious when he made the first call, but less so the second. After a while, it felt almost normal. So far, so good, he concluded.*

*Other items on his list were things that could wait. His lease would last at least three more months, so he had that time to decide to move or not. He thought about moving away from the District, but he liked D.C., and he knew it would probably be easier to meet people here than in other places he might relocate.*

*He was originally from Minnesota, and he knew he did not want to return there. He got to D.C. after doing an internship while still in college. He was drawn to the whole ethos of the place when he was young: it was fast-paced but friendly; there were lots of people his age; it was surprisingly easy to find a job, which he did right after college.*

*He met Suzanne here. She was a native Washingtonian, which was one of the reasons he had a hard time picturing her in Ohio. They started dating the first few months he moved here, and it seemed natural to Adam that they would get married. He wondered if Suzanne felt the same way. He knew he had been incubated in the Upper Midwest, and the values he had from his upbringing, though nearly invisible to him, may have been different from those people, such as Suzanne, who grew up in a more cosmopolitan environment. He remembered the first time he brought up marriage. The look on Suzanne's face wasn't exactly shock, but something like acute curiosity, as if the prospect of marrying someone after more than a year of dating seemed new and quaint.*

*"Really?" was her first response.*

*"Well, yeah. Isn't that what people do?"*

*"Some people . . ."*

*"People like us?" said Adam hopefully.*

*Suzanne chuckled, as if she were enjoying a new toy that someone had given her.*

*"I guess so," she said. "People like us," she repeated in a way that suggested she found the expression quaint.*

*Adam recalled how happy and relieved he felt, and how being with Suzanne in those early days was such an adventure. They did everything together. They both went searching for a place to live and ended up renting the house Adam was still in. They even went grocery shopping together and prepared dinner most of the time. They talked all the time they weren't working: in the kitchen, in the living room, in the bedroom. Communication seemed effortless and constant.*

*Adam tried to think of when all that togetherness came to an end. It obviously did, given the state of his soon-to-be-extinct marriage. He had a vague notion that things had changed after about a year together. It wasn't a sudden thing; no one called for an end to togetherness. It was something that gradually slipped away. He thought of it as a misty time when one style of life imperceptibly morphed into another, one that did not exactly feel consciously chosen by either person but at the same time did not feel unnatural. Not until the end. Not until it died.*

*Now looking back on the courtship—that's what they called it in Minnesota—Adam saw a young and foolish twenty-something who sharply underestimated what lay ahead of him in working out a marriage. This in itself did not trouble him so much; he would learn from this, he was sure. But it did remind him of how it was ending up, the pain that was still recent, the wound that was still unhealed. That made him shake his head. He would do anything to keep that pain at bay.*

*He put these thoughts out of his mind and focused on the present. So many young people, and I tie myself down to one person so soon. It all seems naïve in retrospect.*

*And he allowed that Suzanne might be feeling the same way. They were about the same age, so perhaps she also found marriage confining. He didn't really know; the couple never talked about things like that. Adam wondered idly what they did talk about. Not much lately, he concluded. Not much that was true anyway.*

*He glanced down at his list and saw his tentative goal of finding another girlfriend. He shook his head. That is going to take some time, he thought.*

*All of a sudden, he realized that he had not spoken to his parents about what was happening. It all seemed like a whirlwind, and he did not think of contacting them until this moment. He was a little uncertain. Is this something you talk with your parents about? What if they didn't approve?*

*You're overthinking this, Adam, came a voice inside his head.*

*I sure am, he thought. It was perfectly natural for an adult son to tell his parents that his marriage was ending, and it was of no concern to him if they did not approve. He decided to call them in the morning.*

## 50

Not too far from Riley's apartment, Edward was still smarting from the mysterious phone call he received from a woman he did not know. He knew his determination was not reduced by it—he promised himself it would not be. But practically he was at a loss.

In the midst of his uncertainty, Edward realized this was all about how Riley hurt him and how he vowed not to be hurt again or to be derailed from his desire to inflict harm on the woman he loved. Still, he had trouble thinking of many options. What can I do? I could assault her (leading to my possible arrest); I could kill her (ditto); I could burn her building down (ditto); I could pour acid on her—all of these had the definite downside of possible jail time. Most of them risked what would no doubt be serious jail time. Or worse. Plus, all those options made him sick to think about.

Edward had never knowingly committed a crime. In fact, he regarded himself pretty much as a model citizen. I teach social studies, for Christ's sake!

He was hesitant to Google 'taking vengeance on your girlfriend' because he had heard that stuff on the Internet stays forever and someone might find it if he did something wrong and got caught. Of course, he could find a public computer and check it that way. Having no other ideas at the moment, he thought that was a good one.

He went to the public library, where he knew there were computers for public use, and found an empty one with no trouble. He sat down and started to log in. It asked for the number of his library card. Shit, he thought. Same problem. He got up, acted as if he had forgotten something, and fled the library.

He was walking down the street when he had an idea that he thought maybe lots of people had but not many people acted upon. He did not want to have it: it made his face contort to think about it, and it put a sour taste in his mouth. But it was not out of the realm of possibility.

The obviousness of it would not leave him. For the first time, he understood why people might take their own lives: it is a form of revenge. Especially if he did it somehow in front of Riley. That would hurt her. She would probably feel guilty for the rest of her life.

But that would be the end of mine, came a sensible internal reply.

That's a consideration, he decided.

But other ideas started floating through his mind, as well. While he had some distant relatives whom he almost never saw—and hadn't seen as an adult ever—he was the last of his line. His parents were deceased: he shuddered at how hard their loss was for him. There were no really significant relationships in his life now save the one he just lost with Riley. He was just a teacher and could be replaced easily. There were lots of teachers. And the school administration knew how to fill vacancies quickly.

The more he thought the more he could not think of many good reasons not to do it. This saddened him because he did not want to die.

Maybe I am being melodramatic, he thought. Killing myself in order to hurt someone? That's reasonable?

No, came an internal voice. It is not reasonable at all.

But other voices persisted. Have you not been listening to yourself? You just did an objective appraisal of your situation, and it doesn't look good. Why stick around here? What's in it for you?

Edward shuddered again as he approached his apartment building.

## 51

*Suzanne made it to Dayton without incident. She actually felt relieved as she parked her car at the extended stay hotel that would be her home until she found an appropriate apartment. That shouldn't be too hard, she thought.*

*She checked in, dropped her luggage off in her room, and went to find something to eat. Not only was she hungry, but she wanted to focus on something besides the messy traffic she had endured for the eight hours it took to get here. In between cursing at other drivers who struck her as unusually inconsiderate or just plain stupid, all she could really think about was Ellie and her death. Once in a while, her mind would flash on Adam, but she really did not know what to think about him.*

*Adam was a nice enough guy. Well, he was nice, but he left a lot to be desired in the 'enough' category. He was obviously well meaning, and he had talent; but he seemed too willing to allow situations to take their own course rather than taking charge. This was a charming thing early in their relationship, but as the years went it spelled tedium to Suzanne.*

*She could not put her finger on the precise time the relationship, the marriage, went south. It was sometime after the first year or two: she had some good memories of those early years. But something changed after that. Something important. And the good times and warm feelings they had together before simply went away.*

*Suzanne marveled that she actually married Adam. It must have been his warm-hearted Midwestern style that more or less dictated* that he at least propose to her. And, truth be told, she found that charming. A little foreign, but charming.

But now there has been too much water under that bridge for Suzanne to feel sad or nostalgic about all that. It was really Ellie who opened her eyes to what was possible in a relationship. Before Ellie, she had had some sexual experiences with other women and with men, but, whether it was true or not, she saw those people as desperate—almost as desperate as she—and she could never see herself building any kind of life together with any of them. Mostly, they were road-warrior relationships. One-night stands.

But with Ellie it was different. They worked together; they got to know each other over a fair amount of time. They often, in those early months, found themselves finishing sentences for each other. That was the first time she noticed how special Ellie was to her. And she learned soon enough that Ellie felt the same way.

This is delicate territory, Suzanne, she said to herself in a stern, motherly tone. She could feel the sadness she felt about Ellie's death rise from inside her guts up to her tear ducts. She shook her head to forestall breaking down and crying. She took a deep breath.

When she looked around her, she found herself standing right in front of a chain restaurant that she had not noticed before. Wow, I must have gotten close to the edge, she thought. This place was not too far from her hotel, she realized, so she went in and sat down. There were free tables, but she could see people parking their cars in the large lot. She timed it just right.

She sat and stared for a while at the overly colorful menu trying to focus on something to eat. The upsurge of emotion that she just experienced had dulled her appetite, but she knew she should eat. Tomorrow she goes to the Dayton office for the first time, where she will take up the director position. She needs to take care of herself.

Suzanne choked down the lingering sadness and forced herself to focus on the task at hand, as if ordering dinner at a chain was a complicated business deal. It felt that way to her.

The server came up with a glass of water. "Just one this evening?" the young, overly eager young woman said.

Suzanne nodded. "Just one." Her eyes glazed over unexpectedly. "Allergies," she said to the server who no doubt did not care.

The young server stood there for a moment, unsure if Suzanne was going to say anything else. Suzanne looked up at her and, tightening every muscle in her upper body, said, "Give me a few minutes."

The server accommodated and walked away. "I'll check back in a bit," she said cheerfully.

I hate cheerful people, Suzanne thought.

She glanced through the many choices on the menu and opted for something simple but sustaining. A small filet sounded good. So did a glass of red wine.

As if reading her mind, the server returned immediately. "All set?"

Suzanne ordered without looking at the server; she stared at the menu as if it were written in hieroglyphs she alone could decipher.

The server left without another word.

Jesus Christ? Why are these simple things so difficult?

She knew why. She shook her head and thought that being in public just now was a poor choice. I'll just sit here and hold my breath, she thought.

She realized she couldn't do that. "Miss," she said as she spotted her attentive server. "I'd like my order to go, please. And I'll pass on the wine."

"Sure," replied Ms. Cheerful.

"Thank you."

It took rather longer than Suzanne thought—she was tempted to just get up and leave—but just when she was about to do that, Ms. Cheerful returned with her order, all wrapped in a brown paper bag. She pulled out her credit card and handed it to her before the check hit the table. Fortunately, the server had a portable machine that could handle the transaction quickly. Suzanne tipped her the normal twenty percent, gathered up dinner, and walked quickly out of the restaurant.

She did not make it much beyond the door before grief fell on her like a death blow. Her whole body was in rebellion. Tears bubbled up and ran down her face, her gut roiled, and she became nauseous. She realized she was going to vomit about a second and a half before she *actually did. If she had felt anything close to normal, she would have been mortified. As it was, she just did not give a damn what anyone else thought at this moment.*

*She pulled herself together enough to continue walking to her hotel, which fortunately was only about half a block away. She walked past the clerk behind the front desk without saying a word or even looking at him. She was able to make it to the elevator without throwing up again. She thought maybe she smelled bad from vomiting the first time, but she really did not know. All she wanted to do was be alone. And she was as soon as the elevator door closed.*

Riley pushed back from her desk. Jesus. Poor Suzanne. Then, she thought back to what a duplicitous character she was and decided not to feel too sorry for her. 'About time' replaced whatever sympathy had crossed her mind.

Riley got up and looked at the clock. Not time for a break yet. She sat back down.

*When she got to her room, Suzanne threw her dinner on the desk and herself onto the bed. She cried a little, took deep breaths, and wondered idly what that funny sensation inside her was.*

*And then it hit her. She was angry. Pissed. Outraged even, that Ellie had up and left her. How could she do this to me? Why would she do this to me? Then, a cavalcade of feelings surfaced all at once: rage at being left; shame for her behavior; guilt for being rewarded because of a tragedy; and fear that the strength of these feelings would not leave her and would ruin the rest of her life.*

*She threw up again, but this time she made it to the toilet, where she deposited what was left of the contents of her stomach as well, she hoped, as the feelings that had taken over her entire body.*

*She sat on the bathroom floor loathing herself. Some way to start a new job, she thought grimly.*

*She did not know how long she sat there. She noticed that it was getting dark outside because she had not turned the lights on in the room when she entered. She noted this dispassionately, the same way she was surveying her emotional life. She did not want to do anything but watch the spectacle of her life playing out in her mind's eye. It wasn't exactly captivating, but it was all she was capable of at the moment. The entire process was oddly non-judgmental: she wasn't saying anything was good or bad, preferable or not. She was just observing, as someone would do in a lab to an imprisoned rat.*

*Why are lab rats always white? She wondered idly. That thought had the same heft as all of her thoughts at the moment. That is to say, some weird combination of ponderous and inconsequential.*

You've got some deep digging to do, girl, Riley thought as she glanced at the clock again. Now it was close enough to the time she could stop. She looked at her screen for a moment, sighed, and shut down her work for the day. She was exhausted.

As Riley went to her kitchen to figure out something to eat, she began thinking about the situation with Edward. Maybe she's been overreacting to the whole thing. Maybe he was just a lovesick puppy who wandered by her apartment because of some immature but compelling impulse to be near to her again. The kinds of things teenage boys often do; even some men have been known to do stuff like that. Even I've been known to do similarly childish things, she thought sheepishly. She reddened slightly at some memories that she did not wish to entertain.

She forced herself to focus her attention on the situation with Edward. It occurred to her that the brief conversation she had with him at the coffee shop might have taken him completely by surprise. Maybe he expected something else. The two hadn't had that much contact, so when she invited him to her table, he probably did not know what to expect, but if he did, he probably thought it would be something positive. That would not be a surprise, as she gave no indication that she was going to drop an emotional bomb on him. No matter what he expected; what he got was something he couldn't handle, so he fled. How many times have I wanted to run away from difficult situations? Isn't that what I did when I left Cameron?

No, it wasn't, came a sensible voice inside her head. You opened your mouth and at least attempted to have a conversation. You made plans and kept him posted. You kept in touch with him. You did not run away. You simply left.

Sometimes—often, really, especially lately—Riley has found herself thinking things that did not seem quite like her. She was familiar with her anxious, obsessive, sometimes panicky self, but the reasonable, considered part that made periodic appearances seemed slightly alien. Not completely: it still felt like her, but an advanced form of the personality she usually identified with. Is this the new normal?

Maybe those therapy sessions helped me more than I thought. Or maybe I'm just growing up. Odd thing to think at my age.

Her mind turned back to Edward. I wasn't really expecting him to show up, so whatever I said, and however I said it, is kind of a mystery. I was flying by the seat of my pants, and I was as unprepared as he was for a serious conversation. Maybe I came across more harshly than I intended. I did not set out to hurt his feelings; I just wanted him to know where I stood with him. And where he stood with me. The notion that maybe she was too forceful, too accusing, or too something would not leave her head. She scared him. He seemed frightened. And then he scared me. Intentionally or not.

This was a novel way of thinking about this sordid little situation. It was, after all, just a roll in the hay one highly-charged afternoon. Surely Edward has other people he can couple with from time to time? None of my business, really.

It's been a couple days. Maybe he's had a chance to settle down a bit. Perhaps it's time to at least try to have a more levelheaded conversation with him; it might be appropriate or even helpful. She had his number, his home address, and the place where he worked. She was hesitant to meet up with him: after all, if he was truly stalking her, he might not have the best of intentions. But even if he weren't, she did not want to expose herself to whatever strong feelings he was having in person, and it was obvious to her that he was having strong feelings. She shivered a bit when she thought this. The thought that somewhat might want to hurt her, even if it was unlikely, scared her. In fact, she could not recall being this frightened.

That thought caught her off guard. She felt her pulse rise. She started taking slow deep breaths. Frightened? Yes, I guess I am. I have never been the target of anyone's wrath before. Her parents were not shouters; when they corrected her or even punished her—although she could not recall a specific instance when they did that—they did so in an even voice, patiently explaining why such-and-such a behavior was inappropriate and helped her understand what she could do differently.

Even when she had the panic attack the other night, she did not label that as fear-driven. She thought her body was just rebelling from confronting such a wildly irrational situation, one in which she bore more than a little responsibility. To her mind, it was a matter of a lot of feelings colliding inside her. Now she recognized that fear was a big driver of those reactions. Her responsibility for creating this mess and her ignorance of her own reactions made her blush with shame. I'm supposed to be an adult.

Then act like one, came a not-unfamiliar voice.

Mom again. Okay, what would a mature person do? Face her fear, that's what. And what specifically was she afraid of? I am afraid of being hurt somehow by Edward. All this seemed clear and obvious but might not be true. So, the choice she faced was this: do I wait around for him to do or not do something to me and confirm my worst fears or do I take the situation in hand and ask him what exactly he is up to?

The more she thought about this, the more appealing the latter option appeared. Even Jennifer had not unearthed anything violent in Edward's past. He has been a teacher for many years; he was apparently respected by his colleagues; he had no criminal record. There must be a difference between how I have been casting him and how he actually is.

Riley realized she could be mistaken about this. Maybe I should call somebody before I do anything precipitous, she thought. She considered talking to her attorney about it, but that cost money, and she could always do that if she needed to at some point in the future. But for now . . .

She dialed Jennifer's number.

Voicemail. Ugh. "Hi, Jen. It's me. Call me. There is something I'd like to run by you."

She hung up and wasn't sure if she wanted Jennifer to call back or not. On the one hand, she did because she thought it was a really good idea to get somebody else's reaction. On the other hand, it felt a little like being a kid asking for direction from a parent. Not what an adult would do.

Nonsense, came a potent voice inside her. Adults all need and want feedback.

Yes, they do, she concluded; she went to get a bite to eat while she waited for Jennifer to call her back.

It did not take long. After the preliminary pleasantries, Riley explained to Jennifer what she was thinking of doing and invited her to tell her what she thought.

Jennifer listened patiently and did not respond right away. "Let me think about this a minute, Riley," she said. After a few minutes, she said, "I think there is something to this plan. It's safe to talk over the phone, and you can block your number." Another thoughtful pause. "But, you know, I would ask someone with experience in these matters. Maybe either your lawyer or someone who deals with these things, such as somebody who works at a woman's shelter."

That last suggestion struck Riley as an excellent idea. She was amazed she had not thought of it herself. "That's a good idea Jen. I'll do that. And I'll keep you posted."

When they hung up, Riley picked up her laptop and started searching for women's shelters in the D.C. area. She was surprised how many there were. She counted ten on a resource page. She imagined there were others. She went through the list and checked off those sponsored by religious groups. She thought she might feel more comfortable with secular agencies. She was going to narrow her list down further by their proximity to her apartment because she might want to meet with somebody in person. But she soon noticed that addresses were not listed on any of the websites. That's probably a wise idea, she realized. She ended up with three places she could call for starters.

She glanced at the clock on her screen. It was almost 5:00 p.m., so she thought it best to wait until morning. But her comfort level was increasing about managing her situation in a more straight-forward way.

She spent the evening watching TV, reading, and just relaxing. She listened to some music. Then she thought about Cameron. Maybe I should tell him about this? She could not decide. She had had enough decision-making for one day. She put that issue off until another day.

## 53

Cameron had a rough few days. For the first time in his life, he did not commit early in the morning to maintain his happy-go-lucky demeanor. He thought the timing on this was not great, as he had just started a new job, but it did not seem to him that anyone at the office where he now worked cared about his mood. All they really cared about was getting the job done. That's how it should be, he concluded.

At first, the inscrutable look on his face did not feel exactly right. It did not feel phony or inauthentic as his happy face sometimes did, but nor did it feel entirely natural. If it were natural, he thought, it might not be so blank; it would be furrowed, grim, and just tortured.

Because that was how he felt. His emotional firestorm of the day before had brought to life a simple but nearly unbearable fact: that his marriage—and probably his relationship—with Riley was over. That felt like a piece of hot volcanic rock inside his gut, and it made it nearly impossible to even pretend to be happy. The most he could manage was to keep his face blank. A neutral look, if he wanted to put a good spin on it.

He looked at himself in the mirror and decided that neutral would have to do. He got dressed, had a cup of coffee, and set out for work at his new job. He took a different route from the one he had taken the day before. He did not want to risk getting any more upset than he already was.

When he walked into his new office, which was really a set of cubicle workspaces in a large room, the first person he saw was

Evie, the woman whose feelings he hurt on his first day on the job. Ever since that episode, she kept a studied distance from him, watching him closely whenever he was near her. He had tried after that initial episode to be engaging with her, smiling and nodding and trying to have a conversation with her, but he never got much of a response. This morning he nodded to her as he passed and said simply, "Good Morning." No smile, no nod, no engagement.

Evie turned her head sideways, as if something were new or different or unusual. "Good Morning," she replied. They went their separate ways.

He passed a few other coworkers and greeted them in the same low-key way. Each nodded back in greeting, and all seemed to register something different about the new hire.

This did not impact Cameron much, who simply went to his workstation and arranged his things and got ready for a day of work. He was grateful to be here, somewhere safe where it was unlikely that he would feel much of anything once he got his mind around the tasks for that day.

He noticed from time to time that people would pass by his station and, if he saw them, would just nod and move on. When lunchtime came, he closed his computer and went down to the canteen to get a bite to eat. Evie was seated at a table with some of her coworkers talking. They fell silent, however, when they spotted him.

Cameron's eyes scanned the room. It seemed that everyone had stopped talking. He walked to a machine, bought something, paid, and quickly left the room. He did not smile at anyone. He ate lunch alone at his desk.

Cameron could not decide if he was imagining things or if people were treating him differently. He had never been one to worry about office gossip or that sort of thing, and even now it was hard to focus on it. For him, the work itself always remained the focus of his day. He liked being productive.

At the end of the day, Cameron collected his things and got ready to go home. He was not looking forward to it.

Jennifer hung up from her conversation with Riley and was impressed. Riley had become pretty unglued the night before, and she realized just now how concerned she was about her friend's mental health. Just how much wasn't clear until her conversation with Riley this afternoon, when she seemed not only rational but positive. The contrast stood out: no neediness; no tears; no wild thought storms. This all seemed good to her, and she was enormously relieved.

I think I can trust her more than I think. Jen had not realized how worried she was. She shivered thinking about it.

She went about her business feeling a little less responsible for Riley. She was concerned about her friend, but not excessively so. And Riley seemed to take the suggestion to talk to a professional seriously. Jennifer was especially glad about that: for one thing, it took her off the hook.

She found a book she had started a couple months ago and abandoned, not because she did not enjoy it but because other things—life, so she thought—intervened. She plopped down on her couch and began to read, wrapping herself in a throw she kept there for precisely that purpose. She was feeling like the normal version of herself she liked.

She read until she realized she was falling asleep on her couch. Feeling warm and fuzzy, she removed herself to her bed and fell into an even deeper sleep.

Riley started calling women's shelters the next morning, postponing her writing out of deference to how important this task felt. The first woman was not in and wasn't expected until later in the week. The second was with a client. But the third answered the phone. Her name was Mildred, who introduced herself as a psychologist who had worked at such shelters for over ten years. She was the program director.

Riley launched into the history of events and her concerns in a voice that was almost incomprehensibly rapid. Until Mildred interrupted her. "Slow down, Honey," she said. "Let's take this slowly. I'm not as young as I used to be."

Neither am I, Riley thought. "Sorry," she said to Mildred. "I'm just so happy to be talking to someone about this." She felt her anxiety level drop.

"I understand. Let's take it from the very beginning."

Like a sinner who finally resolved to come clean, Riley took a deep breath, slowed down, and told Mildred the whole unexpurgated version of her contacts with Edward. She included the parts about her friend Jennifer trolling him online and coming up with important details.

Mildred had some questions: Is where you live safe? Have you spoken to the police? Has Edward ever been violent in your experience or to your knowledge? These questions seemed serious to Riley, who felt genuine relief when she answered each of them: yes, no, and no.

There was silence on the phone for a while, and then Mildred said, "From what you are describing, Riley, it does not appear that there is a high likelihood of violence. However, there are a couple of things I would like you to consider moving forward." She paused for a moment. "First, I'd like you to come here and visit our facility so you know where it is in case you need it." She did not hesitate to add quickly, "We all hope that will not be necessary, but there is someone here 24/7, and we have security. Second, if you make contact with him—and I think that's a reasonable path for you, do so on the phone with a blocked number in a place where you are comfortable. It might be a good idea to have a close friend with you. Take notes when you talk to him and record the date and time. Documentation in these situations is very, very important."

Riley had begun taking notes on what Mildred was saying and was nodding to herself alone in her apartment. This was all making good sense.

Mildred continued. "When and if you talk to Edward, listen closely. Remember what he says. Also listen for his tone of voice: if it seems stressed or angry or sad or whatever. Since you'll be on the phone, you won't be able to observe him, but listening closely on the phone can be very instructive."

"Also, if he does not respond or stops talking, ask him gently what he's thinking or feeling. Apologize only if you feel a genuine need. Be the grownup in the conversation."

Riley liked that last idea. It confirmed her agenda with Edward, with Cameron, and with herself. She wanted to be a grownup; she was tired of being a child.

When Mildred was finished, Riley said with utmost sincerity, "Mildred, thank you so much. This has been very, very helpful, and my plan right now is to follow through. Is this afternoon a good time for a visit?"

"What time, Riley?"

"Say 2:30 or so?"

"Perfect. Tell the front desk to fetch me when you come." She gave her the address of the facility.

Riley was happy to have taken this step and was looking forward to meeting Mildred. She liked her voice on the phone and her no-nonsense attitude.

But it wasn't exactly elation that she felt. She felt sober, self-possessed, and cautiously optimistic. She had not realized how fearful she had allowed herself to become over all of this and how much of a toll it was taking on her mood and even her body. She shook herself, as if preparing for a new beginning.

She glanced at the clock. Still time to do some writing, she decided.

*Despite a night of off-and-on sleep, Suzanne awoke the next morning with sufficient time to get ready for her first appearance at the Dayton office. Fortunately, she had visited it once, so getting there was not going to be a problem. She wasn't sure if she had met the assistant director or not. She couldn't place him.*

*What she wasn't so sure of was whether or not she could spend a whole day of work while recovering from her meltdown the day before. While the storm had passed, she felt Ellie's absence acutely in her body, the very cells of which felt heavy and mournful. She wasn't sure how she was going to manage once she got to her new job site.*

*She drove slowly to downtown Dayton, where the office was located. She parked in the open lot to the side of the building, gathered up her things, and looked at the office building where she was scheduled to enter the higher levels of employment in her company. That thought did not relieve the distress she felt inside. Today, it was just another job.*

*Slowly, she got out of her car and walked toward the building. The company's offices were on the third and fourth floors of the building, and there was a receptionist in the lobby on the ground floor. She checked in with her, gave her name, and told her where she was going.*

*"Of course, Ms. Wilkerson," the receptionist said. "I will let Mr. Collins know you are here. He would like to escort you to your new office."*

*Suzanne did not know what to make of that. I guess a new boss is some kind of 'event,' but she did not know what kind. She decided to play it by ear. She tried smiling in preparation for Mr. Collins, but it felt both artificial and out of place, so she decided to wait to see if she could ramp up a smile when he actually showed up.*

*She did, a little. Mr. Collins—call me Dave, he said immediately—was all smiles and warmth. Sickeningly so, Suzanne thought. While still shaking her hand, he pivoted sideways and put his other arm on her back to guide her to the elevator. That might have been an innocent gesture, she thought, but it felt intrusive. She pulled back a bit and took several steps toward the elevator. Dave, who did not seem to notice her reaction, pushed the button.*

*"The staff is really looking forward to you coming," he said, pointedly not calling her by name. Then, he paused as they stepped into the elevator car. "We were as shocked as anyone to hear about Elizabeth." Nothing about his tone of voice sounded sincere. Suzanne just nodded knowingly. Or what she hoped was knowingly.*

*When the elevator door opened on the third floor, she immediately noticed that everyone in the office, a couple dozen people, turned to get their first glimpse of their new boss. Suzanne straightened her back, stretched as imperceptibly as possible, and stepped into the room. Again she attempted a smile. She suddenly realized it would be a good idea to say something to all those people watching her.*

*Before speaking, she dropped her smile and gestured for everyone to gather around her. There was an open space in the large room. She turned to Dave. "Could you ask the people from upstairs to come down, please?"*

*Dave did not question the request, which he knew to be a command. "Sure," he said. And he picked up his cell phone and pushed a speed dial button.*

*Within minutes, there were about forty people squeezed into a space that was designed for maybe half that number. Intimate, thought Suzanne. She looked around before speaking. She had given up smiling altogether. It was not, she determined, an entirely happy event.*

*She looked around at the faces of the people watching her. She knew this was the right thing to do. She introduced herself, giving her name and a little bit of her history. Then: "As you all know, I am here* because of a tragic circumstance." She looked around. "As you may or may not know, Ellie and I worked together a great deal, and I came to respect her as a professional, a woman, and a friend." Another pause. "She would have been a great leader."

While Suzanne was talking, she thought her voice barely sounded like her. She wondered why it was so even. She must have cried every emotion out of her body the evening before.

"Her loss leaves a big hole in the organization. It is my intention, my determined intention, to make up for any deficits I bring to this job and to be worthy of her." She realized it would probably have been preferable to say 'it,' meaning the job, but what she said was more candid. "To that end, I will be relying on each of you to bring me up to date or give me information necessary to make decisions. I will actively solicit your input. I want your honest feedback. My desire is to live up to the leader that Ellie would have been, had she been given the chance."

Suzanne looked around. Everyone seemed to be listening intently. No one signaled any opposition at all. She felt a quiver in her body and wasn't sure how much more she could do just now. "Thank you," she said. "I look forward to working with you. Please go back to what you were doing."

She nodded to Dave, who nodded back and led her to her new office.

# — 57 —

'Dave is a snake' was the thought Riley had as she checked the time and shut down her computer. She wanted to get something to eat before she went to meet Mildred, but she was so excited about the visit she was not sure she could. She went to the kitchen to look around. I should spend a little more energy planning meals, she thought as she surveyed the empty shelves of her refrigerator and her food pantry. There wasn't much there.

She grabbed her purse and her phone and decided to get a quick bite at a local diner. She also wanted to spend some time just thinking about how Mildred could help her, her own reactions, and her goals for talking to Edward. It occurred to her that Edward might just refuse to talk to her. Cross that bridge when we come to it, she thought.

The part about goals was easy: she wanted him to stop following her around. Is it 'following her around', or is it stalking? Truthfully, Riley wasn't certain; maybe there was no difference, although the latter suggested malevolence. She just wanted all of it to stop, malevolent or not.

She sat at a table for one in the diner and ordered a salad. She wanted to eat something, but she did not want to consume anything heavy. When it came, she ate it slowly, almost thoughtfully, as if it were her last meal.

There was a unmistakable sadness in all this. She recalled again that Cameron was not up to date about this situation, and she wondered if it would be appropriate to tell him about it. She had no idea what his reaction might be, but a nagging voice suggested that maybe she was hiding something. What? Oh, I know what. Sex is involved. Sex with someone other than Cameron. Not only is it involved, but Riley had the distinct feeling that it was at the heart of her current difficulties with Edward. Unwise move to tell Cameron about it, she thought yet another time. And for another time, she concluded that this was part of her life and was none of his business.

She decided to walk to the shelter. It was more than a mile; but the weather was fine, and she had time. She was in no hurry. She paid her bill and left the restaurant, headed in the direction of the address Mildred had given her.

She found the non-descript, mid-twentieth-century building easily enough, but there was no signage or anything indicating what it was. Simply an address. Makes sense, she thought. She walked up to the door and pushed a button she presumed was a doorbell.

"Yes?"

"Um, I'm Riley Cotswald. I'm here to see Mildred." She realized that she did not know Mildred's last name.

"One moment please."

The door clicked, and Riley pushed it open. It led into a long narrow foyer with a desk in the middle, making it even narrower. The narrowest part had a gate. There was a young woman sitting behind the desk.

"Sign in, please," said the pleasant young woman.

Riley duly signed her name and noted the time.

"I'll let Mildred know you're here."

Riley nodded. She looked around trying to gauge what kind of place this was. It smelled vaguely of babies, but that smell coupled with a lot of disinfectant. It did not smell entirely pleasant. She thought she heard the sound of a baby crying, but it was distant, and she wasn't sure.

Her thoughts were interrupted by the arrival of a young-looking forty-something woman, who extended her hand and said simply, "Hi, Riley, I'm Mildred."

The warmth of the welcome and the handshake and the tone of Mildred's voice put Riley at ease immediately. This woman certainly looks the part, she thought.

Mildred motioned for Riley to follow, and the pair walked to the end of the foyer, through a door, and down another hallway. They stopped at what appeared to be the back of the building. Mildred opened the door to her office and motioned again for Riley to follow. She did without hesitation.

She entered a room that was filled with light from large windows on two sides, which gave out to a small, courtyard-like area surrounded by a tall masonry wall. Charming.

Mildred noticed her appraising the scenery. "They don't pay much, but there are perks," she said simply. It wasn't a resentful statement, merely an observation. Warm, just like her initial welcome.

"It's lovely."

"Please have a seat, Riley." She directed her to a couch across the room from her desk; it faced the windows with the admirable view. Mildred took a seat on a chair at the end of the couch.

"So," began Mildred. "You brought me up to date on most of the particulars when we spoke this morning. Is there anything new that's developed? Or is there something that you realized later you may have omitted?"

Riley shook her head. "I don't think so, Mildred." Then, she added, almost as an afterthought. "By the way, I don't know your last name."

"Johansen," Mildred replied. "Scandinavian origin."

Riley nodded. Mildred continued. "I wanted you to visit because I think if this situation does escalate somehow, it would be helpful for you to have a safe place to go. This is what we offer women who are abused or being stalked: a safe place."

Riley took Mildred's work for this, although she did not see any intrusive security with the possible exception of the locked front door and the gate in the foyer.

"I appreciate your seeing me, Mildred. Truthfully, I've only shared this story with my lawyer, who offered some good perspective with regard to the law and restraining orders but could not offer any personal help. And I shared it with Jennifer, who is a good friend. She was the person who went online to find out basic information about Edward, the information I shared with you earlier."

"Has Edward made any attempt to contact you by phone, email, or letter?"

"No, he hasn't," Riley said, shaking her head. "But I am not sure he has contact information about me."

Mildred looked at Riley askance. "Um, Riley. It did not take long for Jennifer to find out Edward's contact information. I think we can safely assume that Edward has that information about you. After all, you are a published author, which pretty much makes you a public person."

Riley wondered how Mildred knew that. Then, she blushed slightly and nodded in tacit agreement. "You looked me up," she said.

"Yes, I did. I like to think I'm reasonably up to date with current technology, although I must say my skills are not well developed." She looked at Riley over her glasses. "But I found you pretty easily." There was that same warmth in her voice that Riley found so disarming.

Riley shook her head. "I suppose that's true; I just never think of myself as a public person."

Mildred shrugged as if to say, 'no matter.' "How are you thinking of making contact with Edward?"

Riley explained that she thought it best to pick a time after school was over and call him at home. Of course, the only number she had for him was a mobile one, so he could answer it anywhere. "I believe I told you—and I was so anxious I wasn't entirely sure—that my friend Jennifer called him the other evening."

"You mentioned that, but you did not tell me what she said to him."

"She said that she knew who he was and what he was up to."

"And what was his response?"

Riley shook her head. "I don't know. Jennifer hung up on him."

Mildred was obviously trying to suppress surprise. Her eyes grew slightly larger. "Really?"

"Really."

Mildred looked out the window as if thinking, which was, in fact, what she was doing. "Let's talk about what you want to do," she said, turning her attention back to Riley.

"What I want to do is simple," Riley said. "I want to ask him if he is following me and, if so, to please stop." She thought for a moment and then looked up at Mildred. "But I want to do this in a way which is as gentle and kind as possible. I don't know how fragile Edward is, but if he is following me around at his age—he's thirty-six—it's not a good sign."

Mildred nodded in agreement at this. "You may not be surprised to learn that this kind of thing can happen with men of any age. Or women, for that matter."

It was Riley's turn to shrug. Mildred was the expert.

"Riley, is there any way you can think of that we can help you with this?"

Riley thought for a long minute. "Yes," she said. "I would like to know if I can call you after the conversation so we can talk about it."

"Of course," replied Mildred.

Riley felt her body relax immediately, a signal of how important that assurance was to her. Mildred nodded.

"Okay," Mildred said. "Two more things: Number one: let me know when you plan to talk to him, so I can be available. Number two: Let's take a tour."

And with that Mildred stood up, followed by Riley, and the pair proceeded to visit the facility. For Riley, having Mildred on her side felt like a major boost. She felt she now had the wherewithal to deal with this situation as straightforwardly and as competently as she could. And she had support. She wasn't exactly sure why, but it meant a great deal to her.

They left Mildred's office and took a series of turns that Riley was sure she could not replicate if she tried. The place seemed like a warren of small rooms and odd corridors.

Down one such corridor, she heard women talking; although she could not make out what they were saying. "That's a therapy group in process," Mildred explained.

Down another corridor, she heard children playing and laughing. "Women often do not come here alone. They often fear for themselves and for their children. We take children up to twelve. After that, it's usually a matter for DFS to handle."

"DFS?"

"Department of Family Services."

"Oh."

They kept walking, past a dining room, more living quarters, a communal bathroom that held several showers, and all the other things required for housing women in distress.

It made Riley sad. "I don't know how you do this, Mildred."

Mildred shrugged. "It's something that needs to be done. And I've been doing it for a long time."

Riley got the distinct impression from her tone of voice that Mildred spoke from an experience to which Riley was not privy. It felt private. She did not dare ask.

Finally, the pair came to the foyer near the front door where Riley had entered. Mildred handed her a card. "This has my name and cell number, as well as the office number. It also has the door code on the back." She turned the card over, and Riley saw that she had handwritten the door code on the small business card. "Don't lose it," Mildred said, but she was smiling when she said it.

Despite the smile, Riley knew that she was serious. The last thing this facility needed was a business card with the private phone number of the director and the code that would open the door at any time.

"Thank you," Riley said, taking Mildred's hand in hers. She hoped it conveyed the appreciation she felt inside.

"Stay in touch, Riley."

"I will."

She went to the door and opened it. Outside seemed especially bright this afternoon. She had not noticed how dark the building was, but it must have been quite dark to make the outdoors seem so bright. Before the door closed, she turned to say good-bye once again, but Mildred was gone, and the receptionist was engrossed with something on her desk.

## — 58 —

A few days went by during which Riley began to feel like her old self. Or maybe a new, more comfortable version of herself. She noticed that she felt less frightened or anxious. She decided to take a couple days off from writing in order to absorb all the things that have happened these past few days. She wanted to be as clear and lucid as she could be when she contacted Edward.

She spent the time relaxing: reading, watching a little TV, daydreaming. This last being something she loved to do and felt was important for a writer of fiction.

Sure it is, came a gentle but mildly sarcastic voice from within her head.

Mom again?

Probably.

In any case, Riley wasn't in any rush to call Edward. She had not noticed him anywhere near her apartment since that one time, and thought maybe he had just given up and forgotten about her. This latter possibility seemed remote, but one never knew.

She decided to check in with Cameron. She planned to call him after his workday was over. She had a new appreciation of how important, even central, work was her husband's life: she did not want to disturb him in his natural habitat. She tried, against her inclination, to be nice about it.

She was a little nervous about calling him, but she was determined to do so. It's okay to talk to my husband, she decided, even my estranged husband. She dialed his number around 6:30 p.m.

Cameron looked at the phone when it rang. He had been home for less than ten minutes and was mercifully tired. He knew it was Riley, but he was unsure about answering, so unsure that the call went to voicemail before he could decide.

"Hi, Cameron. It's me. Call me."

Cameron sighed. Same old message. Short, only what was necessary. Still, she wanted him to call her. Why? What did he have to offer her at this point? Self-pity aside, what did she want?

It was this last question that motivated him to press the call-back button.

"Hi," said Riley.

"Hi," replied Cameron.

There was silence on the phone from both sides.

"You called me," Cameron finally said.

"Yes, I did. I'm sorry. You called back so quickly. It surprised me."

"So . . . what do you want, Riley?"

"I just wanted to catch up. I haven't heard from. . .We haven't spoken in a while. I was just wondering how you are."

It was clear to Cameron that this was something Riley had never asked about, although she would perhaps contest that. Maybe she did ask in the early years of their marriage. He could not recall. Certainly not in recent years.

"I'm, I'm . . . Honestly, Riley, I don't know how I am."

Riley sat up a little straighter when she heard this. "What's the matter, Cameron?"

Against all history and normal inclination, Cameron began to cry softly. But he did not hang up. He just held the phone to his ear, bit his lip, and tried to weep as silently as he could so Riley would not notice.

But it was impossible not to notice. This was Cameron. This was a person who, up until this point, had only wept seriously for a job he had inexplicably lost. This was a man who had never shed a tear over the loss of his wife, lover, and partner.

"I'm sorry," Cameron said. "It's been a rough few days."

Tell me about it, Riley said, thinking of her own last few days. To Cameron she said, "Do you want to tell me about it?"

"I don't know. I don't know if I can even explain it." He spoke slowly, as if trying to be as accurate as he could speaking a language he barely knew and seldom used.

Riley was torn. She was hearing the voice of a different Cameron, one that actually touched her emotionally. But she had been so angry, so fed up for so long, that resentment toward the old Cameron felt like a default mode, the normal state of affairs in their relationship. She found herself now perhaps willing to forge a new path but was uncertain how to move forward. She did not want to be cruel, but nor did she wish to be overtaken by habits she hated. That, she believed, entailed honesty and no small amount of courage. Both of which are hard.

"Did something happen?"

"Yeah. A couple days ago . . . I was on my way home . . . just driving back toward the apartment . . . and, I don't know, suddenly it hit me . . ."

He fell silent.

"What hit you, Cameron?"

She could sense that the tears were returning. "I, uh, I'm not sure. I guess I realized, I mean, I really realized that . . . that . . . that you were really gone."

Jesus, Riley thought. It's been six months and he just now gets it that I'm gone. But, then again, this was Cameron, and this thick-headedness was one of the deal-breakers in their relationship.

"I'm sorry, Cameron," she said as gently as she could. She did not know exactly what to say. She had not had a big emotional catharsis after separating from Cameron. She had heard that people do, but for her, it was mostly about relief and the adventure of moving on. That seemed to be enough.

Still no response from Cameron.

"Cameron?"

"What?"

"Is there something I can do for you, something that would make you feel better?"

Cameron thought about this for a moment as his tears dried up. He could not think of a thing. He dared not ask her to come back, although that thought flickered on the edge of his mind. He did not know why. He just knew Riley wasn't coming back, whether he asked or not. On the other hand, he was realizing how familiar and even warm it felt to talk to Riley. It seemed like a long, long time since they had had a normal conversation.

"I can't think of anything, Riley." He almost chuckled. "Believe me, if I could, I would tell you."

Riley also chuckled at the simple incongruity that Cameron might be laughing at himself.

For lack of anything else to say, Riley pressed on about the one thing that had been on her mind these last days. "It's been a little dicey on my end, too, Cameron. I've been dealing with a situation . . ." She really felt in her head that she did not want to proceed and was positive it wasn't a good idea to do so, but she found that she could not close the gate once opened. "It's been difficult . . ."

"Riley, what are you talking about?" The voice was Old Cameron, upbeat but demanding.

Riley took a deep breath. "There was guy I met in a coffee shop a while back. We talked. We had, um, one date. Then he started hanging around my apartment. I got scared, so I talked to my lawyer and to a good friend. Then yesterday I went to visit with the director of a women's shelter . . ."

"Women's shelter!?"

"Yes. I'm . . . I'm in the middle of dealing with this situation, so I thought I should get some advice from . . ."

"A women's shelter? You mean where women go who have been abused? When they run away to escape their violent husbands?"

"Yes, Cameron. A women's shelter." She rolled her eyes.

"Riley," said Cameron with a forcefulness she had never heard from him. "Are you all right? Has someone hurt you?" He was getting more agitated by the moment.

"No, Cameron. No one has hurt me. But this guy has been . . ." She searched for the correct word. ". . . stalking me."

"Stalking you?!"

Riley was pretty sure at this moment that her original inclination to refrain from bringing this up was correct. Really, why would Cameron care? And even if he did, what could he do? He had a job, a life. He did not live close. And now, he seemed positively angry. Concerned; maybe even protective.

"Riley, do you want or need to come back home for a while?"

Riley was glad Cameron couldn't see the shocked look on her face. Come back home? She had not considered their previously shared apartment home for months, but she heard the 'for a while' part clearly. Cameron wasn't, it seemed, trying to finagle her back into their marriage, he was simply trying to be helpful by offering her a place to stay for a while. It struck her as at once generous and kind, if way off the mark. She had not for one instant thought of seeking refuge in what she now regarded as Cameron's apartment.

But the concern in his voice was impossible to miss. She felt a surge of guilt for 'what I did to him,' meaning her decision to separate. But at the same time, she felt a wave of genuine care from Cameron that she had not felt in years. It was her turn for a tear to roll down her cheek. She was touched.

"I'm sorry, Cameron. I am so sorry. Perhaps I should not have told you about this."

"No, no. It is something I want to know about, Riley. I would hate myself forever if something happened to you and I didn't know about it."

This strange, intimate, difficult, caring, and completely unforeseen conversation ground to a halt, even as it continued to befuddle both parties. Neither knew what to say. Both were talking about something so basic to their relationship and how they were together; something so primal words could not do it justice; something so much about attachment and longing and a history of frustration and love that finally they both fell silent from the sheer weight of it all.

At length, Cameron said, "Riley, would you like to meet and talk about this in person?"

Riley did not know what to say. Yes, she did want to meet at this moment. But she was also nearly certain that she would regret the decision either right after agreeing or most certainly after meeting up with Cameron.

"I don't know, Cameron. Let me think about that."

Cameron's nod was of course invisible to her, but she felt it anyway. "I will do whatever I can to make sure you are safe, Riley. I love you."

Hearing that was too much for Riley to bear. She said good-bye before her escalating tears prevented further speech and clicked her phone off. She was speechless.

She sat and wept for some time, realizing how she had never mourned the relationship with Cameron. After she left him, she had been all about the relief and liberation she felt during these months of separation, feelings that culminated in her actually filing for divorce. And now she was faced with the other side of the coin of her decision to leave the marriage.

Abandoning the marriage had been entirely her decision. Cameron had not wanted it; for a long time, he did not even believe his marriage would end, even after she left. Riley did not know about feelings Cameron may or may not have had about their recent conversations, but the past few days—up until today—his voice had taken on an edge that was wholly unlike the iteration of him that she had known for the years of their marriage. Not sunny or happy but terse, even sharp. Angry.

But today was different. He was an actual human being, a whole human being with a variety of feelings. She could not help wondering what had happened to bring this about. Was it when he realized I wasn't coming back, the episode he told me that happened the other day? Could one experience do that?

Riley did not know what to make with any of this. Who is this person I married? Is the current Cameron the same one?

She felt exposed. Why had she told him about Edward? At the moment, Edward's antics slipped into the background of a more potent and more immediate drama. The story of Edward was banished like an incident with a wayward child that, while disturbing when it happens, is quickly forgotten. In center stage now was a transformed Cameron, a man who incomprehensibly came into possession of himself as someone she didn't know. Cameron the adult, the real, not pretend grown-up; the person she wanted more than ever for herself to be.

For the first time, Riley thought grimly; and she felt a familiar surge of anger about the years spent wondering if there was really a person inside the body she lived next to. The sad routine of watching helplessly as the distance in her relationship with Cameron grew; the growing recognition that nothing would ever change. Not while they were together; not while they clung to their practiced roles of husband and wife.

And empty roles they were. Prior to this telephone conversation, she and Cameron had not had an emotionally honest relationship in years. And now they were having one in the midst of the wreckage of their marriage.

So things can change, she thought. At least they seem to be changing for Cameron. But she also saw that the change happened in part because of what she 'did to him', because she found the courage to leave. She mentally applauded Cameron's transformation but also knew that it was too late for what they had together. Maybe someday they could be friends. But that day was most likely not now, not even soon. It was in a faraway future. Years perhaps.

A sensation enveloped Riley that was new to her. It was a heavy feeling with elements of clear-sightedness, sobriety, truth, sadness, and perhaps even wisdom. She sat on her couch for the rest of the evening, saying nothing, doing nothing, thinking nothing.

— 59 —

On a lark, Jennifer called Riley just to touch base. When Riley answered, Jennifer chuckled. "What are you doing answering your phone during the day. Why aren't you working?"

"I'm taking a break. I met with this interesting woman from the women's shelter named Mildred. I felt so much better after talking to her. But I'd been so stressed, I decided to take a few days off to relax and pull back from everything to get some perspective. Especially before I decide what to do about Edward."

She continued. "A lot's happened. I talked to Cameron—that's a whole different story—and we had a good conversation, something we had not done in, I don't know, years. Maybe ever. I have not seen or heard from Edward at all. I look out my window in the late afternoon, but he is nowhere to be seen. So I'm feeling much better about everything. It's nice."

"Wow! A lot *has* happened. How about we meet for happy hour later?"

That sounded like the perfect thing to Riley. "I would love to. Name the place."

Jennifer suggested meeting at some place other than Carter's, their usual haunt. "How about Nellie's?"

"Nellie's?"

"Yeah. It's a new-ish place on U Street. It's supposed to have great appetizers during happy hour and half-price cocktails."

"Sounds good. See you there around 5:30?"

"Deal," replied Jennifer.

## 60

Jennifer and Riley met at precisely 5:30 at the trendy new place that already had most seats taken. Fortunately, they found a small table in the corner of the bar area with high stools and settled in. Within seconds, a server came up and plopped down a food menu, an appetizer menu, a cocktail menu, and a wine list.

"Hmm. Paper-heavy," commented Jennifer. "How last century."

"No kidding."

They felt compelled to at least peruse the multiple documents that lay before them, commanding all the real estate on top of the small bar table. Jennifer glanced at Riley. "I think I'll have the usual."

"Me too."

They did: martini for Jen and a gin and tonic for Riley. They ordered the top two appetizers on the list and finally cleared the table of all the excess paper. They faced each other eager to talk.

For a while, they talked of catch-up stuff: work, Riley's progress on her manuscript, the goings-on at Jen's office. Jen looked Riley straight in the eye. "So, you talked to Cameron?"

"I did," said Riley, exhaling loudly. "It was something."

"Tell me about it."

Riley paused, trying to decide where to start. She settled on an old writing principle: Start at the beginning. "Well, I called him because I hadn't heard from him in a while, and I had been debating whether to talk to him about the situation with Edward." She shook her head back and forth as she said this last part. "So I call him, and he doesn't pick up. Then he calls me right back, and I ask him how he is, and instead of Standard Response One, which would basically be some version of 'I'm fine,' he hesitates a bit and says 'I don't know how I am' and that it had been 'a rough few days.'" She took a sip of her drink. "Honestly, I looked at my phone to make sure I hadn't dialed someone else. It was so out of character."

"Then, he tells me that on the way home from work the other day it finally hit him that I'm gone, and he's been having some kind of emotional thing ever since. It must be serious: he sounds completely different from the Cameron I know."

"And then we proceed to have a real conversation, as in a conversation between two adults. Cameron tells me the truth and I, going out on a limb, told him about the situation with Edward." Another sip.

"You told him about Edward?!"

Riley nodded. "Yes, and I regretted it immediately. But then Cameron is all kindness, not in that smarmy way he used to get sometimes, but like a concerned adult. He asked me if I needed a place to stay. And it wasn't like, you know, come back to me. It was like 'If you need a place to stay for a while.' And then . . ." At this point Riley got quiet and looked away for a while. "And then he said he would never forgive himself if something happened to me and . . . and . . . and that . . . he loved me." And at that, a tear ran down Riley's face.

And she was not the only one. Jennifer's eyes were moist, and tears were beginning to escape, as well. She reached over and put her hand on Riley's. "Oh. My. God."

The two sat there and wept softly for several moments. Then they both searched their purses for tissue and wiped their eyes. "And it completely floored me. He had not said that sincerely in a long time. A long time." Riley looked down at the table. Then. she looked up again at Jennifer.

"I know none of this really matters in terms of a future for Cameron and me. I know it would never have happened if we had kept doing the same old thing, living together, tolerating each other. Lying to each other. And that part is so, so sad." She wiped her eyes of the newly arriving tears.

## 61

Cameron did not take any time off from work—that was not in his constitution—but he could not put his conversation with Riley out of his mind. He went to work the next day thinking about it, and it was never too far from his head throughout the day.

Much of Cameron's work was conducted between him and a computer on his desk. Once in a while, he needed to check in with someone, but usually he did that via an in-house instant messaging system, or an email if it was something complicated. It was only occasionally that he had to actually talk to someone on the phone or face to face.

Throughout the day, his mind flipped back and forth constantly between the computer screen, his conversation with Riley, and his relationship with her. I don't know what I did that turned her off so much, he kept thinking. I always tried to be nice. But even he recognized that the conversation they had the day before was different from any they had had previously. He just could not put his finger on what was different about it. So absorbed was he in this knotty issue that, from time to time, his work ground to a halt. He appeared to be staring at his computer screen, although the actual screen he was viewing was the one inside his head. It was in just this circumstance that he suddenly heard a voice that jolted him out of his reverie.

"Uh, excuse me, Mr. Cotswald," came the voice from nowhere.

Startled, Cameron turned his head toward the sound, trying to mask his surprise. He found Evie standing behind him.

Evie blushed. "I'm so sorry," she said reddening. "I didn't mean to scare you."

"No, no, Evie. Don't worry about it. You startled me; that's all."

As she could not think of another thing to say, Evie forged ahead with her assigned task. "Mr. Bullock asked me to ask you if you would be available for a consultation with another office later this week." This sounded like she had been practicing.

Cameron listened intently to what Evie was saying, although in the back of his mind he was trying to figure out what she was talking about and why the head of the office would ask her to convey a question that he could just as easily have asked him. With nothing to stop her, Evie went on.

"He's out of town, and he called me about another matter, and he just asked me to ask you that while he was thinking about it." Her reddening did not diminish much.

"Of course, I will, Evie. Does he want me to contact him?"

"No. He just wants me to let him know if you would be available."

"Okay. I'm available."

"Okay."

Evie turned and walked away, and Cameron shook himself in an effort to come all the way back to reality. He still had a weird, even eerie feeling about this indirect communication from his supervisor, especially after his surprise dismissal a few weeks ago; but he did not have enough experience in this new job to know if it was a sign of trouble or if it was just how Bullock operated. It may have been, as Evie intimated, just a convenience thing.

He tried to refocus on work but soon found his attention being drawn back into his talk with Riley. He just could not get it out of his mind. He glanced at his watch. It was almost 11:00 a.m., too early for lunch. But he was feeling stultified in his cubicle and unable to focus on his work. He needed a break.

Fortunately, the new office had an employee break room for just this kind of moment. This company prided itself on allowing its employees to manage their own time—many often worked from home—so long as they get the work done in a professional and timely manner.

No one was in the small, windowless room, and its features did not provide him much diversion from his cubicle, which at least was open above five feet. The room did nothing to relieve the feeling of being smothered. He grabbed a bottle of water from the fridge and returned to his cubicle.

Evie was right behind him. "Mr. Bullock said that he would discuss this with you when he gets back to the office tomorrow."

"Thanks, Evie. Good to know." What he thought in his head was, 'She is very, very detail oriented.' He liked that about her. He liked it about himself.

I can't stay here today, he thought. He IM'd his supervisor, who was just under Bullock, and informed her that he would be working from home the rest of the day. Ordinarily, ever since Riley left, he always worked from the office because he did not want to spend too much time in what had been their apartment, but today that did not matter. He gathered up his things and left for home.

On his way, he could think about the conversation without the diversion of work. That concept—diverting himself from work—felt alien to him. Work was the most important thing he did . . . It was the thing that brought him a sense of purpose and value . . . It enabled him to live a financially secure life . . . It was everything to him. This was a no-brainer.

And that, he suddenly realized, may be what is at the heart of the problem I had with Riley. Cameron had to admit that he often felt that she was distracting him from his job, especially when he would bring work home or go into the office on weekends. She complained constantly about it.

As he drove along, he felt some barriers drop from his mind, expanding his awareness; he began to see things in a different light. It was tentative at first, but the more he drove and thought, the more space he made for a new realization in his life. Work crowded everything and everyone else out; it was my major, maybe even my sole focus. I did not really take other people seriously. Even Riley, who I loved.

This was a dismaying realization.

Cameron was tempted to pull over and allow this . . . this insight to broaden, but he was wary after what happened the last time he stopped his car in the middle of Washington, D.C. He kept driving, but slowly and carefully, until he got to his building. When he turned off the engine, he just sat there for a while, not wanting to disturb the burgeoning architecture of what his mind was building for him.

After a short time, he gathered up his things, got out of his car, and went up to his apartment. He did not know what to make of this whole concept: that work could be something other than central in his life, or that there could be more than one thing that was central, or that maybe a job was, after all, just a job . . .

This was going nowhere. He just couldn't do it, not yet anyway. He couldn't imagine himself as a human being first and a worker second. It was weird. The whole notion was weird.

## 62

Meanwhile, things were getting weirder for Edward. Ever since the call from that mysterious woman who knew him, but whom he did not know, he had been wary. He went to work every day as usual, teaching his students with the same diligence he always had. He came home and adhered closely to his typical pre-Riley routine: put things away, get a bite to eat, grade papers if needed, prepare for class the next day, and then decide how he was going to spend the remaining time until he went to bed. He purposely avoided the area where Riley lived, the coffee shop where he first spotted her, or any venue that he thought she might frequent.

Edward had some anxiety because the school year was rapidly drawing to a close, and he would have a lot more time on his hands. Especially since he had made a previous decision not to work this summer.

But there were differences between now and his pre-Riley days. He did not touch his computer for several days. Even though he knew better, he had an inkling that somehow information leached out of it, and committing anything to the electronic leviathan might alert a wider audience about what he was up to. A small voice inside him told him that was nonsense, but he did not give that small but reasonable voice much credence.

The truth was he wasn't sure what he was up to. Prior to that phone call, he had considered a number of possibilities, mostly having to do with revenge. These ranged from hurting (killing?) Riley, to doing the same to himself in her presence. But that damned phone call at once put a huge damper on what he now saw to be those idle fantasies. No, he would not hurt himself or Riley. Well, certainly not himself.

In a way, that phone call took a lot of pressure off of him: it short-circuited the feelings and thoughts he had about him and Riley. In an odd, maybe even perverse, way, he felt some gratitude about that.

But he was unsure what to do or what he could do or who was watching him do whatever he did do. The fact that someone might be watching him sapped the energy out of his life. He could still function, but barely: he was anxious all the time, looking over his shoulder, being on hyper alert, not speaking to almost anyone when there was no specific purpose. Not that he was much of a talker anyway, but now he lived day to day in self-imposed silence, save for necessary words to his students, who had to listen to him, or to the school administration, which largely ignored him. He spent his free time reading or staring at the television, something to which he was generally unaccustomed, but it seemed like the safest thing for him just now.

He didn't know how long he could stand this. He was actually shocked at how silly and formulary TV shows were; he hadn't watched a regular sitcom or other TV series in years. He rarely laughed along with the laugh track. And the serious police dramas scared him senseless. He was disgusted by the fact that he was reduced to spending his time like this.

But at the same time, he was deeply uncertain what to do next. In the months leading up to his meeting Riley, he had spent more than a few hours researching her online, reading her book, and fantasizing about her. When the actual experience outclassed the fantasies, he felt that all his work had been validated. That idea was obliterated first by her telling him that she did not want a relation-ship and then by that damned phone call.

He tried to read to distract himself, but he was too edgy and uptight to get through more than a page or two. He tried drinking one evening, but he hated the taste of hard liquor and had never developed a taste for wine or beer. He went out jogging another evening, only to find that his chest was so constricted by anxiety that he only made it two city blocks.

He was a wreck.

And she did this to me.

Or maybe not. Maybe I am the one responsible for this. After all, I was the one who 'discovered' her and followed her, who asked her out, who consented when she returned that happy afternoon. I was the one who spent hours searching for information about her online, looking and hoping and dreaming about her in a way I had never done with anyone prior to this. Maybe there is something wrong with me.

Nah, he decided. That stuff happens when one person gets taken up by another. The fact that it collapsed so spectacularly; well, that happens too. Relationships crash and burn all the time. Perhaps not so dramatically as this one, but they often end in less-than-ideal circumstances.

This is certainly less than ideal, he thought to himself. And now I do not know what to do with myself. He felt a tinge of embarrassment that at the age of thirty-four, he was at sea in his life.

Edward considered his present state. He tried to decide what it was he was facing. All his attention was taken up by the gigantic void at the center of his life, the emptiness that just seemed to go on and on. He felt more depressed just thinking about it.

What to do in a situation like this? Hold on, he told himself. Just hold on.

It was then that an idea struck him that had the hallmark of genius.

## 63

Riley decided it was also time to get back to work.

*Adam did not call his parents the day after it occurred to him that it might be a good idea. Instead, he waited several days to mull it over.*

*Adam's relationship with his parents was always warm, he supposed, as relationships with parents often are; but he equally often bristled at much of the staunch Lutheran culture that served as the backdrop of his Upper Midwestern upbringing.*

*His family were members of the Wisconsin Evangelical Lutheran Synod, or WELS, a very conservative Lutheran group that did not brook contemporary ideas, such as evolution, extramarital sex, ordaining women or allowing any woman to have authority over a man, allowing homosexual couples to marry, and every other item on the standard liberal agenda. To WELS, the Pope is the Antichrist, even the friendly one currently holding that position.*

*The heavy and restrictive attitudes had been too much for Adam, even from a young age. He especially liked girls, whom he knew would grow up to be women. He also had two sisters. They did not seem less intelligent, less moral, or really less anything than men, except that they were, for the most part, a lot prettier. He had no idea why they were locked out of church governance in such a definite and complete way. And as for Catholics, well, he knew some great Catholics who lived not far from him growing up. Friends. Good friends.*

*And truthfully he did not care about all that doctrine stuff. He went along to the weekly church services of his parents; when they sent him to a WELS school, he did not protest. He knew it would not matter if he had; they were clear about what they wanted for him. But when churchy issues came up in class, as they did in almost every one but most especially Religion class, his mind would glaze over and he would have to force his eyes to stay open, at the cost of any genuine attention. It became second nature.*

*Divorce in particular was frowned upon by that church. Adam thought he recalled that there were only two reasons for a valid divorce, according to his upbringing: fornication and desertion. Adam guessed he qualified for both through the benevolent offices of Suzanne, who both fornicated and left town.*

*That was small consolation, however, as he thought about telling his parents. They never seemed like religious fanatics, but they never questioned church doctrine either. And honestly, some of it was hard to support, such as the seven-day creation story and the whole inerrancy of the Bible thing. Myths, Adam thought, as he was sure every sensible person on the planet did; but he never heard a bit of deviation from that strict doctrine or any other from his parents.*

*And it wasn't that his parents weren't educated. Both had finished high school; both had attended college. In fact, his father graduated with a degree in accounting, which he put to good use counting whatever accountants count. He had a reasonably successful career, and he supported his family well, so far as Adam could see. His mother taught school for a while, until the demands of domestic life called and her husband's income had grown suffice for the whole family. He and his two siblings got along fine growing up; and this geniality persisted into adulthood. In fact, his relationships with all members of his family were cordial, even if they would not be called close. His two sisters had both married and still lived in Minnesota. They both had children, whom they were planning to send to WELS schools. That did not bother Adam; it was, after all, not his life.*

*To call his relationships with either of his parents close would also be an overstatement. He loved them. He visited them when he could, which was not often. Actually, he visited them for what he regarded as an acceptable and respectful amount of time. He did not especially relish the visits. He went dutifully, and his parents welcomed him with a matching sense of duty. He did not, oddly enough, go home for Christmas; this was odd because it was such a high holiday in the WELS tradition. That's probably why I don't go, he surmised. Suzanne and he decided early in their marriage that Christmas would be for the two of them; no doubt this was because they both worked and time alone together was spotty early on.*

*So what do I say to them? he wondered. That Suzanne is a fornicator and abandoned me? His parents were skeptical of Adam's marrying outside their congregation, but even they recognized that there were limits to how much they could expect their offspring to remain on what they regarded as the straight and narrow, especially when the offspring in question lived a thousand miles away in city that was generally seen in the pious community as a new Sodom.*

*They had agreed to come and participate in the small but tasteful wedding thrown by Suzanne's adoring parents. They seemed to enjoy themselves. They gave the couple an illuminated Bible as a present, something in which they could record milestones of their lives such as children, baptisms, and the like. Improbable things, in fact. But both Adam and Suzanne thanked them warmly and took possession of the sacred book that lay somewhere at the bottom of one of the closets in the house. Adam wasn't sure exactly where.*

*I think I'll wait to talk to them, he finally concluded. This is still all pretty fresh, and I think a little more time would be for everyone's benefit.*

"Especially yours," said Riley, as she pulled her fingers away from the keyboard for a few blinks and a quick stretch.

*I wish I'd stop thinking about all this, Adam thought to himself. It doesn't help to ruminate about things; nor is there any sense thinking Suzanne might change her mind. Even if she did, which is unlikely, would I really want her back after all that I've learned these past weeks?*

*He could not imagine it. He looked around the rental house. This isn't ours anymore; it's just mine. And it's too much for me. He decided then and there that he would start looking for an apartment closer to downtown, where his office was located—the one he did not see much—and where there was a more active social scene. He did not really look forward to jumping into the life of a single man again, but what was the alternative? Pretend that being alone is what I want? It's not.*

*With that sobering realization, he went online to seek out apartments and, after getting over the initial shock at the exorbitant rents that were listed, did a little math to figure out what he could afford. He found several good prospects and resolved to visit them over the next few days.*

Time for a change, my friend. It's going around.

Riley pulled back from her computer and thought about the characters who were coming to life on her screen right in front of her. She sympathized with them and their struggles. We're all in this sort of, I don't know what. A maze? No, not exactly. A game where the rules are discovered as you go along? And even those are provisional? Something like that. And where the outcome is always tragic? Yes, apparently so.

That seems like an insidious thing, she thought to herself.

Yes, it does, came a sympathetic voice from inside her.

## — 64 —

As the genius idea bloomed in his mind, Edward began to see a path forward. It was complicated, to be sure; and it would require a considerable investment in time, and perhaps even money. Neither of those should be a problem, he thought. It's worth time and money.

At the same time, he was feeling agitated. He had this sinking feeling that he was getting depressed, rather like what happened after his parents died. Shit. I never want to go through that again.

He considered his options. Talk to his doctor? Go on medication? See a therapist? None of these felt right to him. He would be too mortified to talk to his doctor about his mood. Both the thought of taking medication and seeing a therapist were equally repugnant. Go on medication because I feel bad? Aspirin for the soul? That sounded ridiculous to him. And seeing a therapist struck him as something like torture, where session after session he would talk about himself, a topic that held only marginal interest. The thought of it made him want to throw up.

But he did not want to go down the path that he travelled after his parents died, when he spent months just fighting to get up in the morning. He wanted to avoid it if at all possible. Surely there were things he could do that were not the ones that initially popped into his mind. And not the ones portrayed on television.

He went online to search for non-medical treatments for depression. There was exercise, which he already did regularly; meditation, which he knew nothing about; and various plants, herbs, and vitamins that were 'thought to be helpful.' That last item did not sound exactly like the resounding affirmation of what he was looking for, but how could ingesting a few natural substances harm him?

He searched online for a health food store near him and, to his surprise, found several. In fact, it looked as if the District had more than its share of natural herb stores that hawked stress relievers of various sorts, natural cures for mysterious pain, and, of course, pills for depression. Politics probably has something to do with the bull market in those products, he thought grimly.

The choice was to order something online or show up at one of these stores, the nearest one of which was two blocks away. He decided to go to the store and not wait for delivery.

It was a particularly warm day in the District, and the humidity was noticeably high. Oddly, it felt good to Edward, who had been cooped up in his apartment with the air conditioning blowing for the better part of the day. Since he had decided not to work this summer, he was free every day. He again wondered if this was the best choice for what he was going through, although he did not feel unduly anxious.

Instead of complaining about the heat and humidity, he breathed it in. It made him feel . . . natural, human. He felt more grounded. By the time he got to the herbal supplement store, he began to wonder if it was worth going in.

But he did. His intention was to look around. He had taken some notes from his perusal of the web, so he had something to go on. He assumed that, like most retail establishments, service would be spotty.

Not so here. There were only two other people in the store, and one of them was apparently the proprietor. "What can I help you with, young man?" he said amiably.

"I'm just looking," replied Edward.

"Well, if you need any help, just let me know." The man turned back to reading whatever he was reading when Edward walked into the lines of shelves.

Edward walked up and down the aisles looking for containers of the things he had made notes about. What he found was a panoply of herbs, supplements, and various chemicals all claiming to work various degrees of wonder for depression.

It took him a while to find St. John's Wort, which he felt was probably the least controversial supplement on the market. Actual people use it: it's apparently very popular in Europe. He picked up a bottle and walked over to the counter.

The proprietor saw what Edward had in his hand and nodded sympathetically. "We sell a lot of this," he said, his amiability never flagging. "Make sure you tell your doctor if you are on other medications; sometimes it interacts badly."

Edward nodded. He was finding himself self-conscious, but not so much as he had anticipated. What the man said reflected what he had read about the medication in his hand. He thanked him, paid, and started walking home.

Edward was not a fan of medication. As he walked through the heavy air and breathed it in, he felt a little more alive, a little more in touch with himself, with the earth. The thought of taking something that would interfere with his natural experience made him slightly nauseous. Especially now as he was finding a way to do what he wanted and needed to do.

Once home, he pulled the bottle out of his pocket and stared at it for a while. "You'll be here if I need you," he said to the full bottle of pills. Then, he went to his bathroom and put it in the medicine cabinet. He went to his desk, turned on the computer, and began doing research.

## 65

Riley's writing was going well, and a couple of weeks flew by as Adam and Suzanne's new lives unfolded.

*Suzanne took up her duties in her new assignment as competently as she was able, but with a heavy heart. She missed Ellie more than words could describe. She missed D.C., with its frenetic social scene and endless entertainments. She even missed her adoring parents, whom she seldom saw in person but talked to on the phone from time to time. She would like to say that she missed Adam, but the fact was his receding memory seldom made it to center stage in her consciousness.*

*Added to this was a queer similarity in appearance between Adam and David Collins, who was resentfully returning to his duties as assistant director of the office. They were about the same height and weight, had the same color hair, and seemed to share some manner-isms. David was older than Adam, and his hair was receding some. Adam's hair would likely do the same in a few years. Sometimes when Suzanne met with David, she thought of him as an older version of her ex-husband. It was not a comfortable comparison.*

*So far she did not really mind Dayton: it was one of those basic American cities that was not without its charm. It's just that the charm level paled compared to what was routine in D.C. She hoped that the increase in salary and benefits would also include frequent reimbursed travel expenses.*

*As if in response to her desire, she received an email from Jerome Bitworth, her former boss. He was asking her to come to D.C. for a meeting of all office directors in two weeks. Suzanne could not believe her good fortune. She emailed him back immediately, assuring him that she would be there.*

*'Great' came his response. 'Looking forward to seeing you again.'*

*That struck Suzanne as unusual, since it had not been a week since she left the District and Bitworth's office. But she did not care. She wanted to make flight reservations, but then realized she did not know the protocol for that. She messaged Collins to ask about the procedure. He was standing in her office doorway within thirty seconds.*

*He just stood there for a moment staring at Suzanne, who stared back. "Yes?" she finally said.*

*"You just messaged me about travel plans," he said obviously enough.*

*Suzanne nodded. "Yes, I did? And?"*

*"Excuse me, Ms. Wilkerson, but did no one explain the procedures for this kind of thing before you came?"*

*"Only in broad outline, David. What am I missing?" Her voice sounded curt, but David's tone lacked any sense of helpfulness.*

*David noticed her tone too. He straightened up and started reciting something that must have been written down somewhere. "All personnel at the director level and above are to be issued a company credit card on which they are to charge all travel expenses, completely at their own discretion."*

*"Well, that's fine, David, but right now I do not have one, and I am going to D.C. in two weeks, and I need to make travel arrangements."*

*"I will see that you get it today, ma'am."*

*Suzanne cocked her head sideways, still looking at him. "Thank you, David."*

*"You're welcome, ma'am," replied David, who seemed anything but welcoming about what he was doing.*

*Asshole, thought Suzanne as David disappeared from her doorway. She wondered how long it would be before she could replace him. Then suddenly, she said, "David?" to empty doorway.*

*David magically reappeared at her door again. "Yes, ma'am?"*

After a one-second delay, Suzanne said, "You recited what sounded like a company policy a few minutes ago. Is that written down somewhere?"

"Yes, ma'am."

Again, she looked at him askance. "Where?"

"I will bring you the manual right away."

"Thank you."

Without another word, David disappeared from her door and re-appeared within sixty seconds. "Here it is, ma'am." He lay a well-thumbed spiral-bound book on her desk.

"Thank you."

"Ma'am." He disappeared a third time.

Shaking her head, Suzanne threw the book into her briefcase, which was on the floor next to her with the intention of looking it over once she got home. There were just too many more pressing things to do right now.

The thought of returning to Washington so soon made her feel lighter, less condemned to the outer provinces and more in touch with central control. That was vaguely reminiscent of a movie she could not place. She smiled to herself and got back to work. It felt good to smile.

## 66

As Adam looked around the house that he was planning to abandon, he began to feel a tinge of excitement about making changes in his life. *This will be a new start; this will be better.*

His thoughts went back to the day when he and Suzanne finally admitted to each other that they were not happy, that what they had hoped for was not working out, and that they were essentially living separate lives and just co-habitating. He shuddered at how hard that all was, both the conversation and life before it. And, he mused, life immediately afterwards.

But that part of the drama in his life was moving inexorably into the past. And while it had taken Adam some time to move on to the next phase of his life, he felt that he was doing precisely that in looking for a new apartment. *This is what I need to do. I need to let go of this place and all the emotional baggage that goes with it.* He looked forward to that.

It occurred to him that he might not have to wait out the three months until the lease ended. *Why not move sooner rather than later?* He was psyched for it now, ready for a change.

He pulled out the contract he had signed on the house and read it in detail for the first time. In it, there was a section about departing before the term of the lease was complete. To Adam's amazement, all it required was a thirty-day notification to the landlord. He had assumed he was locked in. He wasn't.

*This has been the story of my life,* he thought, chuckling to himself: *thinking I'm trapped when I'm not.*

*He went to work on finding a new apartment. He called several buildings in the northwest section of the District and made appointments to see available apartments. He wrote a notification letter to his landlord, which he would send if he found an appropriate option.*

*All of this made that spark of excitement grow into something of a flame. He found himself smiling for the first time in a long time.*

*The excitement included a distinct feeling of freedom that he had not felt since before he was married. I can do what I want. I could even start dating.*

*Until this moment, seeing other women was something he had relegated to the distant future, sometime after he 'recovers' from his marriage to Suzanne. But why wait? What exactly am I waiting for? The subtext of this was the chilling question: How long to do I want to suffer? He shook his head. I spend way too much time alone as it is; a little company seems like a wonderful idea.*

*He was torn a bit: he sat down and made a list of single women he knew or thought he knew. It was short. He thought about the dating sites that advertise so much on television, but that seemed . . . he did not know what. Dark. Desperate. Unnatural. Elements of all of these. He would leave that alone for now.*

*One thing he could do was spend more time at the office downtown. He decided early on in his work life to do as much as he could from home because he knew he could get a lot more done in a shorter amount of time. That felt like a good investment of his time. But it left him with such a solitary lifestyle that . . . that . . . that what?*

*That I got used to it; that's what! It was self-imposed isolation. And because it's completely self-imposed, I can change it at any time. And who said it had to be all or nothing? He could spend a couple days at the office and a couple at home; he could split his time every day between the two if he so chose. Who knows? Maybe he would like going to the office and being around people more often than he used to think. Doors seemed to be opening everywhere in his mind.*

*All this seems embarrassingly simple, he thought.*

*It is, came a reassuring voice inside his head.*

*I do not want to sit around here one more minute, he decided on the spot. One of the old friends he had reconnected with after*

*Suzanne left had just moved into D.C. and was also on his own. He might also want some company. Why hadn't I thought of this before?*

*Because the time is now.*

*That's right. The time is now.*

Riley stared at the screen where she had just written these words. She could not sympathize more with Adam's predicament and his thoughts. Is that what I've been doing? Sitting around waiting for god-knows-what to happen?

Apparently so.

It's been months!

Yes, it has.

Riley sat back in her chair. Is now the time?

Perhaps it is.

Except for her unwise dalliance with Edward, Riley had not dated or had sex with anyone since she left Cameron. She could feel a certain emptiness in that neighborhood of her mind, but she had shielded it from any serious scrutiny. She just thought, as Adam did, that dating was something that she had 'relegated to the distant future.' How silly is that?

Not silly. You needed some time to heal. Divorce is a big deal. Adam is being a tad cavalier.

Yeah, divorce is a big deal. But that's almost complete. And now I think I'm about to be almost ready to . . .

Could you be any more equivocal?

I could try, she thought sheepishly, but matching the sarcasm that was coming from inside her own head.

So, what is it you want? What is it you are ready for?

I want to go on a date.

Okay. Then go on a date.

Just like that?

How do you think it happens?

Most of Riley wanted to delete the last few interchanges of her mind, but she knew she could not do that, especially when they rang so true.

I'm scared.

Everyone who does this feels some anxiety.

I don't really care what everyone feels. I care about what I feel.

That's a great start.

She hated when her own thinking reflected things she learned when she was in therapy. But what was she doing there, anyway, if not learning?

So learn. That, of course, involves some risk.

Yeah, yeah. I know. You can stop now.

As if to make sure her internal conversation would stop, she reached back to her computer, saved her work, and shut the machine down.

She grabbed her keys and purse and headed out.

## — 67 —

Riley walked down the street from her apartment to a bar she knew was there but had never visited. She wasn't really a big drinker but going to a coffee shop and burying herself in her laptop while she got buzzed on caffeine did not seem appealing. Nor did it seem like a way to meet people. She was not really a pro at the bar scene, but she thought she would give it a try. It was a step. And what did she have to lose?

Mindful of what Jennifer had gone through at lunch a few weeks ago, she found a place at the bar and ordered a tonic and lime. There were a few other customers at the bar, mostly men—government types by the look of their off-the-rack suits—and mostly older than she. She did not care. She wasn't sure what she was looking for, but she knew it was something that was different from what she had been doing.

It did not take long for more people to file in and fill up all the bar stools. There were tables scattered around the room, and these started filling up also. Riley glanced at her watch: 5:36. I got here just in time, she thought.

Nor did it take long for her to be noticed. The guy sitting next to her on one side was involved in an apparently engaging conversation with another man; he did not even seem to notice her. But on the other side, a man about her age had sat down by himself a few minutes earlier and was already nursing something in a martini glass. She could feel him glancing her way occasionally. A few other guys in the bar also signaled in that primal male way that she was noticed.

Riley turned to the man next to her and smiled. She could not think of a single thing to say that did not sound stupid or trite or both. So she added a nod to the smile.

He nodded back. "Hi."

"Hi," she replied.

Riley was thinking this man was about as shy as she was. But what could she say? 'Do you come here often?' 'Nice place?' She was running through similarly goofy options when he spoke. "My name's Adam," he said.

Riley had taken a sip of her drink just before he said this; it immediately erupted from her mouth and splattered across the bar. After wiping her mouth and the bar top with a napkin and letting her obvious mortification show, she turned to him and said, "Really?"

She was dying to ask him his last name but did not really want to explain why that was so important.

Adam looked puzzled. Riley was wondering if he was thinking something like: Do people lie about their names in bars? Truth be told, he did not seem like much of a frequenter of drinking establishments. "Yes," he said after a few moments. "Really."

He tried to smile but the effort produced a look more akin to skepticism.

Every bone in Riley's body wanted to say that her name was Suzanne, but she could not bring herself to do that. "My name is Riley," she said simply. She nodded as if to confirm it.

Adam nodded back. He seemed to find that name curious. "Really?" he said with a smile at his opportunity to mimic Riley.

"Really," replied Riley. "I know it's a bit unusual."

"It must be. I've never known anyone with that name."

"Listen, the reason I was so surprised about your name was that . . . well . . . I'm a writer, and the book I'm currently working on has a main character whose name is. . ."

"Adam?"

"Adam."

A minute ticked by.

"I'll be damned." Then, he blushed slightly and said, "I mean, what a coincidence."

"Yes," said Riley. Quite a coincidence."

"What's he like?"

Thoughtful question. Riley looked at her now-empty glass for a moment. "Well, he's kind of a regular guy. You know, he's not one of those characters who was at the top of his class at Harvard or who made a billion dollars by the time he was twenty-five, or who was the most handsome guy in his class; you know . . . He's just a guy. Has a job. Works hard. Was married but divorced toward the beginning of the book . . ." She stopped because she felt she was talking too much and maybe giving away too much of the plot. Of course, if there was a plot, she knew as little about it as anyone.

"Another coincidence," remarked Adam.

"You're kidding."

"No, I'm not."

"I'm sorry," said Riley, who wasn't really sorry but who was having a visceral reaction to this seeming coincidence. She was a little confused and wasn't sure what was happening exactly. It was as if the rock-solid line that had always separated reality from fantasy was slipping a bit, and she could sense it in her visual field, her mind, and even her body, which felt chilly.

"No need to be," said Adam. "It's for the best. We didn't have any children. We both have careers and decent jobs." He took a sip of his drink. "It's just something that happened."

'I know' is what Riley thought, but she found herself unable to say anything. Riley signaled the bartender. "I'll have whatever he's having."

The bartender nodded, and within sixty seconds she was sipping on a vodka martini.

The two sat quietly for a while, sipping their respective beverages, looking straight ahead. Riley had a feeling that she might look to her left and find an empty bar stool. She closed her eyes for a moment and then opened them. She glanced sideways, only to find Adam—a real Adam—still sitting there.

"This is a little weird," she said, with remarkable understatement.

"Yeah, maybe more than a little."

More silence.

"Um, I'm curious. What is your character's wife's name?"

No, I can't tell him. If it's the same, this feeling will just get worse. She glanced at him and then looked straight ahead. "I'm sorry," she said after a few moments. "I'm having kind of a weird feeling about all this. I mean, I'm not that superstitious, but what are the odds?"

Adam nodded. "Yeah," he said. "What are the odds?"

Then, he swiveled his whole body to face hers. "My wife's name is Suzanne."

## — 68 —

Riley did not say anything. She just stared across the bar into the bottles aligned against the wall and said nothing.

Adam sat there for a while, sipping his drink. He waited patiently for a while.

He had finished his drink and ordered another when he decided he should do something. First, he had to decide if this kind of behavior was just a brush-off. That was possible, he thought. He wasn't the most attractive man in the place.

But before he could conclude that, he decided to give the conversation one more try. "Riley," he said gently, trying to get her attention. "Are you all right?" He touched her gently on the forearm.

Riley seemed to wake up with a start. Surely, she could not have fallen asleep, he thought. But he watched as her eyes widened, she took a deep breath, and turned toward him.

"I'm sorry," she said. "I'm not sure what happened."

"What do you mean?"

"It's just that. . . It's just that, um, Suzanne is the name of the Adam character's wife in my book."

"That is creepy," Adam said.

He wanted to keep the conversation going, but he was uncertain exactly how to proceed. He began to wonder if Riley was this woman's real name. It could be an act.

"So, Riley. Are you really a writer? Are you really writing a book about a divorcing couple named Adam and Suzanne?" He said this in the softest voice he could muster and combined it with the most sympathetic look he could manage.

Riley look at him askance. Does he think I'm lying? She pondered for an entire minute whether to respond or not. First, she had to decide if these questions were insulting or not.

"You don't believe me?"

"No, no. It's not that. It's just that the odds on these being a string of coincidences are astronomically high."

And he thinks I'm making it up.

"And you think I'm making it all up?"

Adam shrugged. "It is one possibility."

Riley thought that to be true. She tried to put herself in his shoes. That was not really so difficult, as she felt she had been in his shoes for some time. Still, the whole situation was not getting any less confusing.

"I guess so," she said at length. She motioned to the bartender for another round. He nodded.

She turned back to Adam. She felt her mind clearing some, and then some more when she took the first sip of her second martini. She wanted to know more about Adam and Suzanne.

"Tell me she doesn't work in Dayton."

"How did you know?"

Jesus Christ! That blurry feeling started to come back.

"Let's try this from another angle. What are you doing here?"

Adam shrugged a little. "Um, I was sitting around my house and decided I needed to get out more, so I called a friend and we were going to meet here. But when I got here, he texted me and said he couldn't make it."

He took a sip of his drink.

"And since the only seat in the house was next to you, I sat here and ordered a drink." He half-smiled sheepishly. "I think this is the first time in my entire life I've gone to a bar alone for a drink."

"I actually did not know that," said Riley with some relief. She could not recall it showing up in the manuscript. It was a small thing, but still . . .

Adam also felt a little relief when he noticed Riley relaxing.

Then, Riley started thinking of all the things she did know about the fictional (or not so fictional) character she thought she had created. The initial shock was wearing off, and the vodka helped quell her anxiety a little, so instead of being totally freaked out, she got curious.

"Okay," she said, turning her attention back to Adam. "Let me tell you what I know about my character, and you tell me if it's accurate with respect to your life."

"Okay," replied Adam, but he was not at all sure it would be okay.

"So, you are from Minnesota?"

"Yes."

"You were raised Lutheran?"

"Yes."

"The Wisconsin Evangelical Synod?"

Adam nodded.

Riley poured out all the information she could recall from her manuscript: his relationship with his parents, the fact that he had two sisters who were practicing Lutherans, how he ended up in D.C., his unhappiness with his marriage, his approach to his job, and recent decisions he made about his life, such as spending more time at the office.

Yes, all the way down the line. She noticed that Adam's hands were trembling and his complexion was changing colors.

Adam stared into his drink for a long while. This whole situation was getting weirder by the moment, and he was beginning to lose his bearings. He did not like the feeling. He did not get the point of any of this, and he felt a sudden need to get away.

He motioned the bartender for the check and took thirty dollars out of his wallet.

Then, he glanced in Riley's direction. "It's been nice chatting with you, Riley." He slid the check and the cash toward the bartender. "Good luck with your book." He got up and walked out of the bar without looking back.

Riley sat there pondering what happened. Or what she thought happened. What is going on here? Why did he leave? Is this a dream, or my imagination?

She looked around the small room. It looked and felt real. Nothing else had changed. There were the same people around her she had seen minutes before.

She took a sip of her drink before deciding that more alcohol was probably not a good idea just now. She waved for her check and paid it promptly.

Before leaving, she swiveled on her stool and looked around the room one more time, as if grounding herself in a conventional reality. She massaged the part of her arm that Adam touched. Except for him, everybody here seemed normal, even if they were unknown to her. At the moment, she did not want to know any of them. She slid slowly off her stood and walked toward the door. She stepped out into the sunshine—it was still light out—and started walking back toward her apartment.

'I thought Edward was weird' was a thought that went through her mind. I think I owe him an apology. This is the most bizarre thing that has happened to me in my entire life.

The rest of her short walk home was mentally vacant. She did not know what to think. She was not even sure what she knew. Her mind was cluttered with what she believed to be real things that she knew were not possible.

Once inside her apartment, she sat down on the small couch and stared at the wall across the room. She began to sense the shock morph into feelings of fear. Fear that she was losing her mind.

## — 69 —

She sat on the couch throughout the entire night. The fear came in waves: sometimes it hit her like a storm surge, and her body reacted by shaking, becoming nauseous, and holding onto herself with her arms tightly across her chest. At other times, it was as if the life force abandoned her completely, and she felt invertebrate on the not-very-comfortable couch. She could not make heads or tails of the ideas going through her mind. The incongruities were just too big; the impossibility of it all too clear; the collision of these two things was monstrous.

Is this what losing one's mind feels like?

Sometime near dawn she fell asleep. Not a restful sleep, but one of sheer mental and physical exhaustion.

She awoke about nine o'clock. She could see the clock on her desk and shuddered to think that this was the time she would ordinarily start writing. Now even the idea of touching her computer just compounded her anxiety.

What happens when a person just can't go on?

Silence.

I asked you a question.

A small, distant voice inside her head said quietly, 'people go on.'

Riley remembered how irritating her internal voices could be, often cajoling her, challenging her, helping her. She often resented it. But the distance she felt from this tiny voice in her head now made her feel closer to the edge, less connected to reality.

She tried to clear her mind using a meditation technique she had learned years before: it entailed repeating a mantra, a nonsense syllable, over and over in one's mind to the exclusion of everything else.

She had not meditated for several years but fortunately found the skill still available to her. It was even helpful. She felt her body calming down, her mind becoming more tranquil, and the muscles of her body relaxing.

She did not want to stop but felt that sufficient time had passed. She needed to decide what to do. And she needed to decide soon.

"How did it go?" Edward asked 'Adam,' whose real name was Todd.

"Fine," he replied. "I think she bought it completely." He glanced down at the table. "But it was getting weird for me. I think she was having a hard time with this. It was as if she believed it, like she wasn't acting."

Edward nodded. "Excellent," he said. "As I told you when we were prepping, it is vital that each character in the scene not know who the other actors are or when they show up. I understand that this can be troubling for all the participants at times."

It sure can, Todd thought, but what the man said made sense: he had indeed prepared him that way, but it still freaked him out more than he thought it would. He wondered vaguely if there was a future in acting for him, after all.

Edward pulled out an envelope from his backpack and handed it to Todd. He felt satisfied that Todd had sold the persona of Riley's character Adam well enough. Edward knew this because he had listened to the entire conversation between the writer and her character-come-to-life. He had a triumphant feeling of satisfaction that he had rarely, if ever, had before in his life.

"I want you to know how important this has been in my overall project," he said, following the script he had prepared beforehand. "I will let you know more when it is completed, as we discussed."

The young man nodded and put the envelope in his inside jacket pocket. He needed the money badly and was glad to get it.

The pair stood up. Edward looked at him. "The microphone?"

"Oh, yes," Todd said. He pulled it from the inside of his lapel and handed it to Edward. The two shook hands. Todd went one way; Edward sat back down and watched him leave. Only one of them knew that they would never meet again; the other did not care.

Edward had found Todd at an actors' studio in Norfolk, a town that was a far enough from D.C. so as not to have an obvious connection. Edward had contacted him with an offer to play a part in a documentary he was doing, which was in fact a fabricated narrative, the sole but unspoken aim of which was to cause Riley the kind of mental anguish she had visited upon him. In short, he wanted to drive her crazy, or as crazy as possible.

This was his genius idea, a thought so intoxicating that he did not understand how he hadn't thought of it sooner. He spent too much time with silly, made-for-TV fantasies of getting back at Riley before he realized that he could create his own unique method by using her own creation against her.

It had taken time and money, as he had anticipated, but he did not mind that. For a period of several weeks, he immersed himself in his new project, devoting all of his time to assembling the necessary parts of the plan. He found someone in Maryland to teach him how to hack into desktop. This enabled him to read her unfolding novel. His hacking mentor also taught him how to remotely activate the camera and microphone features on her machine, a feature that enabled him to keep an eye on Riley whenever he wanted. He had a good sense of when she would leave her apartment.

And this was the genius part: to obliterate the line between reality and fantasy. Few people, Edward reasoned, could bear that experience intact. And it was his sincerest hope that Riley would not.

He learned where to buy small microphones specifically designed to surreptitiously record conversations and how to set them up properly. He had arranged for Todd to have one active during the entire time he was with Riley in the bar, enabling him to listen and record the entire episode.

All of this had been quite a learning curve in addition to being an elaborate fabrication; but it was an exhilarating ride. And it was surprisingly easy to find assistance in these matters, many aspects of which were probably illegal.

Edward was as sure as could reasonably be expected that he had covered his tracks well. He had never been so thorough about anything in his life, and he was by temperament a thorough guy. He was proud of himself.

And he could now feel that revenge was being served. It was such a delicious feeling, he could not help but do something to celebrate, so he stopped at a bar on his way home and ordered a Diet Coke. He just wanted to be around other people. He felt like one of them: one man among many, a vindicated man. A man who knew how to visit punishment upon those who wronged him.

# — 71 —

It took the better part of the following day for Riley to feel something akin to normal, albeit with caveats. The waves of fear had receded with meditation and additional sleep. It helped to eat something, which she often forgot to do when stressed. She took deep breaths and recalled some yoga poses that she had learned in the past. In short, she spent a rudderless day doing deliberate things to take care of herself in any way she could think of.

She considered contacting her last therapist, but then decided that this might not be the best course of action. As she recalled, she left her last session with that woman feeling at loose ends and never went back to clear those up. She just did not think she was the right person for the moment.

She thought of Jennifer, but she felt the prospects there were mixed. True, Jen had helped her get a bead on who Edward was, how to contact him, and all the rest. She even called the guy to tell him to back off. . .

Riley stopped. Edward. Could this whole thing be an elaborate ruse? An evil, deliberate plan? Could Edward be behind this somehow? Was this whole thing some sort of sick set-up? She had been so focused on 'Adam,' even though she tried mightily to push him out of her mind, that she had not considered the larger picture. Mostly what she had been thinking about was how engaging 'Adam' was, how sincere he seemed. How real.

Seemed. Another word that gave her pause. There was no doubt in her mind that she had believed everything that person, whatever his name was, said. She saw no reason to doubt him. She still didn't, despite the fact that the whole thing was too preposterous to be true.

Her thoughts turned back to Edward. She had no idea how he could have or would have contrived to do something like this, but he was the only person she knew who might have such a powerful grudge against her. She thought back over her history, going back to her childhood, trying to list the people she thought she hurt. It was short. She was always a nice kid.

But how? How would Edward possibly know what was only on her computer?

She looked across the room at the desktop that now seemed radioactive. That is the only place where the story is written. Then she realized it was also on a flash drive in case of a computer crash. She got up and checked to see if it was still in the drawer where she kept it. It was. She pulled out her laptop and booted it up to see if the manuscript was there. It was not, as she kept that machine purely for personal purposes.

She felt not so much relieved as enlightened a bit. This prospect did not exactly move anything forward very much, but it gave her another angle to think about.

Riley felt she still needed to talk to someone. This is too crazy for one person to handle.

Mildred popped into her mind. A sensation of warmth flashed across her body, and a light went on in her mind. I can talk to Mildred.

She got up to look for the business card Mildred had given her with her private cell number on it. It also had the door code for the shelter.

She pulled out her phone and hesitated a bit. Then, she forced herself to dial the number. She glanced at the clock: 4:30 p.m. Riley did not know what kind of hours Mildred kept.

"Hi, Riley."

"Mildred, hi. Thank you for picking up." Riley started to cry, something she had not anticipated. "Uh, um, I'm sorry . . . I have a situation . . ." Then the tears kept her from being able to speak.

"Riley, where are you?"

"At my apartment," Riley chocked out.

"Can you come here, or do you want me to come there?"

Riley felt like a child alone in the woods. Her adult self was mortified, but she could not help herself. "Could you come here?" she said in a small, quivering voice.

"Give me your address."

Riley complied.

"Ten minutes."

"Thank you," Riley squeaked.

She clicked off and through all the embarrassment and unanticipated emotion felt relief. All I have to do is make it through the next ten minutes. She went over and pulled the plug of her computer out of the wall without touching any other part of it.

Mildred arrived in precisely ten minutes.

Riley recognized her voice over the intercom and pushed the button to open the building door. She listened intently as the elevator made its typical noises. When she heard the final bell announcing the floor, she opened her door and saw Mildred, who spotted her immediately.

Riley threw her arms around her before the pair even went inside the apartment. "Thank you so much for coming," Riley said.

Mildred did not say anything. She held Riley for a few moments. Then she pulled away and looked Riley straight in the eye. "I know trouble when I hear it," she said gently.

The pair walked into Riley's apartment and sat on the couch.

The two women held hands. Riley noticed absently that Mildred did not look around, as most first-time visitors to her place usually did. She is entirely focused on her.

"Tell me everything you can about what happened."

Riley nodded and started tentatively. "I've got to say first that what I am about to share with you is preposterous and possibly deranged. I am not quite sure of my sanity just now." Riley realized that her throat was dry and that she had not offered Mildred anything to drink. "Excuse me," she said, and stood up. "I am thirsty. Would you like something to drink?"

Mildred shook her head. "No, but go ahead."

Riley went to the kitchen, where she poured herself a glass of water. Mentally, she was trying to construct a coherent narrative of events that made no sense to her. She returned to the couch, sat down, and looked at Mildred mournfully. "I can't tell you how much it means to me that you are here. I did not know what to do." Tears filled her eyes.

Mildred nodded and took Riley's hand. "I am glad to be here, Riley," she said softly.

Riley took a deep breath. "Okay. Here is the situation. I've been working on a book about a couple named Adam and Suzanne. The story picks up during the later stages of their relationship; their marriage is falling apart. They separate. Things happen." She shook her head as if she were watching a video of the action in her manuscript. "The last thing I wrote was about Adam was that he decided to get on with his life and meet up with an old friend." She paused and took a sip of water. "They were to meet at a bar."

Riley look across the room, as if embarrassed by what she was going to say next. "So, I sort of took a cue from my character, and in a sort of muddled conversation with myself—I talk to myself a lot—I decided I wanted to start making connections with other people." Another sip of water.

"So I shut down my computer and walked down the street to that bar on the corner. I'd never been there before. In fact, I'd never been to a bar by myself before. I just wanted to be around people. I didn't even want to drink; I had a tonic and lime."

Riley stared at the floor for a moment. "The place starts filling up, and this guy comes and sits down on the stool next to me. I smile at him; he says 'hi;' we start talking."

"After a while, he mentions that his name is Adam, which is the name of the character in the book. And then he says he's recently divorced." Riley looked toward the ceiling. She did not know if this made sense or if she made it up or if it was a dream. She stared until she felt Mildred squeeze her hand gently, just enough to get her attention.

"What happened then, Riley?"

Another long exhale. "I start feeling really, really weird. Like this can't be happening. I recover a bit, and I say to him something like 'Let's see about other stuff.' And I start listing everything I know about Adam and Suzanne. And he confirms every detail I come up with."

"So, then I get even more weirded out, and he gets up and leaves." She paused a moment. "I think I scared him; I think he was kind of freaked out."

"So, then I came home, and I've been pretty much on this couch since that happened yesterday."

"Jesus," exclaimed Mildred. "Riley," she continued. "How are you doing right now, at this moment?"

Riley shook her head. "I'm not sure. Okay, I think. Better. It feels so good that you're here." She shook her head some more. "This all sounds so crazy, but okay. I think."

"Good." Mildred looked down for a bit, as if arranging her thoughts.

"Let's start at the beginning." Then she turned and glanced around the room for the first time. She focused on the desktop computer. "Is that thing on?"

Riley shook her head. "I unplugged it right after I called you."

"Good. Let's take that a step further." She got up and took a towel from the kitchen and covered the computer screen. "I understand that it is even possible sometimes to turn these things back on remotely." She returned to the couch.

"When we met, you told me about a man by the name of Edward McAlister. Do you remember?"

"Yes, I remember."

"Do you think he is capable of doing something like this?"

Riley thought for a moment. "I don't know," she said. "But I thought of him earlier, before I called you. I was wondering who to call, and I thought of the conversation Jennifer had with him, and I stopped cold at his name. Then, I started thinking of people who might have a grudge against me, and he was the only person I could think of who might." She looked at Mildred. "I tried to talk to him a while back, but he ran away before I could explain myself."

She continued. "After you and I spoke, I was thinking of how to approach him again. But I hadn't come to any firm conclusions about that. In fact, I sort of let it go, as I felt so much better after we spoke." She took a sip of water. "I really didn't give Edward much thought until earlier, as I said."

Mildred had an intense look on her face as she listened closely to what Riley was telling her. She was also thinking. After a few moments, Mildred said, "Usually the most obvious explanation is the correct one." More thinking. Then: "But first, let me be clear about this: This was no coincidence. This was a planned . . . " she searched for the right word. "A planned assault on your sanity." She shuddered slightly. "It's despicable. It may even be criminal."

Riley listened intently to what Mildred was saying, and she wanted with all her heart to believe her. But the past eighteen hours of questioning herself, feeling waves of fear and dread, and questioning everything she knew had taken a toll. She wasn't sure what to believe.

She did not say anything.

Mildred did not take her eyes off her. "Somehow—and we do not know how right now—but somehow, somebody, probably Edward, figured out a way to get ahold of your manuscript and coach someone to play the part of one of your characters."

When Riley did not say anything, Mildred added. "Trust me, Riley. This was a deliberate assault."

Riley looked at Mildred with a hint of skepticism she could not disguise. "How do you know?"

Mildred exhaled. "I've never seen anything quite this sophisticated, but I've seen people in relationships devise ways to make their partners feel crazy, to make them question everything they know, to degrade their ability to think clearly." Her eyes bored into Riley's. "Sometimes it's deliberate; sometimes it's unconscious. But it's always heinous. It can be worse than physical assault. Nothing is more important to a human being than the ability to think clearly and objectively about ourselves, our lives, and our relationships."

A silence descended on the room as the two women sat together without speaking. Mildred did not take her eyes off Riley; in her mind, she was hoping that Riley had not been so damaged by this incident that she would not believe her. Riley kept shaking her head, unsure what to think.

It was Riley who spoke next. "This all sounds so crazy." She paused a moment. "So what can I do?"

"I cannot emphasize enough how important it is to do precisely what you're doing right now. Talking. Being honest. Sharing details. Letting somebody in." She patted Riley's hand gently. "This is not something you should deal with by yourself. We need to get to work."

## — 72 —

The work did not look to be easy. First, they had to establish whether someone hacked into Riley's computer. Then they had to figure out a way to identify the man Riley met at the bar. And then they had to figure out if Edward was indeed the person behind this.

It quickly became a tall order with unclear details about precisely how to do the tasks involved. Mildred asked Riley if she knew anyone who was familiar with computer security.

"I am not sure, but maybe my friend Jen. She was the one who found Edward's name and details online. It took her no time, and she had a bead on him. It was impressive."

"Call her," said Mildred.

Riley looked at Mildred with dismay, as if she weren't ready to move away from the safe space the two had created. But Mildred's face bespoke a firmness that gave her some courage. She picked up her phone and dialed Jennifer's number.

"Hi, Honey," said Jen.

Riley felt the blood drain from her face as she started talking. "Hi, Jen. Um, something has happened. I am here at my apartment with Mildred, the woman who runs the shelter I told you about. We . . . I have a problem."

Jennifer's ears perked up. "Riley, what happened?" When this was met with silence, she said, "What can I do to help you? You know I'll do anything."

Riley paused and glanced at Mildred. "It might be best if you could come over?"

"I'll be there as soon as I can."

"Thanks, Honey." Riley clicked off and stared at the phone for a moment; then she returned her gaze to Mildred.

"Thank you so much for being here, Mildred. I have been beside myself for the past twenty-four hours."

Mildred responded with a cross between a nod and a shrug. "This is what I do, Honey. And the fact is I was relieved when you called. It let me know that you are capable of trusting someone." She looked into Riley's eyes. "I think it's a good sign that you reached out for help."

Riley did not know exactly what that meant or even what it might mean, but she nodded thoughtfully.

Fifteen minutes later, Jennifer was at the front door of her building. Riley buzzed her in and waited in silence until she got to her floor. The pair hugged each other tightly.

Then Riley introduced Jennifer to Mildred, and the two women hugged gently.

Riley went through the whole experience another time to bring Jennifer up to date. Jennifer listened carefully, her mouth open and her eyes widening as she listened to tell the story. She did not want to interrupt, but she could hardly believe what she was hearing. She kept thinking this was not possible.

When Riley finished there was silence in the room, each woman having her own thoughts.

Finally, Mildred spoke. "I asked Riley if she knew anyone who could tell whether her computer had been hacked. Your name came up right away."

Riley spoke up. "I was so impressed when you tracked Edward down so quickly a while back. I thought you might be able to tell."

Jennifer thought for a moment. What she knew that the other two women didn't was that she had exhausted her pool of computer skills that evening she worked furiously to track down Edward online. She did not want to disappoint her friend or this other woman, but she figured this was no time to equivocate.

Jen shook her head "I'm sorry, Riley, that is beyond my capabilities." She thought for a moment. "But I might know somebody who has the skills to do this or could at least tell us where to go."

Mildred and Riley looked at Jennifer expectantly.

"Let me check," Jen said, and she picked up her phone. But before she dialed, she had a thought. "Are you sure Edward hacked into your computer? Could he have bugged this place?"

The three women exchanged glances and simultaneously stood up. "Good thought," said Mildred.

A kind of tribal techno awareness descended upon the women as they prepared to leave. Each one independently powered down their respective phones and silently filed out of the room. They wordlessly descended in the elevator. When they stepped outside, they looked at each other and exhaled simultaneously.

"Well, there are uses for paranoia," said Mildred. The other two women chuckled humorlessly as they kept walking. "My place," Mildred said, pointing down the next street. "We'll be safe there. It's swept for electronic surveillance routinely. The safety of our clients is our number one concern.

Edward sat at the bar for some time, savoring his triumph and wondering how Riley's downfall would play out. He figured that it would take some time, but he was in no rush. In the meantime, he could not help replaying every step of his path toward victory. He recalled just where he was and what he was thinking when the Big Idea came to him. He felt the rush of the frenetic activity that followed: finding and contacting people on the fringe, people he would never have considered seeking in his life but for Riley. He recalled the fear he felt as he began this journey and how that fear was overcome time and time again by his commitment to the vengeful path that he had chosen for himself.

He realized right away that there would be a lot of prep work before he could start turning his Big Idea into a reality. The last thing he wanted was to get caught or expose himself, and in order to minimize that possibility he had to put distance between himself and whomever he might meet. At minimum he had to forge a new online identity. He had heard about virtual private networks but did not know much about them. He did some research, which informed him that it would prevent anyone from tracking him online or locating his computer. He signed up immediately. He would also need an untraceable phone. The local drugstore had just the thing: a no-contract, 'burner' phone that had a set amount of data and talk time that he could buy with cash. Then he set up a dummy business and gave himself a phony name and a different email address. Each of these things proved surprisingly easy to do.

Edward smiled as he thought about how simple it was to set up a phony identity and a fake business. He went so far as to rent a mailing address at one of those postal stores and registering a company name with the Department of Consumer and Regulatory Affairs. Now, for all intents and purposes, he was legal. Sort of. What made it illegal, he imagined, was the nefarious purpose behind all this commercial activity: to inflict pain; to take someone down.

He felt a rush of emotion of a type he had never experienced before. It was a kind of physical and emotional excitement that he had read about in crime novels. Edward had never done an illegal thing in his life, and he wondered from time to time whether this was something he was missing. He was beginning to appreciate its appeal.

But that was just preliminary work. Once that was in place, his next step, of course, was gaining access to Riley's computer. He thought this would be the hardest part, so he chose to tackle it first. He started searching online for hackers and how to find them. He knew enough about computers to do this using the VPN and a 'private' setting on his browser so as not to leave a trail. And what he discovered amazed him at first and then thrilled him. He hooked into the dark web, where hackers actually advertised their services. Some not only hacked, but also gave lessons on how to do it. It was a whole cottage industry about which he knew absolutely nothing before he started.

He arranged to meet with a man in Maryland who went by the name of Bomber17; apparently, this was some vague historic reference Edward neither knew nor cared about. They met up at a shady bar in an even shadier part of a small rural town. Bomber17 was a scruffy, chunky, forty-something-year-old man; these features surprised Edward, who assumed all hackers were emaciated millennials. But despite Mr. Bomber17's throwback looks, he could not have been a more articulate or enthusiastic teacher. Edward wondered how he ended up giving people clandestine hacking lessons but thought it unwise to ask. Despite the issues this meeting would have raised for Edward in the past—the probable illegality of what he was doing, the fact that he was dealing with someone he would never choose to talk to in any other context—he forged ahead, dismissing them all. This got surprisingly easy to do once the duo began working on the mechanics of learning how to hack into someone else's computer without that person's knowledge.

Bomber17 did not pretend that what they were doing was legal. But he was an excellent teacher, and Edward was a student on a mission. They met for three days running—something which cost Edward more money than he had ever spent on any one thing in his life—but he relished every minute of the time. And, he reasoned, what is money for if not to use on one's own behalf?

At the end of the third day, Edward felt confident and Bomber felt flush, feelings that culminated in a kind of warmth between them. Enough so that Bomber hugged Edward when they parted and told him to contact him at any time if he hit a snag. They parted in a cloud of cozy friendship that was completely unfamiliar to Edward, partly because he could not recall ever being hugged by a man, and partly because the man in question fit comfortably in the deplorable category, despite his extensive knowledge base and solid pedagogic skills.

Edward left that meeting with what he felt was a firm grasp on the skills he needed to proceed to the next step. And that entailed accessing Riley's computer, putting those new skills to good use. He was nervous at first and attempted it during a time when he figured Riley would not be in her apartment. This meant that he had to do some in-person surveillance to determine her habits. He donned a broad-brimmed hat—just like the spy novels—and took up a position as far away from her apartment building as possible. He figured she often went for coffee after her writing in the afternoon, and this turned out to be accurate. After confirming this on two separate occasions, he felt secure that 4:00 p.m. would be the preferred time to try out his new skills.

He sat at his computer and began following the steps he had learned from Bomber17. After a few frustrating unsuccessful attempts, her desktop suddenly appeared on his screen. He inhaled sharply and was filled with a sense of wonder and power, as adrenaline coursed through his body. 'I'm in charge now' was such an intoxicating realization; it amped up his motivation even more and validated his agenda. He was sure he was on the right path.

He found the manuscript she was working on and downloaded a copy of it to a flash drive. Then he read it on her machine just because he could. He read it with close attention, knowing that he had to track what she was writing very closely in order to get the timing right of the next phase of his plan. He kept one eye on his watch to monitor the time. He did not want to overstay his visit.

Before he logged off, he followed Bomber's directions for remotely turning on Riley's camera and microphone. Now he was able to see if she was in front of her machine, and he could listen to the ambient noises, enabling him to know if she was at home or not. The power this accorded him gave Edward chills.

With everything in place, he logged off and felt certain that no trace of his presence could be detected. Bomber17 had shown him just what to do to avoid detection, and Edward followed every step very carefully.

He studied the manuscript for days, taking copious notes and committing every significant detail to memory. When he was satisfied, he revisited Riley's computer in order to find out exactly what was happening in the narrative. He dared not download anything else; he did not want to risk exposure any more than he had to. He just wanted to remain current on what the characters in her book were doing.

The next step was finding someone to play the part of Adam, the character he chose to reproduce in the flesh. It made sense to Edward that it would be natural for Riley to encounter a man in some setting where there could be flirtation or sexual interest: a coffee shop or a bar. Sexual undertones created just the kind of chaos he was looking for, he thought. It could even be a department store or someplace public, but a bar or coffee shop sounded right. It was, after all, a coffee shop where he and Riley met.

Now that Edward had a way to surveil Riley in her apartment, he felt he would have some idea of where she was going or what she was doing. This felt much safer for him than physically trying to observe her, where he might be noticed.

He started searching for acting schools outside the District but within a reasonable driving distance. He did not want to connect with anyone too close. He found numerous offerings in northern Virginia, which to him seemed like an extension of the greater Washington area. He looked further out. Norfolk, a comfortable four-hour drive, was where he found Todd.

Everyone at this particular school had head shots on the school's website, along with basic information about what they had done professionally, what their interests were, and other details that might interest someone looking to them for a gig or for signing up for the school.

He filtered by sex, age, and general appearance. Todd caught his attention immediately. He had done a few commercials and some summer stock, so he had some experience, but no one would have called that experience a career. He looked younger than his age and fit what Adam looked like in Edward's imagination. He was also thinking he was someone who might need money.

Edward sat at his computer composing a message.

*Hi, Todd. I saw your promo on the acting school's website. Am looking for a young man to act in an upcoming documentary. This is a one-time opportunity that may lead to further shoots in the future. It is, of course, a paid position. Please let me know if you are interested. Deadline for application is next week. Randall Sheets, Producer.*

He ended it with his contact information.

Not bad, thought Edward as he sat back and reviewed the message. He hit 'send' and stared at his screen for a while, feeling a rush of adrenaline course through his body. He was surprised when a response came within five minutes. Todd must be hungry, he thought, confirming his suspicion.

Very hungry, as it turned out. Todd had spent the last of his meager savings for the tuition to the acting school he was attending. Edward questioned him on the phone about his experience and goals. Then, he agreed to meet up personally with him to explain the 'project' he was working on.

They met the following day at a coffee shop in Norfolk. Edward found Todd to be engaging and committed to a career in acting. He had done some commercials, as his online entry indicated, but it had been some time since his last gig. He said he thought of giving up on acting but got very excited when he received Mr. Sheets' email.

"Acting is where I belong," he said with more confidence than his experience seemed to warrant. But Edward had to admit he knew very little about forging a career in acting or any of the arts for that matter. His impression of Todd was that he was sincere and not without charm, even if he was somewhat naïve. He struck Edward as earnest but not untalented. He had the ability to engage 'Mr. Sheets' in a spirited conversation about what he was looking for in his life, and he did it in a jocular, self-effacing way that was attractive. This struck Edward as an important skill, as he would need to engage Riley as quickly as possible.

He hired him. When Edward told Todd how much he was willing to pay, his new employee got even more engaging, even excited. The pair spent the rest of their time together talking about the specifics: things Todd needed to know, how he should dress, how he should respond to the woman Edward would arrange for him to meet. "Now it's very important to understand that, while this woman will also be an actor, she will not know you are. This is to guarantee as much realism as possible and is critical to the success of the overall project."

Todd nodded at this as if it were a sensible statement. He must really need the money, Edward thought.

Edward and Todd wrapped up their conversation and discussed the next step. Mr. Sheets would contact Todd when everything was ready, and Todd had to be ready on short notice.

Again, Todd nodded as if this would present no difficulty, and the two parted with an apparently shared goal: the success of the documentary that would further both their careers.

On the drive home, Edward thought about how easy it was to lie to another person. He was not given to dissimulation: it always seemed to lead to more stress and untenable situations. As a rule, telling the truth always struck him as the easiest way to live; in fact, he made this point to his students whenever he caught them lying.

But in this situation, it seemed almost natural. He knew he was being devious and perhaps he should feel guilty, but he didn't. He felt quite normal, in fact, more normal than he usually did. This must be how actors feel when they play a role.

Edward always knew he wasn't like other people. This never bothered him much; it was just the way things were. Maybe most people feel that way, he thought from time to time, but the truth was he did not know and did not care. What he cared about was what he cared about, and at the moment, what he cared about was taking due revenge on Riley for destroying the single possibility of true happiness in his life.

— 74 —

Mildred took out her electronic pass card to open a side entrance of the shelter where she worked. She led Riley and Jennifer to her office, which was only a few steps away. They did not encounter anyone between the door and her office.

She motioned for the two women to take a seat on the couch and then excused herself without explanation. "I'll be back in a few minutes," she said as she walked out of the room.

Riley and Jennifer sat in silence for a while. Riley was struggling with her thoughts and feelings in a way she had never quite done before. Jennifer just looked around the spare but not unappealing space. Riley kept turning the things Mildred said over and over in her mind. She believed Mildred; or rather, she really, really, really wanted to believe her, especially when the older woman seemed so sure that someone, most likely Edward, had set up this entire situation to get back at her.

She wasn't quite there yet. Mildred was certainly firm in her belief, but it all seemed so improbable to Riley that anyone would go to such lengths to hurt her. No one had ever deliberately tried to hurt her throughout her entire life. Never. Unfortunately, that meant that she could not quite relinquish the notion that somehow she had fallen into some weird, previously unexperienced mental state that was outside the spectrum of normal.

She tried to think of all the things that Edward would have had to do to pull off such a charade. Somehow break into her computer and hire people to play characters in her manuscript? It sounded so preposterous. And why? Because she did not want to date him?

295

That seemed like a terrible reason to deliberately attempt to make someone feel crazy and attempt to ruin her life. And she could not even begin to imagine what it would have taken in time and money to do this. Unless, of course, this was something Edward did routinely. She wondered if it was possible that he was that psychopathic.

As if echoing her thoughts, Jennifer, who had been surveying the surprisingly pleasant office of the director of a woman's shelter, turned to Riley and said, "Do you think Edward could really do this? You described him as shy, which is one thing. But this, I don't know, malevolent stuff is on a whole other level." She paused and looked Riley in the eye. "I really don't understand, Riley," she said.

Riley did not know exactly what to say except for the most obvious thing, embarrassing but honest as it was. "Do you think I'm just crazy, Jen?" she blurted out.

Jennifer's eyebrows tented. "You don't seem crazy to me, Honey," she said, reaching across the couch and patting her shoulder. "But you've just been through something that most people mercifully never experience."

This conversation was interrupted by Mildred's return. "Sorry, I just had to give some instructions to the staff." She looked at the two younger women. "Would either of you like something to drink? Water? Coffee? Tea?"

Both women shook their head. Jennifer spoke first. "Where do we go from here, Mildred? What do we need to do?"

"That's why we're here, Jennifer," Mildred replied. "To figure out the best way to proceed."

The three women started discussing the situation in the most specific terms possible based on what they knew, reviewing every detail Riley could remember and anything Jennifer, who knew her better than anyone, might surmise. Mildred and Jennifer asked Riley as many questions as they could in an effort to get ahold of a larger perspective of what was possible, what was probable, and what was just plain unlikely.

This took a toll on Riley, who could not get the idea out of her head that it was too much to think that someone—anyone—would go to such lengths to hurt her. And she held onto this thought throughout the conversation.

Finally, with a tiny hint of exasperation, Mildred looked at her and said, "Riley, there are two possibilities here: either someone set out to deliberately hurt you and make you feel miserable or you have completely lost your mind." She looked at her with an uncompromising expression on her face and a definite firmness in her tone. "Since I have been with you for the past few hours, I have seen no signs of significant mental illness. I see someone who is working through a highly improbable, highly painful emotional experience that she is having trouble wrapping her mind around." She continued to stare at Riley for some moments, who in turn looked back at her with no small amount of apprehension.

"Now I want to ask you a few questions," Mildred said. "What day is it?"

Riley looked at her uncomprehending. "Tuesday," she said.

"What is your name?"

"Riley Cotswald."

"What is the date?"

Riley gave her the date.

"I want you to count backwards from 100 by sevens."

Riley looked at her with a skeptical look and started. "100.93.86.79.72.65. . ."

"Good enough. Now spell 'world.'"

"W-O-R-L-D."

"Spell it backwards."

"D-L-R-O-W."

"Have you heard any voices outside your head that were present when no one else was?"

"No."

"Do you believe you have seen something that no one else could see?"

Riley thought about that for a moment. "You mean, like, apparitions?"

"Yes, like apparitions."

"No, of course not."

"In light of the above, which is what is called a mental status test, something professionals use to determine the extent of mental illness, I conclude that you are not suffering from psychosis. You may be anxious or depressed, but that's it. And even those miseries are not negatively impacting your cognitive functions."

Riley flashed on the word 'supercilious' to describe the look on Mildred's face. "How can you be so sure?"

"Because I am a mental health professional licensed by the District to diagnosis and treat mental disorders." Mildred said. Her facial expression and her tone softened considerably. "I've had quite a bit of experience with this kind of thing."

A kind of gentle firmness returned to Mildred's voice. "I know you are torn about this, Riley, but the fact is you need to get your mind around what is actually happening and stop harboring the irrational notion that there is something mysteriously wrong with you, an idea based primarily, if not exclusively, on fear, which only gets in the way of dealing with a very difficult, even dangerous situation."

Riley looked down. Then, she glanced at Jennifer, whose face was pale. She looked back at Mildred. "I don't know what to say."

"Say what you believe to be true."

Riley looked at one woman, then the other. She could feel anger rising within her, a feeling she attributed to being scolded by an older woman. She hated this. She was angry.

It showed. "So, you're angry," said Mildred.

"Yes."

"Tell me about it."

"No."

"Tell her about it!" interjected Jennifer after a too-long pause.

Riley looked wide-eyed at her friend. Then, she looked back at Mildred. "I'm . . . I'm . . . angry at how you talked to me."

"Anything else?"

Riley closed her eyes. She did not want to say what she knew she needed to say. "And I'm furious that someone would do this to me!" She shot up and walked to Mildred's desk across the room. She turned away from the others and leaned on the desk as much to hide her tears as for physical support. "How could someone, anyone, do this to me?" she shouted toward the window. Her whole body began to shake as the tears fell and the rage leapt out of her. "I hate whoever did this to me!" She stood motionless for some moments.

Jennifer glanced at Mildred, who simply nodded. Jen got up slowly and walked over to Riley. She put her arms around her. "It's okay, Honey. It's okay."

Riley did not look up. "No, it's not, Jen," she said. "No, it's not." She turned to face her friend. "Nothing about this is okay."

The three women were motionless for some minutes. Finally, Mildred got up and walked over to her desk, where she sat down facing Riley. "You are right, Riley. It's not even close to okay." She had the same hard, certain look on her face. "For one person to do this to another human being is evil. It's criminal."

Riley leaned down from the waist and buried her head in her folded arms on the desk. She cried and cried and made guttural noises that Jennifer had never heard from another human being. It was anguish: primal, desperate, powerful.

Mildred did not move. She sat in her desk chair, watching Riley experience what she knew she had to feel. It was tough, but it was necessary.

After a few minutes—long minutes, to be sure—the weeping and screeching began to abate. Riley stood upright, but she did not take her hands off the desk. "I need to sit down," she said, and walked a bit unsteadily toward the couch. Once there, she plopped herself down and just looked dazed.

Mildred stood up and opened a cabinet on the wall near her desk. From it she took out two glasses and a pitcher of water. She filled the glasses and walked over to the couch, where she handed one to Riley and one to Jennifer. Riley took a sip; Jennifer drank hers down.

Mildred retook the chair closest to Riley. "Do you believe me now?" she said gently.

Riley looked at her; then she looked at Jen; then her gaze returned to Mildred. "Yes," she said quietly but clearly. To Jennifer, who was sitting within two feet of her, it sounded like a different voice from the one she had been hearing from her friend. She wasn't sure what to make of that but decided it was better than the emotional maelstrom that she had just witnessed.

"Good," said Mildred. "I have an idea of where to start." Then, she turned her attention to Jennifer. "Jennifer, you said you might know someone who could look into Riley's computer to see whether it's been breached."

Jennifer nodded. "I think so, yes."

"Is it someone you trust?"

Jennifer glanced at Riley and then looked back at Mildred. "Honestly, it's just someone I work with. I don't trust him or not trust him. I don't really know him that well. Except I do know he's a computer whiz."

Mildred looked at both women. "I know someone else who may be able to help us. Someone I trust completely."

She took Riley's hand and then Jennifer's and squeezed softly. Then, she stood up and walked back to her desk. She took a key from her pocket and unlocked the bottom drawer of the desk. Mildred pulled out an old-fashioned address book, the kind people used before computers became so common. She looked up a number and picked up the telephone from her desk.

"Willard Bean, please," she said.

"Hi, Will. Mildred. I've got a situation I need your help with." After listening to a brief response, she said, "There's a woman here who's been the target of a serious mind fuck. We need help finding the perpetrator." More pausing as Mildred listened to his response. "Thanks, Will."

Mildred turned to the two other women. "Willard Bean is a private investigator, one of the best in the District. He can help us."

"What about the police?" asked Jennifer.

Mildred shrugged. "We don't have enough for them to go on. If we went to them now, they would blow you off as a hysterical woman who got dissed in a bar. Will used to be a D.C. cop. Once he gets a bead on whoever did this, he knows how to convey the information to the police in a way that will make a difference. Right now, we just need to trust him."

"How do you know him?" asked Riley.

"Will and I go back a long way. He has helped me deal with difficult situations on numerous occasions. He is a guy who comes through."

This seemed to satisfy Riley, who was beginning the feel that maybe Mildred's judgment had been functioning better than hers these past hours.

It did not take long for Willard to show up. A tall, lanky man of indeterminate middle age entered and greeted Mildred with a hug. She, in turn, introduced him to Riley and Jennifer.

Mildred nodded to Riley, who seemed to understand immediately that she had once again to recount the events of the previous few days. Willard listened closely. At one point, he raised his hand, indicating a pause, and pulled out a notebook and began taking notes. Then, he nodded again, and Riley continued.

He spoke in a steady but soft voice. "What was the name of the bar where this happened?"

"A.J.'s. It's on 14th Street."

Willard wrote that down. "And what time were you there?"

"About 4:15 or so. I was there probably less than an hour."

"Did you have a lot to drink?"

"No. I ordered a tonic and then a martini, but I only took a couple sips of the cocktail."

"Go on."

Riley finished telling the story. Jennifer kept thinking of how different Riley's voice was, how confidant she seemed to be, how certain she was of every detail. She wondered about her own role in this drama but decided that this would become clearer as the four people continued talking.

It did. After Willard finished with Riley, he turned to Jennifer. "And what is your relationship to Ms. Cotswald?"

"I'm her friend," said Jennifer unapologetically.

"Did you know anything about this business before it happened?"

"What do you mean?"

"Let me rephrase it: When did you learn about this incident?"

"Just today, when Riley called me."

Jennifer and Riley glanced at each other.

"There's a guy," Jennifer began, "who was put out with Riley and was stalking her, hanging out in front of her apartment building. We think. . . I think he was following her."

"Do you know who this guy is?" asked Will.

"Yes," interjected Riley. "Thanks to my friend Jennifer here, we were able to find out who he is and where he lives."

"Do you think he is capable of pulling something like this?"

Riley thought for a while as Jennifer looked on. "Honestly, I don't know. I met him in a coffee shop. He was the shy type, but otherwise seemed normal enough. We hooked up one time. He wanted to date me. I told him that was not possible. The last time I saw him and tried to tell him that, he went running, literally running away." She thought for a while and then looked Willard squarely in the eye. "Somebody did this, and he is the most likely."

Willard nodded. "I'll need his contact information if you have it."

Jennifer pulled out her phone and dictated the information to Willard Bean.

Willard was quiet for a while, wrapping his mind around what he had been hearing. He turned to Riley. "So, you are sure this Edward was stalking you?"

Riley did not hesitate. "Yes."

"And you said your friend Jennifer here helped you find out where he lives. How did you two do that?"

"We went . . . Jennifer went online and did some searching, the kind of stuff I really don't know how to do. She found his contact information in under twenty minutes."

"Impressive," said Willard. He turned to Jennifer. "You have pretty good computer skills?"

Jennifer nodded. "Not good enough to take this to the next level."

Willard's eyebrows raised. "Meaning . . . ?"

"Meaning that I can do Internet stuff pretty well—social media and all that, finding people—but when it comes to detecting computer hacks or viruses—all that really technical stuff—that's beyond my skill level." She nodded in Mildred's direction. "I told Mildred I might know someone who can help me with that, but it's just somebody I work with and really don't know that well."

Willard glanced at Mildred and then looked back at Jennifer. "Good. But I have someone I'd prefer to use."

"One more thing," Willard said. "Could you provide me with a photo of Edward?"

"Sure," said Jennifer. "If you give me your email address, I'll send you one right now." He did, and she pulled out her phone, tapped furiously for a few moments, and then sent the picture. "Done," she said.

Willard nodded to Jennifer and then turned to face all three women. "Anything else you think I might need to know?"

The three women shook their heads. Mildred spoke up first. "I think you've got a good picture, Will. I hope you can help us."

Willard nodded and closed his notebook. "I'm sure going to try, Mildred. How soon would you like me to start working on this?"

"As soon as possible."

Willard nodded and looked back at Riley. "I am going to check out the bar at A.J.'s to see if they have any surveillance cameras. If they do, I'll need you to see if you can identify the man who called himself Adam."

Riley nodded. Her anxiety spiked, but not by much. She was ready to do whatever it took. "Okay."

Willard stood up, hugged Mildred gently, and said, "I'll call you as soon as I know something." Then, he nodded to each of the other two women and left the office.

Mildred turned to Jen and Riley. "This may take some time, so don't feel a need to hang around here. I will let you know as soon as I hear from Will." She turned to Riley. "What do you want to do Riley, return to your apartment? Stay here at the shelter?"

"She can stay with me," interjected Jennifer, raising her head to face Mildred squarely.

Riley looked at her friend. "I would like that."

Mildred nodded. "That's fine with me." She looked as if she were about to say something else, but she stopped. After a brief pause, she said, "I'll be in touch soon."

Jennifer and Riley left the office and began walking toward Jen's apartment. "What a day," Jen said.

"Yeah," said Riley. "What a day."

## — 76 —

Edward waited a full day and a half before accessing Riley's computer again. He was eager to see and hear the results of his work, but he knew that being impulsive was a bad idea. He was in charge; he could afford to bide his time.

Around four o'clock, two days after the drama at the bar, he decided it was safe. He logged onto his machine and went through the careful steps to access Riley's computer.

Nothing. It was turned off. Hmm, he thought. This was unusual; she ordinarily kept it on, even if it was asleep. He wondered if her building had lost electricity or something.

He tried again an hour later. Still nothing. Then an hour after that. The same result.

Edward could feel anxiety rising in his body, but he reminded himself that he was in charge, and that all it took for him to stay in charge was for Riley to turn her machine back on.

He considered possible explanations. In addition to a power outage, it could be that Riley had gone to stay with someone else and turned her machine off. But the pesky notion that she suspected something kept rolling around in his head. Rationally, it did not seem likely to Edward, who had been so careful in the planning and execution of his actions.

Could she have gotten a new computer? That did not seem likely either, not in the state he believed her to be in. Could she have gone back to her husband? Another improbable scenario.

He concluded that he would just have to wait until tomorrow and try again. To assuage his gnawing anxiety, he went for a run.

He considered jogging past her apartment building but decided against it. No use drawing attention to himself now. Instead, he headed toward Navy Yard and the new developments along the Anacostia River. It was fresh and new and modern and hip. Just like his new self felt to him.

He ran and ran. He began doing sprints to increase his heart rate; then, he would slow down to an easier pace. He did the intervals five times, and by the end, he found himself walking in a cool-down mode back to his apartment, pleasantly exhausted by his workout and by the quieting of his mind.

Back in his apartment, he stripped off his clothes and got into the shower. Few things feel so good as a hot shower after a good run, he thought.

After getting dressed, he booted up his computer again. He was tempted to check in on Riley's machine, but he did not want to give into the impulse. He could wait another day. Surely she would be back online in the morning. Bomber17 had told him that, once he did the initial hack, he could surveil her computer at will without her detecting his presence, so he didn't have to wait until a time he thought she would not be there. The free access underscored the power he had been feeling since this began, and he looked forward to taking that unprecedented step in the morning.

In the meantime, he surfed around the Internet looking at some news sites and other interesting places. He spent some time on the Dark Web, which he had only recently discovered. It contained things he had never even known about: depraved things, for the most part. Things he wanted nothing to do with.

He surfed until it was time for bed. He turned his machine off and got ready to go to sleep, but his phone rang. He glanced at the small screen. Blocked call.

Edward froze. That woman? Could that be that same woman who called him a while back and threatened him? He looked at his phone. "Not today," he said to the small device. "Not anymore."

## 77

Willard Bean was familiar with A.J.'s. It's an upscale bar in a nice neighborhood frequented by a lot of professional people, government workers mostly, but a fair share of lawyers, lobbyists, and related types of humans who haunted the District. He had been there himself on a number of occasions. Enough to recognize the bartender.

"Hi, Jake," he said, loading himself onto a bar stool.

"Hey, Will," said Jake. "What'll it be?"

"I'm just here for information today. A couple days ago, there was a young woman in here around four or four-thirty: late twenties, pretty, black hair, tall, thin. She was by herself."

"I remember her, Will. She ordered a tonic and spent about half an hour being chatted up by a youngish guy in a suit." Jake glanced around. "Of course, that's not much of a description in a place like this. Then, she ordered a martini, but she didn't finish it. The guy had gotten up and left, I think in kind of a hurry."

"How did he pay?"

"Cash, okay tip," said the bartender.

Will took all this information in without comment. He was grateful for Jake's good memory.

"Do you have any surveillance cameras here, Jake?"

Jake shook his head. "Not in here, but we have some watching the front and rear entrances. Also, the bank across the street has fairly wide coverage with its surveillance system. It sweeps right up to our front door.

"Mind if I take a look at your feeds from two days ago?"

"Not a problem for me, Will. But let me check with the owner." He walked over to the corner of the bar and made a phone call. He returned two minutes later. "No problem," he said. "Come with me." He nodded to another bartender to take over.

The two went to a small back room with the recording equipment for the outside cameras. Jake double checked the time Will needed and pushed some buttons. Instantly, a video came up of several people entering the bar. Will spotted Riley entering the establishment; then he saw a man about the age and general description that Riley had given him. "Is that him?" he asked Jake. He noted the time: 4:25.

"Could be," Jake said.

"Can you fast forward thirty minutes?"

The two men watched the same man leaving the establishment in something of a hurry. He loosened his tie as soon as he left the bar and walked west, facing directly into the camera. A few minutes later, they watched Riley leave also. She looked shaken but steady on her feet.

"That's him," said Jake.

Will nodded. It looked like a match to him. "Let's check the rear cameras."

Jake looked skeptical but loaded the rear surveillance camera feeds for the same time. Nothing.

"Okay. Can I get a copy of those two segments we saw a few minutes ago?"

"No problem," said Jake, who downloaded the segments and sent it to an email address Will gave him.

"Thanks, Jake. This is very helpful."

"Glad I can help, Will."

"Anything else you recall about this woman or the guy she was talking to?"

"Yeah, actually there is. The reason I remember is that the man left in a hurry and seemed kind of agitated, and the woman seemed upset when she left. Almost as if she drank too much, but she only had a couple sips of the drink she ordered." He paused a bit. "I was a little concerned about her, but she made it out the door okay. And then we got real busy."

Will thanked him again and left the bar. He went back to his office to review the videos Jake sent him. As he did so, he dialed the number of a friend in the FBI, where a face recognition database was kept.

He emailed a still photo to his FBI friend and within ten minutes was looking at an image of Todd Wilhaber's face, which graced the front of his Virginia driver's license. "Okay, Todd", he said to his computer. "We will be meeting soon."

But not before doing what he understood most self-respecting millennials would do: he googled Todd to see what he could find on social media and whatever other footprint Todd had on the Web. He found the site of the acting studio and his CV page. He also found Facebook and Twitter accounts; although there did not seem to be much action on either. Willard was only passingly familiar with the newest forms of social media, such as Instagram and Snapchat, but he noticed that Todd used them as well.

In the end, he decided to contact a friend of his in the Department and asked him to run a criminal background check. He got a response within twenty minutes.

Todd had a sheet. That is, he had a history of arrests in his early twenties: assault, minor theft, disorderly conduct. His last arrest was two years ago, about a year before he started at the acting school. It looked as if his last job was about a year before that. Willard wondered how Todd managed to pay for school and support himself without steady employment. He also wondered if it really made any difference.

Will decided to go directly to Norfolk to find Todd rather than trying to contact him by phone. He did not want to spook him, and he felt there was some chance Todd could disappear before Will had a chance to question him.

But before that, he had more background work to do. He had some experience with hackers, but not much. He called another friend in the Department who dealt with computer crimes. He grilled him about how a hacker would do what it appeared Edward, or someone, had done to Riley's machine.

He took careful notes. While he was still on the phone, he searched terms he was fuzzy about, such as VPNs, the Dark Web, and other things he had only heard about. His contact gave him lots of information.

After he hung up, he thought about his next step. He was eager to get to Todd Wilhaber soon, just in case he decides to leave the area. He glanced at the clock on the wall. It was early enough to make it to Norfolk while it was mostly light out. He decided to give it a try.

Willard liked to drive and found the four-hour trip a pleasant distraction from the frenetic activity that had come to typify the metropolis that Washington, D.C., had become. He loved the southern countryside. It also gave him time to think.

And along the way, his mind turned to one of his favorite things: he thought of Mildred, a person who stood as a giant in his life. Mildred and he had shared some time together—what was it now, three, maybe four years? Yeah. That's about right. He couldn't believe it. It was toward the end of an ill-fated marriage that he had gotten into when he decided that he was too old to be unmarried and too young to dismiss such a stupid idea. Mildred helped liberate him from that misguided decision the old-fashioned way: by seducing him in the course of one of his investigations. Actually, he wasn't sure who seduced whom, but as he came to know how strong-willed she was, he was left with no doubt that he was on the receiving end of her feminine wiles. The two dated for a couple years. Even though they ended up parting ways romantically, they kept in touch. There was something simpatico about the two of them, something he had never been able to find elsewhere. He did not quite understand it—truthfully, he had no idea what it 'meant'—but it was a piece of his life he never wanted to give up.

And she helped him a lot, even after the two shifted their relationship into a lower gear. When he found himself waist deep in a bureaucratic entanglement in the Metropolitan Police Department, it was Mildred, sharp-witted as ever, who helped him see how much he liked investigating but not so much the grunt work involved in being a cop. He came to understand that he enjoyed the patient gathering of data, following leads, clearing up situations that are often murky. And she showed him how he did not need to be an officer of the law to do that.

She helped him set up his own shop and get some early clients, although that never seemed to be an issue, as he had been well liked when he was with the department and had left on amicable terms. As soon as he hung out his shingle, business appeared.

The fact that the entanglement in question involved his shooting someone on the job made leaving the Department a lot easier. The whole situation was a nightmare. Even though every friend, colleague, committee, lawyer, and judge he knew said it was not his fault—he was quickly cleared by Internal Affairs—he had a very difficult time taking himself off the hook. He did not sign up to kill people, even bad people; and the fact that he did, even if justifiably, still knotted up his stomach. It was better now—he no longer stayed awake at night grieving for the innocence he lost on that fateful, dreary day—but he long ago accepted the fact that this was something that would never leave him so long as he walked the earth. He tried not to dwell on it, but it was always a presence.

Mildred, being a psychologist by training and in practice at the time, helped him with that, too. He was more open with her than with the department shrink he was required to visit, or anyone else for that matter. And it wasn't all professional distance: she held his hand when he needed it and wrapped her arms around him when the emotional torrents got bad. She stayed up late with him, drank with him, and helped him slay his demons as each made its appearance. He never understood how she could invest that kind of time and always show up to her own job the next day. She was a rock, his rock.

Even after all this time, he was fuzzy about how and why they broke up. He knew he was burnt out on marriage and didn't want another one. He did not really want children. Mildred was powerfully independent and, while he valued the strength that reflected, he had some trouble when she slipped into pig-headed territory.

She was not one to change her mind easily. But mostly he valued her friendship; it was something he just was not willing to relinquish. So when things came to a head he had two choices: fight to keep her as a romantic partner and risk losing everything, or stepping back from the romance and declaring his devotion to her as a lifelong friend. He chose the latter. That made abundant sense at the time, and it relieved a lot of pressure he had been feeling, rightly or wrongly.

He was in the midst of these memories when he pulled up to a Hampton Inn on the outskirts of Norfolk. He was grateful that the hour was late and he would not have to deal with Wilhaber until the next day. He was also grateful to be alone, where he could savor the powerful memories he had of himself and Mildred together. That was not something he could share with anyone in the world but her, and with her only occasionally.

All this history is why to this day, if Mildred calls, he responds. He drops what he's doing and does whatever she needs him to do. That's what he did today. That's what he's done ever since he quit the force and set up his own shop. That's what he will always do.

After he registered and walked to his room, he thought about why he was here, about Riley and Jennifer, and the odd tale they told. A tale Mildred believed. Truthfully, Willard did not know what to make of Riley and her story. It seemed pretty far-fetched, but Mildred believed her, so he believed her, too.

## 78

Jennifer and Riley slowly walked toward Jen's apartment in somber silence. So many words had been spoken, it didn't seem there was much left to say. Riley was grateful that she was going to stay with Jennifer, and Jennifer was grateful that Riley would be with her. She did not know why exactly, but she felt Riley was safer with her.

And perhaps she was safer with Riley. In the back of her mind, she wondered if she had a role in this latest development. Maybe it was precipitous of me to call Edward, she thought, but I so wanted him to know he was not invisible to us, that we knew who he was. I would do it again, she decided.

But the fact that this latest gambit was so sophisticated put a different slant on things. If it was Edward, his computer skills may be much more developed than she had assumed. When she called him, she felt certain the call was blocked; but if he could hack into Riley's computer at will, who's to say that he couldn't trace the call she made to him. It did not seem likely, but it did not seem out of the realm of possibility either.

Whatever worry she had about this situation felt more manageable with Riley near her. Whatever was going to happen next, at least they were together.

When they got to Jen's apartment, it occurred to Riley that she had never been there before. They almost always met up at a restaurant or a bar or even a park, but Jen had never invited her back to her place. Then, she realized that Jennifer had only been to her place once, and that was the time she used her computer to find Edward. It felt like a long time ago, even though it wasn't.

Jennifer was realizing the same thing. For her, inviting an attractive woman back to her apartment meant just one thing, and that one thing had always been off limits when it came to Riley. She felt a little awkward now, even though she had no thought of seducing her. New ground for me, she decided. For both of us.

Riley's thoughts were dispelled when they entered Jen's spacious apartment. It was in an older building with high ceilings and large windows. It had been completely remodeled, with none of the paint-on-paint window panes so common in the older buildings of the District. Plus, it was tastefully furnished in modern themes and colors, appeared pristine in its cleanliness, and had uncovered windows, which gave it a feeling of even greater size. Riley was a little awestruck.

"Jesus, Jen," she said. "This is beautiful!"

Jen smiled and nodded. She loved her place and took great pride in keeping it just the way it was now. "Thanks," she said.

"My apartment looks like a grad student lives there," gushed Riley a little self-consciously. "Or like I'm camping out."

"As I recall," Jen noted, "You just moved into that place six months or so ago. I've been here for five years."

It was Riley's turn to nod. "Maybe so, but now I have something to shoot for."

After a brief tour of the apartment and the pouring of a chilled chardonnay, the two settled in Jen's comfortable couch. Silence descended once again.

"Where did you find Mildred?" asked Jen after a bit.

Riley took a sip of wine before she responded. "After you suggested I contact someone at a shelter, I began searching online. There are a bunch of them in D.C. Her place was only a few blocks from my apartment, so I called her up and went to see her." She took another sip of wine. "And I immediately thought I had found the right person. She did not question what I said; she did not think I was crazy; she listened and took actions in such a smooth and professional manner, I felt right away that I was in good hands."

A little more silence, another sip of wine. "She could not have been more welcoming, warmer, or clearer about how these things go. I was lucky to find her."

The two talked a little more as they finished their wine. After about an hour, Jen announced that she had some work to catch up on before she went into the office the next day, so she went and got some bed linens for Riley and pointed out a fold-out couch in the room that served as her study. The two women went in to set up the bed, made it, and looked at each other.

"Jen, I can't tell you how much your support through this means to me." A tear came to her eye. "I don't know what I would do without you."

Jennifer also had a tear in her eye. "That's what friends are for, Riley. I'm sure you'd do the same for me." She paused a moment. "And as I recall, I think you took care of me pretty well when I sprained my ankle a while back under less than, um, optimal conditions."

They both chuckled at the memory. "I guess so," said Riley. "But thanks again, anyway."

The two women hugged warmly. Jennifer left the room, and Riley fell into bed and was soon asleep.

# — 79 —

First thing the next morning, Willard reviewed what he knew about the case of Riley and Edward. He checked his email and found the picture that Jennifer sent him. It looked a little dated, based on the tie width, but he thought it would do. He also checked Google Maps to find the exact location of Todd Wilhaber's residence.

Okay, I guess I'm ready. He did not think this would take longer than an hour or so, so he packed up his few things, loaded them into his car, and checked out of the hotel.

It did not take long to find Todd's home. It was a duplex in what could generously be called a neighborhood in transition, although it was unclear to Willard which direction the transition was headed. He checked his watch: 8:30 a.m. Any decent person should be awake by then.

He parked a few houses away from the building, got out of his car, and walked casually up to the door, taking in details of the structure as he got closer to it. The outside looked to be decently well kept: no peeling paint, new-ish doors and windows, a small well-trimmed yard in front.

He knocked on the door. No answer. He glanced around the neighborhood. A few people were getting in their cars, probably on their way to work. He was about to knocked again when a crack appeared in the doorway.

"Yes?" said a disheveled-looking thirty-something.

"Mr. Wilhaber?" said Willard, even though Todd looked exactly like the video capture he had in his pocket.

"Yes?"

317

Willard flashed an official looking credential that he was sure made no real difference. "My name's Willard Bean. I'm an investigator looking into an incident that happened in Washington, D.C., a few days ago. I'd like to talk to you about it."

He paused because he noticed a sudden loss of color in Todd's face. "Are you all right?" he said with a look of concern on his face.

Todd nodded as if he were not scared to death. Willard took the nod and the pale face to mean that the man he was looking at knew exactly what he was referring to. "I'd like to talk to you about it," he repeated gently.

Todd hesitated for just a moment. Willard thought he was weighing whether to open the door or not. Whatever internal conversation Todd had, it must have been brief, because he opened the door and motioned for Willard to come in, which Will did not hesitate to do.

Willard Bean was attuned to details by long habit, but he did not need extensive experience to grasp immediately that he was dealing with someone who was in desperate need of money, direction, personal discipline, and improved hygiene. He walked past Todd, who was wearing a bathrobe and smelled slightly rancid; but he was unprepared for the seriously malodorous atmosphere of the room he had just entered, a space that looked as if it had not been dusted, picked up, or cleaned in any way since the Carter administration. He spied a cat scurrying away into what was most likely the kitchen, and he had no doubt that the cat, who was, like most cats, personally clean, added to an already unclean environment. The smell of cat excrement was prominent.

Willard turned to Todd. He decided to question him standing up.

"Todd," he said soothingly. "You seem to know what I'm talking about."

Todd nodded slowly. "Maybe," he said with more élan than Willard expected.

To make sure he could not easily turn around and deny it, Willard pulled out his phone and showed him some stills from the video of him entering and leaving the bar. They were time-stamped. "This is you."

Somewhat to Willard's surprise, Todd's face lost even more color. "I need to sit down," he said.

Willard remained standing. This was not his preferred way to interrogate people, but he just could not bring himself to touch any of the furniture that surrounded him, and he did not think Todd was going to take much convincing to reveal what he knew. "Please," he said gesturing the couch behind Todd.

"Todd, you are actually not the person I am concerned about." He pulled up the photo Jennifer had sent to his phone. "I am interested in this person."

Todd took some low deep breaths. The relief on his face was real if tentative. "You mean Mr. Sheets?"

Willard pulled up a picture of Edward on his phone. "Is this him?"

Todd nodded. His color was returning a little.

"Tell me exactly what happened, Todd. How did you get involved with, um, Mr. Sheets?"

Todd took a deep breath and launched into a minute-by-minute narrative of his contact with Mr. Randall Sheets. He told him about the website for the acting school, the fact that Sheets found him there and contacted him for a documentary. It seemed like a stroke of luck and made sense to Todd. He also mentioned that it was a paid position and that he needed the money. Willard had no doubt about that.

At the end of Todd's narrative, he looked skeptically at Willard. "Did I do something wrong?"

"I don't know, Todd. It does not appear so. But, even if you did, it was a very wise move to tell me everything you know." He paused. "Is there anything else about this that you would like to tell me?"

Todd hesitated. "Only . . . only that I got sort of freaked out toward the end of my visit to the bar. That woman: she was supposed to be another actor, but she did not seem like one. She seemed really, genuinely upset. I was glad to get out of there."

Willard, who had been taking notes through this conversation, nodded. "I need one more thing from you, Todd," he said. "I may need you to testify about what you just told me. Nothing more, nothing less." He looked at the young man with as much gravitas as he could muster. "Would you be willing to do that?"

Todd took in a long breath that he dispelled slowly. "If you need me to, Mr. Bean, I will," he said at length.

"And I need you to keep this conversation confidential. You are not to share what we talked about with anyone." The look on his face was stern.

Todd looked uncertain. "Not even . . .

"Especially not Mr. Sheets. If he should try to contact you, I want you to let me know. Here is my card."

Willard seemed reasonably certain that Todd was sufficiently frightened to abide by his stipulations. He thanked Todd and reassured him that he did not think any of this would likely come back to him, but he reiterated the need for confidentiality. Todd kept nodding until Willard walked out the door.

He left the fetid apartment with great relief: both for getting out of such a putrid place and for obtaining positive identification that the perpetrator of this pathetic hoax was indeed Edward McAlister.

## 80

While Bean was on his trail, Edward was trying to access Riley's computer for the umpteenth time. It remained stubbornly off line. He found himself getting angry, as if Riley was not being cooperative.

"Damn her," he said aloud to his own machine. He checked and then rechecked. He did this a dozen times or so before he pushed himself away from the screen in an effort to calm his mounting anxiety.

She must know that I accessed her computer. No, he replied to himself, she may know that someone accessed her computer. She really has no way of knowing it was me. This sensible idea, however, gave him scant comfort.

The other thing that was dawning on him was worse: If she knew that someone accessed her computer and figured out that the whole meeting with 'Adam' was a ruse, she is probably not suffering. Or not suffering enough. If that is true, he failed.

He spun around in his chair and looked at his small apartment. It was just yesterday that he had felt as if he were whole again. No, even better than that: he felt that he had attained a degree of manliness that he had never experienced before. In one fell swoop, nice, easy-going, bland Edward McAlister had taken revenge upon someone who hurt him, had shown her and the world that he would not take injury lying down. He was a man.

And now that idea was tumbling into the category of quaint. If he failed to take revenge, what was he? A failure who hid behind a façade of forced niceness, an easy-going wimp of a man who was afraid or unable to take control of his own life? The whole idea made him sick.

He knew he was connecting things that may or may not have been connected. He tried to think rationally. Fact One: Riley's computer is off line. Fact Two: I don't know why it's off line. She may be out of town. Fact Three: Someone, perhaps a friend or acquaintance of Riley's, called him to let him know that he was on their radar. If One and Three are connected, it was crystal clear to Edward that he would be the prime suspect in the recent drama. He didn't know what to make of Two, except that it might be a possibility.

The fact that these disturbing thoughts may be connected was yet another assault on the invincible persona he had acquired over the past few days. He was beginning to feel less invincible. In fact, he was beginning to feel downright vulnerable. And of all the feelings in the panoply of emotions to which humans are prone, vulnerable was high on the list of unwanted ones. Even feared ones.

This could not be allowed to continue.

He again tried to force himself to think rationally but found himself awash in thoughts that were anything but reasonable. It was all about fear. Finally, he pulled out a piece of paper and a pencil and began writing reasonable thoughts on paper.

*I must assume Riley figured out that Adam was a ruse.*

*She and whoever is helping her—someone must be helping her—are looking for who is responsible.*

*I am the one who is responsible.*

*How can they find me?*

*They have my phone number, and probably my address.*

*They cannot trace me through my computer.*

*They cannot trace me through her computer.*

*Therefore, they cannot prove that I did it.*

*They cannot trace me through anyone I used to set this up. Bomber17 and Todd.*

Bomber he was sure about. But Todd? Could they find Todd?

He froze in place. If they ID Todd they could find me. Shit. Shit. Shit.

He stood up. He wanted to run away but he had nowhere to go. He could not move on short notice. He could feel the anxiety escalating within his body; it made him feel trapped. I need to do something. I need to put an end to this.

He took breaths in an effort to calm himself down. He closed his eyes and lay supine on his couch. Mental images of Todd passed through his mind. I could call him, he realized. He sat up. Is that a good idea? What if they found him already? How could they have done that, especially so quickly?

Edward could not think of any way that his opponents could ID Todd. He lives in Norfolk, for Christ's sake. It's hours away from here.

Then, it struck him: cameras. In all the planning he did arranging this situation, he did not think once about surveillance cameras. He chided himself for being so careless. He could see now how, in his haste to arrange this drama, he overlooked a critical piece of the puzzle. How could I have been so blind?

But he also knew that this was something he could look into. He could go to the bar where it happened and see if they have surveillance cameras.

But if someone is investigating me, I might be being watched.

No problem, he concluded. I have disguises. I won't go looking like myself.

He glanced at his watch. 2:00 p.m. He wondered if the place was open, but he did not want to look it up online, the way he would ordinarily find such information. It didn't matter. He could go see if they had outside cameras. If they were open, he could look inside.

Edward spent the next hour assembling a disguise that would reasonably prevent him from being recognized. This felt childish to him; but costumes had their uses, and this was one of them.

When he was finished, he looked into the mirror. His hair was a different color. He put on fake glasses with a heavy frame. He even added a moustache for effect. Then he put on the only suit he owned, which he felt made him look older. Finally, he donned a broad-brimmed hat. He was ready.

He left his apartment and started walking to A.J.'s. He knew where it was, but he had never been inside. He knew that it was not far from Riley's apartment. That was no doubt why she selected it. As he walked, he was mindful of the possibility that he might run into her, although he thought it unlikely that she would recognize him. Even so, he was constantly vigilant of the people around him. If he spotted her first, he reckoned, he could take steps to avoid her. The fifteen-minute walk seemed to take forever.

As he turned the corner on 14$^{th}$, he spotted the bar and paused. He continued walking, looking this way and that as if he were a visitor to the area. He noticed the camera aiming out from the front of the building. Because he was scanning the area, he also noticed a larger camera on the bank across the street that swiveled. He had never noticed any of these before. He was glad to be in disguise.

He also noticed that the bar was open. He wondered who frequented bars in mid-day, but that was not his concern. All he wanted to know was whether there were cameras inside the bar or not.

It did not take Edward long to conclude that the only way to determine that was to go inside. He crossed the street and headed for the door, keeping his head down in deference to his newly minted awareness of the ubiquitous cameras. He did not want to be filmed.

There were only a few patrons inside. He glanced around and did not see anything that resembled a camera, but he wanted to be sure. He slid onto an empty bar stool.

The bartender, who was washing glasses, looked over and asked what he wanted. "A Diet Coke, please," Edward said.

"Coming right up," said the bartender. Within a minute, Edward had his drink.

It had always been hard for Edward to strike up conversations with strangers. But he had to know, so he took some deep breaths and waited until the bartender was looking his way.

"I notice you have a camera out front," he said as casually as he could.

"Yeah, us and every other business in the District," replied the bartender good-naturedly.

"That common, huh?"

"Yeah. And ours is good, but it's a bit redundant. The one across the street is bigger and can catch our front door. But I think the owners installed it for insurance purposes. I'm not really sure, but I think so."

His attention went back to the glasses he was washing.

Edward nodded. Finally, as the sweat poured down his body inside his suit, he said, "Do you have them inside and outside?"

"Nah," the amiable man behind the bar replied. "Just outside, front and back." He winked, which Edward thought odd but did not comment on.

Instead, he nodded. He discovered what he came here to learn, so he did not really know what to do. He sat there for a while trying to look as if he were savoring his Diet Coke.

## 81

Riley really, really wanted to get back to her work. When morning came, she asked Jennifer what she thought.

"Do you think it's safe to use my computer?" This was the question Riley desperately wanted some feedback about.

Jennifer shook her head before speaking, giving Riley a pretty good indication of what she was thinking. "I don't think so, Honey," she finally said. "For a couple reasons. It is possible that Edward is still monitoring it, or at least trying to. I guess he really can't if it's unplugged, but I've heard a lot of strange things about what hackers can do. But the real point is that, if there was really a crime here, I think it could be an important piece of evidence."

Riley nodded. That all made sense. She wondered if there was in fact a crime involved. She would have to talk to her attorney about that.

While she was still thinking, Jennifer spoke up. "You have a laptop, don't you?"

"Sure."

"And do you have some sort of back-up of whatever you were working on?"

Riley nodded again. "Yes, I keep a current copy of whatever I'm working on a flash drive."

"In that case, I don't see why you couldn't just work on the portable computer and keep the desktop shut down until all this is resolved."

Of course, thought Riley. Why did that not occur to me? "That makes a lot of sense, Jen. Thanks."

Jennifer was almost ready to go to work. She had done her make-up and dressed in work clothes. She turned to Riley. "What do you want me to do, Honey? Do you want to go to work? Do you want me to stay here with you? I will, you know, even though I'm 'in uniform.'" She chuckled. "I don't mind changing back into street clothes."

Riley looked around for a bit. "I think I'm okay going home," she said. "If something happens, I'll keep you posted." She paused a bit. "Even if nothing happens, I'll keep you posted."

The two chuckled in spite of what felt like a serious, ongoing, and potentially dangerous situation. Then, Riley gathered up the few things she had brought with her, and the pair walked out of the apartment; Riley going home and Jennifer going to work.

At the point where their paths were to actually diverge, Jennifer turned to Riley. "I want you to know that if you need me for any reason, just call and I'll be there. I don't mind leaving work." Her tone was deadly serious.

"Thank you," Riley whispered. "I will."

The two women hugged and went their separate ways.

Riley walked to her building in a trance. It was the first time she had been alone since she called Mildred just the day before, but it felt like a long, long time ago. And emotionally, it was, she thought. Yesterday this time I was freaked out, thinking my mind was going. Today I feel pretty close to normal.

Pretty close?

Yeah, almost healed, but not quite completely. She recognized a lot of feelings inside herself: she was still angry at Edward, who, for all the carefulness of Mr. Bean, was the person Riley was sure was behind this mess. She still felt a little raw from her episode with Mildred, who confronted her so strongly yesterday afternoon. That woman was on the right side of rationality, but this woman was still peeved that Mildred was so firm with her. It was something she wasn't used to.

But she had to admit it helped her get her head on straight about this whole unsavory episode.

Unsavory? That's the nicest thing you can say about it.

Yeah, well, it's at least unsavory. I'm not sure yet what else to call it.

This train of thought wound down as she approached her building. She looked up at her apartment and took a deep breath. It felt like forever since she'd been here, but she knew it was only one day. As she entered the building, it occurred to her how much had happened during the past half year or so she lived here. It seemed like a lot. It *was* a lot.

Ascending the elevator, she did not feel exactly anxious. She was eager to get back home and be surrounded by familiar stuff. After letting herself into her apartment, the first thing she spotted was the unplugged computer covered with a kitchen towel, sitting on the small desk she used to write. It looked both ominous and silly at the same time. She believed that so long as it was unplugged, it was an inert piece of electronic equipment that was incapable of coming back to life on its own. So long as it had the towel over it, it just looked ridiculous. She walked over and removed the towel. Now it just looked ominous. That is okay with me, Riley thought. It is ominous.

She turned toward another small piece of furniture and pulled out her laptop. She found the flash drive where she kept a copy of her work. Thank God I do this, she thought. She set the smaller machine up by the front window, booted it up, and inserted the flash drive.

She felt a rush of relief when the file appeared on the screen. A sentimental wave washed through her body: she felt as if she was reconnecting with old friends. Welcome back, she said to them when it was done getting ready. She could not wait to engage her characters.

*Fortunately, Adam's friend was also looking for some company and suggested they meet up at a new bar that opened on U Street. Adam made notes of the name and address of the place, and the two agreed to meet there around 5:30.*

*Adam was . . . what was the word? . . . Happy? Elated. It wasn't a date with a woman, but it was a step out of his self-imposed isolation. He went to take a shower and get ready, as if it were a date. He felt a bit as if he were about to enter into a foreign country, even though he had lived in the District for nearly eight years.*

*His friend Ryan was already at the bar, drink in hand, when Adam showed up. The two had not seen each other in four or five years, but they were Facebook friends, so they knew pretty much about each other's lives and whereabouts. They exchanged warm, male-to-male hugs when Adam got there.*

*"So, when did you get to D.C.?" Adam asked, settling into the stool next to him.*

*"I've only been here a couple weeks," Ryan replied. "I'm staying in company housing until I find a place. From what I gather, when I do find a place, it will be a big step down from the company place, which is really, really nice."*

*The bartender came, and Adam ordered a Johnny Walker neat. He tried to remember the last time he had a drink of anything other than beer, but he couldn't recall. When his drink came, he sniffed it and savored the fragrance before taking a sip.*

*"You'll like D.C.," he said to Ryan. "It's a happening place."*

*"So I understand," Ryan replied. "But then again, almost anything is more 'happening' than Milwaukee."*

*"Got that right," said Adam, slipping into a version of himself that he hadn't been in for a long time.*

*The two spent an hour or so catching up before Ryan, apparently realizing that he may have been impolite, said, "And how's Suzanne?"*

*A question that Adam perhaps should have anticipated but hadn't. He looked at Ryan and could not think of a single reason to reveal anything but the truth. "I don't know," he said. "We broke up a while back."*

*Ryan turned scarlet, as if he had broached a terrible, terrible subject. "I'm so sorry," he said.*

*"Take it from me, Ryan," Adam said. "It's for the best."*

*The two sat in silence; Adam thinking about how true his reaction was and feeling relieved that the truth was on the table and Ryan unsure what to say next. "I thought you two were so happy," he said warily.*

"*We were for a while,*" Adam replied. "*But gradually we grew apart.*" He swirled the brown liquid in his glass and took a sip. "*And, you know, these things are always messy, even if it's for the best.*"

"*I imagine,*" said Ryan, who had never come even close to tying the marital or any other knot he could think of. The whole idea of commitment gave him the willies. He was eager to get on to some other topic.

"*How are the Nationals doing?*" he said.

"*Great,*" replied Adam, who was also not inclined to go into more detail about his battles with Suzanne. He was thankful that guys could always talk about sports.

After another hour of male bonding, Adam checked his watch. "*Gotta go,*" he said. "*Work tomorrow.*"

"*Me too,*" said Ryan. And the pair split up with assurances that they would get together periodically. Adam offered assistance to his friend if he had any questions about Washington. Ryan promised to stay in touch.

On his way home, Adam felt like he had initiated a new phase of his life. He felt connected to a guy to whom he had been very close at one time, and who he kept in touch with the way people do these days. He knew there were others he could connect with.

He thought back to that fateful day when he and Suzanne began talking about their relationship honestly. He remembered—not without some residual pain—how scared he had been to approach the truth about his relationship with Suzanne, and how blown away he was by her courage and by what she told him. He admired his wife's strength. Picturing her, he felt a twinge of regret, not so much for the loss of the marriage—that had been defunct for some time—but for the lost contact he had with someone he loved once and admired always. He knew Dayton wasn't far, but given what their relationship had just gone through, it might as well be across an ocean.

He pulled up to his rental house, unlocked the door, and got undressed. He watched television for a few minutes before he fell into a dreamless sleep.

## 82

Willard Bean was nothing if not thorough. On the long drive back to D.C., he thought a lot about Todd and his challenging lifestyle. He could not imagine he was that good an actor. Frankly, he could not imagine Todd being good at anything. Anyone who lets himself go like that . . . Will knew he listed toward the critical side, and it was something he also knew he needed to keep an eye on. Even so, he wondered why Edward would consider such a lowlife for a task in which he obviously invested a lot of time and money.

He thought at some point, perhaps soon, he would need to confront Edward, but he was fairly certain that time had not quite arrived. He wanted to be sure of the larger picture, and he wanted more evidence if he was going to deal with Edward in the flesh. Also, he considered the very real possibility that the details of the case might be something he will need to turn over to the police: breaking into someone's computer was a crime, although even Willard could not recall the exact legal assignation. What did his friend call it? Unauthorized entry? Yeah, that was it.

Willard made a mental list of things he needed to do for this case. One was touching base with Mildred, whom he knew wanted to be updated more or less in real time. She was a bear for information. He admired that in her, but she often wanted more details than he had at his fingertips. He hated being unprepared and had promised himself on several occasions that he would not be caught again without all the information she wanted. Hence the list he was working on mentally as he drove across the scenic Virginia countryside.

Willard's mind, however, kept returning to Todd. How could anyone live like that? Will was single himself, but his apartment was neat and tidy. Even allowing for the fact that he was older than Todd and more fastidious than the average single male, he could not picture anyone living in squalor unless he was absolutely without resources. In Willard's experience, even most criminals he had contact with kept their personal nests reasonably need and tidy. Or Todd could be mentally ill. He seemed to have some resources: he attended an acting school, which was no doubt pricey; his place was located in an acceptable if not great part of Norfolk; he apparently cleaned up well enough for Edward to hire him for a delicate task. So what was all that crap in his apartment?

Willard's mind ranged over the possibilities: drugs or alcohol or both, or maybe some other life-smothering addiction, such as gambling, might be part of the picture.

Gambling. That made sense. That would explain why Todd was so desperate for money and perhaps why he was so focused on something other than his living space. Who knows? he thought as the miles slipped by. It could be any combination of these factors and god know what else. It's not that Willard cared that much; it was just that, even with his fairly extensive experience, he found Todd's habitat unusually repugnant, disgusting even, although that may not be strong enough a word to describe being exposed to it.

He promised himself to do some more checking once he got back to his office.

In the meantime, he decided to go ahead and bring Mildred up to date. Whatever apprehension he had about her questioning dissipated in light of the pleasure he took in talking with her. He scanned his dashboard phone entry list, selected her number, and pressed talk.

"Hi, Mildred," he said after she picked up on the first ring. "I thought I'd bring you up to date."

"Great," Mildred replied.

Willard proceeded to tell Mildred everything he knew about Todd: his demeanor, his squalid apartment, his offensive odor. He explained their entire brief conversation, where Todd put up only the weakest of defenses, and how he readily verified Edward from a picture Willard showed him. Mostly, he told Mildred, Todd was concerned about getting into trouble himself, like a little boy caught for doing something bad. "I told him I did not think that was likely so long as he cooperated," he told Mildred.

Mildred listened intently. Willard could feel her nodding through the phone. "Oh," he said before she did, "I'm headed to my office to do a little more background checking on our friend Todd. Something is going on with him; I just don't know what yet. But I'll keep you posted."

"Good work, Will. Thanks," said Mildred, much to his surprise. No questions, no reactions, no requests for additional information. He momentarily did not know what to say.

"Talk soon," finally fell out of his mouth.

Back at his office, Willard decided to turn his attention to Edward, who was shaping up to be the real person of interest in this whole mess. There were some things about him that just did not add up on the basis of what he had heard from Riley. This whole scheme seemed like massive overkill for being jilted, which, as far as Willard knew, was not uncommon among young adults. He could only imagine what Edward would do if someone seriously hurt him.

Touchy guy, he concluded.

## — 83 —

Touchy but dauntless, as it was turning out. When Edward got back to his apartment, he took out a piece of paper and started making notes.

*The bar has a surveillance camera that could have picked up Todd.*

*It is unlikely that he would be in any local D.C. database, as he lives in Virginia hundreds of miles away.*

*It is not impossible if someone has access to a federal database.*

*Conclusion: Possible but unlikely.*

Then he started another page entitled pros and cons of contacting Todd.

**Pros:**

*I would know if he had been contacted and not have to guess.*

*I could find out what, if anything, he revealed.*

*I could find out who that person was who found him and how.*

*If no one has contacted him, I could coach him on what to say.*

**Cons:**

*Contacting him may signal that something is wrong.*

*If no one has contacted him . . .*

Edward stopped. He did not know how to finish that sentence. So instead, he picked up his burner phone, plugged it in because the battery was low, and dialed Todd's number.

Todd answered. Edward thought this was a hopeful sign.

"Todd, hi. This is Randall Sheets. How are you doing?"

There was silence on the other end of the phone. Todd was trying to figure out how to respond. Edward's hopefulness was beginning to weaken.

"Are you there, Todd?"

"Yes," Todd finally said. "I'm here."

"Listen. I'm just calling to follow up. You did a great job for me, and I have some potential contacts that might be able to use your services. . . "

"Mr. Sheets," interrupted Todd.

"Yes?"

Another long pause. "Nothing. I'm just surprised to hear from you."

Edward thought for a moment. He decided to just ask what he wanted to know: "Todd, did anyone contact you about our arrangement?" He wanted to ask about the police but thought better of it. "Anybody asking questions about it?"

Todd's breathing got heavier. Mr. Bean had instructed him in no uncertain terms not to reveal their conversation with any one, but Todd was a terrible liar. The only way he could lie was to pretend he was in character in a role of someone other than himself. He took a few deep breaths, just as he had learned in acting school, and got into character. "No," he said in a different, more confidant voice. "No one. Why do you ask?"

Edward never thought he was the kind of person who read social cues very well, and he thought of himself as generally insensitive to the vagaries of human communication; however, he was having a novel experience. He was absolutely certain Todd was lying.

"No reason. Sometimes competitors in documentaries like to dig up information about the opposition. No big deal." He paused again. "Just checking."

Edward clicked off. Shit, he thought. Someone found him.

## 84

Todd, meanwhile, still felt himself in character for several minutes after the call. He was proud of himself, primarily because the character he chose was a study in how to play a vain, overly confident man who did not give a damn about anyone but himself. He had done this in class, and it was one of the highlights of his experience there. Supercilious, conceited, and extremely self-focused, this character was impervious to the harm or hurt his behavior occasioned in others. It was quite a display, which Todd believed he had mastered exceptionally well, as he did today for about ten minutes.

Then his actual self, his uncertain, frail, hollow self re-emerged with something of a vengeance. He got light headed and had to lean against a nearby table. His stomach started to churn, and he thought he might throw up. He had to do something, or he felt the anxiety would overwhelm him. He needed to talk to somebody, but no one came to mind. No one, that is, who would or could help him.

What about your Twelve-Step friends? Your sponsor in the Program?

Todd shook his head. They can't help me.

Isn't that what they're there for?

Todd let out a long, low growl. He hated, hated, hated depending on Twelve-Step people. They were so sanctimonious, so uppity, so holier-than-thou. He hated them all.

But still, what else could he do? He did not have enough money left to make even a respectable showing at the nearby gambling boats; nor did he want to show up at his regular meeting and admit that he had relapsed after almost eighteen months of abstinence from gambling. Plus, his parents, who were understandably at their wits' end, had informed him in no uncertain terms that one more trip to a gambling house would result in their severing all support.

He threw himself on the filthy couch in the vain hope of finding an alternative solution to the gamble/Twelve-Step dilemma, even though he knew that, for him, one did not exist. He lay there taking deep breaths hoping that the anxiety would at least recede some.

And suddenly, it did. In fact, it went away completely. A third alternative! He sat up and realized that he had done something that was very hard for him to do: he kept his word to Mr. Bean that he would tell no one of their meeting. And he realized, although he wasn't sure, that Mr. Sheets was probably not the name of the person in the picture Mr. Bean showed him.

In short, Todd caught a glimpse of himself as a capable adult male. He liked it.

He got up and decided to go for a walk.

## 85

Suzanne could hardly wait to board the flight back to D.C. The few weeks she had been gone had enabled her to build a suitable base in her new city, but she missed the District more than she ever thought she would.

It wasn't a clean, positive-only vibe. D.C. had lots of good memories and some notably bad ones: Her relationship with Ellie was a high point; her death was definitely in the latter column. She could still feel the pain in her body when images of her erstwhile lover flitted through her mind. Her marriage was okay for a while, but the last few years had been rough.

She tried to put the painful feelings aside, but gently and lovingly. Her desire to get back to Washington trumped all other feelings she was having.

Even though her parents lived just across the border in Virginia, she was not staying with them. The company paid for her travel and related expenses—generously, she thought—and she was there for work. Plus, as much as she cared about her parents, she was mum about large tracts of her life with them, such as her relationship with Ellie. They knew she was divorcing Adam, but only in general terms. They loved and supported her and did not want to interfere with her life too much. They always assumed she would give them the information she needed to give them when the time came. That gentle hand in her life was always something she cherished. It was how she wanted to treat herself and other people.

She did want to stop by and visit her parents while she was so close. It had been some time since she saw them in person: she almost *always called or texted them. But living out of town added a new urgency to seeing them in the flesh. She looked forward to it.*

She thought about getting together with Adam just to see if . . . if what? If he was doing okay? She was not sure she wanted to know. On the other hand, there may be legalities they had to work out relative to the divorce. She promised herself she would call him.

All of these ruminations took place during the one-hour flight from Dayton to D.C. When the full plane landed with a thud on the runway, she did what almost every passenger did: she pulled out her cell phone and started checking emails and making calls. The first one was to her parents. Her mother answered and Suzanne told them she would like to stop by while she was in town. She gave them some times she could get away from work. They planned to meet two days hence for dinner at a favorite restaurant in the District.

Then she looked at her phone as if it would tell her whether to call Adam or not. I should. I don't want to. I should. I don't want to.

Why don't you want to?

Because I was pretty shitty toward him, and I don't think he deserved it. He's a good man, a solid citizen, and I was a philandering bitch.

That seems harsh.

It did not seem harsh to Suzanne. It just seemed true.

She gave up and decided to wait until she was settled in her hotel to call her soon-to-be-ex-husband. That enabled her to sigh with at least temporary relief.

In the limousine that picked her up to take her to the hotel, Suzanne savored the perks of her job. She flew first class; she was staying in a five-star hotel. All of this courtesy of the generous benefits accorded an office director. It amazed her, but it did not displease her one bit.

The other person who popped into her mind was David Collins, the obsequious little prick who was her assistant director. Suzanne could not stand him. He was at once subservient and haughty, using every opportunity to lord his apparent knowledge of office procedure over her. As if knowing the location of the water cooler were critical information.

*The net effect of his behavior on Suzanne was that she was determined to get rid of him. When he practically threw the well-worn book of office procedures at her the day she arrived, she took it home and decided to read it. Then she milked Collins for all the information she could before she implemented a strategy to rid herself of the miserable excuse for a human being.*

*Harsh again?*

*Yeah. So be it.*

*Suzanne had choices for dinner. She could go to the fanciest restaurant in town, or she could eat at her hotel, either in the restaurant or with room service. So many lovely choices. She decided to savor dinner alone in her room, which had a marvelous view of the nation's capital. She just wanted to spend time by herself, neither seeing nor being seen by others, not even strangers.*

*She surveyed the menu and ordered an elaborate meal, which included beet salad and pan-seared Maryland rockfish. A bottle of severely overpriced French wine added a welcome accompaniment. While she was waiting, she patiently unpacked her suitcase, washed her face, and touched up her make-up. Just for herself. Not for anyone else.*

Riley pushed back from her laptop. I don't know if I like you or not, Suzanne.

## — 86 —

Edward's insides were roiling. What to do? What to do?

What about doing nothing? Why do I need to do anything?

Because there are people looking for you, if they know it or not. And because they may find you because you dropped the ball and did not think through this situation thoroughly enough. Suddenly, the omission of surveillance cameras seemed like an Original Sin: something that he most assuredly should have considered but failed to. Failed completely. And now it may be his undoing. Something he could not fix.

On an emotional level, he was going down a road he never wanted to tread. He was already feeling himself beginning to come undone. The grandeur of his feelings the days before were now rapidly slipping into memory, and a taunting memory at that. Edward was left feeling as if the worst parts of him had surged to the fore and taken permanent control over his life. He felt weak and vulnerable, anxious and afraid, alone and unaided. He could not even imagine anyone he could turn to for help.

A lawyer? The idea sounded preposterous. Why would a guilty man hire a lawyer and disclose his crime?

Am I a criminal? Yes, I did some things that probably skirted the law, such as hacking into someone else's computer. But the rest of it . . . wasn't it more like a gag or a practical joke or an understandable payback to a former lover? How serious can it be?

These thoughts struck Edward as pathetic. He knew how serious the situation was: deadly serious.

Edward found himself staring at a blank wall in his apartment, a wall with no pictures, no color, no ornament of any kind. He turned to look out his window. Even though it was a beautiful, early summer day in the District, one of his favorite seasons, he registered everything as colorless and as devoid of art as the walls of his sterile apartment. In the theater of his mind, he pictured times in his life when he wanted something more from himself, when he had goals that he pursued with all his heart. Graduating from college, leaving home, finding a profession, and finding a lover as pleasing as Riley. He hung his head as he weighed the multiple successes against the failures. None of the former mattered; only the latter loomed large in his mind.

He looked around at his humble space. I used to think this was perfect, he recalled. It used to be my place where no one could enter without my consent. In fact, few people had ever crossed the threshold of his small, spare apartment. He could not recall a single time that he entertained someone, cooked for someone, made love to someone in this space. The emptiness of it all hit him as never before. And it left him without hope.

The thought of being discovered, of going through an arrest, a conviction, even spending time in prison: these things had always been inconceivable to him. They portrayed a version of himself he could not recognize. He was a good person, a professional person, a moral person. Even though his parents were long deceased, the thought of public humiliation appalled him. I can't do it, he decided. I won't do it.

He felt finished.

## 87

Willard was on the phone to George Talbot, a lawyer he knew in the District Attorney's office, whom he had called to check out how the criminal profile that was shaping up against Edward would likely play out. He got the earful he was hoping for.

Talbot office ran down the legal scenario. "Someone who hacks into another person's computer could be punished for a number of different crimes, depending on the circumstances. Could be a class B misdemeanor punishable by up to six months in prison, a fine of up to $1,000, or both, or a class B felony punishable by up to twenty years in prison, a fine of up to $15,000, or both. A lot of it depends upon circumstances," he said, "such as how the information garnered is used. If there's no theft of data or identity or unauthorized use of pirated information, then it's more likely to fall in the less serious side. Maybe not a misdemeanor, but no serious jail time or huge fine." He paused for a breath. "Of course, the law specifically authorizes someone harmed by a computer or unauthorized use crime to bring a civil lawsuit against the perpetrator."

"So really," Willard said, "If it's just a matter of spying on somebody else's machine, the penalties could be fairly light?"

"Yeah. Especially if it's a first offense. It would likely be pleaded out; there probably wouldn't be jail time, but that would really be up to the judge. Of course, it all depends on the specific circumstances, but in general, we don't think throwing kids in jail for playing around on each other's computers warrants serious punishment just because it pisses somebody off."

"Thanks, George," Willard said. "This is helpful. If something comes of the case I'm working on, I'll be back in touch."

"Sure thing, Will. Good luck."

Willard sat back in his desk chair and started mentally reviewing the situation with Edward, Riley, and the others. George's reference to kids playing around struck him as apt. To Willard, Edward did not seem malevolent so much as immature, even childish. He couldn't see him going to jail, even though the hacking was criminal. But what stood out in his mind was that it was more . . . silly. Did Edward really think shaking this lady up would harm her permanently or make her change her mind about him? Why didn't he just stand behind a tree and jump out and say 'Boo!'? What was he trying to accomplish with this elaborate ruse? It just did not feel right to him. Something was still off. He couldn't put his finger on it.

He decided to get together with Mildred and talk this through in person. People are different on the phone or in texts or whatever other forms of electronic communication exist. He wanted to run the whole situation by Mildred face-to-face. He wanted to observe her reactions, hear her thoughts from her own mouth, and have the two of them work together to formulate both an understanding and then a plan. They had done this on previous cases, and it had a good track record.

He called Mildred to set it up. She was more than willing to meet as soon as possible. It was clear to Willard that she had taken a personal interest in this case. He knew her to be a passionate woman, but this was a level or two higher than her usual fever pitch. They decided to meet first thing in the morning.

They met at Mildred's office because he had more flexibility than she did, since she was running the shelter. He did not mind. After being buzzed in, he entered her office and hugged her warmly, giving her a peck on the cheek.

The pair sat down in comfortable chairs. Willard began. "Okay, Mildred, here's what I've got. Todd Wilhaber is the name of the guy who portrayed Adam at AJ's. He's in acting school in Norfolk. I identified him from a surveillance camera and an interview with the bartender, who was certain that he was the guy who chatted up Riley. I got some pictures and sent them for facial recognition. Then, I went to Todd's place yesterday morning. He was home, but I've got to tell you: I have rarely seen a house in such disarray. Smelled to high heaven. Todd was in a bathrobe around 9:00 a.m. when I arrived. He copped right away to being the impersonator. I asked him who put him up to it and showed him a picture of McAlister. He took one look and said, 'Mr. Sheets.' Apparently, McAlister went by the name of Randall Sheets."

"I told Edward not to say anything to anybody about this, and . . . " Willard stopped because his phone buzzed. He looked at the screen. "I think this is Todd," he said to Mildred, who nodded slightly. Willard clicked his phone.

Will listened intently, occasionally saying "okay" or "good" and finally, "that was the right thing to do." He repeated this last phrase before he added. "I appreciate the call, Todd. You did the right thing."

Will turned to back to Mildred. "McAlister called Todd and asked him if anyone had contacted him about the 'project' they were working on." Pause. "Todd said he lied to him and said no."

An especially pregnant silence filled the room between Mildred and Willard. Will stared at the floor for a few moments then turned to Mildred and said, "I'm worried about McAlister."

Mildred's eyebrow rose slightly. "Edward?"

"Yes. Here is the deal. I know this was a disturbing episode for Riley and it shook her up. I also presume that it was Edward who hacked into her computer, which is a criminal act. But I think we're overlooking something here. Why did this guy go through all this trouble to strike back in such an elaborate—and not to mention expensive—way at someone who just did not want to go out with him? There was nothing in his history to suggest he is some kind of maniac. He has no criminal record; he has a decent professional job; he is evidently well-regarded by his colleagues. Honestly, Millie, it just does not add up."

Mildred looked at Willard for a few moments with a look that was both sympathetic and patient. Up till now, she had been so focused on Riley that she tended to cast Edward as a bad guy rather than, say, a sick guy. She assumed he was—anyone who would act this way was at least half a bubble off—but her more immediate concern was Riley, who, after all, was the one who came to her for help. But now, Will is basically saying to her that something is wrong with this guy, a point she could hardly protest. But she also knew that sick guys can also turn into bad guys, sometimes on short notice.

"No, it doesn't add up, Will," she said softly. "What are you thinking?"

Will shook his head. "I'm not sure, Millie. I think he's probably a pretty lonely guy who does not have very well-developed social skills. He probably doesn't date much. I can find no evidence that he's ever lived with anyone or been married. He's never been arrested; he's never had a traffic ticket. He's lived in the same six hundred square foot apartment for over a decade. In general, he has a history that seems mostly . . . dull."

Mildred nodded as she listened. "I think maybe more vulnerable than dull, Will. All those things you described are textbook examples of careful, often heavily repressed people who look dull because they restrain their emotional lives so much. Until they don't. At that point, they can be very, um, un-dull. Meaning they can do uncharacteristic, outlandish things. Sometimes violent things. It does not always happen; it doesn't even happen in the majority of cases, but it's not unheard of."

This is something Will appreciated about Mildred: she adds a lot to the conversation. Surely her background as a psychologist helps with this, but she's also a patient and fair-minded observer of humans. Will valued that a great deal.

"But let's give this some more thought, Will. I get that I have been focused almost exclusively on Riley in this situation: she is the one who came to me for help. But let's step back and look at this situation more closely." She thought for a moment. "Do you need more information from Riley about her experience with Edward?"

"Maybe," Will said. "But before that, let's talk about what Edward was actually trying to accomplish with this scheme. Was it just about getting back at Riley?"

"Apparently," said Mildred. "I have thought all along that only a pretty sick guy would go to these lengths to get back at somebody. But I think I discounted the sick part." She paused a moment. "I think you're onto something important."

Will nodded. "My immediate concern is this: he called Todd, so he at least suspects that someone is onto him. I also understand that other woman, Riley's friend . . ."

"Jennifer?"

"Yeah, Jennifer. She called Edward anonymously before the recent events happened. So he knew then that someone knew that he was up to something. So why proceed?"

Mildred thought for a while. "Well, he went to great lengths to guard information that would identify him. He hacked into a computer using a VPN, he went all the way to Norfolk to find Todd. God knows how he learned to do the hacking in the first place, but that could have been a hobby or something. Not so uncommon for loners." She stared down at the floor, sill thinking. She looked up. "Maybe he thought he could outsmart everyone."

"What is clear," she said, resuming the conversation, "is that he was focused on retribution, on getting back at Riley. And he was willing to take some risks and, apparently, spend some money to do it." The look on her face turned dark. "And revenge is a powerful and often destructive motive."

"A strong motive for sure. Todd said that he was paid well for the job."

A ponderous silence filled the room. Will pulled out his notes; Mildred stared at the glass window behind her desk.

Finally, Mildred turned back to Will and said, "I think we are right to be concerned about safety, both for Riley and for Edward." Another pause. "And at the moment, I take your point about Edward. Yes, he might do something to harm Riley, but it seems more likely that he might do something to hurt himself."

Will nodded. He had not put words to it, but that resonated precisely with what his fear had been. If a person was so sensitive and vengeful that he would go to the lengths Edward went to, something was seriously amiss in the mental department.

A shared question that did not even need to be stated aloud arose in the room. What do we do now?

"We could call the police," Will said.

"We could," agreed Mildred hesitantly.

"Or . . ." Will began hesitantly. "I could go talk to him. Or at least try."

Mildred nodded, a behavior that Will rightly interpreted as 'That is the best option, and that's what I'd like to see happen.' He was not that especially happy about that, but if it was what Mildred wanted . . .

"Okay," he said. "What do you think, in your professional opinion, would be the best way to approach this?"

Mildred sank back into thought. "I don't know, Will. Let me think for a minute."

It was actually several minutes. Finally, she looked up and said, "I usually think the direct approach is the best, but I think it's important to be mindful of the likelihood that Edward is most likely a seriously scared and probably irrational puppy."

Will sympathized with the scared part. He was way more comfortable with bad guys than he was with sick guys, who tended, in his experience, to be capable of unpredictable things. Bad guys tend to be fairly predictable.

"And he could do something unpredictable?"

"Yes."

"Potentially violent, toward himself or someone else?"

"Yes."

'Shit' is what Will thought, although that word never transitioned to a vocal sound.

"Should we alert Riley?"

"Yes. That's a good idea. I will do that."

"Anything else?"

"Not that I can think of just now, but I'll think about it some more."

Fair enough, Will thought. But he noticed his hands were sweaty.

Mildred stood up. "I've got to check on some things here in the shelter, Will. I'll be back in a little bit." She walked out of the room and closed the door.

## 88

It wasn't really that Mildred had anything significant to do—there were a few things she *could* do—but what she did have was a need to get some distance between herself and Will. She hated to fudge on the truth, but she learned over the years of her relationship with Will that there were times it was just easier.

She was very fond of Will and valued his friendship. She also knew that he valued hers as well. But being friends with former lovers is tricky, and she was still working her way through the transition, even though it has been almost two years since the lover part of their relationship came to an end.

What she was learning was that having a continuing relationship with a former lover posed some often surprisingly immediate problems. The attraction never really goes away. She guessed maybe it has gotten a little less intense, but she was aware that she had not had another sexual relationship since the breakup with Will that came anywhere close to what they had together. And as far as the less intense part, well, that was mostly something she told herself to get through times when she and Will were working together closely, as they were doing today, when she had to keep an eye on herself.

Walking down the corridor of the shelter, her mind flashed on her history with Will. It was one of those rare instances where she was immediately attracted to someone; and she, considering herself an astute observer of the human scene, believed that he was instantly attracted to her as well, a belief that she confirmed on their second date.

Their relationship had a honeymoon period, and then a conten-
tious period, and then a friends-not-lovers period. Mildred did not
mind the first two: the honeymoon was great, and she did not shy
away from conflict, and believed that healthy disagreement done
respectfully was actually good for a relationship. But that did not
turn out to be the case with her and Will. It just seemed to foster
more contentiousness. Instead of strengthening the relationship, it
had, in fact, eroded it.

The let's-be-friends part hit her hard. It was not her idea. She
did not want it; she wanted to stay and fight for what to her was
a rare and special relationship in her life. But later, when she got
over the initial anger and grief about it, she realized that there
were things about Will that made her straightforward manner less
than tolerable. For one thing, he was way more fastidious than
she recognized at first. There were the typical cues—shirts and
slacks hung by color, season, and level of formality; suits by shade
atop shoes aligned in a similarly precise way. Mildred didn't mind
these compulsive features much: she and most of her friends were
different only in degree in that regard. But Will had another side,
a controlling one. Control can be an attractive trait, but when Will
did not feel in control, he tended to get anxious. Very anxious.
And snappy. Mildred tried to help him with this, but it was as if
the anxiety came from such a deeply buried spring that neither she
nor Will could put a name to it. She tried every way she could to
just accommodate it. Even those attempts did not go over well with
Will; she guessed because it violated his commitment to remaining
in control.

After the shift in their relationship, she understood things about
it more but disliked the outcome the same amount. During those
times when they were together, as they were now, she just closed
down a part of herself that she just knew would interfere. That
would be the longing, hurt side that also wanted to play with him,
cuddle with him, hug him, lie with him, and be with him in all the
ways humans can be together.

She could keep those impulses in check, but it took a toll. And
as much as she still enjoyed Will's company, she had to take a break

from time to time. Sometimes it wasn't an issue, but today it was. Mildred knew that Will had dropped everything to help her with this situation, and she respected that about him. The problem was there were so many things she loved and valued about him: he was loyal to a fault; he was bright; he was hardworking; and he was as honest a person as one could find. Those were big things in her mind. It all added up to a very agreeable package. Too agreeable.

She walked down the corridor, took some deep breaths, and checked with the receptionist for messages. On her way back, she flipped through the pink slips to see if any were important. None of them was urgent. She took another deep breath, stood outside the door to her office for a moment, and then decided there were some other things she could check on before going back.

In the meantime, Will was thinking about was his next step. He did not relish a visit to Edward, and he was uncertain how to go about it. Should he just show up at his apartment unannounced? Should he call first? Maybe he should observe him and approach him on the street. These seemed like flimsy ways to approach a man who is no doubt concerned about getting into a lot of trouble. A man who, until now, had a spotless record. In Will's experience, people like this do not like to be surprised. Plus, they often did not understand objectively the spot they were in, often overstating, but sometimes understating, the consequences of their behavior. Not like a regular thief or philanderer, for instance, who typically knew exactly the consequences of their actions.

But Will knew he was getting far afield and not thinking clearly. He recalled what Mildred said earlier about Edward being scared. Okay, he thought, what would I want if I were scared?

I would want to be assured that I was safe, maybe that I was not going to jail.

What if I were so scared I wouldn't answer my phone?

I might listen to a message.

That seemed reasonable. Will, who hated putting off things that made him anxious, decided to move forward immediately. He pulled out his phone while still in Mildred's office. He was alone and hoped he would remain so for the next few minutes.

The call went straight to voicemail. "Mr. McAlister," Will began in as gentle a voice as he could. "My name is Willard Bean. I'm a private investigator. I am aware that you were involved in an incident concerning a certain Riley Cotswald. I would like to talk to you. I would like to resolve this without the police getting involved, so I would appreciate your giving me a call back. Here is my number." And he rattled of his cell phone number.

Step Number One, he thought, clicking his phone off. He was glad it was over. But he knew he would be anxious until he heard back from Edward.

It was then that Mildred returned to the office, and Will told her what he had done. She nodded that bloodless, noncommittal nod that psychologists are resentfully known for but said nothing.

"What do you think?" Will asked.

"I think you'll be anxious until you hear from him," said Mildred, with a hint of a smile on her face. "I think this is a good first step, Will."

Now it was Will's turn to nod. He glanced at his watch and stood up and stretched. "Lunch?" he said.

"Sure," said Mildred, rather to Will's surprise.

## 89

Not two miles from Mildred's office, Edward was not having lunch; in fact, he wasn't doing much of anything but sweating. When his phone rang, which was a rare event, he always looked at the number and seldom answered. He usually thought it might just a wrong number, and often it was. But today he was jumpy, and the ringing phone startled him. He stared at the device until he heard the signal for a voicemail.

He debated whether to listen to it or to delete it without hearing it. No, I can't do that. It might be important.

That may have been true, but it still took him some minutes before he pushed the appropriate buttons to retrieve the voicemail.

It wasn't a long message, but his body seemed to freeze over as he listened to every word. This is it, he kept thinking. This is it. I am screwed.

He closed his eyes and decided to listen to the message again. And again. And again.

He hadn't moved during all this listening, and his body was beginning to feel stiff and breathing was coming harder. So, he forced himself to do something. He stood up and shook his limbs; he inhaled deeply; he even ran in place for a bit. Then, he went to his desk and wrote down the name and number that the person gave him and booted up his computer to look it up. There aren't that many ways you can spell Bean, he thought.

He found him online right away. In fact, Willard Bean had a website describing his services. It was professionally done and tasteful. Understated even. This enabled Edward to thaw a bit, although he wasn't sure he should.

What he thought was that he should not make a rash decision. He kicked himself for calling Todd impulsively, and, even though he realized his feelings had more to do with what he learned in the call than with making the call itself, he could not easily separate the two. I can wait until tomorrow, he decided.

That left him with an afternoon and evening free, but he had no idea what to do with himself. None of the options that popped into his mind held the slightest appeal. Then, he realized he would remain frozen until he got the deed over with. He picked up his phone, took a deep breath, and entered Willard's number.

God, I hate this.

The call went straight to voicemail. He pondered what to say as he listened to the outgoing announcement. Then he said in his best professional voice, "Mr. Bean, this is Edward McAlister returning your call." He hung up.

The relief he felt was palpable but not complete. He took in deep breaths to compensate for the deficits of oxygen that had piled up over the previous ten minutes or so. His head began to clear some.

Okay, he's a private investigator. He is not a cop, but he used to be, having spent almost a decade on the force. He's not a lawyer. He wants information. Edward had no idea what to say to a PI who wanted to talk to him, but he thought maybe he could just respond to whatever questions Bean had. Or maybe I should think up some alternative stories.

But he could not ignore the notion that was growing in the back of his mind: Isn't this how you got into this mess in the first place? Because you decided to perpetrate a fraud against somebody who harmed you? Would continuing to lie be something you would recommend to your students?

And with the realization that he wouldn't or even couldn't do that, Edward felt shame so intense that tears formed in his eyes.

## 90

Adam was next, Riley decided. This could be tricky.

*Adam found a suitable apartment in a nice, rent-controlled build-ing in Washington, D.C., and signed a year-long lease. When he got home, he notified his landlord by email, text, and a handwritten letter of his decision to terminate their current agreement, effective thirty days hence.*

*The excitement he felt built throughout the day. He realized that leaving the rental house that he and Suzanne shared was a huge step, even a symbolic one: He was striking out on his own with the baggage of a failed marriage behind him. He felt no regret; he felt no real loss; his only feelings were contentment and excitement for the move.*

*And for his life. When he was talking with Ryan, he felt like an insider because of his years of experience in D.C. It bolstered his belief in himself. I can't believe how much time I wasted just going through the motions with Suzanne. It did not seem to be a question of right or wrong or even of anger or resentment: the fact that his marriage disintegrated just felt like a simple fact. Something that happens to a lot of people, to a lot of marriages. Yes, it hurt when it happened. And I was scared. But I think I'm past that part. I am free. And I am young enough to set out on another course for my life.*

*This was all so intoxicating he thought maybe he was getting carried away. He lectured himself on the need to relax, calm down, and take things one day at a time. He still had thirty days left on his current lease, and he had a lot to do. Decide what to take and what to leave. Check again with Suzanne to see if she wants anything from the house. Maybe the Bible my parents gave us? Fat chance, he thought. But there might be other things.*

*Adam hadn't talked to Suzanne in a while, since before she moved to Dayton, and, truth be told, it never occurred to him to call her. What were they now? Of course, ex-spouses. But were they friends? Acquaintances? Or just a couple people whose lives would take other turns and who would never intersect again? That felt vaguely sad to Adam, but not enough for him to call his ex-wife. And they weren't feelings he wanted to indulge.*

*He decided doing something was more important than thinking about doing something, so he set about inventorying everything in the house that he was preparing to leave.*

"Good for you, Adam," Riley said aloud to her laptop screen. She was thinking how important it was to act and not overthink things.

She sat back in her chair. One of the advantages of working on the smaller machine was that she could face the window of her apartment and enjoy the views it afforded. As she was watching the street below through her window, her mind scanned over all the things that had happened recently, and she found herself having different feelings. She missed Cameron a little. She felt a little guilt about Edward, even though she still harbored anger toward him for being so intrusive. She was grateful for Mildred and Jennifer. She even liked Willard Bean, whose name could have been one of her characters.

But mostly she was savoring being back home working on what she was working on. Living her life. She felt safe in her apartment, except that the unplugged desktop cast a shadow in the corner where it resided. For the most part, she avoided looking at it. Instead, she focused on the solid support network she had and the happiness she felt living alone. Sort of like Adam, she mused.

## 91

But not like Edward, whose anxiety continued to bombard him from many directions. His stomach and mind roiled, feelings of impending doom showed up in technicolored scenarios in his imagination. He thought maybe his blood pressure was high, although that had never been an issue, because he was lightheaded. His perception of the world around him shifted incomprehensibly: now one way, now another. He thought his vision was impaired. He thought he might be having a stroke.

He got up and walked around his small apartment. He wanted to leave and walk or jog, but he didn't in case Mr. Bean called back, which he was sure he would. He wanted to talk to him inside, where it was quiet. And he was pretty sure Bean would call him back soon. He glanced at his watch. The noon hour. He could be at lunch.

In the meantime, Edward practiced an imaginary conversation. Since Bean had called him, it would be natural for Edward to ask him what he wanted. Bean said in his message that he wanted to talk. Edward gave this some thought. He did not think he could get around meeting with Will somewhere. He looked around his apartment. Certainly not here, even though he probably knows where I live. Then he had a startling thought. He knows my phone number and my address. Just like that woman who called me.

This thought was not only startling; it was distressing. Are all these people united against me in some conspiratorial way? The woman who called him, Riley for sure, and now a PI named Bean? Edward couldn't be sure what this meant, but it smelled very fishy.

These things can't just be a coincidence. He sat mesmerized by his uncertainty. What does it mean? What *can* it mean?

No answer came to him. But his belief that it was significant did not diminish a bit.

Edward shook his head to file that thought and refocus on the specifics of meeting up with Bean. He wanted to be clear and intelligent about it. Are there questions I should ask him before we meet? Not a bad idea, although, again, he was uncertain what those questions might be. Should we meet somewhere private?

No, came a voice from inside him. Meet somewhere in public. That's what all the spy novels and thriller TV shows do: meet in a very public place where nothing bad can happen.

That part Edward thought was doable. They could meet at one of the traffic circles in D.C., Dupont or Logan. They were large and had a number of benches that were spaced far enough apart to have a private conversation. They were almost always populated by people coming and going or just sitting there watching or reading. A mild but distinct feeling of safety introduced itself into his mind.

He glimpsed a feeling of control. Okay, what about the questions? In fact, there was a question in Edward's mind that was so obvious it took him a minute to recognize it. Is Bean working with the police? He mentioned the police in the voicemail. Maybe he was, and maybe he wasn't. Maybe, because he used to be a cop and no doubt had connections in the department; maybe not, because he was a PI and just used that as leverage. He could not be sure, but he was leaning toward the latter. It seemed like something a PI might do. This was a guess, but it was a more calming one than the alternative.

In the end, Edward could not decide if it was even worth it to try to set any conditions or ask any questions to protect himself. He had just spent time and money trying to keep himself hidden, and it fell apart within a day. All it reaped for him was an unrelenting burden of disquiet unlike anything he had experienced in his life prior to this moment. And given how neurotic Edward knew himself to be, that seemed like a high bar.

He would just have to tell the truth.

His anxiety did not abate, but it not increase either. It just was.

## 92

Lunch was in fact where Will and Mildred were. They had decided to go to a nice little Italian restaurant not too far from the shelter where Mildred worked. It had been some time since the two had done this ordinary thing together, but it felt comfortable and familiar, despite the time lapse.

Of course, mostly they talked about the details of the immediate situation they were dealing with, except that it was in somewhat coded language so as not to disclose confidential information to anyone who might be listening. This was easy for the couple, both of whom watched their conversation carefully when in public. Mostly they talked about Will's call to Edward, trying to strategize next steps.

When their entrées came, the pair ate in silence. When they finished, they both ordered espressos.

"It's nice to see you, Millie," Will said, patting her forearm across the table.

"It's nice to see you too, Will," she replied. She felt her body temperature spike a bit. "It's been a while."

"I know. You've been busy; I've been busy. I guess this is what people call life."

Mildred nodded and took a sip of her coffee. She considered pursuing this conversation, the next step of which would a more intimate one. How are you doing? Are you dating anyone? Do you miss me? Those things that she just did not want to resurrect right now. Not that she wouldn't welcome such a conversation down the line, but now she did not want to divert her energies from the situation with Riley and Edward.

So instead, she smiled warmly and said, "We should be getting back. You probably have a call to make."

Will did not protest, but Mildred thought she sensed a certain disappointment in his face. Will was always agreeable, sometimes to the point of irritating her, but she knew he was a sensitive soul. It was another thing she loved about him.

The two stood up and left the restaurant. To Mildred's surprise, Will took her hand, and to her further surprise, she took his, as well. The pair walked down the D.C. street as any other intimate couple would, speaking softly or not at all. Signaling their closeness but not drawing attention to it. Just another close, satisfied couple.

When they got back to her office, the business at hand re-injected itself, and Will powered his phone back up to see if Edward had called back. He had. He glanced over at Mildred, nodded, and dialed Edward's number.

## 93

"Hello," said Edward.

"Mr. McAlister, this is Willard Bean. I just got your message. Thank you for calling me back."

No response. Will continued after a moment. "As I said in my message, I'm calling about an incident that involved a young woman named Riley Cotswald. Your name came up in the course of my investigation, and I want to meet with you to ask you some questions."

Bean said this in such a matter-of-fact tone that Edward was momentarily disarmed. "Okay," he said, forgetting whatever plans he had thought about. "Where would you like to meet?" Then, he thought better of that. "Wait a minute," he said. "Are you with the police?"

"No, I'm not."

"Are you going to arrest me?"

"No. I am not a police officer. For full disclosure, I used to be, but I'm not anymore."

Edward paused a bit. He couldn't think of any more questions, and the ones he had just asked seemed inane anyway. "Okay," he finally said. "Where would you like to meet?"

"Wherever is convenient for you," said Will reassuringly.

His plans returned to his mind. "How about DuPont Circle?"

"Sure. What time?"

"In an hour?" Edward wanted to get this over with.

"Great. I'll see you there at 2:00 p.m."

"How will I recognize you?"

"I am tall and slender with no facial hair. I am wearing a navy jacket and khaki trousers with plane brown oxford shoes, red patterned tie. But don't worry; I have your picture, Mr. McAlister. I'll recognize you."

Will clicked off and looked over at Mildred, who had seated herself behind her desk, facing the room. "Okay. It's all set. Dupont Circle in an hour."

Mildred nodded. "Okay," she said simply. "I'll call Riley."

She picked up her phone and dialed Riley's number. She described developments since they last met and told her tha Will would be meeting with Edward at 2:00 this afternoon.

"Where?" said Riley.

Mildred put the phone against her shoulder and whispered to Will, "She wants to know where." Will shook his head.

"Somewhere of Edward's choosing," she said, returning the phone to her ear.

Even from across the room, Will noted the silence on the line. Obviously, Riley was thinking about this and was probably wanting to be a part of the meeting. But that was the last thing Will wanted. He wanted to question Edward alone. Maybe the two of them could meet at a later date.

Then Will noticed the conversation resuming. He heard Mildred say, "Yes, we will be in touch with you immediately afterward. Don't worry, Riley." Then she hung up.

She turned to Will. "She wants to know everything."

"She deserves to know everything," Will replied. "I just want to do the questioning without her. It will be a lot easier."

Mildred nodded. Will picked up his notebook and headed toward the door. Before opening it, he turned to Mildred and said, "I'll come straight back here afterward."

Mildred nodded again.

— 94 —

Edward was not nodding. He was conflicted. Bean sounded awfully nice. He reviewed the conversation he had with himself before the call: he reminded himself that Bean was a PI, not a police officer. Dupont Circle was a very public place with several benches spaced well apart from each other, where the two could talk in private and not be interrupted. Actually, Edward thought the location was perfect: there would be people around, so he would feel safe. He could leave at any time, even physically run away if he needed to. And it was far enough away from his apartment. He wasn't sure why that was important, but it felt significant to him. It was as if he did not want to contaminate his personal space with the presence of someone questioning him. The utter irrationality of that did not even cross his mind.

Riley, meanwhile, was watching her cozy, self-satisfied feelings evaporate. She felt a rush of anxiety and then anger. She understood in her head that Will probably did not want her present for the initial interview with Edward, but every bone in her body wanted to pound Edward until he answered every question she had about why and how he singled her out to harass, and why he went to so much trouble to do it. She felt her pulse increase. She couldn't write anymore, so she saved her work on a flash drive and shut down her laptop.

She got up and paced around her apartment. She was not doing well at getting control of her mood, so finally she decided to call Jennifer to bring her up to date. She glanced at her watch: 1:15. She had mixed feelings about calling Jen at work, but Jen did offer, so she dialed her number.

The call went straight to voicemail. Ugh. She did not leave a message.

Instead, she decided to take a walk. She grabbed her keys and her phone. She glanced at her purse. Do I need that? No, I don't think so. She had credit and debit cards in the phone case, so if she needed or wanted to buy things she could. That was enough. She turned and left her apartment.

Riley knew where she was going, but she did not want herself to know that she knew. This, of course, is tricky within the confines of one's mind. But she was, after all, a novelist, and she could tolerate some mental acrobatics better than most.

Nor did she hesitate or take a circuitous route to Edward's apartment. She went straight to it, albeit at a leisurely place, as if she were out for an afternoon stroll. She had never been to his building before, but the address was seared into her mind from the moment that Jennifer first discovered it. She knew exactly where it was.

About a block away from the building, she slowed her pace. Her senses went on heightened alert. If Edward were anywhere around, she wanted to spot him first. It did not even matter to her if he saw her; she just wanted to be first.

And, as if it had been ordained sometime in the distant past that this moment would arrive, she happened to be looking at the front door of his apartment building at the precise moment that Edward himself was leaving. He closed the door and turned right down the street, in the opposite direction from Riley, not even looking around.

Satisfaction swept through Riley's soul. She glanced at her watch. 1:40. He was probably going to meet Willard. Can it be this easy, she wondered? She continued to follow him from what she believed to be a reasonable distance so that he would not notice. The streets weren't crowded, but there were enough people about that she could blend in easily.

At one point, Edward did have to cross an exceptionally busy street, and his gaze pulled in almost every degree of area around him. As if she had been trained for this moment, Riley turned and looked into a shop window to fiddle with her hair, her hand blocking her face. She knew the moment was brief, and when she looked back at Edward, he was still standing at the crosswalk, looking across the street to Dupont Circle.

She stopped and watched. She spotted Willard sitting on a bench on the far side of the circle, just checking his phone, as most of the people scattered around the Circle benches were doing. She noticed that he glanced up from time to time, looking in the general direction of where she and Edward were positioned. Willard knows where Edward lives as well, she thought. She could not tell if he recognized her; he gave no indication that he did.

She wondered what Edward was doing. She saw him glance at his watch and turn right along the next street. Killing time? She figured he was fastidious about time. How would I know that? she wondered. Then she realized that she had constructed a narrative in her mind about how Edward was, and that story line tagged him as a definite OCD type. It made sense to her, even though she had very little data to support her belief. She also noticed that Willard glanced at his watch several times.

Riley turned back. She did not want either Edward or Willard to see her there, but she was torn. She understood that Willard wanted to talk to Edward alone, and she even believed that this was in her best interest. She had too many feelings—she was too angry—to interrogate Edward in a calm, dispassionate manner. On the other hand, her heart was pounding, and she was sorely tempted to insert herself into the Boys Club meeting, where the two of them would be talking about her. That thought left a sour taste in her mouth.

To give herself some time, she lingered for a while at the shop window that she had used for cover and decided to go in. Then, she could at least observe the conversation from a distance, see how long it lasted, and go from there.

She walked around the small curio shop trying to act interested. A thin, late-middle-age woman asked if she needed assistance, and Riley, surprising even herself, gave a candid reply: "Yes, but I'm not looking for anything. There's a private investigator in Dupont Circle who is about to meet up with a man who's been stalking me, and I need a place where I can watch them without being seen."

Riley could not tell if the look on the woman's face was shock, amusement, or some peculiar combination of the two. "Honey," she said after the slightest pause. "Make yourself at home."

Riley smiled and said, "Thank you so much."

"Would you like some tea?"

"I would love some."

The woman went through an opening in the wall near the back of the shop and returned five minutes later with a pot of tea and two cups. In the meantime, Riley stood gazing out the window, looking for Edward and expecting him to reappear at any moment. She glanced at her watch. 1:50. It could be any moment. A ten-minute window is safe for even the most fastidious among us, she thought.

And it was. She and her new shopkeeper friend watched as Edward crossed Massachusetts Avenue and headed for the bench on which Willard was waiting. The two women each took a sip of tea.

"Mr. Bean?" said Edward as he approached the bench in Dupont Circle, where Will was waiting. His heart was pounding so hard he thought he and everyone else around him could hear it.

"Yes. Mr. McAlister." said Willard, standing to greet Edward and offering his hand. "Thank you for coming."

Edward shook Willard's hand and, following a gesture by Will, sat down on the bench. Will sat on the other end. Edward could feel his body shaking; he hoped Will wouldn't notice.

"Mr. McAlister," began Willard, "As I told you on the phone, I've been asked to investigate a situation that occurred recently that concerned a young woman named Riley Cotswald. I believe you are familiar with the details." He paused a bit and looked at the pad of paper in his lap, as if checking his notes. "I spoke with a bartender at A.J.'s, and he was helpful. They have surveillance cameras at their doors, and he showed me a picture of Todd Wilhaber, a man who approached Riley and, apparently, impersonated a character in her novel." He showed Edward the digital image of Todd on his phone.

This simple, clear description of events hit Edward hard. It made everything seem so obvious, so petty, so . . . pathetic. He was beginning to feel both embarrassed and nauseous. He wasn't sure which was worse.

Willard pressed on. "I visited Mr. Wilhaber yesterday, and he verified that you were the one who retained him to engage in this little charade." Will paused a bit. "Not a bad choice, I suppose; he is taking acting classes."

Edward felt this last comment to be as patronizing as it was intended. His embarrassment deepened. He felt his face start to redden.

A development that was not lost on Willard, who felt he was moving in precisely the right direction. He turned and looked up at Edward's face. "You did identify yourself as a man by the name of Randall Sheets and hired Wilhaber to do this?"

While the question was hanging in the air, Edward felt his head bobbing without his consent, tacitly providing a positive response to Bean's question, even though he was unsure if he should agree to anything.

"I'll take that as a yes," Will said.

"Yes," said Edward in the softest of whispers.

The two sat in silence for a few moments. Willard was writing in a notebook and thinking of his next move; Edward was awash in shame. He had never been so mortified in his life.

"And in order to set up this, uh, charade, you had to gain access to Ms. Cotswald's computer, which was the only place her work was located, except for a flash drive she kept in a drawer in her desk." Will's voice became gentler but did not lose its seriousness. "So, either you hacked into her computer or you broke into her apartment and stole or copied the flash drive."

Edward was biting his lip, frantically deciding whether to get up and run or to continue this tortuous conversation. But where would he run? Back to his apartment, where Bean could surely fine him? Out of the District, where he had lived and worked for over a decade? He wrapped his hands around the bench on which he was sitting and decided not to run. His knuckles were white against the dark green wood.

"Which was it?"

Edward turned away. "I hacked into her computer."

"And how did you know how to do that?"

Edward looked away, as though not facing Bean directly would somehow enable him to share what he was about to say with less guilt. "I found a guy in Maryland who taught people how to do it for a fee." His voice was flat, and he could still not bring himself to look at Bean directly. He wondered in the back of his mind if he was supposed to be feeling relief from all this confessional material. He wasn't.

"And his name is . . .?"

Edward was so startled by the question that he turned and looked at Willard. He was embarrassed to give the answer out loud, but he found he could not veer from this path of confession. "Bomber17."

"Bomber17?" Will said, writing it down. "Did he have a real name?"

"I imagine he did, but I never knew what it was."

"You paid him in cash?"

"Yes."

More silence. Will kept writing as if he were taking notes. Actually, he was thinking.

"So, Edward," he said, leaning toward him. "Why did you do this? What were you looking to accomplish?" The look on Bean's face was calm, even solicitous.

Edward again turned his head away and stared at the sidewalk in front of him. "I don't know. I wanted to get back at her. She played me. We had sex and then she dumped me. She told me she did not want to even have a relationship with me." Edward was recounting these things not so much as facts, but as thoughts he grasped out of the air, out of the universe of thoughts that went through his mind when he thought of Riley. They seemed empty now, devoid of meaning, lifeless.

Yet they had driven him to elaborate schemes that had jeopardized his well-being, his freedom, even his integrity. They led him to this ridiculous park bench being interrogated by a man he did not know. He began to feel a sense of depersonalization, the slipping away of a personality he always thought he had or was. He was feeling distance from himself, from Bean, from Riley. From the earth.

"I can't go on," he said abruptly. "I've got to go." He stood up and prepared himself to run.

"Edward," said Bean with greater force than he had used so far in the conversation. "I am not here to criticize you, and certainly not to get you into trouble. I'm just trying to understand."

The tone that Edward heard in Bean's voice was both forceful and gentle. He did not know if he could trust what Bean way saying, but he felt trapped. In truth, even in his attenuated state, he had no place to run, no place to hide. He sat back down.

"Why?" he said, looking at Bean full face.

"Because I am concerned about you," Willard said, surprising himself.

Edward shook his head. "What?!"

"Look, Edward. You must have been in some very difficult place to have done this, to have gone through all the trouble of setting it up. It wasn't easy. But it wasn't really evil, either." He looked at Edward with as much compassion as he could muster, which was getting easier as he observed the raw edge of psychological turmoil in Edward's demeanor, a place where the younger man seemed stuck.

He continued. "I did a little research on you, and what I found was a responsible guy, a teacher, who was respected by his colleagues and led an exemplary life. I could not find a single time when you violated the law, not even the traffic laws." He leaned toward Edward. "So, there must have been something to lead you to do what you did."

Will sat back a bit a let that sink in to Edward's mind. He watched as Edward tried to wrap his mind around what this Mr. Bean was saying.

But he was lost. He did not know what to think, what to believe, whether to trust Bean or not. He just did not know. Anything.

He shook his head.

Will, not wanting to lose the conversation, gently took another tack. "Tell me what happened between you and Riley," he said.

Edward blinked several times as mental images flashed through his mind: the first time he saw her, the first time he Googled her, the time he bought her book, the first time he met her, and the time they had sex. He shook his head.

"It's all a blur," he said quietly.

"Take your time," Will said.

Edward strained against telling the whole truth: how he had tracked Riley before he met her, how he practiced approaching her, how he felt she was his even before he met her, and how he was certain she was his after they had sex. It all seemed so . . . so private . . . so special. He was staring down at the sidewalk as these things ran through his mind.

"Mr. Bean," he finally said, looked up at Will. "This is a long story, and I don't think I can tell you all of it just now." He looked away. "Could we maybe meet another time? I don't want to withhold stuff; I know I screwed up big time. But this is very, very hard for me." As if to confirm this, an unforced tear fell from his eye.

Will nodded. He could see how tormented the young man was, and his heart went out to him, contrary to what he believed was the proper way for an investigator to act. But he was a human being, and he glimpsed in Edward a version of himself that could have materialized if his life had gone just a bit differently. He did not want to make Edward's pain worse. "Of course, we can, Edward. Let's find a time soon. Would tomorrow work for you?"

Edward nodded.

"Say 10:00 tomorrow morning? Where would you like to meet?"

Edward had not thought that far in advance. Tomorrow seemed very soon, but he knew if he waited too long he would just prolong his own suffering. "Tomorrow at 10:00 is fine," he said. "I don't know where to meet. Not in public. Somewhere private. You have an office?"

"I do," said Will, and he handed him a business card with the address prominently displayed.

"Edward," he said gently. "One more thing. Will you be okay this evening? I mean, do you feel safe?"

Edward was startled by Willard's question. Tears started dribbling down his face; slowly, at first, but then faster. The simple expression of genuine personal concern was alien to him. It overwhelmed him: he could not speak; his throat was constricted, and he wasn't sure he was able to move. Finally, he bobbed his head in a display of affirmation, and then got up and walked away quickly.

Will did not move as he watched Edward walk off. He felt his own eyes moisten.

## 96

Riley had not moved much during this entire conversation; nor had she taken her eyes of the two men discussing her. She simply stood in the little shop and observed the silent movie version of Willard and Edward talking through the boutique window. It was obviously intense. Willard looked as though he was conducting a professional interview. Edward looked pale, even from a distance, although, at times, his face turned various shades of crimson. She watched how at one point Edward stood up and seemed ready to leave, but then he sat down again, apparently at Willard's behest.

She could not be sure, but she thought she saw a look of intense sadness on Edward's face as he left the park bench. Was he crying?

Riley wasn't sure what to do. She glanced at the shopkeeper, who had stood near her the entire time. "Go ahead, Honey," the woman said gently. "I think it's okay now." She patted Riley gently on the back.

Riley gave her a sideways hug, told her thank you, and walked out the door headed for the park bench.

Willard did not seem surprised to see her. In fact, he was just sitting there, as if he were waiting for someone.

"I'm glad you did not interrupt us while we were talking," he said, but it was a friendly tone, not an accusing one.

"You saw me across the street?"

"Yes. I saw you go into the shop. The front is glass, you know; I could see you as clearly as you could see me. Glass is funny that way." He smiled.

Riley was a little embarrassed but more grateful that she had not barged into the conversation Willard and Edward had. She sat down on the bench. "How'd it go?"

Willard looked directly into Riley's eyes. He saw no reason to dissemble. "He did not deny anything," he said. "Truthfully, I don't think he knows why he did what he did, but we are going to meet again tomorrow morning at my office to continue the conversation."

He paused and looked at Riley, whose face seemed pained. "I think Edward is a guy in a lot of pain, Riley," he said gently.

Riley did not know what to say. Willard was being honest and objective. She knew that. Some of the original guilt she felt reasserted itself, although not severely. It just made her feel that the situation wasn't just a black-and-white kind of thing. Edward had a part; she had a part. The anger she felt earlier did not depart completely, but the intensity of it wafted away some.

"Mr. Bean," she said slowly. "Thank you for all you're doing for me." She paused a moment. "And for Edward."

Willard smiled. "Let's take this one day at a time, Riley." He glanced at his watch. "I told Mildred I would go straight back to her office when Edward and I finished, so I'm headed there now. Want to come?"

Riley shook her head. She appreciated the invitation, but she felt she had intruded enough. "No," she said. "I'll talk to Mildred later. Thanks again, Mr. Bean."

"Call me Willard," he said.

The pair stood up. Willard went one way; Riley another. Both felt that important things had happened here.

## 97

Mildred was waiting for Willard in her office. She had been trying to find things to do, but really she was just fretting over how the interview was going and wishing she had been a part of it.

She was relieved when she heard the knock on her door. "Come in, please," she said.

Willard entered and headed toward the sofa across the room. Mildred came over, gave him a hug, sat across from him on a chair. "Tell me everything."

Willard described the interview in detail. When he got to the end, the part where he asked Edward if he was going to be okay, his voice choked, just a bit.

This was not lost on Mildred. Her heart melted a little, and she could feel her body relax. Willard felt genuine compassion for Edward. This was a great sign for all concerned, but for Mildred it was yet another indication of why she cared for this man, who could do what he did and still maintain his sensitive soul. She cherished that about him.

"What do we do now?" asked Mildred when he was finished.

"Well, I'm seeing him tomorrow, and we can go from there." He thought for a moment; then turned to Mildred. "Would you like to come?"

Mildred thought about this. Part of her certainly wanted to come so she could observe up close the person who had become the focus of this entire drama. On the other hand, she knew it was unwise to just show up without Edward knowing about it in advance. She shook her head and turned to Willard. "I don't think so, Will. Not this time. But, you know, I'd love to get my clinical hands on him sometime."

They both chuckled. "Let's take this one step at a time," Will said. Then his tone turned somber. "I know Edward said he would be okay this evening, but I'm not so sure. He was pretty upset when he left me."

Mildred thought for a moment. "Of course he was upset. His grand scheme had come off the rails in ways he was totally unprepared for." She looked directly at Will. "Self-harm is always a possibility, but the fact that Edward was honest with you suggests a fairly healthy reaction to disturbing situation. It's a good sign." She looked deeply into Willard's eyes. "And the fact that you felt compassion for him suggests that *he's* capable of being emotionally authentic. That's very important."

Willard heard what Mildred said and wanted to believe her, but his apprehensions did not diminish much. He already knew he would not be getting much sleep tonight. "Well, I guess we'll see in the morning."

"I guess so."

Will shrugged and got up to leave. "I have some thinking to do, Millie. I'll contact you tomorrow after Edward and I meet." He did not wait for a response. He simply turned and walked out the door.

Mildred sat on her chair for a while, pondering what had just happened. In truth, she did not really know. She had never seen Will quite this involved in a case, and she wondered what was going on with him. Being a mental health professional, her mind ranged over many possible scenarios, but she knew she had no way of weighing one against the other in any reasonable way. This is one of the frustrations of my profession, she thought darkly. I want to know, and I don't know. And the only person who could possibly inform me just left.

She stood up, returned to her desk, and started working.

## 98

Edward left the meeting with Willard Bean completely at a loss for what to think. Emotionally, he was a mess. He rarely cried, and to lose it in front of somebody—a stranger no less!—would have been unfathomable to him at any time of his life prior to now. Except, of course, for the time that Riley dropped the bomb of abandonment on him completely by surprise.

He walked home slowly. The emotional storms began to subside a little as he walked. As usual, moving, walking, and exercising were always helpful for him: it lowered his anxiety, cleared his head some, and enabled him to breathe more deeply. He also thought that maybe he was feeling an inkling of the positive effects of coming clean about what he had been up to these past weeks. Not catharsis or euphoria or anything like that, but Bean was less confrontational than he had anticipated, and Edward had been honest with him. No matter what came next, he would just have to deal with it.

But there was something else, something he had completely overlooked prior to today. He had some trouble putting his finger on it, but it was coming together in his head. He felt more whole; he had a sense of integrity. It wasn't euphoria or catharsis or anything like that. It was simply a sense that he had been restored to himself. Simply by telling the truth to another human being. He was now beginning to see how his efforts to get back at Riley—and the devious tactics those efforts entailed—led him to be someone he wasn't: a liar and a hurtful human being. It was only now that he was beginning to see this clearly. He had simply not thought about it when he was going about planning his evil deeds. He shivered a little at how far astray he had gone from how he saw himself.

His mind flashed on the first flush of success and how awesome that seemed, how strong he felt. Now it just seems like a childish boast.

I told the truth. I will need to build on that, although I'm not exactly sure how. I really have no recourse, he thought. I can't try to dress this up and make it something it wasn't. I have to face it.

Lost in these thoughts, Edward passed his apartment building without going inside; he just wanted to keep walking. And thinking.

He had to admit that he did not really know Willard's reaction. He seemed awfully genuine to Edward, but he was an experienced interrogator. He could have been doing it for effect. That did not feel right to Edward, but it did seem to be an option he could not easily dismiss.

The whole business about lying befuddled him. He thought that many people lied frequently, although he could not think of a single instance when someone he knew lied to him personally. Edward never thought he was good at it. It always entailed some kind of cost. This made him wonder how he got it into his head that he could pull the wool over Riley's eyes and deliberately mislead her. He had an explanation, or at least he had one when he was planning the revenge. He was angry; he felt dumped. He *had* been dumped. So my outrage led me to do something I would not otherwise have done?

This notion mystified him. How could that be? Is this what it means when somebody is 'carried away by anger?' I guess so, he concluded. That feeling of shame that he had felt so acutely earlier was beginning to make another entrance. He took a deep breath and picked up his pace. Maybe I can outrun it, he thought.

But he couldn't. He had just gotten up to jogging speed when the shame and guilt and grief hit him again. He stopped at a lamppost and wrapped his arm around it to steady himself. The thought of crying in public in a crowded city dismayed him, but he did not feel he had a real choice. He tried as best he could to swallow his feelings. When he realized he couldn't, he recalled having a pair of sunglasses in his pocket. He reached in and put them on, despite the gloomy weather that had settled over the District that afternoon.

Once the emotional storm passed, he turned, bespectacled, and headed back to his apartment. Wishes flashed through his mind: he wished he had never heard of Riley, that he had never approached her, that he had just gotten over it when she dumped him, and that he had not made a fool of himself in front of the whole world. And most of all, he wished he would not go to jail or have his life upended by being arrested.

What was I thinking?

His thoughts turned to his students. Edward had always maintained a strict demarcation between his professional life and his personal life, such as it was. He was friendly with his students in a formal kind of way. He considered himself a dedicated and fair teacher. He was always prepared for class. He listened to his students carefully when they asked questions and did his best to give them solid answers. Sometimes, those questions were about personal matters. Not uncommonly, the question was, "Should I tell so-and-so about such-and-such?" or "I can't tell my parents x." And what was Edward's most common advice? Consider what it would cost you not to reveal important information to important people in your life. Picture the dishonest alternative and make a choice. Often, the student returned to thank him for giving him good advice.

As Edward made his way to his apartment, he realized how thoroughly he disregarded his own advice; how he had done exactly what he had advised numerous students not to do. And now he was paying the price.

I earned this shame, he concluded. I did it. No one forced me to. This shame is mine.

## 99

*3:00 a.m. Suzanne had eaten a wonderful meal, tasted better than average French wine, and indulged in an evening of simple self-gratification, after which she fell into a perfectly deep sleep. So, why am I awake. And why do I feel like crap?*

She sat up in bed unable to think of anything but the misery of her body, which seemed to be getting worse. And then, not a moment too soon, she leapt to her feet and got to the bathroom with about two seconds to spare before she ejected the contents of that wonderful meal into the oversized porcelain toilet. *Jesus Christ!* she exclaimed through her bile-tasting lips.

She stood up and felt a little woozy, so she sat back down on the same toilet. The room spun, but just a little. *Am I drunk?* She did not feel drunk. She had sipped the wine throughout the evening, and, while she finished the bottle, it had taken her four hours to do so. That, plus the food, made it seem unlikely to her that she was intoxicated, especially since she had also had four hours of sleep since then.

*Food poisoning? Possible.* She had never had that before, so she wasn't sure what the symptoms were. *I could look that up,* she realized. But she needed to be able to walk first, and just now she wasn't sure that was possible.

She sat there for some time before another possibility dawned on her. *No, no, no. It can't be.* She thought back. *Actually, it could be. But not now, maybe not ever.* Ambitious though she might be, she never considered a replica of herself to be a beneficial contribution to the earth.

*She forced herself to think. When was my last period? She couldn't remember. Her mind was battling the residual effects of whatever was ailing her and her growing anxiety about the prospect that she might be pregnant.*

*Of all the thoughts that were tumbling through her mind, one was about sitting in a hotel throwing up, being pregnant, and being alone. This is not something she signed up for. Being alone and being alone with a child were two vastly different things.*

*She forced herself to think back. It was true that she had been spotty with her birth control pills, since almost all of her sexual contact the six months before her separation from Adam was with a woman. She could not discern, however, just how spotty it was. Maybe I missed a few? But she could not recall exactly when.*

*Of course, I have choices. If I am pregnant, I do not have to carry the baby to term. She wished she could recall her last period; it's not as if she weren't regular. She just could not be sure she could pinpoint the very last time.*

*Suzanne knew that there was only one opportunity to have been inseminated, and it was the last night she and Adam were together. Adam. Would he want a child? Under these circumstances? Suzanne found her head shaking no even before she determined an answer. I don't think so. But that may be what I think, not what he thinks.*

*Finally, she felt good enough to stand, so she turned to the mirror in the large bathroom and beheld her image. You look like shit, she said candidly to the image facing her. She pushed back her hair and decided to brush her teeth to rid herself of the awful taste in her mouth. The toothpaste and the mouthwash helped but did not completely eradicate it.*

*She turned and walked back to the bed. She thought of her parents. They would want to know. How would they feel about an abortion? Not great. Nobody wants to be a part of such a thing. Not her parents, not Adam. If I go that route, it would be best to be absolutely quiet about it and tell no one.*

*Or I could carry the baby to term and give it up for adoption.*

*Or I could calm down and wait until I find out if I'm really pregnant before I panic.*

*She decided to call her former OB/Gyn in the morning and see if she could get an appointment.*

*That was enough to allow her to fall back asleep, but it was not enough to stop her dreams.*

*In an especially colorful one, she dreamt she and Adam were driving up Highway One in California, that breathtakingly beautiful roadway that hugs the mountains along the Pacific Coast. Truly one of the most fabulous drives in the entire country. Also one of the scariest, especially if driving south on the ocean side. The drop-offs were sheer, the guard rails few, and the confidence of the driver meant everything. In her dream, the last element was iffy.*

*Which, upon awakening, described her current predicament pretty well.*

Jesus, Suzanne, how could you be so careless? Riley stared at the screen surprised by this development. Pregnant? That's not something I need to worry about, thank God.

She wanted to get back to writing because her mind was so benumbed by the predicament in which she found herself. She wanted to be angry at Edward, but Willard's calm, sensible view of the situation had an outsized impact on her. I have been selfish, she told herself. I've lost objectivity.

That was one of the nice things about writing fiction, she allowed: it permits me to escape the objective world and enter into a subjective one of my choosing. It's a relief to get away from the real world sometimes. Often, she corrected herself.

She had no idea what to do about Edward. She wanted to escape, to run from it. It was not clear; it was messy. She did not want to hurt him, but she was, despite herself, still angry about the whole sorry mess.

Her phone rang. She glanced at the number; it was Jennifer. Thank God. "Hi, Jen," she said.

"Hi, Honey. Just calling to check on you. How're you doing?"

"Complicated," Riley replied. She glanced at her watch. "Can we meet up for happy hour at Carter's?"

"Sure," said Jennifer.

"Great. I'll meet you there in twenty minutes."

Riley was relieved. She needed someone to talk to. Someone who was on her side but capable of objectivity.

## 100

Jennifer was at a table when Riley got to Carter's. This was a familiar thing—seeing Jennifer nursing a vodka martini with exactly three olives in a booth along the far wall of their most frequented restaurant. Riley immediately began to feel better.

She bent over and gave Jen a peck on the cheek, which seemed to surprise her friend, but not in a bad way. Jennifer looked at her expectantly. "Must have been some day," she noted.

"It's been some day," said Riley, who was waving to get the attention of the server. "I'll tell you all about it, but I need a drink first."

Drink ordered, she turned to Jennifer and began telling her about the events of the day: about Willard learning that Edward was indeed behind this business because he tracked down the person who impersonated Adam; about the call from Mildred bringing her up to speed; about observing Willard and Edward talking in Dupont Circle; even about Willard's take on things, which did not exactly extinguish her anger at Edward but gave her a broader perspective. She was trying to be a grown-up about all this.

"Jesus Christ!" said Jen in a voice that ensured that every single person in the restaurant heard her. She noticed that the server was approaching with Riley's drink, snatched it from her, and served it to Riley, who seemed just about to burst. "You're right. You need this."

Jennifer stared at Riley for a while trying to digest everything she had just been told. "So this Willard: he moves fast?"

"Yes, he does."

"He did all this in, like, a day or two."

"Yes."

Jennifer took a sip of her drink. As did Riley.

"Jesus."

"You keep saying that."

"That's only the second time. I might have to say it again."

The two women chuckled.

"Honestly, Jen, I don't know what to make of all this. The day this stupid thing happened, I was weirded out. I thought maybe I really was losing my mind. I guess that's what Edward wanted. But that did not last long. Then I met up with Mildred, who has been nothing but a huge support. And she, of course, brought in Willard. And Willard is a fucking magician. In twenty-four hours, he went to A.J's, identified Todd, which is the name of the guy who introduced himself to me as Adam. He drove all the way to Norfolk to meet up with him. Todd led him straight to Edward.

"Evidently, Edward thought he had all his bases covered, but he did not figure in the surveillance cameras." When Riley said this, her head nodded toward a camera above the bar filming everyone in the place. "Welcome to the twenty-first century, Edward!" She raised her glass.

And Jennifer clinked with hers. She put her glass back on the table. "Tell me about the meeting between Edward and Willard."

"That's where this all came to a head. I wasn't absolutely sure where it was going to be, but I headed in the general direction of Edward's apartment. I was a block away when I spotted him leaving his building." She took a sip of her drink. "So, I followed him to Dupont Circle, where Willard was sitting on one of the benches. I slipped into a little shop so Edward wouldn't see me. He left for a while, then he came back. I knew he was meeting up with Willard at 2:00, but Edward was early. I saw him at about 1:40. He was back on Mass. Ave. at 1:50 and went straight to the bench where Willard was sitting." She took another sip of her drink. "It was as if they knew each other."

"This really nice lady who ran the shop asked me if she could help me, and I told her the truth. I told her I was watching a PI question a guy who'd been stalking me. She was great. She told me I could stay as long as I needed. She got me some tea. We both watched Willard and Edward talk. It was like watching a silent movie. We could tell some things: at one point, Edward stood up and looked as if he were about to leave, but then he sat down again. At the end, he seemed really, really upset—I think he was crying—and he walked away fast. Not a run, but it was obvious he wanted to get out of there."

She took another sip of her drink. "This is good."

Jennifer hadn't said a word and was listening intently to what Riley was telling her.

Riley continued. "So after Edward left, I went up to Willard, who was still sitting on the bench, and he acknowledged that he had seen me before Edward even showed up. So Willard says something like 'Edward is in a lot of pain.' I mean, I guess I figured that, but Willard seemed really, really concerned about Edward."

Then she suddenly stopped. "Wait, let me back up. Willard also said that Edward did not deny anything. He admitted hacking into my computer and hiring this Todd guy to play Adam, coaching him along the way and paying him to impersonate one of my characters."

"Wow," said Jen.

"Wow," said Riley.

After staring into their respective beverages for a while, Jennifer looked up at Riley with one eyebrow raised. "What happens now?"

Riley thought for a while. "I'm not sure. Willard was going back to Mildred's office to bring her up to speed. I think he may be meeting with Edward again. Maybe even tomorrow." She paused a bit. "He asked me if I wanted to go with him back to Mildred's, but I didn't. I already felt I got busted for just watching him and Edward talk. It felt like I was being too intrusive."

Jennifer shrugged as if she perhaps did not quite agree with that assessment, but she didn't say anything.

"So, I have lots of feelings. I still have some guilt about initiating sex with Edward, even though I new when I first met him that he was shy and inexperienced. I'm still really angry that he went through this whole stupid charade just to get back at me, but I kind of feel sorry for him." Another reflective pause. "Honestly, I think

Edward is more than a little on the weird side, but I just don't think of him as a bad guy, a bad person."

It was Jennifer's turn to think a bit. "Well, he's not exactly a good guy, either."

"Apparently, he is. Or he was up until now. You know he's never even gotten a traffic ticket? That's impressive."

Jennifer frowned a bit and shook her head. "I don't think that's so impressive, Riley. I've never had a traffic ticket. Have you?"

"Come to think of it, no, I haven't." She smiled a sheepish smile. "I guess I was being dramatic."

The two women chuckled. They both reached their hands across the table at the same moment and clasped them together. "I'm so glad you're my friend, Jen."

Then she pulled away. "And on top of everything, Suzanne might be pregnant!"

Jennifer froze and blinked twice. She never knew what to say when Riley was being like this; it seemed a little psychotic in a person who struck her as otherwise pretty sane.

## 101

The next morning, Edward awoke after a surprisingly sound night's sleep. He could not recall any dreams he might have had; nor did he feel so awful as he had the day before. He was still concerned, even worried, but he felt more aware of himself somehow. It was an improvement.

But still, he had mixed feelings about meeting a second time with Bean. On the one hand, he had to admit that as time went on from the difficult conversation yesterday, he began feeling better: more centered, calmer, not quite so anxious. Not that his anxiety had left him entirely, but it was much closer to the quotidian type to which he had long grown accustomed.

On the other hand, what was the point? This guy is a PI, not a police officer. I don't have any responsibility to tell him everything about myself—or anything, really. But Edward recognized that he found talking to Bean to be fairly easy, given how constrained he ordinarily felt talking to just about anyone.

He knew in his heart that he would not let himself skip the meeting. That just wasn't like him: he was a responsible person. He felt a huge need to be that person again. It was clear to him, now in retrospect, how carried away he had gotten and how he had not quite deliberately relinquished his responsible self to a very selfish and narrow version of himself that now embarrassed him beyond belief. He was beginning to have trouble even imagining how he had come to that point.

The single time Edward had darkened the door of a therapist was after his parents died, and he was beside himself with grief and depression. He only went once, dismissing the whole enter-prise because he felt only a tiny bit better after the session. But the therapist had used a word that struck him and stayed with him ever after: obsessive. The kindly late-middle-age therapist gently explained that people who were obsessive—and he made it clear in his understated way that he was including Edward in this group—have a particularly hard time with feelings. For most people, feelings come and go, even strong ones. But often respon-sible obsessives seem to believe, unconsciously perhaps, that they must suffer, or at least that they should be extremely careful about expressing their feelings openly, for reasons therapists speculate about but do not actually know. So painful feelings, such as a person experiences in the face of the death of close ones, becomes more like a sentence, a deserved punishment, than an emotional wave with a beginning, middle, and end.

This notion registered with Edward. Since then, he periodically looked up more about obsessive personality. He recognized those features in himself, but he would hardly claim to be an expert. But he knew enough to recognize that he was obsessed with Riley, and that her rejection of him triggered an upsurge in feelings that included rage, guilt, shame, and god-knows-what else, feelings that he could not block or gloss over, and that he apparently tried to manage by weaving an elaborate revenge plot.

Now that all seemed so pitiful and . . . unnecessary. Sure, he was attracted to her; and sure, the sex was great. But he could continue a quest for women he was attracted to. And the fact is Riley has a right to date or not date whomever she wants. Just thinking about what he did embarrassed him so much he felt his face flushing in the privacy of his own living room.

This would be a good reason to skip the meeting, he thought.

Right after he thought that, he started to get ready. He took a shower, shaved, carefully selected his wardrobe, and checked Bean's office location on Google Maps. It wasn't far from his apartment.

— 102 —

In some respects, Willard was almost as nervous about the meeting as Edward. His sleep wasn't so sound: he woke up periodically throughout the night and checked the local news feed on his phone. He knew he was worried about Edward going off the deep end and hurting himself or someone else—Riley being the most likely target—and Will could not bear the thought that he could do nothing to prevent that.

He tried to remind himself of what Millie had said to him: how it was a good sign that . . . that what? Will tried to recall, but in the middle of the night, beset by less-than fully formed fears, he couldn't. That did not help his anxiety.

He finally gave up and got out of bed around 5:00 a.m. He showered, dressed, and headed to the office early. He wanted to review everything he knew and did not know about this entire situation.

It seemed pretty straightforward. Sensitive guy gets jilted and weaves elaborate plot to get revenge on the woman who dumped him. It had kind of a deranged coloring to it, but in some ways it was preferable to the more common forms of revenge, such as assaulting or killing the person, that Willard was familiar with. Comparatively, it seemed almost benign.

But something kept gnawing at him. Despite how silly the thing struck him at first, he could not help thinking that he was missing something, that there was some other reason Edward would go to such lengths to exact revenge on Riley. What kind of person does this? Will did some more searching online to fill out the picture of what he knew about Edward. There were no arrests; no psychiatric hospitalization that he could find, although that sort of information was not readily available due to privacy constraints.

But police records were available, and there weren't any. Many psych admissions start with police actions, and there was no sign of any kind of altercation of which Edward was a part.

He decided to call Mildred. He knew her to be an early riser, so he wasn't worried about waking her up. It was, after all, about 6:30 a.m.

Mildred picked up after a single ring. "Good Morning, Will," she said pleasantly.

"Good Morning," he replied. He waited a moment while he gathered his thoughts. "Millie, I've been going over this case with Edward, and I can't help thinking I'm missing something. Honestly, on one level it seems straightforward, but in another way it seems way over the top. From what you know, do you think there is something I'm missing here?"

Mildred thought for a few minutes. "It's hard to say without interviewing Edward," she finally said. "You haven't heard from him today, have you?"

"No, I haven't. We're scheduled to meet at my office at 10:00."

Silence on both ends.

Mildred wanted to attend the session, but she still felt it would be unfair to Edward if he did not know about her being there in advance.

"You know, Will. I said yesterday that it would be unfair for me to show up without notice at your meeting with him. But I could be at your office, and you could ask him when you're finished if he would be willing to talk to me."

That sounded reasonable to Will on the surface, but he wasn't sure, so he erred on the side of caution. "You know, Millie, I think even that might spook him. Why don't I just suggest to him to talk to you, and then we can set up a time if he's amenable?"

"That makes sense, Will. I'll be available any time that works for him."

"Any other advice?"

Millie thought for a moment. "If he shows up after what you described yesterday, it will be a good sign. If you see something that worries you or makes you suspicious, I think it would be wise simply to share your concerns with him and get his reaction. From what you said, he sounds contrite now, and I think you can rely on that."

"Okay. Thanks, Mil. I'll be in touch." He hung up.

This conversation assuaged Will's anxiety enough to focus on what his concerns actually were. And the major one was that Edward would do something to harm himself. He did not really believe he would hurt Riley: he had tried that, and it didn't work out so well.

Will glanced at the clock on his desk. It was only 7:30. He felt better about the meeting, so he decided to go get breakfast before Edward got there. He had plenty of time.

Edward walked into Willard Bean's office at precisely 9:55 a.m. The receptionist, who had been there since 9:00 a.m., asked him to have a seat and offered him coffee or water. Edward politely declined.

He looked around the office, never having been in a PI's office ever. He could not even recall seeing one on TV, although he probably had; he just did not pay much attention. The waiting room was small, but nicely appointed. The woman behind the desk was maybe in her early 40s, pleasant enough, attractive enough.

The receptionist had pressed a button announcing Edward's arrival, so Willard came out of his office and greeted the younger man in the waiting room and shook his hand. "Come on in," he said, gesturing toward the door leading to a hall that led to his office.

Edward did not say a word; he just nodded. Bean had asked for this meeting, so he just assumed Willard would be the one asking questions, as he had done yesterday. He sat down on a chair in front of Willard's desk and waited silently.

Willard took his seat behind his desk and glanced down at his papers. Then, he looked up at Edward. "How're you doing, Edward?" he said.

Edward shrugged. "Okay," he said.

Willard wasn't sure how sincere that was, but it was enough to get down to business. "Good," he said. "Let's pick up where we left off yesterday. I'd like to know what happened between you and Riley Cotswald."

Edward exhaled slowly and peered out the only window in the office. The small muscles around his mouth twitched a bit. And he was quiet for a minute or so. Then, he nodded to no one in particular, looked across Wil's desk, and took in a deep breath.

"I first saw Riley at a Starbucks, where she goes pretty regularly. I actually started tracking her. I mean, not following her, but watching her there, keeping track of the times she would show up. I teach, so I'm often free in the middle of the afternoon, and I like that location."

Edward observed Bean listening carefully and taking occasional notes. He took another deep breath. "So one day, she paid for her coffee with a debit card and left the receipt on the table and left the restaurant. I picked it up and had her name. I went home and did a little searching online and found out that she was a writer." He paused again as his face reddened. "I bought her book. I started fantasizing about her. Then, one day I finally asked her out."

Willard could see that beads of sweat were appearing on Edward's forehead as he was talking.

"You know, I'm not great with women," Edward blurted out. "Riley just seemed like someone, I don't know, someone I would really like to hang out with. She's really pretty, she's smart, she's introverted. I had never seen her with anyone at the coffee shop. So, I thought I had at least a decent chance." Long pause. "I finally got up enough courage to ask her out." Another long exhale.

"And she did not shut me down. We talked for a while. She asked questions. Then she just explained that she was going through a divorce and wasn't ready to go out with anyone yet, and I felt okay about that. It made sense." He paused a bit. "In fact, it made me like her more. I like honesty in a person."

Willard was taking notes. Edward paused in part to give him time to finish. When Will looked up, Edward continued. Will noticed that Edward's hands had started shaking a little.

"Okay, here's the hard part," Edward said. "The next day I'm sitting in the same coffee shop, and Riley comes storming in—and I mean storming; she seemed really hopped up, kind of angry— and she comes right up to me and asks me if I still want to go on a date, and I say 'sure,' and she kisses me right there in the coffee shop and we go to her apartment, where we make love for the rest of the afternoon."

Edward's face was paler than Will had ever seen before. He did not say anything.

Edward did not speak either.

"And then?"

Edward's eyes widened. "It was the best thing that ever happened to me in my entire life."

As Willard worked to suppress a smile, something clicked in his mind.

"Tell me about it," Will said gently.

Edward did. "It was just great. Everything about it was wonderful. Riley is not just beautiful, she is sexy and aggressive and takes charge and . . . it was like nothing I had ever felt or experienced before."

Will was motionless.

Edward looked out the window. "I know this sounds stupid, but from then on I just assumed we would be together." He turned back to face Will. "Just me and Riley, together."

Will waited without taking his gaze off Edward. "And then?"

Edward's body deflated a bit in his chair. "Then, the next day I go to her apartment. She's not there. I wait for her. When she shows up in a taxi, she asks me what I'm doing there. I tell her I wanted to see her again and had no way to contact her. I told her I didn't even know her last name, much less her phone number. All I knew was where she lived." He looked down. "She was mad."

Edward started looking out the window, unsure of what to say next. He shook his head, as if giving up. "What I told her was not really the truth. The fact was I did know her last name and other things about her. I had looked her up and knew all that stuff." He hung his head. "I lied to her."

"Edward," Will said. "When was this?"

Edward thought for a moment. "It was weeks ago, long before this recent stuff happened."

"So it wasn't this thing that triggered your . . . revenge?"

Edward shook his head. "No, that didn't happen until later. A little while after that incident in front of her apartment building, I ran into her in a different coffee shop, and she told me in no uncertain terms that she would not have a relationship with me." He looked away wistfully. "I was surprised to run into her again. I hadn't seen her for a while. I was so happy to see her. I thought maybe we could hook up again . . ."

"What did you do when she told you that would not happen again?"

Again, Edward shook his head. "I ran out of the coffee shop as fast as I could. I went home." He hung his head. "I cried. A lot."

Will looked at Edward questioningly.

"And that was when I started to get so angry; I knew I had to do something to get back at her."

Will kept writing until he realized Edward had stopped talking. The two men looked at each other. Edward looked as if he were getting angry; Will was wondering what to ask next.

"You doing okay?" Will finally said.

"Yeah . . . No . . . I don't know," said Edward. "What's 'okay'?"

Willard shrugged. "Good question. Tell me something, Edward. What's the hardest part about telling me this story?"

That seemed to jog something in Edward's mind. "It's the whole thing, Mr. Bean. I don't know what got into me. I am so sorry." He stopped and looked at Willard with an intense expression Will had not seen from him before. "She knows, doesn't she? She knows it was me?"

Will nodded. "Yes, she knows."

Edward looked away. "So I'll never see her again."

Will did not respond.

Edward looked at Willard for a moment, shook his head, and got back to his story. He described how he found Bomber17, where they met, how much it cost him. He also told the story of finding Todd and provided similar details.

"Is there anything else that's important for me to understand about this situation, Edward?"

Edward thought for a few moments. "I don't think so, no." He looked at Willard sorrowfully. "Will you be seeing Riley? Will you tell her about this conversation?"

"I am not sure I'll be seeing her, but I might. I will not share the details of this conversation with her. This has been for my benefit, so I could understand why a smart, responsible guy like you could have dreamed up and implemented such a scheme like this."

"Mr. Bean, will I get arrested?"

"That's up to Ms. Cotswald, Edward. She would have to file a criminal complaint. We've not really talked about doing that. That's one of the reasons for this investigation."

"Are you going to, like, make a recommendation?"

"Yes, I will."

Edward stared at Willard for a long moment. "Can I ask what that will be?"

Willard put his pen down and leaned forward on his desk, placing both hands on top of it. "The way I see this, Edward, you were a guy who got carried away, largely because you had such a great sexual experience with Riley. You made a lot of assumptions about a future with her that turned out not to be true. Your plan to get back at her was . . . creative, but it was not a physical assault. You may have tried to hurt her psychologically, although I think she's recovered from that. And there may be some residual effects, such as trust issues with men. I personally would not recommend getting the police involved at this point."

Willard glanced out the window for a moment.

"It's also true that it is illegal to hack into someone's computer without permission. And, as I said, it's really up to Ms. Cotswald how she proceeds.

Edward memorized every word that came out of Willard's mouth. He had never been this open with anyone in his life, and he had a sense that he could trust what Bean was saying, and he also had a very clear understanding that Bean was giving his opinion and that the final determination would be made by Riley. He was as clear as he could be about where he stood. Not completely out of the woods, but with more hope than he had when he walked in the door.

"One more thing," Willard said. "Ever since I started this investigation, the more I've gotten to know you I've been worried." He shook his head as if deciding how far to go. "I am primarily concerned that you might do something to harm yourself." He looked at Edward expectantly.

Edward did not know what to say. And he could feel emotions rising inside of him, much as they did at the end of their conversation the day before but more controllable. "Mr. Bean, I don't want to hurt myself. Ever." He felt the sincerity in his own voice.

So did Willard. "I believe you, Edward. And I am glad and relieved to hear it."

"Just one more thing, Mr. Bean. If you see Riley, please tell her I am so sorry."

"I promise, Edward."

Edward stood up, paused a moment, and reached across the desk to shake Willard's hand. The two men held their hands together for a few moments. "Take care of yourself, Edward."

"I will, Mr. Bean. Thank you." And he walked out the door.

— 104 —

Willard sat back down at his desk to give himself a little time to absorb what he learned. So this was about sex—great sex at that. He allowed himself the smile he had suppressed earlier. Edward's not a bad guy, he decided. A little on the strange side, but not bad.

But he did get carried away. No one involved in this matter had talked about legal action of any sort, and Willard was pleased that this was the case. Nobody's life should be wrecked because of a single episode that got out of hand, even if it got *way* out of hand, so long as no one was permanently injured. He wondered idly if Riley would be satisfied with a simple apology from Edward or if she just preferred never to have any contact with him again. He was pretty sure Edward would provide an apology; he doubted that Riley would go along. She would probably opt for the latter option. Willard really had no basis for thinking this; it was just how she struck him.

He glanced at his watch. It was time to call Mildred. She answered right away and invited him over to her office.

Willard decided to walk. It was a beautiful day, and the exercise felt good. He realized on his way over how worried he had been about Edward. It was unusual for Will to get so emotionally entangled in a case, but he figured relationships were complicated things. They are difficult, he mused, thinking of his experience with the woman he loved more than any other he had met in his entire life. The woman he was going to see now. The woman he had given up being close to in order to hold onto her.

That bargain never struck him as entirely satisfactory. It's hard to turn off the intimate inclinations that pop up, sometimes—maybe usually—at unexpected times. Just yesterday, at lunch, he felt so close to Mildred he took her hand without thinking about it as they walked back to her building. And she did not resist at all. He could have kissed her but didn't. That would be crossing a line he had set up for himself. But it didn't mean he didn't want to.

He was in the middle of these delightful but befuddling thoughts when he arrived at Mildred's building. He rang himself in and went straight to her office. She was standing at her desk talking on the phone when he entered. When she saw him, she motioned for him to sit on the couch. Then, she wrapped up her call and walked over and sat in a chair across from him. "How'd it go?"

"Good," replied Will. "He was as honest today as he was yesterday. I thought he was sincere: he knows he got carried away and seems to feel genuine remorse."

Mildred was looking at Will intensely and nodding occasionally. "Did you ask him about safety?"

"Yes, I did. He assured me that he never wanted to hurt himself. Or anyone else, for that matter."

The two sat with their respective thoughts for a while. Mildred looked up. "Do you think he needs to see somebody?"

Will shrugged. "I'm sure it would help him, but I also think he's not the kind of person who would volunteer for therapy. I got the impression he was as open with me as he had been with anyone."

"What did you learn, Will?"

"It actually came down to something that surprised me a little. Evidently, Edward had asked Riley out at a coffee shop they both frequent. She tells him about her divorce and how she wasn't ready for a relationship. The next day she breezes into the same coffee shop, spots Edward, and tells him that she's changed her mind. She takes him to her place where they spend all afternoon having sex. Edward described this as the best thing that had ever happened to him in his life." He looked at Mildred. "He said he assumed then that he and Riley would be together. But then he went to her apartment the next day, and she got mad. Some days later they run into each other again, and he gets all excited. But she says to him in no uncertain terms that they will not have a relationship. He was crushed. That's when things went downhill." Will was shaking his head.

Mildred cocked her head to the side, as if trying to wrap her mind around what Will was saying. It made peculiar psychological sense, even if it seemed a bit sketchy.

"What do you think pushed him over the edge, Will?"

"I don't know if I have a complete answer to that question, Millie. He did say that he had been 'tracking' Riley for some time before he approached her the first time. He found out her name, Googled her, and even read her first book. So their meeting was not really an impulsive thing; actually, there was nothing impulsive about his first approach." Will paused and looked away. "I really think after that erotic afternoon that he felt he had happened upon something big, something he had dreamt about, maybe for a long time. It was like a dream come true until Riley shattered it by telling him she did not want a relationship." He shrugged. "That's about as close as I can come, Millie."

Mildred thought for a while. "I'd love to know about his background, but I don't imagine that really came up in your conversation with him."

"No, it didn't. Frankly, once he got to disclosing how this all happened, it did not seem so mysterious. Sure it was over the top as paybacks go, but I think it was more . . . what's the right word . . . pathetic, I guess. More pathetic than anything. Almost childish, except that the child had money, was actually an adult, and was willing to be creative."

Mildred smiled at that characterization. Sounded right to her. "What do you think we should do with Riley?"

Will thought for a while. "Edward asked me if I was going to make a recommendation, and I said yes. He was predominantly concerned with the police getting involved, and I told him that would not be my recommendation, but I also told him that it was really up to Riley to determine that."

"Why not contact the police, Will? What he did was clearly illegal. And he set out to hurt her. It might have been emotional, psychological hurt he wanted to inflict, but it was pain nonetheless. And he actually succeeded in that for a time."

Will nodded. He did not disagree with Mildred's point. But he was hesitant. "Basically, it comes down to the police having more pressing things to do, Millie. The fact was Riley did get over it fairly quickly, there do not seem to be any residual effects. It would be low on their priority."

"What about civil action?"

Will looked at Mildred skeptically. "Why?"

"Because he went to great lengths to hurt her, he violated her personal space, he broke a number of laws in the process. And because it might dissuade him from trying something like this in the future."

Will shrugged. "Maybe so, but I think that's already been accomplished, Mil."

"Maybe," she said without conviction.

Will glanced around the room and then met Mildred's eyes directly. "Do you really think it would be in Riley's best interest for her to prolong this with a legal fight that could go on for months or even years?"

Mildred shrugged. It has been her life's work for many years to advocate for women who had been hurt. It was not something she could relinquish easily. "I don't know, Will. I'll need to think about it for a while."

"Okay," Will said, hoping his irritation wasn't showing. "I think my part in this is done, unless you think I should talk with Riley."

"I think that would be a good idea." She turned her head sideways. "I'd like to be there for that."

"I'm sure Riley won't mind. Go ahead and set it up."

Mildred nodded. "Okay."

Will stood up. "Keep me posted," he said. "I'll try to be as flexible as I can." He nodded once more and left the room.

God, relationships are hard, Mildred thought after he left. Of course, she picked up on his irritation. And truthfully, she wasn't sure if she wanted Riley to take any further action; it was just a possibility that popped into her head. And in the end, it was entirely up to Riley whether she wanted to do that or not. She did not like it when she and Will had altercations, even simple disagreements such as this one. But, she admonished herself: it comes with the territory.

Edward's walk home from Bean's office was almost the opposite of the trek he did yesterday after his first meeting with him. Yesterday was an emotional quagmire, but today his feelings seem to have drifted away. He figured they went somewhere, but they weren't immediately available to him. Instead, his mind was filled with thoughts. He walked slowly, breathing in the fresh air, thinking calmly about himself, his life, and his future.

Of all the things he told Bean—and it was a lot—the one thing that stood out to him was his prompt response to Bean's question about doing harm to himself. At the time, Edward responded with what felt to him, and probably to Bean, was absolute sincerity. Edward wasn't sure what to make of that. As he thought about it now, it didn't seem exactly true.

Of course, he had thought of killing himself periodically throughout his life, but he never felt it was serious. A few weeks ago, it was one of the options he considered before he had the idea of driving Riley crazy. He recalled feeling relieved at the time that he found an alternative. The fact was he never got close to actually doing away with himself.

But that was before all the recent stuff happened, before he made a huge mess of things. Even though he believed Bean—he actually felt Bean cared for him, at least a little bit—he knew it was not a sure thing that the police wouldn't be brought in. He didn't know what he would do if that happened. Nor did he know what would happen because of it. Would he lose his job? Would he be arrested? Could Riley sue him? All of these questions loomed large in his mind; but they were just questions, ones that would be answered in due course.

They were troublesome enough. But the other thing that was tugging at his mind was the larger canvas of his life, the backdrop of what was going on now. It did not look encouraging. In his mind, he moved from his current predicament, which had a number of unknowns just now, to the larger picture. Where am I in my life? He shook his head, as he tallied up the pros and cons. He had a job that he valued, perhaps more than liked. But his social life was very, very limited. He had few friends. There was no one close enough for him to talk to about what's been going on. He did not have any hobbies to speak of, with the possible exception of personal fitness. But that didn't seem like a hobby so much as an obligation to take care of himself. Like taking a shower or brushing your teeth. He did not have a girlfriend, and even the thought of that after his experience with Riley made his stomach churn. It might be a while. Maybe never. He didn't know. It didn't seem likely at the moment.

When he got to his apartment, he looked around and saw it in a different light. It was neat and clean—he was fastidious about that—but it was so empty. No mementos, no personal pictures, no wall hangings. It was functional. That was it. And small.

But it was the emptiness that stood out to him; it was a thing that seemed to define his life. He wasn't sad, really. He had probably expelled all the sadness he was capable of in the past twenty-four hours. Now he just felt empty. And the emptiness did not seem to have a bottom.

## — 106 —

Riley put the phone down after talking to Mildred, who relayed what she and Willard thought about meeting with her. Mildred thought it best if she heard directly from Willard about his meetings with Edward rather than from her secondhand account. Riley was happy to oblige. They settled on a time the next day.

All Riley really felt was relief. She sat back in her chair and took a couple deep breaths. She wasn't sure what Willard could tell her that he had not told her yesterday, but she wanted to cover all her bases before she put this whole sorry story to rest.

She also wanted to know as much as she could about the how and why of this situation. Why me? Why was it all so elaborate? What did he do to my computer? She did not know the answers to these questions, but she was sure she would feel better if she did. She also had some things she wanted to discuss with Mildred and Willard. Things like: Where to now? Do I need to do anything else? Is it really over?

For the most part, the situation felt resolved in Riley's mind, but she wanted to make sure. And meeting with Mildred and Willard was the best way to do that. She looked forward to meeting with them.

In the meantime, it was back to work.

*The next day, Suzanne called her former OB/Gyn's office and explained what she wanted. They arranged an appointment for that afternoon.*

*Suzanne was relieved but anxious. She did not want to face the choices that she knew in her heart she would have to face. She put her hand on her still-flat stomach, wondering if the stirrings of life were going on beneath the surface. She did not know exactly what to think. The thought of a new life growing inside her was not without appeal: it gave her a warm feeling that surprised her. At the same time, that feeling was all but overshadowed by the sheer inconvenience of the timing of having a child. She was under a lot of pressure at work to perform, and this was her moment to succeed in this higher-level job or not. Even after just a couple weeks in her new position, she saw just how much of a step up she had made.*

*Plus, she was alone. Sure, she had parents, even some friends, but she lived alone, ate alone most of the time, did solitary things when she had the time. Other people she knew, especially her friends, were busy or had moved away, or were in similar professional situations, where work took precedence over everything.*

*All due to decisions she made and to the tragic circumstance of Ellie's death.*

*That last part was not in my control, she thought darkly.*

*No, it wasn't. But you benefited greatly.*

*Suzanne shook her head to terminate the internal conversation. She did not want to second-guess herself. She wanted to move forward.*

*So she got ready for a day of meetings at her former office, stopped for a coffee on the way, swallowed some ibuprofen, and prepared to go about her day as if nothing unusual were going on. She was still a little queasy, but she thought she could make it until her afternoon appointment.*

*And she did. It seemed to take more out of her than usual to listen to people droning on, especially privileged people—it was a meeting of directors of branch offices—and she fought to keep her irritation in check. She smiled and nodded along with the others, although she had a feeling she was not the only person in the room wishing she were somewhere else.*

*At lunch, she declined the obligatory glass of white wine in favor of water, just in case. She explained in passing that she was a little queasy, which was certainly true. She did not let on about her big suspicion.*

*Finally, the day wrapped up. The other directors were planning to go out for a happy hour at a local bar. Suzanne begged off, pleading fatigue, which was not inaccurate, and wishing everyone a pleasant evening. She was glad to be done.*

*She took an Uber to her doctor's office downtown, which was not far. She could have walked, but suddenly the fatigue she felt seemed to take over. She almost fell asleep in the back seat during the ten-minute ride.*

*She arrived at the office, thanked the driver, and took the elevator to the appointed floor. She walked in, told the receptionist she was there, and sat down on a chair in an empty waiting room. Must be the end of the day for them, she thought.*

*She was actually looking forward to seeing Dr. Desai, a woman who had been her OB ever since she became an adult and left her pediatrician behind.*

*Within a few minutes, the nurse directed her to a small room, where she asked what brought Suzanne in and took routine vital signs. Suzanne answered candidly and shared her suspicion about being pregnant. The nurse just nodded and proceeded with her tasks. Suzanne figured she probably wasn't the first pregnant young woman she had seen today.*

*Dr. Desai came in and greeted her warmly. Suzanne brought her up to date on events in her life: her separation and divorce from Adam, the death of her Ellie, the job change. Even reciting these things wore her out.*

*The doctor nodded and started feeling around Suzanne's body. She felt her forehead, took her pulse, and retook her blood pressure. She consulted the chart. Then she turned to Suzanne and said, "I'm calling an ambulance. You need to go to the hospital."*

*What? The hospital?*

*The look on Desai's face was dark and serious. "I believe you may be hemorrhaging internally," she said. "We need to get you to a hospital ASAP."*

*Suzanne was dazed. Hemorrhaging? She looked at Dr. Desai with uncharacteristic fear evident in her features. She could feel the blood drain from her face. "Am I going to be okay?"*

*Desai took her hand. "We are going to do everything we can to make sure you will be okay," she said. But the look on her face broadcast her concern. "Lie down," she said to Suzanne. "The ambulance will be here shortly." She called the nurse and said something in physician-speak that Suzanne did not understand. She could feel that she was losing consciousness. She had a vague sense of activity around her during her last minutes awake.*

Oh. My. God. Thought Riley, who was feeling as frightened as her character. Please, please be okay.

She pulled away from the screen and tried to calm herself down. This can't be happening. What am I going to do if something happens to her?

She did not know what to do with herself. Finally, she forced herself back to her laptop.

*When Suzanne woke up, she did not know where she was. She looked around the sterile space that could only be a hospital room. She felt something on her hand and looked down to see an IV inserted in her left hand. Jesus Christ? What happened?*

*She tried to think back to the last thing she remembered. She was in Dr. Desai's office, talking to the doctor, who was trying to be reassuring but was obviously very concerned. The last thing she remembered was asking if she was going to be okay. She did not recall the answer.*

*A middle-aged woman swept into the room. "You're awake," she said.*

*Suzanne just looked at her.*

*"Good sign. I'm Natalie, your nurse. You are in intensive care."*

*Intensive Care?!*

*"Why?" squeaked Suzanne.*

*"I'll let the doctor explain it to you. For now, just rest. I'm going to take your vitals.*

*Suzanne wondered why she would bother when she was hooked up to so many machines with LED lights blinking off and on.*

*She cleared her throat. "When can I talk to the doctor?" She had intended that sentence to come out firmly, but it was barely a whisper.*

*"He'll be here soon," Natalie said.*

*Suzanne just nodded. And then she drifted off to sleep again.*

"Thank God," said Riley to her computer screen. Relief coursed through her body.

Riley showed up at Mildred's office ten minutes before the appointed time. She did not want to be late. Willard and Mildred were already there.

She declined coffee or water and sat down on the couch a few feet from Willard. Mildred sat in what Riley now knew to be her chair across from the sofa. She nodded to Will.

"As you know, Riley, I met with Edward twice. The first time in DuPont Circle—his choice—and again yesterday at my office." He paused as if collecting his thoughts. "I don't want to get too specific about all the things he and I talked about, but it was obviously about this whole drama he put into play, apparently in an attempt to get back at you somehow for not dating him."

"As I mentioned yesterday, he did not deny anything. He actually provided a fair amount of detail about how he went about setting up this, um, revenge scenario. The point of it was obviously to cause you distress. I think in the back of his mind he had a notion that somehow it would lead to you and he getting back together, although he never explicitly said that."

"Back together?! We had one encounter; that was it. We were not a 'couple,'" Riley said, gesturing air quotes. She was surprised and more than a bit perturbed about what Willard was saying and how he was saying it.

"Whatever time you spent with him was very important from his perspective," Willard said kindly but firmly. "He described it as the 'best thing that ever happened' to him."

Riley did not say anything. Her ears were tinging red.

Mildred, who was observing this conversation, spoke up. "You seem angry, Riley."

Riley looked at her askance. "Of course, I'm angry. This guy deliberately tortured me and broke probably half a dozen laws to do it." The tone of her voice, the expression on her face, and the look in her eyes did nothing to contradict Mildred's observation. "He hacked into my computer, for Christ's sake! He violated my space."

Silence descended on the three people looking at each other. Willard spoke next. "As far as I'm concerned, you have every right to be angry. What Edward did was unconscionable."

Mildred nodded. "Yes, it was."

Riley sat there with her anger.

No one spoke.

"Is there anything else?" Riley asked.

Willard nodded but did not say anything right away. He was trying to decide how to put it to Riley. It was complicated because she was clearly angry, and, he allowed, for good reason.

"I know this has been an ordeal for you, Riley," he said. "And it was a terrible thing for Edward to do. It's hard to believe he went to such trouble just to get back at you. Most guys would have just gone out and gotten drunk and gotten over it." He paused. "But Edward is not 'most guys'. Not even close."

Riley's eyes narrowed as she looked at Willard. Was he going to defend him?

"To put it bluntly, I think Edward is a mixed-up guy. Very immature in some ways, even though he looks okay on the surface. What he did was not only uncalled for, elaborate, and . . . " Willard was searching for the right word. ". . . evil. It was also the work of a man whose hold on reality is tenuous. What he thought, how he reacted, what he did: these are things that most people would never dream of doing. Even angry, jilted people." He paused again, realizing that he was getting to the hard part. "I think the fact is that this blew up in his face. And I think it set him back enough to realize just how off the beam he had gotten."

"So, you're going to tell me that Edward is suffering, too?!" Her voice was cold.

"Yes, I am," Willard said.

Riley stood up and looked down on Willard, and then glanced over at Mildred. "I don't want to hear it," she said in a bitter voice. "This guy broke into my computer, disrupted my life, and tried to hurt me. He stole my manuscript. I am not giving him a pass just because he was surprised or sorry it didn't work out the way he planned."

Her expression was hard and piercing. She started breathing heavily. No one spoke.

"I don't need this," she said, and she headed for the door.

Neither Willard nor Mildred made any move to stop her.

The sound of the door slamming echoed in the silence.

After a few minutes, Mildred turned to Will. "She's right, you know."

Willard sighed. He knew she was right. He had just been hoping that things would be resolved peaceably, and everyone could go back to living their lives. Everybody. Including Edward.

Now he doubted that would be the case.

## 108

Riley walked and walked and walked. She walked past her apartment, past Lincoln Circle, past shops and restaurants, past everything she was familiar with, until she got to a large open green space. A city park, the name of which she had never known. She kept walking.

After a while, she found herself in Georgetown, strolling down Wisconsin Avenue. She could feel the intensity of her emotions moderating a little, her heartbeat slowing down some, and her mind clearing.

She could not recall any time in her life prior to this that she had been so angry. Well, maybe after that famous conversation with Cameron, when it became clear what his priorities were. But this time, it was worse. Not only was she mad at Edward, but she felt betrayed by Mildred and Will. These people offered to help her: she opened herself up to them and thought—assumed, really—they were on her side. The bitterness of the feeling made itself felt in her mouth; it felt as if that sensation would take up permanent residence.

She shook her head. Now what? Do I go to the police? Do I hire a lawyer? She wasn't sure. And to make matters worse, she did not even know a person to ask.

She felt herself slowing down and went into a coffee shop to rest, think, and sip some coffee while she was at it.

As Riley sat there, she tried to focus on something else. Why beat a dead horse? I know I'm angry. I feel I have every right to be angry. But she was tired of dwelling on it.

She turned her attention to the large window giving onto the street and idly observed people walking up and down busy Wisconsin Avenue. People who did not seem angry or upset or anything. Just normal, going-about-my-business kind of people. She envied them.

Her feelings continued to abate, but slowly. But they did not change focus. She was clear about this: she was wronged by a person who deliberately set out to hurt her. Badly. In the process, he violated her personal space. No, it was more than that: a person can violate your personal space by standing too close. No, he invaded my private domain and read a manuscript he had absolutely no right to. God knows what else he stole from my computer. And he used the information he stole against me. And I'm supposed to just walk away?

She took a gulp of coffee. It was bitter, but that matched the prevailing feeling in her body.

I've got to do something. I'm going to the police. No one can stop me.

She sat for a while sipping her coffee and watching the normal people through the window. Her decision settled her down even more. She began to think more clearly. If there is retribution to be had, that is the only way.

## 109

Riley sat at the table in Georgetown for some time. Her thoughts ranged over all the events of the past six months: her separation and pending divorce from Cameron, her relationship with Jennifer, her fling or whatever it was with Edward, his outrageous response. Her manuscript.

At the thought of her book in embryo, she paused. It struck a different note: not bitterness, not frustration. Just a sense of connectedness, of warmth. These are my true friends, she thought. These are the people I care most about right now. I want to see how their lives work out. I want to be part of them. And most of all, I want them to be okay.

This all sounded true and odd and a more than a little embarrassing for Riley, who knew she could not share these thoughts with anyone else. Not even Jennifer, who always looked at her with a puzzled expression when she talked about her characters. God knows what she thinks about all that, Riley thought. She had no way of knowing, but she suspected it wasn't good.

Then, she thought about Cameron, whom she had not spoken with since she told him about Edward. He had asked if she wanted to meet and talk about it, and she said she'd think about it. But the reality was that she never gave it another moment's thought. Oddly, that seemed natural. That must be what I did all those years being married to him: I just never thought about what was or wasn't happening in our relationship. Not until the end. Riley marveled at how little real information she shared with Cameron and how much a habit that became. How perverse, she now saw in retrospect. She was not certain what marriage was supposed to be, but she was pretty clear that her experience with Cameron in recent years would not qualify. She knew there were some close times early on, when they were dating. It seemed back then that they talked all the time, sharing the kinds of things that young lovers share: hopes, dreams, fantasies. She wondered how long that phase lasted. Not long, she concluded.

Should I call him? That question gave her pause. Do I want to call him? That seemed like a better way to pose it. But he was no doubt at work, and it's probably not a good idea to interrupt him there. But it was coming up on the lunch hour, so maybe she could catch him eating at his desk or taking his lunch however he took it. She debated for several minutes.

Reaching no firm conclusion, she shook her head, picked up her phone, and punched in his number.

Somewhat to her surprise, he answered. He must have known it was me, she thought.

"Hi, Cameron."

"Hey, Riley. What's up?"

Pause. "I was just thinking about you. We haven't spoken in a while. I was wondering how you were doing."

Cameron thought for a while. "I'm doing okay, Riley. I'm on my lunch break." He paused so he could swallow the morsel of his sandwich that remained in his mouth when he answered his phone. "My new job is working out pretty well."

Riley listened closely to what Cameron was saying, even though it felt as if she were talking to someone she barely knew. The fact that he did not advert to their last conversation got her attention. She turned her attention inward, listening closely to how she was responding, what she was feeling, what she was thinking, what her body was telling her. She thought of bringing up recent events in her life but didn't.

She noted how little she cared about what he was doing, how his new job was working out, or how he was doing. At the same time, she had a distant memory of warmth that had existed one time between them. It was something she had not felt in a long time, but it came to mind now, not as a feeling but simply as a memory. She thought about updating him about the situation with Edward, but it just did not feel right to do it just then. That was information for someone she felt closer to.

"Well, listen," she said. "I just wanted to touch base. Glad about your new job. Maybe we could get together sometime and, I don't know, finalize everything."

"Yeah, sure, Riley. Thanks for calling." He sounded sincere in a way she knew she did not.

She hung up. She could feel sadness rising in her, but she wasn't sure why. Maybe it was because of the phone call, the lack of connection to somebody she was married to for years. Maybe it was that she felt so alone. Maybe . . . she really didn't know.

She collected her things, stood up, and walked out into the Georgetown sunshine.

## 110

Cameron was surprised to hear from Riley. After he hung up, he returned to munching on the sandwich he had brought for lunch, idly looking at his computer. But his thoughts kept returning to Riley. He tried to pinpoint how long it had been since they'd spoken. But he could not place the exact time. Days, surely; maybe weeks. It seemed like a long time ago.

It actually felt good to hear her voice. It stirred feelings he had pretty much avoided during these past weeks. His fondness for her, his attraction; even the pain he felt at the divorce . . .

Then, midway through these warm and fuzzy thoughts and halfway through his sandwich, Cameron recalled their previous conversation. The one where she told him about being stalked. The one that stirred up powerful protective feelings on his part and reminded him of how much he loved her. The one that completely slipped his mind when he was talking to her just a few minutes before. The hand with the sandwich slowly dropped down to the top of his desk as shame shot through his body. How could I be so stupid? He picked up his phone and stared at it. Should I call her? What would she think?

What do you think?

I think I'm an idiot.

What will you think if you don't call her back and make this right?

Cameron gave that just a moment's thought. Right now, I feel like a fool, like someone who deserves to have lost her. If I call her, it will be awkward, but if I don't, I'll be stuck with this judgment of myself forever.

He silently scanned what he recalled of his history with Riley and was struck with how little they communicated important stuff in recent years. I was all wrapped up in work and just did not give our relationship the time or attention it deserved. Was I scared?

Like I am now, he thought as he dialed Riley's number. Unsurprisingly, she did not pick up.

Shit, he thought. He closed his eyes and began constructing a voice message before the dreaded beep appeared.

"Riley, it's me. I appreciated your calling, but I did not ask about how the situation was going that you described to me last time we spoke. I am so sorry. It must have just slipped my mind." He knew his time was almost up. "Call me back. Please." He clicked off.

He put the phone back on his desk and stared at it for a while. A certain melancholy drifted over him. Not overpowering, but distinct nonetheless. He was glad he called Riley back but sad that she didn't pick up. I could text her, he thought. But that would just be a repeat of the message he left. He knew there was no way he could control whether Riley called him back or not.

He threw the remainder of his sandwich into the trash, straightened up, and got back to work. But the melancholy flitted in and out of the gaps in his attention to work, something he would ordinarily never have allowed. It was a bittersweet feeling: fond memories of Riley along with painful feelings about their separation, or even before that of the alienation that he had not recognized. And guilt for failing to attend to such an important development in Riley's life. The call assuaged that guilt some, but hardly all of it. He felt like a heel.

The other idea that floated around in his mind was his desire to see her. He wanted to with more desperation than he thought was healthy, but that very desperation forced him to keep the desire under strict wraps. It's one thing to fall apart alone in a car; it's quite another to do it in front of someone. And he knew he might not be able to control his feelings if he were actually to meet up with Riley in the flesh.

## 111

Riley saw that Cameron called but did not pick up. She found their brief conversation of just a few minutes before so vacuous she saw no point in continuing it.

She mellowed a bit when she heard the message. In fact, she felt some relief. A remnant of a relationship flickered in her mind, providing at least some hope that the recent changes she observed in Cameron were still on track. She hoped so. But still, she decided to postpone another conversation until some other time. She did not know when. She put Cameron out of her mind, noticing how easy it was to do that.

She started the long walk home. She was a bundle of feelings with little clear direction except to do all she could to make Edward pay for what he did to her.

It took her a couple hours to get back to her apartment. She was tired, and just wanted to rest before doing anything else. It was still midafternoon, but she couldn't imagine herself doing any work or taking any action today. She would need to think about it more before proceeding. She did not want to make a mistake.

She was so wrapped up in these thoughts she did not notice Willard sitting in his car across the street from her apartment. But he saw her and got out of his car and approached her.

"Ms. Cotswald," he said as he approached her. "Can I have a minute?"

If Riley had not been so fatigued, she would have told him to go to hell. As it was, she simply said, "What for?"

Willard stood directly in front of her. "A couple things. I know this morning was difficult for you, and I wanted to check and see how you were. Also, I want you to know that, if you should decide to take this matter to the police, I will cooperate fully with them and provide them with any information I may have discovered about Edward and what he did."

Even through her fatigue and lingering resentment, these sounded like reasonable things to Riley. They did not match up with the situation she found herself in this morning with Willard and Mildred, but those feelings seemed oddly distant just now. She nodded. 'Thank you' did not seem quite appropriate, but she was grateful.

"And one more thing," Willard said, hesitating. "I promised Edward I would tell you that he said he was sorry." Willard paused a bit and glanced down; then looked at Riley full face. "And I believed him."

Willard handed Riley a card. "Call me if there is anything I can do to help you," he said. And he turned, walked to his car, and drove away.

Riley stood in front of the door to her building holding the card in her hand. She just did not know what to make of this brief encounter. Obviously Willard was not the bad guy she had been thinking he might have been. But she wasn't sure she could trust him either.

She opened the main door to her building and went up to her apartment in something of a daze. This little encounter made things more confusing rather than less; and she was so tired of thinking, all she wanted to do was sleep. She lay down on her carefully made bed, tried to put all thoughts out of her mind, and closed her eyes.

— 112 —

Willard drove away feeling that he had done the right thing. The right thing for Edward, for Riley, for Mildred, and for himself. He too was tired of focusing on this one issue, one so fraught with such powerful feelings. He wanted a break.

Rather than going back to his office or to his apartment, he thought he would stop at A.J.'s for a drink. Willard was not a big drinker, but there were times, such as now, when sitting at a bar anonymously and having a bourbon neat was the only thing he could do that made sense.

It was a new bartender that served him—a woman, an attractive woman at that—and Willard was glad to see a pretty new face. He sat and nursed his drink. He glanced at his watch: 4:30. A little early, he thought, but not too early. He kept thinking of the people he had been thinking about all day, but in a removed, maybe more objective sort of way. Bourbon helps with that.

The truth was he wasn't sure where to go from here and what the right thing was moving forward. Willard always kept 'doing the right thing' as his lodestar, the one rule by which he lived his life. It led him to quit the police force and open his own PI firm; it was at the heart of his decision to terminate his romantic relationship with Mildred; it was what led him to spend several hours this afternoon waiting for Riley to show up at her apartment so he could discharge his duty to Edward and to her.

And when he came to the point where he no longer knew what the right thing was to do, there was always bourbon.

Willard did not want the police to be involved, but Mildred was right: this was a police matter. He had hoped beyond hope that it might not come to that, but he found himself resolved to the extent that he was able to take his ego out of the picture. It is not my call to make, he realized.

That thought makes almost no one feel better, and Willard searched his mind for another way to frame this situation. Look at this like this, he told himself: you were just trying to help Mildred in one of her frequent causes, and you did a creditable job: you tracked down incontrovertible evidence of Edward's involvement in the criminal behavior in which he indulged to hurt Riley. All in a matter of a couple of days.

That was it, Willard saw. It was criminal behavior. No matter how much his heart may have gone out to Edward, the poor, conflicted, socially problematic loner; Edward had gone way past any line that Willard would consider sane, much less civil. This raised other questions in his mind. Was Edward simply a skilled sociopath who could elicit sympathy in others who would then overlook his behavior? Willard was accustomed to following his instincts in these matters, and those instincts told him that Edward was sincere. But instincts are not infallible, as many people seem to think. They are as fallible as any other human faculty, which is to say they are often mistaken.

Willard ordered another drink. This prospect was making more sense to him. He was mildly embarrassed to think that he may have been snookered by Edward. He knew this happened from time to time, but he found himself more willing to feel sorry for Edward than he should have been. He accepted the story Edward told him, not really challenging Edward about anything he said; he simply asked him how he did what he did and accepted the answers. Realistically, these accorded with the facts as he knew them: he had tracked down Todd who identified Edward, and Edward admitted as much. Will made a mental note to check out Bomber17, the one loose end he knew nothing about.

Sooner rather than later, he thought. He picked up his cell and contacted a former colleague on the Metropolitan Police and asked him to look up a hacker who went by the name of Bomber17. His colleague said it might take a day or two, but Willard was in no rush. He hung up feeling certain that he could track down whoever this was. It made his bourbon taste better.

And it felt a little better to be back on the trail with a clear direction. Up until this moment, he had been thinking he was done with this case. He had followed up with Riley, whom he was certain would not contact him despite his invitation to do so; and even Mildred seemed at a dead end. This was fine with Willard: he preferred action to just being passive, and letting loose ends go was not his specialty. He liked the hunt.

Riley's phone rang at 8:22 p.m. and woke her up. It startled her, and at first she did not recall where she was, but a cursory glance around her confirmed that she was in her bed in her apartment in her clothes. It was a little confusing because darkness was settling over the District. She sat up and tried to shake herself awake. Then the events of the day came flooding back, but that ended when she saw Jen's number on her cell phone.

"Hello."

"Riley?"

"Yes?"

"Hi, Honey. I'm calling to check in. What's happened? Did you meet with Willard? How did it go? Details, sister."

Riley sighed. "It's a long story. I just woke up. I did meet with Mildred and Willard, but it went kind of crazy, so I spent the day wandering around and then crashed this afternoon." She paused a bit, surprised that she got that much information out of herself. "Would you mind coming over?" She wasn't sure why she asked that, but it felt right.

"Glad to," replied Jennifer. "I'll be there in twenty."

Riley felt relieved but wasn't sure why. Some primal instinct told her she needed to talk to someone, principally because she wasn't making any sense in her own head. She tried to recall the dreams she was sure she had during her long nap but was unable to remember anything but that they were tumultuous. She could tell because she hardly felt rested. But she did feel awake.

She got up and went into the bathroom and splashed water on her face. She looked at the mirror and deemed her appearance less than appealing. I should get my hair cut, she thought.

But it's only Jennifer. Riley saw the mirror image cock its head. You're talking about your best friend, it said.

I know, but just now I'm having trouble trusting anyone. Or even caring about anyone.

Even Jennifer?

I don't know. I'm torn. I'm glad she's coming over. Maybe . . . maybe we can figure something out together.

You're not doing so well on your own, the mirror said.

That much is true, she concluded. Then picked up her tooth-brush and started brushing without looking at the mirror.

Two minutes later, she heard the buzz from the front door.

Two minutes after that, Jennifer breezed in and gave her a hug.

Jennifer looked at Riley and said, "Are you okay, Honey?"

Riley did not even know how to answer. She did not even know why Jennifer was asking her that. She had combed her hair. She didn't think she looked great, but she thought maybe okay. "I know you just got up, Riley. I'm not being critical." She smiled at her friend. "Let's talk."

Riley nodded and the pair proceeded to the couch.

"So, tell me what happened today."

"You know, Jen, it's a bit of a fog. I went over to Mildred's place and she and Willard were there. I don't know. It did not go well. I thought they were taking Edward's side. Willard acted like he was sympathetic to him, and I did not get that. They did not at all seem to understand that I was the one whose life was affected by this crazy guy."

Jennifer listened intently. She had a hard time picturing how what Riley described actually transpired. In her experience with Will and Mildred, they were solidly on Riley's side. She did not say anything; she just waited.

"I got angry. I got up and left. I spent the next four hours wandering around Georgetown . . ."

"Georgetown?! You walked to Georgetown?"

"Yeah. And the more I walked the more I felt I had to do something." She paused a bit. "No, that's not right. I mean, I do have to do something, but that wasn't what I was feeling when I was walking. I was just so angry, and I felt so betrayed . . ."

Tears began to flow from Riley's eyes. Jennifer reached over and took her hand. "It's okay, Honey."

Riley wiped her tears with her free hand. "So I thought I should go to the police. After all, Edward did hack into my computer. He basically stole my manuscript. And I began to wonder what else he may have taken." She glanced over at her still unplugged desktop.

She tried to organize her thoughts. "All this started when Willard was telling me about Edward in a very sympathetic way. Toward him. That's what started getting me so angry. But then, when I got back to my apartment, who was waiting for me but Willard. He said he wanted to check on me; he assured me he would cooperate if I went to the police; and he offered to be of any assistance he could. I mean, he was really, really nice. More than nice. He did the right thing."

Riley looked at Jennifer. "But it all left me, I don't know, confused, I guess. Honestly, I am lost. I don't know what to think, what to do, whom to trust. I'm a mess." She got a tiny hint of amusement in her eye. "I even called Cameron."

At this, Jennifer smiled. "You did? How is he?" The look on her face indicated clearly that Jennifer did not care much about how Cameron was. But she cared a lot about how her friend was.

"Apparently, he is fine. He talked about moving to another apartment, which will be closer to his work. I guess a fresh start. But you know, I heard him talking about a lot of stuff, and truthfully I did not give a shit about any of it. It felt like talking to someone I did not know rather than somebody I was married to for years." She looked down. "He did not ask me a single question about me, even though I had told him some time ago what was happening with Edward." She looked up at Jennifer. "It was kind of sad. Not really, really sad, but sad nonetheless."

"Sounds like the way I feel about someone I break up with when it's past time to break up. Like: What was that all about?"

Riley chuckled. "Yeah, something like that." She had no idea what that was like.

"He called me back after a little bit, when he apparently remembered our previous conversation. He even apologized." She shrugged. "That was nice, I guess, but it didn't make me care anymore."

The two women looked at each other without saying anything. Neither was sure the conversation was so helpful, but they were both holding onto the thing they each had at the moment: each other. "I hate this, Jen," Riley said. "I hate feeling so confused, so lost . . ."

Jennifer nodded. "I can only imagine, Honey." She squeezed Riley's hand gently.

Riley squeezed back; then she moved closer and lay her head on Jen's chest. She tried to push all thoughts out of her head.

Pretty much like every other thought she had today, that one did not feel exactly right; it could even have been a little crazy. What she wanted—no, what she needed—was the thing that comes with being close to someone regardless of what comes out of the other person's mouth. She just needed to be with someone. And right now, that person was Jennifer.

She scooted over to Jennifer just to be closer to her. She could feel the warmth of her body and smelled a slight scent of something familiar. She put her arm around her. Jennifer did not protest. In fact, she wrapped both of her arms around Riley and squeezed gently. Riley lay her head on Jennifer's shoulder. "I love you," she said.

## 114

Willard did not have to wait long for a response from his contact in the MPDC. He got a call at 8:00 a.m. the next morning after he asked for the information.

"Funny that you should inquire about this guy," Jack, his contact, said. "He has been on our radar for some time. Lately, even the FBI has gotten involved. A real shady character."

"How can I find him?" Willard asked.

"Probably his mother's basement," Jack replied, chuckling. "The guy is something of a nomad. No current address. It appears that he stays with friends a lot and works odd jobs for them. Mostly illegal odd jobs. He pretty much stays off the grid as much as possible. Only uses burner phones; TV shit like that."

A piece of work, thought Willard. "Age?"

"Graduated from college in '05, so I'm guessing mid-thirties." Pause. "Correction: he dropped out of college in '05 after spending a year and a half there. So maybe early 30s. University of Maryland. That's where he grew up."

"Parents?"

"Dad's a prison guard; mom's a secretary. Small-town Americans. Nothing remarkable. One sister, from whom he's apparently estranged. It looks like he does float in and out of his parents' house. They live in . . ." He consulted his file. "Sykesville. Same house Bomber17 grew up in." He gave Willard the address, who wrote it down.

"I almost forgot, Jack. I presume Bomber17 was not his given name."

Jack chuckled. "No, it's just one of a number of aliases. His real name is Stuart Stonecraft. I guess that was too fancy for him."

"Anything else?"

"Yeah, a couple things. One of the reasons he's been showing up lately on everybody's radar is that he appears to be a person of interest in several disappearances. No concrete evidence that I could find, but he was acquainted with a number of people who went missing over the past year. In several cases, he was the last person to see them."

"How many people?"

"Seven."

"That would be a huge coincidence." Willard said. "And the other thing?"

"Nobody believes that this is a coincidence. But the other thing is that the FBI has had him under surveillance periodically, but he's a fairly slippery dude, if you know what I mean."

Willard knew exactly what he meant. He was evading capture.

Jack continued. "And lately, the info coming out of the FBI is getting spottier. That could mean the trail went cold or . . ."

". . . Or they're closing in," interjected Willard.

"Exactly."

"Okay. Thanks a lot, Jack. I'll keep you posted."

"Good luck with this one, Will."

The pair hung up. Willard, who was in his office, stared out the window wondering about Stuart and Edward. At first, he was only vaguely worried about Edward getting hurt. But the more he turned it over in his mind, that vagueness gave way to a clear possibility that harm could befall Edward because of his tie to Stonecraft. This thought was enough for him to touch base with Edward again.

## 115

It never occurred to Edward that he would have any further contact with Willard; so he was surprised when his phone rang, and he saw the PI's number. He could feel the sweat under his armpits.

He debated several moments before answering it. "Hello?" he said finally.

"Edward, this is Willard Bean. I just ran across some information I think you should know about. It's about somebody you worked with."

Edward shook his head. What? He was probably referring to the hacker he hired, since he was the only other person he 'worked with' besides Todd. But who cares about him? "Why?" he said.

"It's not something I want to discuss over the phone, but it is a matter of some urgency. Could you meet me at the office this afternoon?"

Edward's sweat glands dried up a bit. Willard was treating him respectfully, so he agreed to meet. "Okay," he said.

Even though he was no longer sweating, his apprehension did not vanish. He had a hard time picturing how this current situation could get any worse, but he had a sickening feeling in the pit of his stomach that he was about to find out.

He agreed to meet Bean before lunch, so he took a shower, dressed in a similar manner as their previous meeting, and in general, made himself presentable. As he went through his ministrations, he wondered what Bean meant when he talked about 'a matter of some urgency.' He did not have a clue, unless it had to do with the fact that hacking into someone's computer was no doubt illegal. Maybe somebody went to the police. He doubted it was Willard.

From Bean's website, Edward knew that he had been a D.C. cop before opening his own office as a PI. That meant that he probably had access to a lot of information that was not generally available to the public. Edward did not exactly feel panicky, but the queasiness in his stomach was not getting any better.

While Edward was prepping for the meeting, Willard was busy collecting information about the nature of the FBI's interest in Stonecraft. He made some calls and searched online. It appeared that these disappearances all involved the theft of important information obtained by hacking into victims' phones, computers, and other electronic devices, something that Bomber17 excelled at. In the worst case, it looked as if Stuart could be eliminating witnesses and evidence. A grim possibility, but one that Willard could not dismiss. On the other hand, the people who vanished each had his own shady history, so the possibility that Stuart's presence was just background noise in the criminal culture of which he was clearly a part could not be dismissed either.

But there was something about this case that troubled Willard. While the MPDC was helpful as always, the FBI was less forthcoming with information. And in Bean's experience, the more serious the case, the tighter the information control. And based on what he was learning, the control around Mr. Stonecraft was tight indeed.

Willard felt that he made a good call alerting Edward to all this. He was glad Edward agreed so quickly.

Edward got to Bean's office at 11:00 a.m., and Bean met him in the waiting room immediately and ushered him into his office.

"Thanks for meeting with me, Edward," he began. He looked down at the notes on his desk; then turned his attention to Edward. "I recently learned that the guy you knew as Bomber17 is a person of interest in a number of disappearances recently in the D.C. and Maryland area."

Edward blanched. "Disappearances?"

"Yes. And there is a good possibility that they are of the kind that usually end up permanent."

"I, I don't know anything about this."

"I did not think you did, Edward. I am telling you this because there is a slight chance—and I think it's only a slight chance—that you could end up on his radar."

Edward's head turned sideways. "Why?"

Willard looked at him with a very serious expression. "You met with him over several days, did you not?"

"Yes."

"And in this process, he basically taught you how to hack into someone's computer?"

"Yes."

"And during those days, did you disclose any personal information about yourself or your electronic devices?"

Edward looked at Bean quizzically. "Like what?"

"Like mobile phone numbers, computer ID numbers—I think they're called IP addresses. Or other private info: social security number, passwords, your home address, where you work. Anything really."

Edward thought for a while. "At first I blocked my number when I called him, but once we started working together, he asked for it in case he needed to call me. I thought it was a convenience thing." He was silent for another few minutes. "Ordinarily, I worked on his computer . . ."

"What?" Bean said.

"I may have used some passwords on his machine to access some of my accounts, the ones I needed to use for hacking." His face began to pale even more. "And I was with him when I first did a dry run on Riley's computer." Edward froze. "Oh, no," he said.

Willard looked at him intently. "Oh, no what?"

Edward looked up at him. "I think he may be able to access Riley's computer."

A new level of seriousness settled over the two men, reflected first in kind of heavy silence, during which both were digesting new information of a most chilling sort.

Willard was the first to break the silence. "Okay. This is important information" He then picked up his phone and called Riley.

The call went straight to voicemail. "Ms. Cotswald, this is Willard Bean. I have some new information that I need to share with you. Please call me." He hesitated a bit. "Also, I recall that you had unplugged your computer when you realized what was happening. Please keep it unplugged until I talk with you. If you have already plugged it in, please unplug it again. In either case, please return my call. It is a matter of some urgency."

He clicked off and turned back to Edward.

"Is there anything else you might recall that could lead Stuart to track down you or anyone else you know?"

"Stuart?" asked Edward.

"Yeah, Stuart Stonecraft is the real name of Bomber17."

Edward nodded. He sat for a while thinking of any other information he might have shared. He shook his head. "I can't think of anything, but I'll keep thinking about it."

Then he turned to Willard with the most serious look on his face that Will had ever seen on him. "I will do anything I can to make sure Riley is not a target for this guy."

Willard returned the look. "So will I, Edward. So will I."

His attention turned back to his notes, while Edward turned to peer out the window in Willard's office.

"Do you do online banking? Paying bills and stuff like that?"

Edward nodded.

"The first thing I want you to do right now is turn off your phone. Remove the battery. The next thing I want you to do when you go back to your apartment is turn off your computer. Unplug it; don't just shut it down. Then, find another one—at an Internet café or someplace like that; maybe a friend's house, whatever—and check to see if your accounts are undisturbed. If there is anything amiss, I want you to contact me immediately. As you do this, change all of your passwords." Willard had just exhausted his knowledge of computer safety.

Edward stared at Willard unbelieving. "Why . . . why would he do this?"

"Steal? Because he is apparently a thief. And maybe worse."

Edward slowly withdrew his cell phone from his pants pocket and turned it off.

"The battery?" said Willard.

"I don't know how to do that," Edward said weakly.

Willard reached out for the phone, opened his desk drawer, and produced a tool for this very purpose. "This is how," he said.

Edward's ashen face was immobile. When Willard handed him back his phone, he stared at it on the desk in front of him without touching it.

Then he turned and looked at Willard. "Mr. Bean, this scares me."

Bean nodded. "You would have to be a robot not to be concerned about this, Edward. Now let me say this: I do not think it is likely that he would do anything, but I think it's possible. And I think it is worth our attention." He looked at the quivering young man in front of him. "It is a scary prospect," he said. "But let's take this one step at a time."

"Okay," said Edward meekly.

## 116

Riley did not answer her phone because she was working.

*It would have been hard for Adam to be any more surprised by the phone call from Suzanne than he was. He stared at the number before answering.*

*"Hello?"*

*The voice on the other end of the line was almost a whisper. "Adam? This is Suzanne."*

*"Suzanne, hi. You don't sound like yourself."*

*"I'm in a hospital in D.C." It suddenly occurred to Suzanne that she did not know which hospital she was in.*

*"Something happened. I'll explain it . . . when . . ."*

*Adam's heart started beating faster. "Suzanne, what hospital?"*

*"Hold on," she said. A minute later, she came back on the line. "George Washington," she said. Then she fell silent.*

*Adam's mind was racing. Okay, it was one thing to go through a divorce, but Suzanne sounded more than a little sick. "Look, I'm on my way." Then, because he could not refrain from saying it, "Please be there when I get there."*

*Adam was so shaken, he could not even think of how to proceed. He did not have a car, so he called for an Uber. He thought he might change his clothes, but he did not want to lose time, so he went to the bathroom and splashed a little water on himself. He did manage to put on a fresh shirt. Just as he was closing the front door to wait for his ride, the Uber drove up. He got in. "George Washington Hospital," he said unnecessarily.*

*When he got to the hospital, he went straight to the information desk and asked for Suzanne's room. The receptionist looked at her computer. It was obvious when she found Suzanne's name because the expression on her face immediately took on a serious cast. Adam's heart sank.*

*She turned to look at Adam. "She's in intensive care. Only close relatives can visit."*

*"I'm her husband," Adam said for the first time in a long while.*

*"Okay, can I see some ID?"*

*Adam handed her his driver's license.*

*She nodded and scanned it and handed it back to him.*

*"Seventh floor; take that elevator and check in at the nurses' station."*

*Adam was trying, despite himself, to wrap his mind around the idea that he may lose his wife not only to divorce but also to death. He hoped he was catastrophizing, but he couldn't help himself. Suddenly it did not matter that they were estranged or that he did not want to be married to her or that she made a decision to get involved with someone else or that she decided to move to another city. All that mattered was that she would survive whatever this was.*

*He could barely breathe during the short elevator ride. The car stopped at every floor before seven, where he finally got off and went straight to the nurses' station three feet away.*

*"I'm Adam Wilkerson, here to see Suzanne Wilkerson."*

*The nurse looked Adam over and said, "Follow me."*

*They walked about ten feet to a small room, which was not really so much a room as it was a space open to the center station save for a curtain of questionable utility. Susanne was at the center of the space; she was lying pale as the sheet that was covering her with her eyes closed. He stopped just before the cubicle and put his hand on the nurse's elbow.*

*"What happened?" he whispered to the nurse.*

*"Ectopic pregnancy," she said. "Often, they are not so serious, but this one was. She had a rupture; she was bleeding internally." She gathered her thoughts for a moment. "It was lucky that she got here as soon as she did."*

The nurse rattled the curtain aside as much as to signal her presence as for any other useful purpose. Suzanne's eyes were closed but fluttered open when she heard the curtain noise. She saw the nurse first, but then her gaze turned to Adam. She whispered his name.

"Oh, Suzanne," Adam said through tears he could do nothing to stop. He grasped the situation instantly when the nurse told him what it was. He was pretty sure that the timing was right for the last time they had sex. He took Suzanne's hand gently. "I am so sorry, Honey," he said.

"Me too," Suzanne whispered.

The nurse quietly left the couple gazing into each other's eyes and reconnecting emotionally in ways that they had not done in years. Maybe ever.

"When did you find out?"

"About the pregnancy?"

"Yes."

"Yesterday. I woke up the night before feeling terrible, throwing up. I thought it could be the kind of thing that women do when they get pregnant—you hear stories—so I went to my OB/Gyn, the one here in the District, and she confirmed it and sent me here immediately."

"Thank God she did," Adam said.

Suzanne nodded an equivocal nod.

Then she turned her head and looked at Adam full face. "Thank you for coming, Adam. I just called to let you know, but I am glad you're here." She squeezed his hand with the little strength she could muster.

Riley stopped typing and wiped tears from her eyes. She was glad Adam was there, too.

It was almost lunch time, and she glanced at her phone. She saw that whoever called had left a message. She clicked on her voicemail and listened intently to Willard's voice. Now what? she thought.

Willard sounded earnest. Scary earnest, she thought, although she could not imagine why. She debated for only a moment before calling him back. New information? That intrigued her enough to hit the 'call back' button. Willard answered on the first ring.

He reprised the telephone conversation he had had with Edward earlier that morning. But after his meeting with Edward, his voice had taken on an even more urgent tone. "We need to meet as soon as possible," he told Riley.

Jesus Christ! Will this never end? But she could not bring herself to refuse a request from a man who had redeemed himself to a substantial extent by following up with her in such a kind way. "Sure," she said. "Where?"

"How about my office?"

"I don't know where that is," Riley said, completely forgetting about the business card lying on her desk.

Willard gave her the address and general directions. It wasn't that far from Dupont Circle, so she agreed to meet him there at two o'clock.

"And you got my message about your computer?"

"Yes."

"Is it still unplugged?"

"Yes."

Willard's sigh of relief was audible over the phone line. "Good."

Riley clicked off, wondering what could possibly be happening that made Willard so . . . so urgent. He did not seem like the type that scared easily. She shook her head, decided to eat something for lunch, and went about getting ready to go meet Willard at his office.

This has been quite a time, she thought as she was changing her clothes. Her mood was much improved from yesterday by her contact with Jennifer, who stayed the night with her in the same bed. Nothing sexual happened, although Riley felt so close to Jen that the thought of becoming more intimate floated through her mind. But mostly she just wanted to be next to her, within reach, as she was. Just having her this close throughout the night enabled her to sleep soundly, wake up refreshed, and lighten the load of emotional weight that she had amassed the day before. She actually felt lighter. Almost normal.

Jennifer left first thing in the morning to go back to her apartment and prep for the workday. The two women hugged each other deeply before Jennifer walked out the door. The night together was a pleasurable experience for her as well, even if a novel one. She assured Riley that she would be there for her and left feeling as if she had done something good. New ground for her, but good ground. Solid.

## 117

Edward walked home more slowly than he thought he should. He felt eager to unplug his computer, but he also felt a new, weighty sense of guilt for the way this situation was developing. It all came down to him. He was the one who hired Bomber . . . Stuart. He was the one who may have jeopardized Riley's life. It was very close to too much to bear.

He walked slowly, carrying these heavy thoughts as if they were real physical things, as if he were carrying something he could barely lift. He felt that way all the way to his apartment.

The first thing he did when he got home was reach back and pull the plug out from the machine. He needed a computer; like most people, he had become dependent upon it for routine chores, such as banking, but also for his work, his communication with other people, and even his entertainment. Now, with both his computer and his phone disabled, he felt more cut off than he had ever felt. And that was a high bar to start with.

The weighty thoughts did not lighten. If anything, the more he thought about this, the heavier they felt. And the guiltier he felt. I am guilty, he thought. There is just no way around it. And if something were to happen to Riley, I could not, would not forgive myself. Yeah, I wanted to hurt her when I was so angry, but I never wanted her to die.

His mind returned to the dour assessment of his life that he had begun yesterday. What am I doing here? He still had no answer.

Edward lay down on his couch and stared at the ceiling. What can I do to help this situation? Bean was right to tell me about this—and he wasn't exactly blaming me for putting these things in motion—but Bean was short on what I can do now, other than disconnecting from the online world where most people, including me, live.

Edward already felt so disconnected from the world; this was like a final step into an abyss. I thought it was bad yesterday. Today is ten times worse. Somebody could get hurt, and that somebody could be Riley. Or me. At the moment, he would gladly have volunteered to be the one. It was, after all, his doing. He deserved it.

He fell asleep in the midst of these dreary thoughts but woke about ten minutes later with a start. He realized he needed to check his accounts, as Bean had directed him. He thought about possible places he could go. He did not feel close enough to anyone to ask to use their computer, so he was left with public options. Did they still exist? He recalled Internet cafés in the past, but he couldn't recall seeing one recently. And he could not go online to check. Not only was his computer shut down, but his phone was also out of commission. Shit.

Edward got up and looked around. I'll just have to go look, he thought. He left his apartment in a search for an Internet café where he could rejoin the land of the connected. He had heard of such places, but he had never been in one.

He walked around his neighborhood trying to recall where he had last seen one. It's been a long time, he thought.

He walked around for about twenty minutes before it occurred to him to stop and ask someone. He slipped into a convenience store and asked the clerk if there were somewhere nearby that had computers to use or rent.

The clerk did not skip a beat. "The only one I know about with actual computers is a gaming center on P Street." He shook his head as he tried to think of others. "The old-type Internet cafés are almost all gone. The most you can do now is find free WIFI."

A gaming center? Edward thanked the clerk and headed toward P Street. He found a place that was populated with glitzy machines with large screens and inscrutable controls. Fortunately, each station had a keyboard. He checked in with a young man at a front desk and asked for prices and what he could do. "So, can I use one of these machines to access the Internet?"

"Sure," the young man said, looking at Edward as if he were several generations removed from himself. "Nobody really does that except to play a game with someone else online, but there's no reason you can't."

Fortunately, there were not many people in the place, but Edward was sure that would change after schools let out. He slipped into a chair in front of an elaborate console and started accessing his personal accounts. Fortunately, he had an online password utility, so all he had to remember was the password for that. No problem. Soon he was able to reconstruct his online life. He felt a wave of relief.

For the next hour, Edward surveyed everything he could think of: his bank accounts, credit card accounts, his PayPal account, his email. He took special care to review each bank account, credit card account, and online bill pay setup to make sure there was nothing amiss. Then he changed the passwords for all of his accounts; this took some time.

As he worked, he could feel the tension in his body dissipate slowly. At least he had a sense of being in charge, in control of his life in a way that had been badly damaged after his conversation with Bean. And being reconnected to the Internet allowed him some breathing room. It felt normal.

He wanted to share his small triumph with Riley, something which surprised him, wracked by guilt about her as he had been. But what he really wanted was for her to be safe, no matter what.

After about an hour, Edward got up and left the game center as teenagers began to file in. Just in time, he thought. It did not make him feel old exactly, but it made him feel like the sole adult in the room. Pretty close to how he felt with his students.

On his way back to his apartment, he spotted a Verizon store and decided that one of those things was to get a new phone. He hated not being able to communicate with people, even if the people with whom he communicated were few. Plus, a smartphone also gave him as much access to the world as a computer, and he missed that sorely. He decided to go into the shop and inquire about getting a new phone.

After an unexpectedly short period of time, he was in possession of a fancy new phone with a new telephone number. He learned that he could trade his old phone in for a surprisingly high dollar figure, so it did not seem like a complete waste of money. It was an easy transaction.

## 118

Riley was not overly concerned about meeting with Willard, and her walk to his office was not unpleasant. She breathed in the warm summer air, and it felt good to her. She had always loved the seasons changing, and, while she did not relish the trials of winter, she was mindful of how even those, challenging as they could be, would eventually give way to spring again. She felt in tune with the cycles of life.

She also thought about Willard. Yes, she was angry at him for taking Edward's side. But except for that one episode, he had always been kind and gracious to her. She understood that he spent some time waiting for her yesterday; only a truly good person would do that.

So she was a little surprised when she walked into the office. She glanced around, and her first impression was that it reflected what she knew about Bean exactly: spare but not untasteful; neat and well-kept. But the receptionist seemed anxious, and when she spotted Riley entering the waiting room, she quickly picked up the phone and alerted Willard, who showed up ten seconds later. The look on his face was drawn: he was worried about something. He thanked her for coming and ushered her into his office.

Riley sat down on a chair across from Willard's desk, the same one recently vacated by Edward. She put her hands on her lap and waited.

She did not have to wait long. "Ms. Cotswald," Willard began. "I have run across some information that might impact you, and I wanted to share it with you as soon as possible." He looked down at the papers on his desk as he arranged his thoughts in his head. "It appears that Edward McAlister solicited the services of a certain Stuart Stonecraft to teach him how to hack into computers. Edward's agenda, of course, was to implement the twisted plan he had devised to get back at you." More looking at his notes. "It appears that he found Mr. Stonecraft on the Dark Web. He advertised his services as a tutor of sorts, teaching interested parties how to manipulate the machines of other people."

None of this surprised Riley, who was getting a little impatient at what she considered a needlessly long prelude to whatever it was that Willard wanted to tell her.

"After some checking, I learned that Mr. Stonecraft has been a person of interest to local and national police agencies, including the FBI." Willard shut his eyes and opened them. "He is suspected of being involved in theft, as well as the disappearance of several people."

Riley's eyes widened. "Are you telling me he is . . . dangerous?"

"I'm afraid so."

Riley's face blanched a bit. "What does he know about me?"

"We don't know exactly. But I am thinking one of the things he may know is your computer's IP address, the one that Mr. McAlister accessed. So long as that has no power to it, it is useless to him."

Riley exhaled slowly, but her relief was far from incomplete. She had a million questions.

"You said he was involved in the disappearance of several people? What does that mean?"

"It means that a number of people with whom he was involved have gone missing. No one knows exactly what happened to all of them, but one of the common denominators in all of these cases is that they all knew Stonecraft, and he was invariably the last person seen with each of them." Will coughed, looked down, and returned his gaze to Riley. "None of those incidents, by the way, were in the District. They took place in Maryland and were largely centered on unsavory characters. Criminals, most likely, or at least people who were involved in shady operations."

He looked at her gravely. "Authorities believe that several of them are dead."

Riley blanched. "Jesus." She looked across the room toward the single window. "Why are you telling me this now?"

"Out of an abundance of caution." Willard bit his lower lip. "And because I believe it is always better to be careful and safe rather than dismissive of possibilities, even if they are unlikely."

"What?" Riley said.

"Better safe than sorry," Willard replied.

"I thought that's what you meant," said Riley with a hint of a smile on her face. She looked away, thinking that maybe this wasn't the time or place for humor of any sort. Oddly, she did not feel exactly threatened by the news Willard was sharing with her. She was unsure how to feel about it.

After some moments, she turned to look at him directly. "So, what do I do now?"

"The first thing you can do is keep your computer unplugged until you explain to a tech person that you need a new IP address. Then that person can help you resurrect your computer safely. That should take care of the problem." Willard hesitated a moment, focusing on something in his mind. "And I encourage you to check any accounts that you have online to see if they've been tampered with." He looked straight at Riley. "Check them carefully."

Riley's face lost a little more color as she returned his gaze. The silence in the room felt tentative.

Riley swiveled her neck and looked around the room, trying to digest exactly what this all meant to her. She wasn't sure how concerned Willard was, but his anxiety was palpable, despite his reassuring words.

"Mr. Bean," she said at length. "Do you really think I could be in some danger here?"

Willard frowned and returned her gaze. "I don't think it's likely, Ms. Cotswald. But I think you need to have all available information about this situation."

Riley nodded. "I appreciate that."

Riley squinted through her next thoughts. I'm not a criminal; I don't live in Maryland; my computer has been shut down for some time. She could not bring herself to feel that she was in any imminent danger.

The most challenging part to her was finding a 'tech person,' whatever that was. She did not think there was much to do about what Willard was concerned about. It sounded like something to be aware of but not overly concerned about, sort of like a tax audit. She thought of herself as a careful person in general and wasn't sure how much more careful she could be. She decided not to worry about it so much.

Her thoughts were interrupted by Willard, who said, "If you need a tech person, I can give you a name."

Riley nodded. "Okay, that would be great." She thought for a moment. "Is there anything else?"

"I think it would be a good idea for you to be more attentive than usual to your surroundings. Again, I don't really think the prospects are high of your drawing this guy's attention . . ."

"But better safe than sorry."

"Exactly."

Riley took a deep breath. "Okay, then." Then, she looked at Willard warmly. "I want to thank you for all you've done about this, Mr. Bean. It has not been easy, but you handled everything very professionally. And I am grateful." And Riley believed every word she said.

"You're welcome, Riley," said Willard. "You have my card. Call me if you need me."

"Will do."

Riley stood up, reached across the desk to shake Willard's hand; then she turned and left the office feeling neither frightened nor unconcerned. She just felt grounded. It felt good to know what she was dealing with.

## 119

What Willard told her did not *really* hit Riley until later that day. She was back in her apartment, sitting on her couch and staring at the unplugged computer, which suddenly looked dated and past its prime. She thought it might be easier to just throw it out and get a new one. But she wasn't really sure if that was safe.

She found her body shivering a bit when she realized that she might be or might have been in physical danger she knew nothing about. It was such an unusual experience. She had only occasionally been frightened or concerned about her safety—she was something of a nervous flier—but the prospect of someone out there wanting to inflict actual physical harm on her was a whole different thing. She assumed a sense of safety in her apartment, which was in a mid-century high-rise and housed people more or less like her, single for the most part, although of varying ages. She had never heard of anyone being hurt or robbed or in any way importuned. The most serious thing that happened was some people getting angry when their rent was raised. But in a rent-controlled building, even that was muted.

She stood up and tried to shake the feeling of anxiety away, but she could not stop thinking about what might be lying in wait for her. She knew she had to do something, so she dialed the number that Willard had given her for the computer technician. She left a voice message with her return number.

She set about checking her accounts on her laptop and carefully examining every bank account, credit card account, and other things where she thought she would have a chance to see if something was amiss. She didn't notice anything unusual, but that fact did nothing to improve her apprehension.

With few other alternatives coming to mind, she turned to what she knew.

*Vising hours in the ICU were strictly limited, and soon Adam found himself headed toward the waiting room, unsure of what to do next. The tears were still streaming down his cheeks. He didn't really want to leave her side, but Suzanne clearly needed her rest, and he was, after all, a husband in name only.*

*Still, he felt a care for her that had not been there for a very long time. He found himself clinging to the feeling, even savoring it. It reminded him of how he felt about her during their early years together, plus a new feeling of connection that they had perhaps never had together. It gave him hope; but it was a hope that would surely be lost in the sheer improbability of any kind of reconciliation. This made him sad. But perhaps it was not a hope for somehow resurrecting their marriage: that was simply not going to happen. He wasn't at all sure he wanted it to happen. But he would welcome a relationship with Suzanne that was separate from marriage, a kind of friendship that would be special because of their history not in spite of it. Adam had no idea what that might look like in fact; he had never had anything similar in his life before. But wasn't life about forging new paths? Isn't that what he was doing anyway by moving and starting again? Yes, he thought. A feeling of settledness came over him, a feeling that changed the sadness into something resembling a realistic hope. A new path.*

Hmm, Riley thought. Is that even possible?

*He called for another Uber to get home, but the same feelings bedeviled him throughout the ride. Once home, he found himself looking around the house, the one that he and Suzanne had occupied happily and unhappily for the years of their marriage. A house that he was about to give up. He was scheduled to move the following week, and up until now had been greatly looking forward to it. Now the excitement was nowhere to be found. In its place was a kind of sobriety or perhaps a respect for how life changes. It can be difficult at times, but life remains precious even in difficult circumstances. Of that he was sure.*

This all struck Riley as pie-in-the-sky. Is it really improbable? What was he talking about anyway? But she did not touch the delete key. Rather, she put her fingers back to work.

*Suzanne, meanwhile, had fallen back asleep the moment Adam left. It was largely a dreamless sleep, the kind induced by high levels of body-numbing drugs of the type rarely seen outside a hospital. When she awoke several hours later, it was late evening.*

*She deduced this from the clock on the wall rather than any firsthand experience. There were no windows in the ICU, but there were clocks everywhere. So when she read 9:00 o'clock on the analog device, she assumed it was nine o'clock in the evening.*

*She was wrong. In fact, it was 9:00 a.m. the next morning, as the nurse who came in informed her. "How am I doing?" she asked her. Her voice sounded stronger than the day before. It was no longer a whisper. It was her voice.*

*"Coming along," the young woman replied, reading from a chart at the end of the bed. "The doctor will be here in a few minutes, and he can explain everything to you."*

*Suzanne turned away and did not interfere with the nurse doing whatever nurses do in ICUs. She lay back on her bed and checked in with her body. It definitely felt better. She was greatly relieved.*

*She looked down at the IV stuck in her hand, noting that it was attached to what appeared to be a supply of blood. I must have lost a lot, she thought.*

*This was confirmed by the physician who stepped into the room a moment later, picked up her chart and scanned it for perhaps ten seconds, and then turned to face his patient directly.*

*"You are a lucky young woman," he said. He went on to explain the course of her condition in words she mostly understood but which were not devoid of doctor-speak, that curious language physicians often use to communicate with each other that is often only dimly comprehended by lay people such as herself. But she got the gist: she*

*had been in a bad way, got treatment in the nick of time, and would make a full recovery. But it would take some time.*

*That was fine with Suzanne. She found the business meetings she was in D.C. for boring and largely unnecessary. Mostly an unarticulated celebration consisting of people whose luck was slightly better than many of their equally qualified colleagues. Not that Suzanne minded being in the select group, but no one else seemed to understand just how much indifferent fortune played a role in their positions.*

*"How long?" she asked the doctor. And he rightly interpreted this to mean "How long before I can return to work."*

*"Give it a week," he said. "And then start back slowly. No heavy exercise. You can walk when you feel able, but no running or biking or strenuous activity for at least two weeks." He looked down at her chart and then back up to her face. "Take care of yourself. You've been through a serious medical situation. It will take time. Think gradual in all things."*

*Suzanne nodded and thanked him for his concern. "One more thing, Doctor," she said. "How long will I be in here?"*

*"We're transferring you out of the ICU today, but we'll observe you for another day or two in hospital. Then we will discharge you home."*

*Suzanne wondered where home might be, but before she could give that any more thought, she fell back asleep.*

Riley pushed back from her laptop, relieved that Suzanne was okay but wondering what in the world would happen next.

As if in response, her phone rang. It was the computer technician she had called earlier. She explained the situation and an appointment was arranged for the next day. Fast service, Riley thought. She wondered if Willard had alerted him.

She checked in with herself. The acute anxiety she had felt earlier simmered into a low-level sense of apprehension. She recognized that she did not feel in any immediate danger, and that awareness coupled with focusing on work went some way in tempering her panic.

## — 120 —

Jennifer was glad to have been able to help Riley, who had seemed to Jen to be somewhat distant these past few days. But that ended last night, when the two spent the entire night together. She understood it had been an eventful time for her friend, and she was glad to be able to be there when Riley needed her. She also marveled at her own ability to be so close to an attractive woman and not at least try to break down barriers to sex, but she also knew that Riley was fragile in a way she had seen her only rarely. The last thing she wanted to do was add to Riley's stress.

Still, she was relieved to be back at work, focusing on other things. She enjoyed her work: there was a creative side to it; she interacted with interesting people; and it paid sufficiently well at this point for her to enjoy a decent life in the expensive Washington area. She was grateful for all of that.

But she was uncertain whether the excitement of Riley's life was enough to satiate her own appetite for adventure. In fact, she was sure it wasn't. In the back of her mind, she found herself rolling over various options to attract more excitement, which she felt she had not really had in what was beginning to feel like a long time. She reflected a bit on her experience with Matthew, but that was a kind of excitement she did not care to repeat. It gave her the shivers just thinking about it.

Jen knew that her free-wheeling lifestyle was not without risk. But, then again, excitement isn't exciting without some level of danger. Jennifer had always found willing partners, despite the recent drought. It always seemed to her that there was something magical about finding someone. It could happen anywhere: at happy hours and bars, of course, but also in connections through work or in chance encounters in stores. On one occasion, she ran into a woman in the street with whom she struck up a conversation and then a torrid encounter. It was a single-episode relationship, but it was something she never regretted.

In fact, she never regretted any of the escapades she had had. This was how she chose to live her life, and it made perfect sense to her. Giving it up, especially for fuzzy, questionable moralistic qualms, seemed silly to her. And undoable.

One thing she knew for sure. She was not going to meet anyone sitting around her apartment thinking about it. So, after work, she went home, refreshed her make-up, changed her clothes, and went to have a drink at a bar she favored on P Street. It was a place she had visited with some regularity in the past, but she had not been there for some time. It was down a flight of steps into a windowless space that was frequented by a steady clientele of people not too different from her.

And when she walked in, the bartender spotted her immediately and smiled. A couple of other heads bobbed their approval of her return, as if she had just returned from a long voyage. She felt at home.

She found a seat at the bar, greeted the bartender whose name she could not recall, and ordered her favorite martini.

"It's been a while," said the nameless bartender.

Jen nodded. "Been busy." She took a sip of the drink that appeared in front of her. "How's business been?" In the back of her mind, she was searching for the name; she knew it was in there somewhere. It was a little bit unusual; maybe it was foreign.

"Great."

Jen turned to scan the room. It wasn't a large space, but it was big enough so that she had to make a complete 360 degree turn to make sure she saw everyone. No immediate prospects, but it was early. A few male patrons smiled at her; she smiled back before turning back to the bartender. Then it dawned on her: Benjamin. Not Ben or Benny or B; always Benjamin. That's what felt so curious about it.

"There was a woman in here the other day asking about you," said Benjamin.

"Really? Who? Do you know her name?"

The young man—truthfully, he was not so young as he wanted others to believe, but he was young-ish in the general scheme of things—scrunched up his face as if trying to recall her name. "Maria, um, Maria something. Hispanic."

Maria Esposito, Jen recalled immediately. It had been a long time. "When was she here last?"

"Just the other day. Tuesday, I think. Yeah. Tuesday."

"Did she say anything else?

Benjamin shook his head. "Not much, but she was disappointed when I told her you hadn't been here in a while."

I bet she was, Jen thought. She recalled the lovely Mexicana with stunning black hair, high cheekbones, bottomless dark eyes, and a lovely full figure who wanted everything Jennifer had to give and then some. Fiery, possessive, easy to take offense: she was a handful. A passionate handful, to be sure, but the constant demands and intrusiveness finally wore down even Jennifer's adventuresome spirit. They parted on what Jen considered amicable terms; although, that was probably not fully descriptive of the tearful, clingy, hot-headed way Maria reacted when Jen told her it was time. She had not spoken to her since. As per her usual MO.

But sitting in a dimly lit bar nursing a cocktail after a long dry spell tests the resolve of even the most stalwart temporarily abstemious. She tried to think back to when she and Maria were together last. It was months; maybe a year. Seems like a long time to wait for a re-do.

She sipped her drink and took a deep breath. She was beginning to feel centered again.

She pulled out her phone to see if Maria's name was still in her contact list. This was a formality, as she knew it would be: Jennifer was not one to delete the contact information of former lovers. You never knew when that information would come in handy.

She hesitated just a few moments longer before she hit the number.

Maria answered immediately.

## 121

Edward stared at his new phone eager to put it to good use. He felt a surge of relief being reconnected to the online world. Physical isolation is one thing, but being cut off from the Internet was a burden no modern person should have to bear. So he thought.

He was tempted to get back into the Dark Web to see if he could locate Bomber17, but he wasn't sure that was a good idea. He felt a powerful urge to . . . what? . . . tell him off? Strike out at him somehow? He needed some time to think about what to do next. But revulsion, rage, and an enormous desire for revenge was growing in the pit of his stomach, and nothing he could think or dream could extinguish it. It wasn't exactly the same reaction he had felt toward Riley—that experience had faded from his mind and body and was something he remembered but no longer felt— but it was at least equally intense. Maybe more so, as the stakes seemed higher.

Edward started fantasizing about how he could get back at Bomber17, but he knew it would be hard to track him down without revealing his own location. The fact that this very kind of thinking led to the disastrous situation with Riley was completely invisible to him.

He forced himself to distract his attention away from what he felt was inevitable. He spent the greater part of the evening bringing his new phone up to date with his regular bookmarks and contacts. He was able to check his email and follow up with ones he thought were important. His vengeful impulses lurked behind every move he made, however, and had not lessened during that time; they simply took their place at the table of his mind. Revenge seemed like the only sensible path. In part, the motive was noble: he did not want anything bad to happen to Riley. But he could also taste how delicious revenge would be for him. He could not wait to come up with a plan.

In the meantime, he thought he might give Bean a call to let him know that he had a phone and could be contacted if anything else came up. He dialed the number, and his call went straight to voicemail. He explained that he had gotten a new phone with a new number and invited Bean to contact him if he became aware of any new developments. He wasn't sure how Bean could be helpful to him, but he was the one who told him about Stonecraft, so he could not dismiss the prospect of Bean's providing him with more information as things unfolded. He had turned into something of a source, perhaps even a colleague.

Finally, as evening fell, Edward was satisfied that he had done enough for one day. He sat back on his couch and picked up the remote control of the TV and flipped it on. He knew an idea would come to him soon.

## 122

Once Suzanne learned that she would be discharged the next day, she contacted her parents for the first time. She had told them she would be in the District and had planned to get together with them later in the week, and that was true; but the scene she would set would be far from the casual visit by a successful young adult child to her adoring parents. On the contrary, she was hoping they would not mind nursing her back to health for a few days.

Of course, they did not mind and said so after the shock of learning that she was in the hospital receded a little. As any parents would be, they were worried sick that their only child had been in the ICU. It must have been something very serious. And there was no problem at all having her stay with them for as long as she needed for her recovery. Suzanne was vague about the exact nature of her illness, but she informed her frightened parents that there had been some internal bleeding and she needed time to heal. They knew enough not to push for more information.

It was not as if Suzanne would ever tell them the details: that was something her parents had learned about her long ago. Suzanne was a bright woman, who apparently had a great need for a level of privacy that was beyond what her parents would have preferred. Privately, they hoped that she would become more open as she got older, but she was apparently not old enough yet.

They arranged a time to come pick her up and met her at the entrance of the hospital; she was waiting for them in a wheelchair with an attendant standing nearby. Suzanne's mother, Liz, almost fainted when she saw her; her father, Gene, looked the same on the surface, but Suzanne could tell he had subtly grown several levels more serious. It was something about his eyes and mouth and furrowed brow that gave it away: small changes that signaled deep concern. She learned this a long time ago as an observant only child.

*I must look like hell,* Suzanne thought. She felt much better than she had when she first went to Desai, but even she knew her recovery was just starting. She did not feel like her fully functioning self.

As far as her parents knew, Suzanne and Adam were separated, and Suzanne was living in Dayton. They were not privy to the details of their divorce, much less of their relationship. That was fine for Suzanne. She loved her parents dearly, but their version of parenting could be smothering at times. Often, in fact; something she realized while still in middle school. She smiled and waved as they approached and helped her into the back seat of their mid-sized sedan.

"What happened?" her father finally asked as they started back into traffic.

"I think it was something I ate."

Gene nodded, a curious response, as he did not believe a word of what his daughter just said.

Meanwhile, Liz was fidgety. Several times, she turned around to look at Suzanne, who was absently staring out the window. "Do you need anything special, Honey? Food-wise? Or medicine? Should we stop at the drugstore?"

"No, Mom," Suzanne replied. "They loaded me up with drugs when they discharged me. I should be fine."

The threesome fell into less-than-comfortable silence, her parents not wanting to push and Suzanne not wanting to provide any more detail than was absolutely necessary.

Stalemate, observed Riley. Like so many things.

She glanced at the clock. It was almost time for the computer tech. She put her laptop away and grabbed a cup of coffee. She sat on the couch to wait for him, trying not to think about all that had been happening in her life or in her novel.

At precisely the appointed time, her doorbell rang, and she buzzed the tech into the building. She waited at her door until she heard the elevator, whereupon she opened her door to welcome him.

As soon as she spotted him exiting the elevator, she began to blush. She had assumed that a computer technician would be the type she often saw portrayed on television: skinny, nerdy-looking twenty-somethings with big glasses, bad hair, and worse clothes. Instead, a tall, obscenely handsome thirty-year-old in khaki slacks, a white oxford shirt, and faultlessly shined loafers sauntered down the hall toward Riley and her open door.

"Hi, I'm Rick," he said extending his hand.

"Riley," she said, shaking his hand.

She paused a moment too long before gesturing for him to enter her apartment. Rick seemed not to notice and walked in ahead of her. "Thanks," he said, nodding.

It was not hard to spot the unplugged computer: it had a large screen that was only partially hidden by a bath towel and was the focal point of the room. "This is it?"

"Yes."

"So somebody hacked into your computer, and you unplugged it to safeguard the loss of any additional information?"

"Yes."

"May I?" he said, gesturing to the dead machine.

Polite to boot, she thought. "Of course."

She sat down on the couch, which was across the room from her work place but not far. She found her heart beating a little faster, both as an animal attraction response and because she had grown accustomed to her machine being inert. She was a little nervous when Rick picked up the cord to plug it in. It felt as if he were resurrecting a vampire or some other kind of monster.

"How long has this been unplugged?" he asked.

Riley tried to think. She wasn't sure. "I'm not sure," she said. "Maybe a couple weeks?"

The time did not seem to make much difference to Rick. He took out a thumb drive and plugged it into a port on the side of the machine. "I'm going to boot it up from this drive," he said. "That way, we'll be able to check your data without interference. It won't be accessible to anyone else."

To Riley's mind, that bordered on the miraculous. How could that be, she wondered. Was it really that simple? "Okay," she said.

Rick plugged the machine in, and for the first time in a long while, Riley listened to the familiar sounds of the machine whirring back to life. It calmed her down a little, but her anxiety did not disappear.

Rick's eyes were glued to the screen. Riley wondered what he was looking for, but only absently, as she was back to assessing his good looks, confidant demeanor, and overall attractiveness. This was the last thing she expected.

Rick launched into a description of what he was going to do. It was laced with techno-babble, but not overly so, and Riley got the gist of it. He was going to clean her hard drive, change her IP address, install a powerful firewall to prevent further attacks, and make sure there were no traces of whatever the hacker used to gain access to her machine. That sounded like precisely what Riley needed and wanted, and the confidence of his voice allowed her to relax a little.

"Sounds great," she said. Then, realizing that her schoolgirl reaction had overridden her good manners, she asked Rick if he would like some coffee or water. "No, thanks," came the reply. He smiled as he said it.

Riley found herself smiling back.

He worked through whatever routine he was doing without looking at her. His eyes were glued to the machine and occasionally to the keyboard.

Riley was beginning to feel a little unneeded during this and got up to go the kitchen to find something to do. What she wanted to do was find a bottle of wine and two glasses, but that seemed a little forward. She just poured herself a glass of water, leaned against the counter for a while in an effort to keep herself focused on the task at hand. Now whatever stress she was feeling was not about the machine, but about the machine's current handler.

Of course, getting a glass of water took only a couple of minutes, and then it was time to walk back into the room where Rick was working. His eyes were still glued to the screen, the black background of which was filled with a lot of incomprehensible letters, numbers, and symbols. She sat back down on the couch.

Finally, after what seemed like a very long time but wasn't, Rick turned to her and said, "I see that someone had access to a Word document on this machine. It still has residual traces on it. I don't know if it's important or not."

"It's important."

"Do you have another copy?"

"Yes, I do. It's on my laptop," Riley said, gesturing with her head to the laptop on the small table in front of the window.

"Okay," Rick said. He reached inside a case he carried and pulled out another thumb drive. "Could you copy it onto this drive, and we'll delete the original and replace it with the copy. That way, there will be no residual traces."

"Sure," Riley said, and stood up and took the drive from Rick's proffered hand. She swore she felt a spark when her hand inadvertently touched his. She quickly booted up her laptop, inserted the drive, and copied the manuscript, which was, of course, the most current version. She ejected the drive and handed it back to Rick.

He took it from her hand, and her hand sparked again. She bit the inside of her lip to keep from giggling.

He inserted the drive, rebooted the computer, and reglued his eyes to the screen. After a few minutes, he pushed back from the now live computer and said, "Okay. All set."

Riley looked at Rick and then at her newly refurbished machine. "That's it? Is there anything I need to know or do now? Is it safe?"

"Yes, it is. And no, there is nothing special to do except renew the anti-virus software I installed on it every year. Put it on your calendar." He handed her a piece of paper with the name of the software company. "That is the single most important thing you can do. This is the best anti-virus software in the business." Then, he glanced over at the laptop. "I presume you do not have any such software on the laptop?"

"I don't think so."

"Would you like me to check?"

"Please," said Riley, momentarily more concerned about her portable computer than her houseguest.

Rick rolled the chair over to the table by the window where the laptop was waiting and reprised whatever he did on the desktop machine. Riley was pleased with this, as it took roughly the same amount of time.

In what she thought was about the half-way mark, she again asked Rick if he wanted something to drink.

Without taking his eyes off the screen, he said, "Yeah, you know, some water would be great. With ice if you've got it."

Riley felt as if she had rounded first base. She jumped up and got the water with ice and came back into the room. She waited to hand Rick the glass, but he did not seem to notice, so she set it on the table next to him.

"Thanks," he said without turning his head. He picked up the glass and took a hefty gulp.

Riley was of two minds. On the one hand, she really, really wanted to strike up a conversation with this man. On the other hand, she did not want to overplay whatever hand she was holding; nor did she want to disturb his concentration on the work she knew was so important. In the end, she decided not to disturb his concentration. She did not think he would like that; nor did she want to touch her laptop without his imprimatur.

So she sat and waited.

Willard was getting tired. He remembered the early years of his career when he could work for hours or even days and hardly feel fatigued at all; such was his devotion to the whole process of investigation. Some people say it's like a puzzle, but for Willard it was way more than that. It was a calling, a vocation, an essential part of the civil life of the nation, and it absorbed every talent and investment of time and energy he could bring to bear on the successful completion of every case he was involved in. All details were equally important, no matter how trivial or seemingly insignificant they might appear.

When he pushed back at the end of the work day, he blinked hard several times to keep himself focused; then he went to get a cup of coffee from the small kitchen area of his office. The moving around was helpful in reinvigorating himself, as was the strong black liquid that he poured into his cup.

While doing these mundane things, he ran through what he had accomplished over the past few days. He had discovered that Bomber17, Stuart Stonecraft, was most likely a bad actor, or at least a person of interest to multiple police jurisdictions; he had appropriately warned both Riley and Edward about him and gave them each instruction for how to minimize any damage that may have been done or that Stonecraft may have contemplated doing. He had also healed a rift with Riley, who had been very angry with him for appearing to take Edward's side.

Willard still had equivocal feelings about that. He did not think that he was taking anybody's side; he always thought he was on the side of the truth. But he did allow that, for some reason, Edward's predicament touched him: the young man seemed so cut off from normal life, so solitary, and therefore, so susceptible to doing monumentally stupid things. Willard's sympathy for him probably did show up in his meeting with Riley and Mildred, at least creating the impression that he was partial to him.

Mildred. Where did he leave it with Mildred? In her own concise way, she told him that Riley was right. Willard was not fond of such rebukes, and it smarted more coming from someone he respected as much as Millie. But he had to admit she was right. No matter how sympathetic a character Edward was to him, he was also the bad guy in recent events.

After listening to Edward's last voicemail, however, he also realized that Edward was more resourceful than perhaps Willard had thought. It took him no time to get a new phone, and he was self-aware enough to change his number. It was undoubtedly a smart phone, so it enabled him to get back online. In the scheme of things, that seemed like a good immediate solution, but Willard had to acknowledge that his initial sympathy for Edward may have blinded him to other aspects of the younger man's personality.

This seemed like a good thing to discuss with Mildred. And since he wasn't sure about how she felt about their last conversation, he thought it might be as good an excuse as any to touch base with her and review recent events. Besides, he had not brought her up to date on the situation with Stonecraft.

He looked around his office. I don't want to do it here. I don't want to do it at her office. I think it's time we discussed this over dinner.

That seemed like a perfect solution. Willard picked up his phone and dialed Mildred's number.

"Hi, Will," said Mildred.

"Hi, Millie," he replied. "I've been thinking. A lot has happened over the past few days, and there have been some new developments. How about you and I get together for dinner this evening and catch up?"

Mildred hesitated for a moment. She was grateful for the call and wanted to catch up. But dinner? It had been over a year—or was it two?—since she and Willard had done anything outside their respective offices. She recalled on one occasion they met for coffee, and the other day they did have lunch, but even that normal-seeming thing resurrected feelings she wasn't sure she wanted to revisit. But her qualms lost out. "Sure," she said.

Whereupon they made plans to meet at an old haunt of theirs at Will's suggestion and Millie's acquiescence.

After hanging up, Will decided to freshen up. Fortunately, he kept a change of clothes at his office and had a small private bathroom where he could change, shave, and spruce himself up without returning to his apartment. He too was aware that it had been a long time since he and Millie had dinner together. But they had serious things to talk about. This rationalization was so thin even he smiled at his reflection in the mirror.

He had selected a place that the two of them had frequented with some regularity when they were a couple. It was within walking distance of his office. It was a nice place with a good bar and white tablecloths in the dining room. Good food; decent service: there were a lot of good reasons to go there, but none quite so beneficent as his desire to be with Millie outside the pure demands of work. He walked slowly through the streets of D.C., savoring the warm air and breathing in new possibilities.

As hard as it was to put an end to the romantic aspects of their relationship, Willard could not simply dismiss the love he had for this woman. He still longed for her as an intimate partner. It was a constant struggle to keep those feelings in check. He knew that taking her hand the other day after lunch was crossing a line he had established for himself. And it just made him want to take the next step. She did not protest then; he hoped she would not protest now.

The protocol for dinner had not changed, even though it had been a long time since their last shared evening repast. They would meet at the bar, have a drink, and start reviewing events since their last meeting. They would slip into the thing they did most naturally: comparing notes, sharing information, and huddle over a joint mission—to make sure everyone involved in the sad story of Riley and Edward was safe.

Willard had reserved a table for later in the evening, but he enjoyed the first part the most: just hanging out with a woman he admired, cared for, loved. The fact that he had found their intimate relationship so difficult was at this moment a mere historic artifact, having little bearing on what he hoped was about to transpire.

Mildred, on the other hand, was more apprehensive. She too held Will in high regard. The breakup hit her hard. It surprised her; it wasn't what she wanted; she had a hard time even understanding it, a feature especially maddening for a psychologist. But she had several painful months to think about the whole affair, and, with some help from a sympathetic colleague, was able to see how some of her behavior may have been difficult for Willard. As she reflected back on the serious relationships of her life, she recognized that there were things about her that upset many of the men she dated. This was all unpleasant stuff to learn, but she was, after all, a professional, so she forced herself to be open to unsavory truths about herself. It was small consolation at first. Gradually, she got used to being without Willard the lover and settled for Willard the colleague. She adjusted, just as she had after previous relationships; but it was never easy, and it had yet to become second nature. It was especially galling to her that this arrangement was not her decision.

But on this evening, all that pain and anguish she went through was past. She looked forward to being with Willard, and sitting with him in the bar trading information was as comfortable as an old coat. Sure, she had a hard time simply dismissing the attraction she felt for him, but this was work of a sort. Still, in the back of her mind, she could not help lecturing herself: Do you want to be hurt again? Do you really want to risk more emotional turmoil just for the pleasure it might bring tonight? In spite of herself, the answer to all those questions was an unequivocal yes.

Willard was already at the bar when she arrived.

"Hi, Will," she said.

"Hi, Honey," he replied.

Mildred ordered a fortifying bourbon neat. She barely noticed her qualms slipping away as they headed toward the ill-advised destination that both of them wanted.

# — 124 —

The next morning, Edward woke up with a start. He had had some terrible dreams, and he thought he heard a loud noise, something that was rare in his old apartment building. It was a quiet place. But he couldn't tell if there actually was a noise or if it came from inside his dream.

He tried to piece the dream together. What was it? There was a mirror, and he was looking into it. It suddenly turned into the kind of mirror you see in old-fashioned carnivals that distorted the image greatly, turning the observer into a grotesque version of himself. In an actual carnival, this might be a fun thing to do; in his dream, it was terrifying.

He noticed that he was sweating when he awoke. What else about the dream? Where was he and why was he there? He tried hard to bring it back, but, as with so many nocturnal phantasms, it dissipated just as quickly as it emerged. He cursed aloud and got up and went to the bathroom.

There was something scary about it. What was it? He could not put his finger on it, but he found himself hesitant to look at his image in the bathroom mirror that sat above the sink. When he did, he stared hard at the image to make sure it did not change into anything distorted. But his mind kept asking what scared him the most.

He stepped back from the mirror and posed a sensible question to himself. What is scaring you the most right now? He thought he knew the answer to that.

He turned back to the mirror and spoke aloud: "What scares me now is that I may have caused Riley a lot more hurt than I bargained for. It also scares me that I may have drawn even more trouble to her and to myself without even knowing it." He stared harder at his image in the mirror. "And I am enraged that I lost."

Lost? Yes, lost. The whole point of this dangerous enterprise was to inflict misery on Riley but not really hurt her in any important way. But the real motive, the one he barely revealed even to himself, was that he wanted to be with her. He loved her. She gave him something no other woman—no other person, really—had ever given him: an eroticism so intense it swept him away. And he thought—not so consciously, he supposed—that shaking her up would make her see that he was the one for her.

Edward took a step back. All true, he thought. True but pathetic. He proceeded with his morning hygiene routine, staring at his image the whole time. What are you going to do about this? came the silent question from the mirror. He knew only a part of the answer to that question. The part where he kills Mr. Stonecraft. This idea seemed so clear and simple during the morning grooming routine that Edward found it odd it had not occurred to him before. Doing away with Stonecraft removes the danger to himself and to Riley. It might also win her back.

The fact that murder was a capital offense and posed some daunting logistical problems seemed like minor considerations. Of course, he would not want to get caught. He would also have to select a method and be a lot more careful than he had been in the complicated mess with Todd and Riley. But the elegant simplicity of doing away with this evil man held center stage in his mind. In addition, he knew that most murders weren't solved; he also knew the deed would be over quickly. No one would mourn such a man; doing away with him would strike a blow for the general welfare. And even if it did not result in some kind of reconciliation with Riley, it would give Edward the eternal consolation that he had *done* something, that he had stood up to his fate and not cowered in darkness and fear.

Even if the whole thing went to hell and he was caught, prison did not seem like such a terrible alternative to the life he was living. It was not something he wanted, but it was a risk he would just have to accept. In fact, it felt more like a possibility than a probability.

He finished his morning routines, dressed himself with more care than usual, and left his apartment. He considered returning to the video game place for anonymity, but still recalled how old he felt amid the young people there. He decided to give the public library another shot. He thought he might know a way around entering any identifying information. The goal was to gather information anonymously. On the way, he considered how to do what he wanted to do.

Rick finished up his work on Riley's laptop. "All set," he said. He took out a pad of paper and started scribbling an invoice. Riley waited silently. She was deliberately controlling her breathing to keep her wayward impulses at bay. Or at least out of sight.

He handed her the paper. "This covers today's visit," he said. "If you have any other issues with either of these machines, just call me." He pointed to the printed name, address, and phone number on top of the paper.

Riley was relieved to get the contact information and smiled a little too widely. Having that information took some pressure off the moment. She went over to her desk to retrieve her credit card and handed it to Rick, who was looking straight into her eyes.

He took the card and swiped it through a small reader that attached to his smartphone. He asked for her email address, and she gave it to him. "I'll send the receipt to your email," he said casually.

For the life of her, Riley could not determine if Rick's friendliness was simply a professional thing or if he was flirting with her in an understated way. But since she had his contact information, which, she observed, contained his cell phone number, she decided she did not have to do anything right now. Besides, she wasn't sure she could trust herself at this moment not to look foolish. Instead, she took a surreptitious deep breath.

"Thank you so much for coming and doing this so promptly," she managed to say in a reasonably calm, warm voice. "I can't tell you how much this means to me."

"Glad to help," Rick said, nodding. "Thanks for the water."

Riley shrugged. "No problem."

Rick collected his things and headed toward the door. "Have a good day," he said cheerfully.

After closing the door, Riley leaned her back against it and smiled; the tension in her body began to dissipate, leaving her with feelings of, what was it? Oh, yes. Happiness. It's been a long time, she thought, since she found herself attracted to someone, since she's been happy, since she smiled at a future prospect, no matter how distant.

Two things worked together to brighten her mood. One, she was attracted to Rick, who was no longer three feet away from her. Two, her dead computer was now alive. It felt as though her world was opening up.

Riley was surprised at how relieved she was to have her desktop back in operation. It had sat on her desk defunct for what seemed like forever, as if defining an endless, dark period of her life.

And her animal feelings toward Rick reminded her of something that her recent experience had shoved into the background. She was free to date, to explore other relationships with men again. She stood in her apartment realizing how the grotesque experience with Edward had colored her life for the past months.

She shook her head. The sooner I am done with that, the better.

As her thinking cleared, she wondered if she and Rick would ever hook up. It did not seem at all like an unpleasant prospect, but neither did it feel as if it were something that *had* to happen. She could take her time.

This last thought was accompanied by a sense of liberation that she did not know she was looking for.

Not wanting to get lost in overanalyzing things, Riley bounded across the room, sat down at her newly refurbished desktop computer, and booted it up. She had every confidence it would work flawlessly. It had been touched by the hands of an angel. She inserted her thumb drive, copied her manuscript, and placed her hands over the keyboard. She felt those hands reunited with her machine as they flew across the keyboard.

*Suzanne spent the balance of the week being cared for as if she were still a child. She slept much of the time, took her medications faithfully, and gave out information sparingly to her too-eager-to-please parents. They prepared her meals and brought them to her in the bedroom she grew up in.*

*By the third day, she felt strong enough to eat with them at the dining table, where they had dinner every evening. After the expected expressions of encouragement—"This is great; you're finally up and around."—the threesome chatted amiably for a while. Then a silence descended upon the small family. With an uncharacteristic cock of his head, Gene looked at Suzanne and asked in a serious voice: "What really happened, Suzanne?"*

*This question was so unexpected and delivered so firmly that Suzanne just stared back at her father for several moments. She was torn. She had a long-established habit of not letting her parents know everything about her. To her mind, only children do that, and she was most assuredly not a child anymore. At the same time, her father's tone was one she could not recall ever hearing before. It signaled a level of seriousness and legitimacy that she sometimes felt in her own voice but never from either of her parents. She glanced over at her mother, whose face was inscrutable.*

*"I had an ectopic pregnancy, dad," she finally said. It surprised her that she said it, and she had no idea how her parents would respond. In the brief moments of silence, it dawned on Suzanne that her parents deserved to know, not only because they were her parents, but also because they were going through a great deal of trouble caring for her now. "I'm sorry." Tears rolled down her cheeks.*

*Her father, whose eyes were dry, reached over and put his hand on hers and said simply, "No need to apologize, Honey. I'm just glad you told us."*

*The three adults sat at the table motionless except for the tears streaming down Suzanne's face, which were soon accompanied by those of her mother. "Adam?" her father said in that same new voice.*

*Suzanne nodded. "Yes."*

*"Does he know?"*

*"Yes. He came to the ICU the first day I was there."*

*Gene and Liz glanced at each other. Suzanne had no idea what that meant.*

*She was tempted to get up and leave, but she could not decide where to go. It was an old impulse, one that she now saw as more childish than adult. One she relied on often in the past to shield herself from the kind of disclosure that was now happening. Oddly to her mind, a part of her felt closer to her parents than she had in a long, long time. Perhaps ever.*

*"You know you can stay here for as long as you need, Honey," her mother said.*

*"I know, Mom." She looked from one parent to the other. "Thank you for all you do for me." She paused again. "Thank you for all that you have done for me while growing up."*

*Her dad shrugged. "It's what parents do for their children, Honey," he said. "It's been an honor for us. It still is."*

*Suzanne stood up slowly. She walked over to her dad and put her arms around him. "Thank you," she whispered. She repeated this gesture with her mother.*

*She stood there for a while, not knowing exactly what to do. Stay? Leave? "I am lucky to have you for parents," she said softly. "I think I need to rest now."*

*Her parents both nodded, and Suzanne returned to her bedroom. Gene and Liz looked at each other. "Thank you, Gene," Liz said.*

*Gene shrugged. "She's a strong woman, Liz. I think she'll be all right."*

*Liz nodded. I hope so, she thought.*

I hope so too, Riley thought. She pushed back from her computer and luxuriated in her reconstituted relationship with the pile of metal, plastic, and wires that was the rightful home of the characters she cared so much about. It has been too long, she thought. It felt like a homecoming.

She allowed that perhaps some of these feelings had to do with Rick, but she noticed something else. And that was her desire to move on with her life. In the scheme of things, she saw that, whether something happens with Rick or not, at some time in the future, perhaps the near future, she will have another relationship with someone. She will care for someone and allow someone to care about her. She will be as honest as her character Suzanne is struggling to be. She wanted to live, not as the frightened child she often felt herself to be, but as an adult who savored life, as Suzanne was learning to do.

She hoped so.

*Suzanne sat on the unmade bed where she had spent the last few days and found herself awash in grief: for the pregnancy she lost, the marriage she lost, the lover she lost, even for the city she no longer inhabited. But mostly she thought of her parents. She realized that she had never thanked them for raising her until the ripe age she was now. This shamed her. But it also allowed her to see clearly, perhaps for the first time, that a lot of the things she used to do to establish herself as a grown-up were in fact the actions, thoughts, and behaviors of a child or maybe an adolescent. She saw how those habits followed her into adult life and worked havoc on her relationship with Adam. She pretended with him. She pretended with him just the way she pretended with her parents. She pretended that she was an adult when she wasn't, that she loved him when she didn't, and that everything was okay when she knew it wasn't. All those things led her to this moment. It was all panoramically, painfully clear.*

*She lay down on the bed. I feel more like an adult that ever before, even if I'm an emotional mess just now. And it is up to me, to determine the kind of adult I want to be. She lay her head on the pillow and stared at the ceiling. And I want to be a real one, an honest one, she thought as she drifted off to sleep.*

## 126

Edward was frustrated at every turn. He was able to get around the security protocols of the library computer; but when he tried searching for information about Stuart Stonecraft, aka Bomber17, he found nothing. As he reflected about it, it did not seem so surprising. Surely Stonecraft was able to deal with his online presence in any way he liked. He certainly had the skills to make his online self disappear.

Edward wondered if Bean could be helpful for him. It seemed far-fetched, and he, of course, could not disclose the reason for his inquiry. He tried to think of reasons he would want to approach Stonecraft, reasons that he could share with Bean. None came to mind.

He stood up and stretched, casually looking around the library. As a child, he had always liked these places: they seemed like neutral spaces empty of parental eyes. So long as you did things quietly, something that came naturally to Edward even at a young age, you could pretty much do anything you wanted. He used to think that somebody must train the clerks because they were uniformly nice and tolerant with young people. He hadn't thought of that in a long time.

But in the present, his plan was going nowhere. He gathered up his things and started to leave the library and head home. Then he realized something.

He turned around and rebooted the computer he had just been using. He glanced around the room to make sure no one was watching and entered the Dark Web.

This was something he could do on his home computer at his leisure, but most public ones set limits on what you can access. But as part of what Bomber17 taught him, he learned how simple it was to get around those restrictions.

He sent Bomber17 a private message on the utility he had used with him before and sat back and stared at the machine. Sure enough, within a few minutes, he got a reply. *Hi, Buddy*, it read. *What's up?*

Edward could hardly contain himself. *Been busy using those skills you taught me. All worked out perfectly. Time for another lesson.*

*What can I help you with?*

*Let's meet and talk about it?*

*OK.*

*When? Where?*

They agreed on a time and a place. It was later in the week in the afternoon. A small town in Maryland. Perfect, Edward thought. He had a couple days to come up with a very specific plan.

He erased the history on the computer, logged off the web, gathered up his things, and left the library. I can figure out the rest, he thought.

And he spent the remainder of the day doing precisely that. It appeared there were so many options, so many ways to end the life of another. The more he thought and looked, the more obvious this path seemed: it was definite; it was final; there would be no more lingering danger. He could feel his pulse increase as he saw that Bomber's end was near.

It was heady stuff, once he got past the bourgeois prohibitions against murder. Guns, poison, knives, bombs, chemicals. A panoply of choices. All he had to do was choose the perfect one.

And in the end, I will be free, and Riley will be safe. Edward felt blessed to know those two simple things.

## 127

Mildred woke up the morning after dinner with Will feeling a mix of things. She had a delightful sense of contentment and mirth mixed with certain knowledge that she had made a big mistake. It was odd, even to her, that she was unconcerned about that for the moment. She glanced over at Will, who was happily snoring away. She looked at the clock: 6:30 a.m. All she had with her was what she had when she met Will at the restaurant; this fortunately included essential toiletries.

The evening went as both wanted but neither planned exactly. They talked and compared notes, they flirted a bit, they touched lightly. They drank a little too much, just the way they used to when they met up for dinner when they were together. Neither brought up the next step: it was something they danced around. And it was such a lovely dance with such an inevitable and delicious end that neither could really have forestalled it if they had somehow changed their minds. But neither mind changed.

He volunteered to walk her home. "Your place is closer," was her whispered response. Will wasn't surprised. Neither was Millie at that point. So, the two people, a couple again for the moment, went to Will's place and did what they had not done in over a year, perhaps two; something one or the other of them had wanted at various times to do but never did; something that was off limits until this particular night, for reasons neither of them fully understood or cared about.

Will began to awaken. He extended his hand across the bed and felt Mildred's nude body. "You're still here," he said feigning surprise.

Millie took a pillow and plopped it over his still-shut eyes. "It appears we are both still here."

Millie got up to go to the bathroom without bothering to clothe herself. A little late for prudishness, she thought vaguely. Besides, she didn't mind being naked.

The situation that the two fully grown adults had created was a conundrum: they had agreed to set limits on their relationship, limits that broadly defined themselves as friends, a feature that implicitly prohibited sexual contact. And for the most part the new rules seemed to be working. Until last night. Now they were in the wake of incontestably sexual contact, something both of them wanted, flouting the rules as if they were, perhaps, only suggestions.

And while both of them were thinking similar things, neither knew exactly what to do or where to go from here. The glow of the evening before was too fresh, too savory, too wonderful to bother with disruptive conjecture.

"How about breakfast?" Millie heard Will say through the thin bathroom door.

"Great," came her reply. "In or out?"

"I think in," he replied. She could hear him getting out of bed and dressing himself. For a fastidious guy, Willard made a fair amount of noise.

She came out of the bathroom and looked at Will, who was almost completely dressed. "Going somewhere?" she asked.

She walked over and stood in front of his seated, mostly clothed self.

"Guess not," he said, slipping off his shirt and wrapping his arms around her bare waist.

"I thought not," Mildred said. And they continued doing what they had started the evening before.

## 128

Knives, Edward decided. Definitely knives. They were readily available, easy to conceal, easy to surprise someone. A knife can be applied and reapplied until the task was complete. Also, it's an inexpensive option. There were some downsides: concealing it until the right moment; getting close enough to complete the task; getting clothes soaked in blood. But these seemed manageable. Bomber always struck Edward as a sociable guy who was unconcerned about how close he got physically to another person. And as far as the clothes are concerned, he could easily bring a change of clothes along, with some suitable solvents to clean any residual blood from his body.

The tricky part, it seemed to Edward, would be getting Bomber alone. That was going to take some thought. In the past, they usually met at some bar or restaurant where there were people around. Since they always met in out-of-the-way rural places, there weren't a lot of people, so they had a good balance between being in public and having some privacy. It now occurred to Edward that the staging was probably deliberate on Bomber's part.

Edward could not bring himself to call Bomber17 anything but Bomber, even in his mind. 'Stuart Stonecraft' did not really seem to fit him. He was more than a little on the scruffy side, indicating that his breeding and lifestyle left something to be desired. Even if he were one of those people who cast himself as a counter-cultural hero, his personal hygiene was subpar. Also, Edward did not want to let on to Bomber that he knew his real name. So, Bomber it was and Bomber it would remain.

Edward got up to assess his collection of knives, which were suitably housed in the kitchen where he sometimes used them. He counted three different kinds: small paring-type knives, steak knives, and butcher knives. He was first attracted to the smaller ones, as they would be easier to conceal; however, their utility as a murder weapon was limited to small cuts only. He did not want this task to take too long. It would have to be a larger one: the butcher knife had special appeal, given the task at hand. Or maybe a chef's knife.

In the midst of these challenging decisions, Edward stopped. He stared down at the array of cutlery on his small kitchen counter. Really? I'm really going to cut up Bomber17? End his life with kitchen tools, as if he were a piece of meat I'm prepping for dinner? The absurdity and the silliness of this idea crashed down all around him. He could even see the dark humor in this light-bereft situation.

He picked up one of the knives and observed how long, thin, and sharp the blade was. He took out a ruler and measured nine inches of blade. This could do the job. He scrunched up his face as he tried to keep the dying concept alive.

Nothing could save the fantasy. The notion of turning himself into a murderer was too much for even him to bear. The whole notion evaporated in his mind.

I can't do it. I won't do it.

He retreated from his kitchen after returning the equipment to its rightful place and took up a position near the window. He sat staring out as night fell across the District.

After a while, he thought about the impulsive meet-up he had arranged with Bomber17. So what about that?

What about it? I just won't show up. Or I could cancel. Suddenly, it occurred to Edward that texting Bomber was probably not a great idea, given how much interest law enforcement had in him.

This telling notion landed atop a pile of wrong-headed ideas to which he could claim fatherhood: The recently deceased idea of turning himself into a sadistic murderer, the phony bravado he felt just minutes before, the hope for redemption, the swagger that he had momentarily acquired. All vanished. And in its place was the same maddening and relentless feeling of impotence that he had felt ever since he ran into Riley Cotswald.

Did she do this to me?

Of course not.

Who did?

Nobody did.

Somebody did.

Who might that be?

I did.

This internal dialogue wasn't much consolation for Edward, whose own assessment of his life in his most lucid moments ran toward the mediocre. This whole experience, just like his plan for dealing with Riley, was now just another pile of rubbish.

He turned his face away from the window, glanced around his tiny apartment, and hung his head in a shame that would not stop burning through his insides.

*The next morning, Suzanne got up feeling a little better than she felt the day before. And not just physically; on an emotional level she felt more balanced and freer. She got dressed and went downstairs, where her parents usually had breakfast.*

*She found them where she had always found them at this time of the morning, even before they had retired: seated at a small breakfast table off the kitchen with windows giving out to a neatly manicured lawn that was presently withering under the summer sun. She knew her father would probably spend the day tending to it.*

*Gene and Liz fell silent at her approach, not in a suspicious way but in a solicitous, even welcoming one. "Good Morning," Suzanne said.*

*"Good Morning," her father said.*

*Her mother nodded and looked her over. "You're dressed," her mother said. "Feeling better?"*

*"I am. Thank you."*

*A few moments of silence as Suzanne went to retrieve a cup for coffee and fill it from the machine in the same corner of the kitchen where it had always resided.*

*She returned and did not wait for either of her parents to initiate a conversation. It was, after all these years, her turn.*

*"I want to thank you again for being so kind to me about . . . about everything." She looked down for a moment. "And I want to bring you up to date on some things that have been going on in my life, things you probably do not know about."*

*She looked at her father. "After last night, I realized how childish I had been. And all the while I thought I was being grown up. I realized how important it is to be honest with significant people in my life." She looked at one parent, then the other. "And you two are the most significant people in my life right now."*

*Suzanne took in a large breath and launched into a PG13 version of her life over the past few years. Everything she told her parents was true, but she left out some details that were too personal to share. But the things she did tell them reflected a major change in her self-disclosure. Most importantly, she told them about Ellie and her relationship with her, how it developed while she was still married to Adam, and how it served as a beacon for her, a way to feel okay about herself. "I thought at first it was just a thing, a one-time bit of exploring." She looked down at her hands. "But it turned out to be so much more."*

*She spoke tearfully of Ellie's tragic death and the enormous loss that was for her. During this part of the conversation, she was often lost in thought, looking at her hands and only occasionally glancing above the heads of her parents. It was hard. In fact, she thought even as she was saying it, it was one of the hardest things she had ever done.*

*When she was finished, she took another deep breath and looked at both her parents. Both had tears in their eyes.*

*"Oh, Suzie," said her mother, lapsing into what she had often called her as a child. She reached across the small table and took her hand in hers.*

*Her father took her other hand. He spoke haltingly. "I've been hoping for this moment for a long, long time," he said. He paused and looked over his daughter's head before leveling his eyes with hers. "I count this as one of the greatest moments of my life," he whispered. "You know we love you no matter what you choose in your life."*

Riley found a tissue and wiped the tears from her eyes. What great parents. Her hands returned to the keyboard.

*The three family members sat in a warm, intimate silence for some moments. No one dared to speak. Suzanne was checking in with herself. She was happy in a sober kind of way, but she could also feel fatigue setting in. She slumped a bit in her chair.*

*"Are you all right?" her father said.*

*Suzanne nodded. "Just tired," she said.*

*Liz stood up. "I think you need to eat something, Honey," she said. "I'll make you some breakfast." Before moving into the kitchen, she patted Suzanne's hand.*

*Suzanne started to feel a little dizzy. "I think I need to lie down," she said. She went over to a couch and lay down fully clothed.*

Riley froze in her seat. Oh, no. She stopped typing. Her mind was blank. Then, she forced herself to go on.

*Gene came over to the couch and took his daughter's hand. "Are you all right?"*

*Suzanne looked at him. "Yes," she whispered. But it was clear from her voice and her body that her energy was waning. Gene reached into his pocket and pulled out his phone. He dialed 911.*

"No, no, no, no! This can't be happening. I want to her to get better. I want her to live. She has to live."

Riley positioned her hands above the keyboard again, but no amount of prompting from her internal control center allowed them to start typing. She sat there frozen for some moments.

Bereft, she pulled herself away from the computer and stood up. She didn't know what to do. On an intellectual level, she knew that she had created these characters, and if she wanted them to live, she could make that happen in the narrative.

But on a more visceral level, she knew that her characters wrote their own story lines. They had lives, just as Riley did, just as everyone did. And for her to stand in the way of their choices, their fates, would kill the entire project.

She sat down on the couch and wept.

## — 130 —

Willard managed to make it to his office sometime after 11:00 a.m. He nodded a Good Morning to his secretary and observed her looking at him askance. She knew something was different but could not quite put her finger on it.

Willard didn't care. He was happy to keep her in the dark. In fact, he was just plain happy in a way he had not been since he and Mildred broke up. Or did whatever they did, all of which now seemed kind of quaint, or at least naïve. Judging from last night and this morning, definitely naïve.

But last night and this morning didn't seem that way at all. It felt honest. He was glad he had cleared the hurdle to having a more intimate relationship with Millie. Looking back over the past year or two, he wondered how they managed to stay so separate, so business-like. Last night seemed more authentic, more natural, more real, and just about more everything good. He couldn't even imagine letting it go again.

He sat down at his desk and listened to his voicemail, checked his email, and started looking at some cases that interested him. His phone rang. It was George Talbot from the FBI office.

"Hi, Will," said George.

"Good Morning, George."

"Just learned that the FBI picked up Stonecraft this morning. Thought you'd want to know."

Willard leaned back in his chair. "Thanks, George. I do want to know. Tell me what happened."

George proceeded to share with Willard everything he knew about the apprehension of Stuart Stonecraft. He was apparently picked up early in the morning, when the suspect was driving his parent's car on I-70 headed west. The feds, who had been tracking him with increasing interest, thought he might be fleeing Maryland for parts unknown. They did not want to risk losing him.

"What triggered this, George?" Willard asked.

"The arrest was triggered after his DNA showed up on a knife linked to the killing of one of his known associates, whose body was found a couple days ago. It was fresh, and the feds didn't want to postpone the arrest any longer. They were afraid he would skip town. And they were right: that's exactly what he was planning to do. They don't know why he decided to leave, although he may have figured out that he was a suspect. Also, he was remanded without bail this morning."

"Well, this is great news, George. Thanks again. Keep me posted if you hear anything else."

"Sure thing, Will."

Willard turned his chair away from his desk toward the window behind it. He was relieved that Stonecraft had been apprehended. He would, of course, alert Edward, who had a right to know what had happened. But there was time for that. Willard had to get his own thoughts together, and he wanted to run the situation by Mildred before he took any action.

He called Millie, but his call went straight to voicemail, so he left a message bringing her up to speed about his conversation with George.

After he put the phone down, he decided to go ahead and call Edward without waiting. The poor kid was probably worried sick about Stonecraft. He dialed his number, and Edward picked up after the second ring.

Willard explained what had happened to Stonecraft. He imagined Edward would be pleased. What he got by way of response, however, was silence.

"Edward?"

"Uh, huh?"

"This is good news. He will no longer be a threat to you or Riley or anyone else."

"Uh, huh."

"Do you have any questions?"

"No."

"Okay then. I just thought you'd want to know."

Edward clicked off. Willard put his phone down and shrugged. You never know about people, he thought. He picked up some cases from his desk and started reading.

Edward, on the other hand, did not shrug. In fact, he did not move. After clicking off, he resumed his post by the window and stared off. He was not beyond feeling a touch of relief from the news he had just heard, but it did little to change his searing self-assessment. It solved the immediate problem of his meeting up with Bomber17, if that was indeed a problem.

He smiled humorously. I was worried about the meeting I had set up? And Bomber was on his way out of town, probably permanently? He probably would not have showed up for our meeting. What a fool I am.

It also removed the threats he felt about Riley and about himself. He wondered if this would be a time to call her and see what her reaction was.

That idea felt so far out of left field he could barely keep it in his mind. I've never called her. I've only talked to her in person, and then only on a few occasions.

Edward shook his head. I've had it. I've had it with Riley, with Willard, with revenge, with . . . what? Women? Yeah. I've probably had it with women.

He sat there for a long time. The thoughts in his mind seemed heavy and immobile. He could not will them away if he wanted to.

After a while, he moved his head to look out the window of his apartment. Oppressive summer heat had taken complete hold of the District, as attested to by the withering trees and shrubs along the street below him. He sat and watched as the hours slipped by.

He felt once again the anguish he had over the botched attempt to get back at Riley, something that now seemed so pathetic it was embarrassing. And now he was deprived of his one hope to make a difference in her life. The irony of the situation was not lost on him: wanting to protect the woman he tried to hurt. The whole drama turned his stomach.

He knew this was the end. No more joy, no more excitement; just failure upon failure to build a life that made him feel alive. At the moment, he did not feel alive, so the next step was merely a technicality. He had no feelings of fear or anger or sadness. Just the simple clarity that this life that he had was no longer worth living. He did not see an alternative; in fact, he did not even want to consider one. He did not want to seduce himself into thinking that there was hope for him, only to have to dashed again. All he saw was bleakness everywhere.

## 131

Riley got up off the couch and wiped the tears from her eyes. It is up to me to stand up to my fate, she thought. Just as it is Suzanne's to stand up to hers. She went back to her computer and resumed typing.

*The ambulance arrived within five minutes, and the paramedics went to work immediately. Their professionally grim faces did not change during the procedures, and soon they lifted her onto a gurney and carried her out to the waiting vehicle. "We have to get her to a hospital as soon as possible," one of them said to Gene, whose face was stony. He had strong suspicions about what was going to happen next.*

*Behind his stolid face, he could feel a tsunami of sadness and grief, but he had to be strong for Suzanne, for Liz, and even now for himself. He did not want to distract the medics in any way if there was to be hope for his only daughter.*

*"Go with them," he said to Liz as gently as he could. "I'll follow in the car."*

*Liz grabbed her coat and did exactly as her husband instructed her. The door to the ambulance closed, the lights and siren burst the quiet Fall morning, and in less than a minute it was gone.*

*Gene got his coat and his car keys and headed toward the door. But before he opened it, that tsunami broke through his feeble decisions and took hold of him. He burst into tears and slid to the floor weeping. He wished he were not so sure about what was happening right now, but he couldn't shake the feeling that an immense loss awaited him.*

*After some time, he got up, fought back the tears, wiped his eyes, and left the house, certain in the knowledge that the home he would be returning to would be eternally altered. The sadness would not leave him, but he was able to hold back the tears that were still screaming to fall.*

*When he got to the emergency room, Gene went to the desk to ask about where his wife and daughter were. Before the nurse on duty could answer, he spotted Liz walking out of one of the treatment rooms. She was walking slowly, her eyes downcast, confirming in Gene's mind the worst. He walked towards her; she fell into his arms wordlessly. The two stood in the middle of the busy emergency room impervious to all the activity around them.*

*Liz pulled back and grabbed Gene by the arm to lead him back to the treatment room, where the doctor was just coming out. He paused and waited until the parents got there. "I am so sorry," he said, and there were tears in his eyes.*

*He turned and opened the door to the treatment room so that the now-grieving couple could pay their respects to their beloved daughter. No words were spoken; none existed that could come close to capturing the immensity of grief that settled upon them, a dark wave that would color the rest of their time on Earth.*

It's done, thought Riley. She wiped the tears from her eyes and sat back and beheld the tragedy that emanated from her soul. She wondered if this story had some mystical meaning she was not aware of, whether it portended something ominous in her life she knew nothing about. She hoped not, but she felt a distinct sense of courage to face whatever was in front of her.

This did not make her happy, but it did make her feel more solid as a person, more willing to go on. It was a willingness to let life be life and a recognition that she would deal with whatever her future held. As she thought back over the previous months, she saw how she had, in fact, done this; how she had dealt with her life in ways that were perhaps not always the best but that were at least honest and at times assertive. She was glad about that.

The phone rang, and she saw that it was Willard. She picked up, greeted him, and listened to him explain the reason for the call.

When he was finished, she told him how much she appreciated the call, what a relief it was, and how grateful she was for all he had done on her behalf. And in truth, that was the way she felt. She knew she had been angry at him, but that was distant now. Now this whole sordid situation can come to a close.

The more she thought about this good news, the more she reflected on what she was in the midst of learning. About Suzanne, about herself, about people in general. She was neither elated nor euphoric. She took the news in stride, glad that it turned out the way it turned out but taking no personal joy in the matter.

## 132

Neither did Willard. He hung up the phone thinking that Riley's response was in some ways similar to Edward's. She actually did seem a little more pleased than Edward was, but in a distant, thoughtful kind of way.

Willard had contacted her just to be thorough, just as he had contacted Edward for the same reason. But Edward's vacant response still hung like a cloud and dampened whatever enthusiasm he had about this recent development. He tried to tell himself that he could now lay this whole sordid matter to rest, but something told him that he may not have heard the last from this cast of characters. What he really wanted to do was meet up with Millie and talk to her about it.

Meanwhile, Millie was listening closely to Willard's message. She had hoped that he would include some kind of personal endearment, but it was simply a here-is-what's-happening message.

Not that she wasn't glad to be in the loop. She had been worrying this case for weeks and was glad to hear that the person who seemed to be the real bad guy in the drama was now in custody. But she couldn't get Will's tone out of her mind. She deliberately waited to call him back to give herself some time to process the situation.

But 'processing' a situation like this, with so many rational and irrational components, meant little. Usually that tiny piece of psych-talk meant something akin to analyzing a situation, but not exactly. It added a kind of psychological aura to a normal human function, like so much of psychological discourse. Vanity, noted Mildred. So she focused on analysis.

She began by determining exactly what she knew: she knew that Willard and she had re-embarked on a romantic tryst that may be a stand-alone episode or may signal some kind of ongoing involvement.

Wait a minute, she thought. What is it that I'm analyzing? The information that Will gave me or the fabulous time we had last night? I'm obviously not ready for calm, rational thought. In fact, I can't even get my mind around any of it. Armed with this clarity, she picked up her phone and called Will.

"Hi, Honey," he said, seeing her name on caller ID. That move, perhaps a bit too clever, made up for the ghastly professionalism in his previous voicemail, but Mildred was not about to forgive all just yet.

"Hi, Will," she replied evenly. "Tell me everything about what you learned today." What went through her mind was: we'll deal with the 'honey' part later.

Willard did. He told her about the call from his contact in the Bureau, George, the odd conversation with Edward, and the emotionally neutral conversation with Riley.

"Tell me exactly what Edward said, Will," Millie said.

"It consisted exactly of three comments: two 'uh-huhs' and one 'No.'

"Huh," said Millie.

Silence on the phone for a while. It was Will who broke it.

"Let's get together and talk about this."

"This?"

"Yes, this. Everything."

More silence. Everything? "Okay, let's talk about everything."

Willard chuckled nervously. He cleared throat. "Seriously, Millie. I want to go over this situation, especially with Edward." He paused just a bit. "And I think it's time we, um, recalibrated our relationship."

It was Millie's turn to chuckle. "I'm open to that," she said, feeling fairly certain that there was no way to avoid dealing with last night or their relationship or the case they were working. It all seemed curiously intertwined.

"How about my place after work? I'll make dinner."

"Sounds great."

The newly reconstituted couple clicked off at precisely the same moment.

## 133

Adam sat stunned on the couch in the midst of the chaos of his new apartment. He had just put down his phone after talking with Gene, Suzanne's father, who told him what happened. Adam was instantly transported far from the mental spot he had been inhabiting. Instead, his mind flew into a state of utter denial, turmoil, and shock all wrapped into a single experience the likes of which he had never felt in his life.

Suzanne gone? Not possible. I just spoke with her a few days ago. The doctors said she would be okay. Truthfully, he did not recall what the doctors said, but that was his takeaway. He had not for a moment thought that the life of his wife was in danger. Even though they were on the edge of divorce, her death occasioned an instantaneous reassessment of his life, of their life together, and of his future.

But first he had to surmount the huge numbness that settled into his body and prevented him from moving at all. He sat in one place and did not move, images of his life with Suzanne flashing through his mind. Mental images of first meeting her, getting to know her, having sex the first time, meeting her parents, taking trips, sharing notes about their careers: doing all the things that people do when they meet and marry their spouse. They were so vivid the concept of her no longer being in existence left him awestruck and gave him chills.

Adam did not have much of a relationship with Suzanne's parents. When he and Suzanne lived together, he saw them periodically, and everyone was amicable, but it would never have occurred to Adam to *treat them like friends or advisors or anything other than the perhaps overly indulgent parents of his lovely but entitled wife.*

*Like many people, Adam did not want to speak ill of the deceased; but he was aware amidst all the things running through his mind that his relationship with Suzanne had hit the shoals long before they split up and long before the topic of divorce was even broached. And for all the distance he had come since those difficult conversations, he knew he still harbored more than a small amount of resentment about how Suzanne was: she had always been a person who wanted what she wanted and did not care much about the feelings of other people. That may not be exactly true, he realized. What was true was that she did not seem to care about my feelings. But then again, I rarely showed her my emotions until the very end.*

*Almost everyone else who knew her had a completely different view of his now-deceased wife. Most people found her gracious, even charming. She could be the life of the party and could read people pretty well. It was all so confusing.*

*Adam knew that even Suzanne's death did not take away the anger he still felt toward her. He wished it weren't so, but he now understood for perhaps the first time in his life how much he neglected his emotional life and how disastrous that was for himself and for his marriage. He mentally reviewed the time he learned of her infidelities, especially of her ongoing relationship with Ellie and was shocked into wordlessness. It took him some time to recognize just how angry he was at those things. The fact that they made some kind of sense in retrospect did nothing to quell his anger about being cuckolded; the power of these feelings had mostly eluded him until this inconvenient time, as lots of emotions began competing for his conscious attention.*

*He was afraid of the sadness he felt. He sensed it on the horizon of his mind, but he saw himself keeping distance from it. I don't want it; it is too powerful; I will get swept away. But his thoughts and feelings would not be forestalled, and in a powerful moment of uncontrollable emotion, he burst into tears and groaned a loud primeval sound that was closer to animal than human. And not just once, but over and over until the puss of his grief had wracked his body and he found himself doubled over in pain on his hands and knees. His forehead was on the floor.*

*He wasn't sure he could move. He did not really want to move. He wanted to join his wife wherever she was.*

*He remained there for some time; he had no idea how long. Then slowly, he got up, sat back down on the couch and looked around at the disarray of his apartment, a feature that reflected what he was feeling inside. Chaos. Lost. Uncertain. Unavailable to life.*

*Did he take delight in this tragedy? The mere thought of such a thing shamed him. He could not bring himself to admit that he would find any pleasure in his wife's death; he did not even think that likely. But he knew as he sat on that couch that his feelings about his marriage and his wife's death were strong and complicated. He had no idea what to do about any of it.*

*So, he didn't do anything. He sat there and watched the mental video over and over again. The sorrow, the joy, and profound bitterness in the pit of his stomach; the anger and resentment, the loss of everything, and the endangered, just-now-budding recovery. His plans for himself now seemed like empty promises that could never be fulfilled. He didn't care really. At the moment, he didn't care about anything.*

Riley cocked her head at the computer screen. It's hard to know what to do. And just at that moment, she was possessed of a sudden urge to talk to Cameron.

She dialed his number, and he picked up immediately.

"Riley," came a surprised voice.

"Hi, Cameron."

Pause.

"To what do I owe the pleasure?" There was a note of lightness in this comment, as if he were teasing her.

"A lot has been happening, and I've been writing, and I just had a sudden urge to talk to you."

"Okay," Cameron said in the same tone. "Let's talk."

"Could we meet up somewhere and talk in person?" Riley said.

Cameron softened his tone just a bit. "Sure, Riley, where would you like to meet?"

The soon-to-be-divorced pair decided to meet up at a place that evening in between their respective apartments, a small place on U Street that neither of them had visited before.

After hanging up, Riley thought more about Cameron. She remembered how apathetic she felt toward him the last time they talked, but that apathy was nowhere to be found now. It must have been my agitated state when I called him last, she thought. She glanced at her computer screen, knowing that she was sympathizing with Adam's predicament. Maybe I'm confusing Adam and Cameron, she thought. The irony of that, given her experience with Todd and Edward, was not at all lost on her.

Riley wasn't sure exactly why she called Cameron or how she felt about him. It is not as if her defunct apathy was replaced by loving kindness. It was more like an attachment she felt toward him, a frayed one but an attachment nonetheless. She decided that was enough for now.

Cameron too had mixed feelings, but similarly came down on the side of seeing Riley. It has been so long, he thought; pretty much he put her out of his mind on a day to day basis. In addition, he had so thoroughly cleaned the apartment where there was no trace of her left. No toothbrush, no errant hairs, no female smells: nothing to remind him of the woman he lived with for years as man and wife. It all seemed kind of surreal.

He wasn't sure how to proceed. He was unaware of any protocol for meeting up with an estranged spouse. It wasn't like a work thing, where he would put his best foot forward. Or maybe it was. He was uncertain. He wanted to be honest, and that meant that he wanted to share some of the feelings of loss he had about Riley, how much he missed so much about being with her, and how sorry he felt for neglecting her.

It was now clear to him that this was precisely what he did. Work always came first for Cameron, and, if he were honest with himself, he knew that was unlikely to change much. But at the same time, he figured there had to be a way for him to carve out more space in his life for relationships that mattered to him. And he thought that his relationship with Riley, despite the upcoming divorce, qualified for one of those, a relationship that mattered to him. He hoped so.

Cameron had not seen Riley for over half a year, and he began to wonder if she had changed, how the separation had affected her, if she still had feelings for him.

On the other hand, maybe he didn't want to know that.

Cameron found himself a little too aroused at the prospect of seeing the woman he had not seen since she moved out half a year before. He attributed this mostly to the perils of sexual abstinence, and to the fact that he had never lost his physical attraction to his wife. He did not want to get all sentimental with Riley, whom he began to understand was a singularly unsentimental woman.

He was cautious. He decided to get to the place early so he would be there when she showed up. He also took special care with his hygiene and dress. Business casual, he decided: no jeans, no tee-shirts; just a tasteful pair of dark slacks, white open collared shirt, and blue sport coat. The kind of thing any young professional had always at the ready, the kind of thing a young professional would wear on a first date. After looking himself over in the mirror for the third time, he decided he was ready.

Riley was not so concerned about how she looked. She brushed her hair and put on a tiny bit of make-up, but she wasn't going to meet with Cameron for anything but ... well, she wasn't sure what. But it wasn't to rekindle anything. She was doing it, she decided, so she could bring him up to date on the events of her life. And perhaps hear if anything was different in his life, as well. She was not hopeful that this would be the case.

## 134

Riley spotted Cameron as soon as she entered the small restaurant on U Street. He was sitting at the bar, nursing a beer. She slid onto the stool next to his and leaned over and gave him a passionless peck on the cheek. "Hi," was all she said.

"Hi," was all he replied.

A little awkward silence settled in. Riley and Cameron both chuckled nervously; neither was surprised.

"This is so odd," Cameron said. "I was trying to think how long it's been since I've seen you, and I realized it's been over six months since you moved out." He shook his head in mock disbelief.

"It has been a long time, Cameron." She waved to get the attention of the bartender. "A lot has happened."

Cameron looked at her with just a touch of suspicion and surprise. "Are you involved with someone?"

Riley chuckled. "No, nothing that simple."

Cameron shook his head. "Are you all right?" The concern in his voice, which reflected the upsurge of feelings he was having, surprised him a little.

"Yes, I'm fine. It's been, I don't know, it's been quite a few months." The bartender put her gin and tonic down in front of her.

"Tell me about it," Cameron said.

"You know, we talked on the phone a while back, and I was telling you about Edward, that guy who was stalking me?"

Cameron nodded.

"Well, the story got even weirder."

Riley proceeded to detail events about Edward. She referred to having a 'single date' with him, and then his stalking her. Then she revealed her experience at the bar, where a guy who had the same name, background, and job as one of the characters in her novel showed up and how weird that was. She noticed that Cameron's jaw was, quite literally, dropping.

Riley stopped. "Cameron, your mouth is open."

Cameron shook his head. "Riley, I can't believe this," he said, putting his open mouth to use. "What did you do? How did you react?" He stopped and glanced down a moment. "And what was he trying to do? Make you go crazy?" He took a sip of his drink. "This is really, really bizarre."

Riley shrugged and nodded at the same time. Cameron would not get an argument from her about the bizarre nature of what Edward did. In the back of her mind, she realized that if someone had told her this story, she would likely not have believed it. Fortunately for her, all the principal characters in her life believed it immediately. But that did not make it any less peculiar.

"It was very bizarre," she said, taking a sip of her drink.

She went on to describe the major players who helped her with it: Mildred, Jennifer, Willard.

"That was Mildred from the women's shelter?" Cameron asked.

Riley nodded, a little surprised that Cameron remembered that from their last conversation.

The pair sat and sipped their drinks quietly for a few moments. Then Riley resumed her story.

"It turns out that Mildred knew this private investigator who was a huge help. That was Willard Bean. He tracked down the guy who played the part of Adam, who told him everything. Then he got in touch with Edward." Riley scrunched up her face a bit. "And you know, the other odd thing is that Willard, I don't know, felt sorry for Edward or identified with him somehow or something. At one point, I thought for sure he was on his side." Another sip. "As if this were a matter of taking sides," she allowed. "That turned out not to be true."

"But the other thing is that the guy who taught Edward how to hack into my computer was a 'person of interest' to the police and the FBI. He was apparently a suspect is the disappearance of several people with whom he was involved. In fact, the police picked him up yesterday. He was on his way out of town. He's now in jail. Probably won't get bail because he's a flight risk."

Cameron didn't know what to say. For no good reason he could think of, he was feeling guilty about the things that Riley was telling him. This would not have happened, he opined, if they had been together. But those thoughts seemed inappropriate to mention, so he just continued to look at Riley with a stunned and befuddled expression and said nothing.

As the shock of Riley's tale wore off, and as there wasn't much else to say about it, the conversation turned to their relationship. Riley surprised Cameron by asking how he was doing. He never thought she cared that much.

"Okay, Honey . . . Sorry. Old habit. But really, I'm doing okay." He stopped and looked across the bar. "Not that it wasn't hard at first, Riley," he said, turning his gaze to look directly into her eyes. "Then, you know, I changed jobs, and I started to realize how much work had taken over my life. I mean, I think it had been such a priority that I lost sight of other things that were important." He took a sip of his drink. "The big one was you."

Riley nodded because she did not know what else to do, because she was glad Cameron was having a flash of insight, and because she did not want to tell him how liberating it was for her to no longer live with him. "Divorce is a hard thing," she said with as much conviction as she could muster.

Riley wanted to move the conversation on and began asking about Cameron's family, other people they knew, his work, and anything she could think of. This did not take up much time, and soon the conversation faltered, much as it does on a first date that will remain such.

"Well," Riley said at length. "It's getting late. Thanks for seeing me. It's been a long time."

Cameron nodded. He had no illusions about just how difficult this visit was, and he was as glad as Riley that it was drawing to a close. He got off his stool, gave his wife what he figured would be a last hug, and watched her depart the bar.

He sat down to finish his drink and think about his relationship with Riley in what he hoped was a more realistic, if sadder light.

— 135 —

Riley walked home slowly, turning her visit with Cameron over and over in her mind. She was not exactly sorry she met with him; despite the awkwardness, there was something that was actually comfortable about it. It's true that whatever passion they used to have was absent, but that was hardly a surprise. But the relation-ship was familiar, and there was enough residual warmth to make it bearable.

At the same time, she could not conjure up a suitable compar-ison or way to think about Cameron. Apart from the genuine concern he seemed to have for her—and it was obvious he did—she couldn't imagine him as someone she would even date now.

Entering her building, she again acknowledged that she had somewhere along the line postponed dating at all. She kept calling her torrid afternoon with Edward a 'date,' but it wasn't a date; it was a lurid but not unpleasant mix of outrage, anger, pent-up sexual urges, and a fanatic desire to do something different than be her normal, boring self. Riley never regretted that afternoon as such—it was something she enjoyed, even if it was a one-off thing in her life. But she figured it probably would not have played well with all the people who have been helping her these last months. And, of course, it led to some very unsavory experiences with Edward, who no doubt did not take being jilted well. For the rest, well, that was her secret.

That was candid, she concluded. The fact was that when she thought about that afternoon, images of it would flash across her mind. She usually tried to dismiss them but often couldn't. Just

510

now, she was missing sex more than she thought. Not the raucous kind she had with Edward, but the warm, intimate kind she and Cameron had early on. The notion of cuddling up with someone and just being close held great appeal to her. This was especially clear to her now, in part because of the contrast with Cameron, for whom she felt not even an inkling of sexual interest.

She thought of Rick, the computer technician. He was handsome, to be sure; he seemed like a possible next step. She had his contact information but had not as yet made any effort to get ahold of him. The truth was she had mixed feelings. After he left her apartment, she noted her instant attraction, but she also began to think that Rick seemed to know a little too much about his impact on women. That made Riley mistrustful. Maybe she could meet with him for a drink somewhere, but her heart wasn't in it just yet.

Do I need more time? I don't know. Maybe. Maybe not. What she really wanted was to visit with her friend Jennifer, whom she had not seen in what felt like a long time. She glanced at her watch. Too late for this evening; it was after eight. She made a mental note to call Jen in the morning and arrange a time to get together.

That thought allowed her to relax a bit. She did not want to work any longer this evening, so she flipped on her television and sat back to watch anything but the images scrolling through her mind.

## 136

The next morning, she did catch Jen before work and arranged to meet up afterward at Carter's. That felt freeing to Riley, who then went about her work day.

She put her fingers over her keyboard and got ready to start writing. But they did not move. What? That has not happened in a long time. She may write terrible prose, but she is always capable of writing something. Then, an odd thought appeared out of nowhere. She was done.

No, that can't be right. It's not long enough. Adam is still in the throes of grief.

But Suzanne is gone. And there's no more story about her parents except the incalculable loss that will be with them for the rest of their days.

But she couldn't let it end right there. She forced herself to type.

*Adam sat in the same spot for several hours. Darkness descended upon the District, and he was emotionally depleted. He had wept so many tears; he had felt the chill of death run through his bones. He wanted no more of any of this.*

*He dragged himself to bed and plopped onto the mattress with no evening ritual. He hoped for sleep but doubted that it would be easy.*

*And he was right. He tossed and turned. Around 1:30 a.m., he got up to get his tablet to read to distract himself. He could barely get through a sentence without yet another useless torrent of grief coming over him. What's the point? he kept thinking.*

*No point, came a response from somewhere inside him. It's just a process.*

*Well, it's a long one.*

*You're just getting started.*

*Adam suspected that this was true. After all, he only learned of Suzanne's death the day before. He imagined that, despite their separation and imminent divorce, he would feel her loss for a long, long time. He wondered absently if he should get in touch with her parents or call people who knew her. As his mind began to clear, he thought those were appropriate steps. At least to check to see who Gene and Liz had contacted. He felt he had some responsibility here.*

*These thoughts had enough of a sobering effect on Adam to allow him to sleep for several hours.*

*Around 5:00 a.m., he got up, the weight of grief still heavy on his soul and body. He went through his morning ministrations, crying occasionally and letting those feelings be what they were. He knew there would not be a 'last time' for them anytime soon.*

*He stared at himself in the mirror. A widower at barely thirty years old. He thought he noticed some gray hairs sprouting near his ears.*

*"I want this to be over, and I know it won't be for a long time," he said to his image in the mirror.*

*"No, it won't," he replied, taking both sides of a lonely conversation.*

*Halfway through his shave, he thought today was probably not a good time to go to the office. Instead, he wiped the foam from his face, picked up his phone, and informed the office in a voicemail that his wife had died and that he would not be in. He hung up, sat down on his bed, and resumed weeping.*

Okay, Riley thought. That makes sense. She forced herself to continue.

*After a while, he decided to call Suzanne's parents. Gene was the one who had called him, and Adam hoped he would be the one to answer the phone. Fortunately, he was.*

*"Gene, I'm just checking in to see how you are. And to ask if there is anything I can do to help with . . . well, to help with the arrangements for Suzanne's funeral. And if there are people you'd like me to contact, I'd be . . . willing to do that, too."*

*Gene did not say anything right away. Adam pictured the grief-stricken older man barely able to speak. He sounded a lot older than Adam remembered him. But speak he finally did. "Thank you, Adam," he said. "Let me talk to Liz, and I'll get back to you." Another pause. "I think I've contacted most people, including the people she worked for, but . . . but . . . I don't know. If you can think of someone else, let me know or call them or whatever you want to do."*

*Gene's tone was so forlorn, so moribund, so grief-filled, that Adam could not bear to continue the conversation. He thanked Gene and repeated that he would be willing to do anything necessary. And then clicked off and felt something he recognized as relief.*

*He tried to think of friends and acquaintances of Suzanne who might not have been contacted by her father. He went to his desk and began making lists. He came up with a half-dozen names of people— some her friends, some his, some friends of both of them—who might reasonably expect to be informed of such a tragic event. It struck him as a small number, but he knew that their social life had withered in recent years, something they attributed to their busy schedules but was no doubt more about their sinking relationship.*

*He decided to contact each person via email so he would not have to break this sad news face to face. Thank God for technology, he thought.*

*When he was finished, he looked around his apartment. What am I supposed to do? Hole up here and cry my eyes out all day and all night?*

*No, he replied to himself. I won't do that. Not even Suzanne would want me to do that. I will have a life. I will not drown in grief. I will go on.*

*These thoughts had the effect of lightening his mood a tiny bit and increasing his mental clarity in a similar measure; but they were not without their own baggage. Guilt was still there, warranted or not; shame did not vanish, even if he couldn't think of a single thing he had done to warrant it. But relief was also there, and he knew he would have to slay the emotional dragons one at a time. And persist through everything.*

*He forced himself to think. There were reasons for the relief: no more awkwardness; no more marriage. No more pretending. Adam observed that he had already been feeling free of those things, but*

*Suzanne's death actually bolstered that freedom, even if the reason was tragic. It was a little dizzying. He was not sure what to do— maybe for now he did not have to do anything but keep putting one foot in front of the other—but he knew that as his life unfolded he was free to mold it the way he wanted it. He vowed to himself not to repeat the mistakes of his past.*

*Adam surveyed the chaos of his new apartment and decided setting up house was a worthy next step. He grabbed a box and started unpacking.*

That's more like it, Riley thought, pushing back from her computer.

## 137

Later that day, Riley and Jennifer finally met up at Carter's. Riley was feeling much more solid, much more like herself this time than she had last time she contacted Jen, when she was so distraught and confused she didn't know where to turn. She looked forward to being with her friend with a version of herself she liked better.

She felt battle-hardened. As bad as the weird business with Edward was, along with all the other characters that drama swept into its narrative, Suzanne's death was equally troubling. She did not feel it so acutely just now, but she knew there were still feelings of grief that hovered just over the horizon on her mind. And what followed—the reactions of her parents and Adam—weighed on her as well. She felt sorrow for all of them. She wasn't so emotional about it as she had been, but she still felt the heaviness of it in her body.

What complicated matters was that she was uncertain about how much of that she should share with Jennifer, who usually looked lost when Riley talked about emotional ties she felt to her fictional characters. But she did not want to withhold it. She had a lot of feelings about Jennifer: she was very fond of her; she found her unfailingly supportive; and she just enjoyed her intelligence, wit, and even her follow-her-own-path lifestyle. She had grown to respect the bond between her and her best friend, and she did not want to lose any of it by watering down what she wanted to share with Jen. It was worth whatever risk was involved.

As Riley was entering the restaurant, she mentally flashed on all the things that Jen had done for her. Always responding to her when she needed time and attention, giving her sensible advice when she was confused and distraught, helping her sort out the situation with Edward. The most recent thing was spending an entire unplanned night with her just for support. That counted for a lot in Riley's mind.

Riley slid into the booth where Jennifer was nursing her cocktail. "Hi, Honey," she said.

"Hi, Riley," Jen replied. "How're you doing?"

"Okay," she said. "For a change." The waiter came up and took her drink order. Both Riley and Jen settled into a familiar routine, exchanging pleasantries and catching up.

But then there came a point in the conversation when Riley had to make a decision.

"I think I'm almost finished with my manuscript," she began a little tentatively.

Jennifer nodded.

"One of my main characters died unexpectedly."

Jennifer's eyes focused a little to the left of Riley's face.

Riley almost laughed. "I know you think this is stupid."

Jen shook her head as her eyes returned to Riley's. "I don't know that it's stupid, Honey. I just don't get it."

Riley nodded. Maybe it was a hard thing for non-writers to get. She wouldn't know.

"I understand," she said. But she still felt a need to talk about it. "It's just that . . . it's just that it's weighing on me now, and I wanted you to know that." Her eyes bored into her friend's. "You are so important to me."

Jennifer did not know exactly what to make of that, and an unusual, weighty calm descended on the table, a silence quite uncharacteristic of the venue. Two friends breathing shallowly and lost in their own thoughts, neither knowing what to say next but both wanting to honor their bond.

Finally, it was Jen who spoke. In a firm but low voice, she looked straight into Riley's eyes and said: "If it's important to you, Honey, it's important to me. Even if I don't completely understand it." Jen's voice was authoritative, honest.

Riley was so touched, she bit the inside of her lip to keep from crying. She had done so much of that over these last days, she wanted dry-eyed sobriety to take the lead.

"I feel the exact same way about you, Jen," she said at length, not taking her eyes off the eyes across the table. At the same moment, they each reached for the other's hand. "I can't tell you how much I have appreciated all you have done for me or what your friendship means to me.

"And your friendship means a lot to me," said Jen in the same serious voice. "I love you." These words seemed to surprise even the person who spoke them, and Jennifer looked at Riley, searching for clues to her reaction.

"And I you," Riley said. And she picked up Jennifer's hand and kissed it lightly. "Your being with me the other night made a world of difference." A tiny smile appeared on her face. "It even helped me get through the rough part of the manuscript, where Suzanne's health went downhill."

Even Jen smiled with relief. "I'm glad I was able to help you with that," she said in a lighter, more mellifluous voice.

The two turned back to sipping their respective beverages. Jen glanced around the room. "I hooked up with an old friend this past week," she said.

Riley's eyebrows rose at the surprisingly candid piece of information. "Oh?"

"Yeah, it was someone I dated a while back." She stared at Riley over the top of her martini glass. "I know I never talk about that side of my life much," she said. "But you and I are . . . I don't really know what we are . . . friends, I guess; but we have grown to be so honest with each other. I like it. It scares me a little, but I like it." She paused and glanced down at her hands for a moment. "I'm more open with you than anyone else I know."

Riley's insides reverberated with every syllable that came out of her friend's mouth. What Jen just said echoed her own sentiments about their relationship, and she felt welcomed into a very private place, a sanctuary of sorts, a place where few are allowed. Oddly, she felt not a shred of fear or of jealousy about whomever Jen was telling her about.

"Friends, yes," she said. "I'm so honored you told me this, Jen," she said. "And our relationship does not scare me one bit."

Jen was shedding the nervousness she was feeling. It was a risk to be so casually personal with someone who was a friend rather than a lover, but here she was. New ground for her, as much of her experience had been over these past weeks. It was actually something that had been happening from time to time ever since she met Riley. But the die had been cast, and, while she wasn't exactly sure where it would land, it seemed to be alighting in a lovely space.

"What are you going to do now?" she asked Riley, in part to shift the conversation into a lighter mode.

"I don't know exactly, Jen," Riley replied. "I think I'm over wanting to go to the police about Edward. I mean, yes, he did illegal things, but if nothing more happens about this, reporting him would just prolong a part of my life that I would prefer not to keep dealing with. I want to move on." She took another sip of her drink.

Riley thought for a while. "And there was this guy I met, a computer technician who worked on my computers to clean them up: a very handsome, personable guy. So handsome I was nervous just being around him when he was in my apartment working. It was so embarrassing. I think he liked me. I have his contact information, and he has mine. I was thinking maybe reaching out to him casually." Another sip. "It's been ages since I've dated anyone. And god knows it didn't work out so well with Edward." Another sip. "If you can call that a date."

Jen smiled, partly in an effort to hide the touch of jealousy she was feeling. It was not lost on her that Riley was really straight, despite Jen's fantasies about her; but, except for the incident with Edward, Riley never talked about men. And Jen had never met Cameron, her ex-husband. It was all new information, more new ground.

"So, I don't know," Riley continued. "He seemed like one of those guys who knew exactly the effect he had on women: a little too handsome, a little too polished, a little too tall. A little too magnificent." She laughed.

"Maybe I'm not ready for this," she said after a moment.

Jennifer laughed too, but she felt some relief in the humor. It was a new place for her to be, and it felt right.

The two women spent the remainder of their time on more casual subjects. They both ordered some light fare and finished up the time together feeling closer than either of them had before. It was warm and solid and real to each of them.

At the end of the evening, they paid the check and left Carter's. Both were hesitant to let go of the warmth and closeness that had colored the evening, making it special in a deeply emotional way. They hugged warmly and went their separate ways.

## 138

Mildred hated it when she got nervous around men. Truth be told, it did not happen much, but it had been happening with some regularity lately around Willard. She was standing in her kitchen preparing dinner for the two of them when it struck her.

What are you going to do, girl?

Before she could respond verbally, she broke into a smile. I guess that answers my question.

Then she got serious with herself. Number One: I am not a girl. I am a grown woman. Number Two: It is up to me entirely what I want to do with Willard.

That is not entirely true, as all relationships require mutual consent.

Yeah, she thought. There's that.

She continued tinkering with the dish she was making: eggplant parmesan, one of Willard's favorite dishes, as she recalled. One of hers, too.

She glanced at the clock. It was only 4:30. She had left her office early so she could stop by the store and get the things she needed to make dinner. She started cooking as soon as she got home.

She slid the pan into the oven. I have half an hour, she determined.

She went into her bathroom, showered quickly, and started applying her make-up. She selected a casual pair of slacks and a top that favored her figure. She slipped on some jewelry, looked at herself in the mirror, and deemed herself ready.

Just in time, as the door buzzer sounded.

There was a time when Willard had the access information to enter her building as well as a key to her apartment. Mildred wasn't sure if he still had these things or not—given how fastidious he was, however, he probably did—but she noted that it was wise on his part not to use them.

This wasn't a big problem. She trusted Willard as much as she trusted anyone on the planet. The fact that he was sensitive enough not to use the information even though he had it; well, that was just another thing she appreciated . . . loved about him.

She opened the door and saw him standing there with a bottle of Amarone, the first bottle of wine they had shared together. She smiled at the wine and put her arms around Will. They kissed while the door was standing open.

After a length of time expected in first-time lovers but was perhaps a little long for the middle-aged variety, they entered Millie's apartment and shut the door. "I see we're off to a good start," Will said.

Millie smiled. Yes, she thought. We are. She took the wine and walked it over to the counter, where she pulled out an opener.

"We were going to talk. About everything," she said as she uncorked the wine. The apartment was suddenly filled with the smell of sangiovese, a scent she loved and one that she knew Will loved also.

"Yeah," Will said. "Let's talk."

Mildred looked at him with one eyebrow raised. This could go in several different directions. She did not want to ruin the moment, but she was level-headed enough to know that an important conversation was in the offing.

But Will had only one direction in mind. He sat down on a stool at the counter as Mildred put two glasses on it. He picked up the bottle and poured small amounts into each glass. He raised his glass; Mildred raised hers. The two clinked glasses in an air that was suddenly thick with an uncertain outcome.

"I made a mistake, Millie."

Mildred cocked her head to the side.

"I made a mistake when I told you a year and a half ago that we should not be lovers because of . . . reasons that honestly don't make any sense to me now." He took a sip of wine. "I don't know what got into me. But these last weeks—and especially these past few days—have made it clear as could be that . . ." He looked at her with utter seriousness in his eyes. "That I love you. And that, even though there are things about you I had trouble with, those are small things. The fact is I want to be with you all the time. Now. Tomorrow. And the tomorrow after that."

Millie hated it when she lost control, but she could do nothing to stop the tears from falling down her face. Partly in an effort to hide this, she threw her arms around Will. She did not say anything.

The two lovers held that position for a while, each breathing in each other's scent, warmth, honest affection.

After a while, Will said. "I think it's your turn to say something."

Mildred chuckled. "I concur that you made a mistake."

"I want to fix that," Will said soberly.

"Me too," replied Millie.

Dinner was postponed.

## — 139 —

Late summer was especially oppressive in the District. After days of depression, anxiety, suicidal thoughts and a general malaise, Edward found his mood barely rising to the level of apathy. This was not a great emotional place to be, but it was better than the relentless onslaught of despair he had been feeling.

It was all about failure: he had failed to re-ignite his relationship with Riley; he had failed to strike back meaningfully at her. He had also failed in his lame effort to make things right by murdering Bomber17, whom he loathed all the more with each passing, depressive hour.

Edward saw two alternatives. The first, the one he feared the most but felt was the more justifiable, was killing himself. He did not really want to die, but death had the distinct advantage of putting an end to the pain he could not escape and the horrible self-judgements that inhabited every corner of his mind. Death meant an end to suffering. It was not without appeal.

But it would also be another failure. Not that anyone perhaps would notice, but if anyone did, they would shake their heads at the logical end to a wasted life. Edward did not think he could bear another failure in this life or the next.

So that left him with the second alternative: returning to work and allowing his life to proceed, wounded though he was. He had mixed feelings. Part of him wanted to return to work; although, when he thought about it, it felt alien to him as it never had, like something he had done in another life. He knew it had only been the previous semester, but it felt so much more distant.

The administration of his school was, of course, expecting him to resume his duties. He could hardly disclose the reasons for not returning to the school administration. What would he tell them? That he had nearly destroyed his life and was still in a mess about it? That he would likely kill himself after the start of the semester?

With a crushed, heavy heart, Edward decided that he would return at the start of the upcoming semester. While this decision was devoid of the normal anticipation he felt at the beginning of the school year, it at least provided him with a direction.

He wasn't returning because he loved it so much. He was returning because the alternative scared the piss out of him and because sitting around his apartment after a series of utter failures was something he could not bear any longer.

Edward begrudgingly dug out his materials and went through them, flipping through old notes and lesson plans, tests that he barely recognized, and textbooks that felt kind of alien to him. Finally, he dumped all the old materials and began organizing and arranging lesson plans from scratch.

I know what I'm doing, he thought impatiently. How long have I been a teacher? Fourteen or fifteen years? Long enough to know how to plan.

As he set about this work, he began to feel twinges of something that was at first hard to identify. After a few days of preparation, it finally occurred to him that this inchoate feeling was purpose. He was a teacher. He was doing what teachers did. He was preparing. This was not exciting, but it was real. And it was removed from the despair from which he feared he would never escape.

When the new semester started, Edward rose at 5:30 a.m., as had been his habit throughout all the years of teaching. He groomed himself fastidiously, dressed with great care, and noticed that this ritual was unchanged from what he always did at the beginning of a new semester.

The sense of purpose did not leave him. On the train to his school, he wondered if it would be enough to sustain him over the long term. But he found himself clinging to it as the one thing that wasn't about self-destruction.

When he arrived at his appointed stop, he walked the few blocks to the school—the same blocks he had walked for years paying no attention. He got to the building, looked up at its neoclassical façade, and wondered if this was a beginning or an end.

As was his custom, he was in the classroom before any students showed up. He was anxious and knew it, but, then again, he was always a little nervous at the beginning of an academic semester. He had gone over the roster and knew some of the kids, but a lot of them he didn't.

"Okay, everybody. Welcome to 'U.S. Government and Politics.' If this is not the class you were expecting, please see me afterward." He chuckled. Something he had not done in months. And his voice—this even, sonorous sound that came out of his mouth—sounded new to him. But he recognized it as the same classroom voice he had used for years. He recognized it as his teaching voice.

He kept talking, taking the roll, announcing the syllabus and where to find it, clarifying the expectations around homework and projects, listing the frequency of tests, and explaining how grades would be calculated.

He looked around. All the young eyes in the room were on him, and he felt in charge.

God, it's great to be back.

# — Acknowledgements —

I would like to thank all those who contributed to making this book possible. On the personal side, I want to thank my wife Patty, who patiently read the initial very rough draft and made helpful comments. I would like to thank Pattie Cashman, who read the manuscript and provided much-needed support and insight into the narrative. I would also like to thank Tom Cotter and Patrick Cacchione, ardent fans of my previous work. They both provided much-appreciated support along the way.

On the professional side, I would like to thank my editors, Michelle Aschenbrenner and Kathy Clayton, whose invaluable feedback and close attention to the unfolding of the story enhanced its readability considerably. A special thanks to Peggy Nehmen of Nehmen/Kodner, whose candid feedback and constant availability was and remains much appreciated.

# DEAR READER

Thank you for reading *Riley*. I hope you enjoyed the book. Please visit my website at paulmidden.com to take a look at my other books:

*Absolution*
". . . *Absolution* is a superbly crafted novel, replete with memorable characters, psychological insights, ecclesiastical dilemmas, and a riveting story played out within the context of priestly vows and human emotions. Very highly recommended reading, *Absolution* is as entertaining as is thoughtful and thought-provoking.
—*Saint Louis Post-Dispatch*

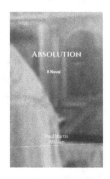

*Toxin*
". . . this novel clicks. . . the senator and the beautiful insider come across as complicated, sometimes contradictory and often unpredictable people, just like you and me. They give *Toxin* an edge on much of the thriller competition.
—Henry Levins, *St. Louis Post Dispatch*

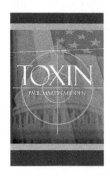

*One Voice Too Many*
"... extremely thought-provoking and a potential intimate look into a "criminal mind" as it develops and ultimately snaps into actions. Highly recommended.
—Glenda Bixler, *Bixler Reviews*

*Indivisible*
"... a frightening convergence of passion, greed, lust for power and control in this gripping, all-too-real page turner... populated with real, multi-dimensional characters who come alive in the novel's pages..."
—BigThrill.org

*Allegiance*
This fast-paced political thriller describes the struggle between home-grown insurgent elements and the federal government. Greed, a desire for power, and religious fanaticism combine to take down the federal government and break up the United States. Follow-up to *Indivisible*.

CPSIA information can be obtained
at www.ICGtesting.com
Printed in the USA
JSHW020842070120
3417JS00004B/10